FAY

by

Mirabelle Maslin

Augur Press

Lightning Source

FAY

Author of:
Beyond the Veil
Tracy
Carl and other writings

British Library Cataloguing in Publication Data.
A catalogue record for this book is available from the British Library.

ISBN 0-9549551-3-7

First published 2005 by
Augur Press
Delf House,
52 Penicuik Road,
Roslin,
Midlothian EH25 9LH
United Kingdom

Printed by
Lightning Source

FAY

With thanks to my editors

Chapter One

She had seen it years ago in a dream – a ruined building, surrounded by huge deciduous trees. It must have been substantial before it had begun to crumble, because it appeared to be at least a hundred and fifty metres long and fifty deep. She could be sure of that from what she could remember of the remaining stonework. As she wandered in her dream state inside its shell, she was aware of the musty smell of deterioration – a smell that she disliked, but one that evoked her imagination. A selection of small ferns nestled in the damp corners, and she found them familiar and curiously comforting.

Why had this dream come back into her mind that day? It was after all an unremarkable evening – an ordinary Wednesday evening in February. Why? she asked herself again.

Fay had been unwell for three months now. It had been an unusual pattern of illness – one she had not encountered before. It had begun with a peculiar sensation in her right lung. Remembering that the last bout of flu she had suffered four years previously had left her with a weakness in that lung for many months, she immediately took care to look after herself. She stayed indoors as much as possible, and if she had to go out she wore a fleece scarf round her nose and mouth and also covered her head with a hood. But two weeks later she began to feel much worse, and had to go to bed. She felt sick, she could not eat and she could not stand up.

At first she wasn't worried. After all, she had heard that there was plenty of flu about, and there were many people who were unwell. Surely she could rest over the Christmas break and she would soon feel better again. Her husband, Don, had done all he could to encourage her to rest and try to relax as much as she could. But the weeks crept by with Fay feeling dizzy and sick. Her head felt very strange and her right lung continued to cause her concern. Sickness is a common symptom when feeling dizzy, but the kind of sickness that Fay was experiencing was more than that, and the only food she could bear to nibble was very small oatcakes. She felt as if her brain had been poisoned.

As time went on, she began to realise that most of the people she knew who had had flu were well again; but she was still far from well, and Don arranged to take her to see her doctor. After two courses of an antibiotic she was in a better state, and began to look forward to being able to go out a little.

However, it soon became clear that it was not as simple as that. Fay found that every attempt she made to expand her daily life beyond sitting in a chair and pottering around the house only led to her feeling very unwell again. Friends encouraged her to try various alternative approaches to improve her health, and they helped her to choose a number of supplements to add to her diet, but nothing resulted in any identifiable improvement. She encouraged herself to think positively and believe that if she had not been taking such good care of herself she would have been even more ill. This seemed a good way to view her situation, but she found that she could not cling on to it for long, and she frequently descended into bouts of fear about what was happening to her. What was it that was affecting her?

On that particular Wednesday evening she had been sitting reading the opening chapters of a book. It had been a relief to find that she could concentrate on it, and could lose herself in the story as the lives of the central characters began to emerge.

Why should the memory of this particular dream come back into her mind, she wondered. It bore no relationship to the lives of the people in the book. Perhaps it was nothing to do with the book? Maybe instead it was something to do with the events of the day? Yes, that could be it. If that were so, then her concentration on the book had perhaps relaxed her mind, and allowed something to come into her consciousness that had previously been obscured. She sifted through what had happened that day, but could not identify anything that seemed to be relevant. She even retrieved the newspaper to see if something had caught her eye without impinging on her conscious awareness, but she saw nothing that gave any clue.

The memory of the dream had come to her straight after she had put her book back on the pile she kept by her chair. She thought again about the feeling of relaxation she had enjoyed while reading it. The book was not challenging in any way, but it was interesting. The characters voiced thoughts and perceptions that were slightly out of the ordinary, and she had found this refreshing. The book provided a basis of something familiar, something with which she could identify, but in addition it provided a focus for thought.

As she pondered this, she suddenly realised that as soon as she had put the book down she had been overwhelmed by feelings of intense fear about her illness. She had wrestled with this fear as best she could, and calmed herself enough to ask herself what she should do next about her predicament. It was then that the memory of the dream had come into her mind, and it had been so clear and so insistent that she had forgotten both her fear and the intensity of it as she viewed the ruined building and the trees once more.

The building seemed so familiar to her that it could have once been her home, she thought. How ridiculous, she chided herself. She had lived in a series of quite ordinary semi-detached houses, nowhere else. But the sense of 'home' lingered on, and she began to feel disturbed enough by it that she stood up and went to the kitchen for a glass of water. She sipped the water meditatively, while in her mind she explored the ruin.

While she was thus engaged, another memory came to her. As a young woman she had lived for a short time in part of some old stone-built farm buildings. As far as she had been able to glean at the time, this had been part of the home farm for a mansion house that had been damaged irretrievably during the war, so that it had to be demolished soon afterwards. Not long ago she had come across a book of historical photographs of that locality, one of which was of that very mansion house. When she first saw that picture she had felt very excited, almost like a child who was coming home after a long time away. And when she looked at the photograph a few days later, it still had exactly the same effect on her.

On impulse she put down her glass and went in search of that book. It was not easy to find, but she eventually located it amongst a row of book-sized catalogues and books that had been lent to her by friends, on top of the record cabinet where she and Don kept old vinyl discs and even some original '78's. She smiled as she remembered the old recording she had of 'How Beautiful are the Feet' from Handel's Messiah. She wanted to hear it, and made a mental note that she and Don must try to get something that would play it, as their old gramophone had given up many years ago.

Eagerly she searched the pages of the book for that photograph. Yes, there it was, and she had the same rush of feeling about it. How strange, she thought, as she returned to her chair with the book still open. What could this mean?

No recognisable answer came, and she began to explore other thoughts and questions that came to her. Was the feeling she had in the dream about the ruined building the same as the feeling she had about this picture? she wondered. But when she tried to re-enter the dream she could not do so.

The clock on the wall told her that it was now much later than she had planned to go to bed, and she decided to put all thoughts of the dream and the photograph out of her mind for now, and concentrate instead on getting a good night's sleep. After all, she had read that the best repair of damaged tissues takes place during sleep. Perhaps sleep would be the best medicine.

Fay was glad to settle herself in bed. She did not sleep straight away, and she lay and thought about the years she had spent here. Her two children had left home more than six years previously. Her daughter, Helen, had since become an optician, and her son, Jack, had studied geology. Since he had obtained his degree he had travelled to many distant locations around the world in the course of his work. In some ways it was very exciting to hear all his news, but in other ways it was difficult, as Fay herself had hardly travelled at all, and she felt envious of his freedom. She smiled as she thought of Helen, and of Peter – the man who was to become Helen's husband later that year. He was just the sort of person Fay might have chosen for a son-in-law, and he and Helen were certainly well suited. He too was an optician, and being a few years older than Helen was more established in his career. Neither of them had spoken about having children, but Fay sometimes wondered what it would be like to have a small person in the family again, and how it would feel to be a grandparent.

These days she had no difficulty in understanding how older people used to speak of the years rushing past. She remembered being irritated by hearing this way of talking when she was younger, feeling that it was contrived. She looked across at the photograph of herself holding Helen when she was a newborn baby, and saw a young woman holding her tiny daughter. The years had certainly flashed past since that time, and when she looked at herself in the mirror she saw someone who reminded her more of her mother than of the person she had been when Helen was born.

As she switched off the bedside light she said goodnight in her thoughts to her husband, Don. He usually phoned each evening when he was away, but this evening he had a meeting that would finish too late for a conversation, and they had decided they would give up the idea of speaking on this occasion. She had missed him, and looked forward to the following evening when she would hear his news. Although partially retired, he was chairing an inquiry that would probably last for weeks, and Fay did not expect to see him for some time to come, except perhaps for an occasional weekend.

Chapter Two

When Fay finally woke the following morning she was aware of having been very restless in the night. ‘So much for the healing effects of good sleep,’ she muttered crossly to herself. Despite the fact that the central heating must have come on at the pre-arranged time, she felt cold, and decided to get up.

Since becoming ill, Fay had found getting up in the morning to be a slow and tiresome process. As soon as she started moving about, the dizziness usually seemed to decide for itself how disabling it would be that day, and she had no way of predicting how she would fare that morning.

As she made her way to the bathroom, she decided that she would take some of the medication her doctor had provided to reduce the sensation of swimming along in entirely uncharted waters. She swallowed two of the small white tablets with a glass of water, and perched on the side of the bath for a few minutes, steadying herself by clutching on to the washbasin with one hand and a bath tap with the other.

She gradually became aware of a vague sense that something had been happening during the time she tossed and turned in the night, but try as she might to pin it down, all fragments of memory eluded her.

She dressed and made her way downstairs, trying unsuccessfully to pretend she was enjoying a swim in a choppy sea on a summer’s day. She saw that the newspaper had arrived, and she spread it on the kitchen table to read while she nibbled the oatcakes she put out on a small plate.

This plate was one she had bought from a charity shop. It was more square than circular, and it had a series of small floral motifs painted at intervals near its edges. In particular she liked the one that appeared to be woody nightshade flowers. Woody nightshade, or bittersweet as it was sometimes called, was a plant that she had always enjoyed seeing in the hedgerows when she went for walks with her family as a child, and later when she took Helen and Jack for walks.

Its delicate flowers, like small purple versions of tomato flowers, never failed to draw her attention; and in the autumn the lovely red berries appeared, although it never seemed right to her that they should be poisonous.

The stories in the newspaper were of the usual kind – more allegations of deception by the government, an earthquake in Turkey that had left hundreds homeless, the AIDS crisis in Africa, paedophile rings… Fay shuddered. She wished she knew how best to contribute to global crises, and how to challenge political deception, but she felt unable to help anyone because she needed all her energy for herself. She had had to discover this reality, step by painful step. She had a generous and spontaneous personality, and loved to be able to contribute to potentiating good outcomes, but she had had to acknowledge that for now at least she had to reduce her output to a minimum. She felt very sad about this, but accepted that she would have to live very quietly and wait, hoping for better times.

Paedophile rings… She found reports of such organisations repulsive, but they drew her attention. The subject was like a series of horror stories, each of massive proportions, and she found it hard to grapple with the fact that every story was true. She tried to imagine how a human being could abuse children in this way, but she always failed. She had some idea of how it felt to be abused, since she had never forgotten what some boys in the park had done to her when she was young.

Having finished her oatcakes, she went to the fridge to get a carton of pineapple juice. She half filled a glass, and then added filtered water to it from the jug she kept on the draining board. She turned to an article in the paper about diet, and about the strain on the NHS caused by the health problems of people who were very overweight. At this she allowed herself a hollow laugh. She remembered how, as a student, she had been coerced by her GP into taking a slimming drug which was subsequently banned. It had been proved to cause damage to heart valves in some of the unlucky people who had used it. At the time when the drug was prescribed for her she could hardly have been termed overweight. But although the whole of that situation had been a cause of considerable anger to her, she was aware that globally the issues concerning food, diet and body weight were immense. There were those who had no food, and those who had more than enough. It was clear to her that those who apparently lived in a land of plenty were really very deprived in some way, if every day they found themselves eating much more than they needed. She wished there was something she could do about raising people's awareness to the wider situation in all its perspectives, but she reminded herself that for now she must conserve her energies solely for herself.

Fay was looking forward to the afternoon, when friends would be calling round with some shopping for her and would stay for a couple of hours. Joan and Jim lived only a short drive away. She and Don had met them at the childbirth classes they had attended before Helen was born, and they had been friends ever since. They had shared their lives through their years of rearing children by supporting and helping each other in times of trouble, and enjoying many holidays and celebrations together. Joan and Jim's daughter, Diana, had been born only a few days after Helen. Sadly, there had been serious complications soon after Diana's birth, which had resulted in Joan having to undergo a hysterectomy.

Fay thought back to the long discussions they had had about whether or not Joan should return to work when Diana was small. She had been inconsolable about the loss of her ability to bear another child, and she had later become very depressed, while struggling to do her best to care for Diana. Joan was a skilled dentist, and suitable employment was readily available, so they had all begun to wonder if it would help her to be able to spend some time at work. Fay and Don had decided from the outset that Fay would be a full-time mother for as long as they thought it necessary, so she offered to care for Diana three days a week, at least until she was old enough to go to school. In those days nursery places were few and far between, and the only chance of help was to find a childminder.

After much deliberation, Joan and Jim had taken up Fay and Don's offer, and the arrangement had worked very well. Joan had quickly acquired work in a small team that was running an experimental dental service for the housebound. It absorbed her energies and attention for half the week, and she was deeply committed to it. For the rest of the week she was able to give spontaneous love and affection to Diana, and to be genuinely interested in everything she did. In this supportive environment, she gradually became accustomed to the fact that she would not bear any more children.

For her part, Fay had found that she revelled in caring for the 'twins', Helen and Diana, for part of each week. Some years before Helen was born, she had given up her job with the bank, and had become self-employed as an accountant, working from home. After the 'twins' were born and Joan had returned to work, Fay had retained only a few of her clients, to keep her hand in. When Jack was born, Joan had taken time off work, including some unpaid leave, so that she could care for Helen and Diana until Fay was able to look after them as well as Jack.

Fay's thoughts came back to the present, and she reflected upon how lucky it was that she was working from home, as this had meant that throughout her long illness she was still able to keep abreast of some of her work. She was glad, because she felt it helped her to keep in touch with the world outside her home. It did not really matter that she had had to hand some of the work on to others. She was confident that she could bring more work in once she was well again. Here she stopped, deciding to be truthful with herself. Maybe I won't get well again, she thought. Then she proclaimed determinedly, 'But in any case I have enough work for my current situation, and I'm not going to worry about the future at the moment.' This pleased and satisfied her.

After this, she put away her breakfast things, took out a pile of papers, and switched on the computer. She smiled as she flicked through the papers. Danny, her neighbour's son, had written an intriguing novel, but because his English was not up to scratch, Fay had offered to correct the first few chapters before arranging a meeting with him to discuss the changes. It was a very satisfying task, and Fay soon lost all track of time as she immersed herself in the tale.

It wasn't the kind of book she would ever have thought of writing, she admitted to herself as she worked her way through the first page. It certainly had most of the characteristics of a good horror story – if indeed she could ever describe a horror story as 'good'. She supposed that it was not uncommon for a young man of Danny's age to write about this kind of thing. She stopped typing as she tried to remember how old he must be now. About twenty-five, perhaps? He was certainly a bit younger than Helen and Jack.

Fay was so absorbed in what she was doing that the sound of the door bell made her jump in her chair. She saw it was already two o'clock, and she guessed that it must be Joan and Jim. She went to the door.

'Hello,' she said with a delighted smile as she saw them on the path outside. 'Come on in.' She glanced at the bulging bags they were carrying and added, 'Thank you so much. It's such a help to have you bringing things in for me. Let's put the bags out of the way in the kitchen, and then we can say a proper hello.'

Joan and Jim deposited the bags on the worktop and then each hugged Fay in turn.

'I must admit that I enjoyed hunting for the items on your list,' Jim said.

'Yes,' Joan confirmed. 'And actually, it was fun watching him ferreting them out!'

'It certainly makes a difference to me,' said Fay gratefully. 'I can manage on what I have here, but it's so nice to have a bit of a change if there's something I fancy.'

'Well, don't hesitate to phone us any time,' Jim assured her. 'We want to keep helping as much as we can.'

'That's right,' Joan agreed. 'And if you fancy a change of scene, we can give you a run up to our house for a couple of hours. As you know, we're around quite a lot. I reduced my hours back to part-time recently, and Jim's got his office at home. There's usually one of us around.'

'Thanks,' replied Fay. 'I'd like to take you up on that offer, but I know I'm not well enough to be away from the house yet. When Don was home last Saturday, he took me to the precinct for an hour. I was glad to have the change of scene, but I felt much worse afterwards, and that lasted for a couple of days. It's lovely to have you here, and I've been looking forward to a chat. Why not help yourselves to something to drink and we'll sit down and catch up a bit? I'll close the computer down.'

'Shall I get something for you?' asked Joan.

'Oh, thanks. A glass of pineapple juice would suit me.'

The three were soon relaxing in the easy chairs in the sitting room.

'Now,' Fay began in businesslike tones. 'You said on the phone that you had news of Diana, but that you would tell me about it when you came over. What is it?'

Joan smiled across at Jim and said, 'Who's going to tell her?'

'Actually, I think I can guess,' said Fay. 'I think she's going to have a baby.'

'Right first time!' exclaimed Jim, and Joan clapped.

'It wouldn't need a detective to work it out,' said Fay modestly. 'She's been married to Paul for two years now, and ever since she was small she has said she wanted to be a mother.' She smiled warmly at both her friends and said excitedly, 'I'm *so* pleased for you all.'

'Now, don't go leaving yourself out,' Jim insisted.

'He's right, you know,' Joan went on. 'You've been another mother to Diana, and we all know that any child of hers will be just as special to you as to us.'

'You're right, and thank you for saying it,' said Fay with tears in her eyes. 'You know, I still miss them all, even though it's years since they grew up.'

'We do too, don't we Jim?' said Joan. 'So you'll be glad to hear the rest of the news.'

'What's that?' asked Fay.

'Paul's got promotion, and he's being moved to a job that's based only three miles away. It's at Bonningham,' Joan explained.

'You mean he's got work at the big depot there?'

'Yes. And of course Diana was due to give up nursing quite soon anyway,' Joan continued. 'She'll finish up just before Paul starts his new post.'

'Have they been looking at houses yet?' asked Fay.

'They've made a start,' Jim replied. 'But we've told them not to worry about it. If they get on with selling their own house, they can move in with us once Paul starts at Bonningham, and they can house hunt from here.'

'Yes,' said Joan, 'and we can put most of their furniture into store while they're with us.'

'Don and I can take some of it here,' Fay offered. 'And if there's anything else you think we can help with, don't hesitate to ask.'

'Remember, you've got your health to think of,' Joan reminded her. 'But there might be a few treasures that Diana would prefer to leave with you. I'll let her know. And of course it's always a great help to have you and Don to talk things over with.'

'It makes me feel useful,' said Fay.

'I know,' Joan sympathised. 'But we've got to ensure that you don't overdo anything. The more careful we are, the quicker you'll be well again. Now, tell us a bit more about how you've been since we saw you last week. You said you had a couple of bad days after your outing on Saturday. How have you been since then?'

'I've had no energy to do much, but I've been able to get about the house, and I've been eating a bit more. That's why I phoned to ask you to bring one or two things. I suddenly had a longing for plenty of fruit! I don't know if I'll eat it all, but I knew it was sensible to have it here so that I had that option.'

'You're right,' Jim agreed. 'You've lost quite a bit of weight over the last weeks, and if you feel you want something, you should just have it.'

Fay fell silent, and after a while Joan asked, 'Is there something on your mind?'

Fay started. 'Oh… I'm sorry. My mind was drifting. What did you say?'

'You looked as if you were thinking quite deeply about something,' Joan prompted her. 'Do you want to tell us about it?'

'There's not much to say,' Fay replied. 'I was thinking about a dream I had some time ago. It came into my mind last night for no apparent reason, and it was on my mind again just a minute ago.'

'That sounds interesting,' said Jim. 'We're all ears.'

'I feel a bit silly,' said Fay. 'It's because it doesn't seem to relate to anything. Well… it does and it doesn't.'

'Tell us whenever you're ready,' Joan encouraged.

'It was a dream about a large ruined building with trees around it. What was left of it was built of stone, so I assume that the whole building was like that before it slid into disrepair. I remember wandering through the ruin and seeing ferns growing there. And there was that damp musty smell of deteriorating stonework.'

'Was there anyone else there?' asked Joan, fascinated.

'No. There was no one in sight, and when I think about it, there was no sound at all except for a faint rustle of leaves.'

Jim was sitting forward in his seat. 'What time of year was it?'

Fay thought for a moment. 'I think it must have been early

summer,' she replied. 'That would certainly fit my memory of how the ferns appeared. They were quite well grown.' She stopped for a moment and looked puzzled. 'But if it were early summer, surely there would have been birds singing,' she added. 'How strange…'

'I dream about all sorts of things, don't I, Jim?' said Joan. 'But I can't remember anything like that!'

Jim laughed. 'Yes, I've sometimes had to save you from wild beasts that were chasing you, and once you were on a boat that capsized. I got you out of that scrape too.' He looked at Fay. 'I think Joan's dreams would fill a book, but there's never been a ruined building.' He groaned.

'What's the matter?' asked Joan and Fay together.

'All this talk about dreams. It's reminded me of my exam dreams.'

'Oh, yes,' said Joan. 'Jim's exam dreams are quite unpleasant. He has them in the late spring nearly every year.'

'Yes, and it must be about forty years since I last had that kind of exam!' Jim complained.

'What happens?' asked Fay.

'He wakes me up because he's shouting and fighting the bedclothes,' Joan began.

Jim continued, 'All I can remember is that I am in a panic, trying to fight off piles and piles of books that seem to be engulfing me. It's horrible!'

'That sounds bad,' Fay sympathised. 'You haven't mentioned it before. I had no idea.'

'It's something you don't think of talking about,' said Jim. 'You wake up feeling horrible, but it passes because it's so obvious what it's about, and then you just get on with the day.'

'I'm glad you told me, though. It makes me feel better about discussing my ruin dream,' said Fay.

'Is there anything else about it that you can remember?' asked Joan.

'Not about the dream, but there's something I feel about the building that's been puzzling me,' Fay replied.

'Aha! A mystery,' said Jim. 'Tell us everything.'

'There's not much to tell,' replied Fay. 'It's just that when I was thinking about it last night it seemed so familiar that I felt it could once have been my home.'

'Home?' echoed Jim. 'You mean you really felt you had lived there?'

Fay pondered for a moment. 'I know it sounds silly, but yes.'

Joan stared at her. 'But you can't have done!' she exclaimed. 'I've known you for more than thirty years, and I've seen photos of all the houses you've lived in, and I've met your mother at one of them.'

'I know there's no way of explaining the feeling I had,' agreed Fay, 'and all I can say is that I had it. But there is one more thing.'

'What's that?' asked Jim eagerly.

'Just a minute and I'll get some photos to show you.'

Fay stood up and went upstairs. She returned with a packet of photographs, which she handed to Joan while she took the book from the top of the record cabinet. She opened the book to find the photo of the mansion house, and then passed it to Jim.

'Keep it open at that page,' she said.

Joan was looking through the contents of the packet that Fay had handed to her.

'I don't think I've seen these before,' she remarked as she sorted through the photos of what looked like a number of farm buildings.

'I think it's unlikely that I've brought them out before,' replied Fay.

'What exactly is this place?' Joan asked.

'I lived there for a short time.'

'Show me which part you were in,' Joan encouraged her.

Fay pointed to a door in the corner of a courtyard consisting of stone buildings. 'That was the way in,' she explained. 'The window to the right of it was the window above the sink. I didn't have a proper kitchen – there was just a sink and a cooker. The tiny window to the right of that is the one that lit the pantry.'

'There's a window above the door. Is that your bedroom?' asked Joan.

'Yes. There were two bedrooms upstairs. The top of the stairs led straight into the one that faced out to the back of the building, and there was a door just to the left that went into the bedroom I used.'

Joan passed the photograph across to Jim.

'What's this window here?' he asked curiously.

'It didn't have a room behind it,' Fay replied. 'If you look carefully, the end of a brick wall comes close up to it inside. There was no way into it. I haven't a clue when the changes to the structure were made.'

'Where was the bathroom?' asked Joan.

'It was under the stairs. And the living room was through a door that led off the hall just behind the outer door. The only other part of the house was about half way up the stairs. There was a small door to where the water tank was housed.'

'Have you ever been back there?' asked Jim.

'Only once,' Fay replied. 'Don and I heard that it was going to be demolished, and Don took these photographs for me. If you look at the picture in the book I handed you, Jim, you'll see the mansion house for which these buildings were the home farm. I never saw the mansion because it was demolished many years before I was there. I got these out to show you because when I first saw that picture in the book I felt excited. It was as if I were a child coming home.'

'How strange,' said Joan slowly. 'That means there are two large stone buildings that you have had a "home" feeling about – one here in this book, and the other in your dream. But you haven't lived in either of them, or even *seen* either of them.'

'That's right. And yesterday evening I was trying to work out if the feeling I'd had about each of them was exactly the same. But when I found I couldn't get back to the feeling in the dream, I gave up and went to bed.'

'I'm rather partial to a good mystery, as you know,' said Jim. 'What are the other clues?'

'There aren't any,' Fay replied.

'But there *must* be!' exclaimed Jim. 'There have to be.'

'Well, I'm sorry to disappoint you. There aren't.'

Jim sagged in his chair theatrically and grinned mischievously. 'What a let down,' he groaned. 'But never mind… you'll let us know when anything else emerges, won't you?'

'I promise I will,' replied Fay. 'I'm glad I've told you about this, and you can be sure I'll be straight on the phone if I think of anything.'

'If we've finished talking about your dream for now, we mustn't forget to mention our idea for a wedding present for Helen and Peter,' said Jim.

'Yes,' Joan agreed. 'We've spoken about it quite a lot, haven't we Jim?'

Jim went on: 'We've thought of a number of options, and in the end the one we were most keen on was a digital piano.'

Fay started to speak, but Jim interrupted her. 'Wait a minute! I haven't finished yet. I know it isn't on the wedding-present list, but we thought it's the kind of thing that's right for the sort of relationship we've had with her and hope to continue to have in the future.'

'What I was going to say is that something like that is really too expensive for a wedding present,' said Fay worriedly.

'We've thought it through, and we don't feel it is,' Jim replied. 'We haven't been sitting trying to make any comparisons with your gift to Diana and Paul, but you were certainly very generous. You gave them that lovely antique chest of drawers, and you insisted on contributing towards the reception.'

'But... after all... she's like a daughter to us,' Fay insisted.

'Precisely!' Jim replied. 'So you'll have some idea of how we feel about Helen and *her* wedding. Now, before you say anything else, I want to ask you and Don to run our idea past Helen and Peter and let us know their reaction. Apart from being keen to get one for them, I have contacts who can advise me about the different makes, and I can probably get a good deal. But don't rush at it. There's plenty of time.'

'Yes, all right. And I meant to tell you earlier that they've confirmed the date at last. Remember how they were given the option of September 21st or 28th? Well, they've chosen the 21st,' said Fay.

'Good, we'll put that in the diary,' said Joan. 'And not wanting to leave anyone out today, tell us what the latest is about Jack.'

'He called at the weekend when Don was here. They had a long talk, and then I had a few minutes with him afterwards. He won't be back in this country for at least a few months, so we won't see him at Easter this year. He sounds really busy – working all hours, but loving every minute of it. Don told me afterwards that he was talking over some plans he's got for the next year or so.'

'That's good news,' said Jim approvingly. 'He always was a bright and eager youngster, and that's bound to show in his work. If all goes well, he should have a good career.'

'Joan,' said Fay, suddenly. 'I meant to ask you about that reading group you joined last autumn. How's it going?'

'I'm enjoying it immensely,' said Joan enthusiastically. 'There's no pressure about it. We meet once a month to discuss a book we've all read the previous month, and to choose the book to read next. Actually, it's fascinating to see what each person makes of each book. It certainly opens my eyes. I get much more out of what I read as a result. Now that we're a little more established as a group, we're beginning to think about inviting an author to one of our meetings. Do you think you might join us? We've still got a few spaces before we close the group.'

'I'd love to!' exclaimed Fay longingly, and then looked very sad. 'But I'm just not up to it at the moment. I can't plan anything. Every time I do, I end up being disappointed because I can't make it… and evenings are not a good time for me.' She stopped for a moment, and then rallied herself to appear more positive. 'Are you going to go, Jim?' she asked.

'No, it's not my cup of tea,' Jim replied. 'And,' he continued perceptively, 'don't try to hide from us exactly how bad you're feeling. It won't help, you know, and it's not what we would want. Is it, Joan?'

'Certainly not,' Joan agreed. 'You must be honest with us about it, Fay. It's the only way we can work out the best way of helping. And if the main help is listening to how ill you feel, then that's what we want to do.'

Fay felt her eyes begin to fill with tears, and she made no attempt to hold them back. 'I feel worried that I'll never be well again,' she admitted. 'I'm doing my best to live quietly within what reserves I have while trying to keep my spirits up, but at times I feel quite frightened.'

'I'm not surprised,' Joan sympathised. 'I think I'd feel much the same. Are you any better at all, or does everything seem stuck?'

Tears ran down Fay's cheeks and she said, 'Sometimes I think I'm a little better and I try to do something different, but then I have a setback – just like I did after Don took me to the precinct. I wasn't out for very long, and I didn't think I was overstretching myself, but then look what happened. That sort of thing frightens me a lot, and I end up thinking I shouldn't plan anything at all.'

'It's certainly a problem,' Jim reflected. 'What's the position with your GP at the moment?'

'I'm due to go for another appointment next Wednesday.'

'How are you getting there?' asked Jim. 'Is Don going to be back?'

'No, and if I'm not well enough to drive by then, I'll get a taxi.'

Jim took his diary out of his pocket. 'What time's your appointment?' he asked.

'It's at ten.'

'I'll come round for you at nine thirty,' he said in a voice that allowed no argument.

'That's one of the things we've been talking about, Fay,' said Joan, clearly concerned. 'Jim and I know that you find it difficult to think about asking for help, and we were so pleased when you rang to ask us to bring some shopping.' She hesitated, but then went on. 'Actually, we were wondering if it might be one of the reasons why you've been ill for such a long time.'

Fay opened her mouth as if to protest, but then shut it again, and her friends waited quietly. When she spoke she said, 'I think you might be right. In fact I've started wondering about that myself.'

'I've an interesting idea coming into my mind,' said Jim.

Fay noticed that he looked quite impish.

'When's the next reading group meeting, Joan?' he asked.

'It's a week today,' she replied. 'Thursday evening. What's in your mind?'

'You wanted me to join the group, didn't you?' he said.

'Yes, I did… very much, and to be truthful I was quite upset when you wouldn't,' she admitted.

'I know you were,' said Jim, 'but I just couldn't face being stuck in a room with a group of people I hadn't met before, talking about a book I might have no interest in. However…' – here he engineered a pregnant pause – 'I'll try coming that day if Fay would like to come too.'

'But I've just said I don't think I can,' said Fay. She sounded alarmed.

'I want you to listen to the rest of my plan before you make your decision,' said Jim. 'I'm not putting any pressure on you, but I'd like you to think over what I'm going to say, and then phone me in a few days.'

Fay looked relieved. 'Go on then,' she said.

'Joan could ask the group if they'd mind if you and I went along just for that evening, and only for a short time. I would come and collect you, and we'd stay only for as long as you felt you wanted to. After that I can either bring you home, or you could stay overnight with us.'

'It's good of you to offer,' said Fay slowly. 'I feel a bit panicky, but I'll certainly think about it and let you know.'

'It should work out okay from the point of view of the group,' said Joan. 'I'll check with them anyway, but there have already been occasions when someone has brought along a visiting friend or relative just for one evening. It's all pretty informal.'

'What are you reading at the moment?' asked Fay. 'I've been finding it hard to concentrate enough to allow me to read a whole book.'

'It's a book that might suit you very well then,' Joan replied. 'It's called *Russian Voices*, and it's a collection of short interviews with a range of Russian people in all walks of life. I've found it fascinating. It was published around 1990, I think.'

'Yes,' said Jim ruefully. 'Many have been the nights when I've woken up to find the light still on and Joan asleep with the book over her face. I've had to mark the place, put it to one side and switch off the light, while she's snoring gently.'

Joan laughed. 'I've had to do the same for you in the past – so it's your turn now,' she said good-naturedly.

Jim looked at his watch. 'Maybe we should be going now, Fay,' he said. 'But be sure to give us a ring if there's anything, and of course you'll have to let me know your reaction to my plan.'

'It's cheered me up having you both here. Thanks for coming,' said Fay. 'I'll get on with the book I was working on when you arrived.'

'What's that?' asked Joan, immediately interested.

'It was written by a neighbour's son. His ideas are good, but his English isn't,' Fay explained. 'I've offered to tidy it up for him. It's not the kind of thing I'd be writing myself, but it's very interesting for me to see what's in the mind of a young aspiring author!'

Joan and Jim gathered their things, and Fay waved them off at the door. As she stood and watched them get into the car, she reflected on how she had always envied Joan's figure – the kind that ensured she would find a range of suitable clothes quite easily, and never need to have them altered. By contrast, Fay was several inches shorter in height, with a wider frame. Jim, like Don, had aged well. Both men were fit and carried no spare weight, and surprisingly, neither of them had many grey hairs.

'Now, remember to phone,' Joan reminded her. 'And if we don't hear anything, we'll give you a ring.'

Fay returned to her computer and switched it on. She had felt warmed and encouraged by the visit from her friends; and comforted by this, she soon became absorbed in her task once more. She did not look at the time until the phone rang and jolted her back out of the work in which she had become so immersed. It was six thirty already! It must be Don.

She lifted the phone and heard his familiar voice.

'Hello, how are you getting on? I missed you yesterday. These dry round-the-table meetings need some normality to break them up.'

'I've got some news for you,' replied Fay. 'But can I go and get some oatcakes? I've just realised I didn't have any lunch.'

'Of course. I'll hang on. Take your time.'

Fay leaned back in an armchair with her food on the low table beside her and spent the next hour exchanging news with Don. He was obviously pleased and relieved that Jim was being quite directive with her. 'It's difficult to get you to ask for help and to accept it when it's offered,' he confirmed. 'I'm very relieved he's going to the doctor with you next week. And when I'm home on Saturday evening you can let me know what you've decided about the reading group.' He went on to tell Fay about some of the events of the last few days. There were always some occasions when potential problems were only just averted, and these were sometimes very entertaining to recount in confidence.

'I was working on Danny's book when you rang,' Fay told him. 'I'll let you see some of what I've done when you're here. I'd like to know what you think.'

'I'll look forward to that,' Don replied. 'But most of all I'm looking forward to seeing you again.'

'But I'm just a wreck at the moment,' Fay groaned. 'And I can't do much. But I suppose I could try to do some baking for when you come.'

'Absolutely not!' said Don firmly. 'You don't have to do anything at all. Being yourself is quite enough. You've no idea what a relief it is to talk to a well-balanced person like you. I'm not always having to second-guess what I'm being told, or watch my back.' He paused and then went on. 'This is the evening that Helen will be phoning you, isn't it? Give her my love, and say I'll speak to her when I'm back at the weekend. And it sounds as if you've had a long day, so why not go to bed before she rings?'

'That's a good idea. I'll get myself ready when you ring off.'

She was safely in bed before Helen phoned. They had their usual lengthy exchange of news, together with some lively discussion about politics and social issues. After this call, Fay felt herself begin to relax into a deep sleep.

Chapter Three

Fay got up late the following morning. Unusually for her, she had found it easy to lie and doze after she had woken up. She felt very deeply relaxed after the visit from her friends, her conversation with Don, and then her phone call with Helen. She could tell that it was bright and sunny outside, as the light was pouring into her room round the edges of the curtains. She was very fond of those curtains. She and Don had chosen the material together when they were first married, and she had made them up herself. It was only the second pair she had ever made, and she enjoyed the challenge of matching the floral pattern as she joined two widths for each curtain. It was while she was making them that she realised why she liked the pattern so much. It was reminiscent of the curtains in the sitting room of the house where she had lived for many years with her parents and her brother.

Her mind slipped back to the memory of when her brother, Martin, was born. She was six years old. His pram was put in the sitting room, and that was where she first saw him. She remembered coming home from school and finding her mother back home again, together with a tiny baby in the huge pram. Her mother had been away for a long time, Fay remembered. The thing that had fascinated her the most was the size of her brother's fingernails. They were minute. She had stared and stared at them.

She reflected upon what a strange woman her mother had been, and the intense conflict that she had felt during her final illness. At one and the same time she had felt for her mother's pain and distress and had longed for at least one authentic exchange before she died. And when she died, Fay had been distraught, knowing that her last faint chance of real communication with her mother had been taken from her forever. That had been when Helen and Jack were still quite young, and she had to get on with life and not dwell on her pain.

When Helen had been born, Fay had worried whether or not she would be able to form the kind of bond with her that she knew instinctively should exist between a mother and daughter. Don had reassured her by reminding her of what good friendships she had formed with her women friends over the years – the kind of friendships that her mother had never been able to develop. However, she had been able to put all her anxiety and upset on one side when she saw how distressed Joan was after her hysterectomy; and she had soon become completely immersed in the care of Helen and Diana, who right from the beginning she had thought of as 'the twins'.

She knew how much she treasured the relationship she had with Helen. If she had not had such a difficult time with her own mother, perhaps she would not value what she had with Helen in the way she did, she reflected.

There was so much to look forward to. Soon Diana would return to the locality and would be having her own baby, and not long after that would be Helen's wedding day. 'I *must* get well,' she said aloud, as she sat up and began to get out of bed.

Helen's wedding was to be at the small church nearby. It was of Norman origin, and Fay had always valued its simple design. Inside it she felt there was peace and right thinking, as if in its long history it had never been tainted by wrong deeds. The current vicar, Reverend Howard, was an honest man who never shirked from preaching about the many intractable problems in the world, and he would urge the congregation to pray for enlightenment and guidance about what could be done. He argued that even if a person could not engage in prayer, good intention in their thoughts would have a beneficial effect, and however small this effect was, it had immense value. Because of his attitude he drew to his church visitors from many denominations, and indeed other religions. Even people who were agnostic, or perhaps atheist, came to hear him speak. The church seated only around two hundred and fifty people, with little standing room at the back; and there were days when it was full, with people standing in the porch with the doors open, even on a cold day.

There had been no question of whether or not Reverend Howard would agree to marry Helen and Peter in the church, although they were currently living a good three hours' drive away. He had known Helen through most of her young life, and having discussed with her and Peter their plans to marry, he was satisfied that they had a good grasp of what marriage truly meant, including their views about their social responsibilities.

Fay looked in the mirror as she combed her greying hair. She generally avoided looking in the mirror, because the appearance of her face reminded her so much of her mother's, and the thought of being like her was horrifying. I must trim my eyebrows, she thought. Some of the hair twists in exactly the same way as my mother's did, and at least I can have some control over that. Control… Somehow that word had a particular ring about it this morning – one that seemed new to Fay. But was it really new? She shuddered, and replaced her comb on the small chest in the bathroom before making her way downstairs to the packet of oatcakes and the carton of pineapple juice. But before she sat down to eat she took a small number of grapes from the bunch that Joan and Jim had brought the day before, and to her surprise she found that she enjoyed them.

After she had finished eating, she cleared away her plate and glass and wondered what to do next. Throughout her illness the TV had held no attraction for her. Even at the best of times she and Don watched very few programmes. Occasionally there was something interesting, but since she had become ill she had found even these programmes unbearable. It was something about the effect of the rapid changing of the scenes, and the close-up shots. These made her feel disorientated, and she disliked the unnatural sound of the voices. Briefly her mind flashed back to a childhood nightmare of her mother's face coming closer and closer to hers, and then seeming to explode in her face, before receding in a flash, back into the distance, only to come towards her again, and again. She shivered, despite the warmth from the central heating. The dizziness had not been so pronounced this morning, but now she swayed a little and clutched the edge of the sink to steady herself. She longed for the feeling of fresh air on her face.

She went into the dining room and stood at the window for a while. She loved looking out into the garden. It was not what one would call a formal garden. Over the years she had tended to allow plants to explore, and a deliberate layout was largely non-existent. She had a small vegetable patch, and there was a dilapidated greenhouse that was very useful, in that it sheltered the more fragile plants and herbs. At the bottom of the garden was a stone wall, behind which were the grounds of what used to be a cottage hospital, but had recently been converted into offices. With developments in communication, more businesses were content to have premises many miles from main towns; and this was an attractive site, with plenty of parking and green space. A bud of her small rowan tree seemed to be bursting – she could see that the end of it was a pale grey instead of brown.

Steadied by the natural appearance of her garden, Fay decided to spend some time on Danny's book. Her accounting work was up to date, and there would be little of that to do over the next few months. She had noticed that thus far Danny's book had an air of menace about it, created through apparently normal images. Actually it was rather cleverly done, she reflected. The characters were the kind of people one might meet on any ordinary day, and in any ordinary place; but Danny had a way of indicating that things were never quite what they seemed to be, and this had an eerie effect. She switched on the computer, and was soon engrossed once more in her task.

As before, time slipped by unnoticed, and it wasn't until Fay began to realise that she was hungry that she looked at her watch and discovered that it was already nearly three. Better stop and have something to eat, she thought. It was unusual for her to feel hungry, and she regarded it as a good sign. She went into the kitchen and chose a selection of fruit. She was surprised to find that she could manage it all, and that she enjoyed it. Perhaps this was the beginning of a change for the better.

She had just put her plate in the kitchen when she heard the doorbell. 'I wonder who that can be? I'm not expecting anyone,' she murmured. When she opened the door she found Reverend Howard smiling at her.

He greeted her formally. 'Good afternoon, Mrs Bowden. I know you've been unwell for a long time and I thought I would call round to see how you are.'

Fay was pleased that he had come, although his visit was entirely unexpected. After all, she did not attend his church regularly, even when she was well. Seeing him standing there reminded her once more of how much he seemed to embody her image of Friar Tuck. He had no tonsure, but his waist was certainly the broadest part of his ample frame.

'Thank you for calling,' she said. 'Do come in if you have time. I'll put the kettle on.'

He stepped into the hall. Fay shut the door and showed him into the sitting room before going to the kitchen. She returned carrying a tray, and handed him a china mug.

'I hope you like it black,' she said.

'That's fine for me,' he replied. He balanced it on one knee while steadying it with his right hand, and began by saying conversationally, 'You'll be looking forward to the wedding of Helen and Peter.'

'Very much so,' Fay replied. 'I sometimes worry about whether I'll be well enough by then, but then I speak to myself firmly. After all, it's more than six months away.'

'I can understand how you might be feeling,' he said. 'Once a person has been ill for a number of weeks, it can seem as if the illness will go on for ever.'

'That's exactly what's happened to me,' Fay confided. 'But on the good side, I felt hungry today for the first time since I became ill, and that must be a promising sign.'

'It sounds like it,' he agreed. 'I expect improvement will be slow, but perhaps it has begun.' He paused for a moment and then continued. 'Incidentally, I heard on the grapevine that Diana will be coming back to the area soon.'

'Goodness, news travels fast!' Fay exclaimed. 'I only heard about it myself yesterday. As you know, her parents, Joan and Jim, are very old friends of mine, and they told me when they came round.'

'I heard earlier this week from some friends of Diana's who are members of the church.' Again he paused. Fay thought he seemed to hesitate before saying apologetically, 'I must confess that in addition to finding out how you are, I have an ulterior motive for calling round.'

Fay was intrigued. She had felt out of the swim of daily life for so long that she could not guess what he had in mind. She waited.

'Now, there's no pressure on you to make a decision, or indeed ever to take up our offer,' he began.

Fay said nothing, but looked at him with interest.

'The person who has been doing the church accounts for many years is moving away towards the end of the year. We wondered if you'd be willing to take the job on. We have an established system where all the papers are filed and prepared by an administrative assistant, but we need someone like yourself who is qualified to collate them and deal with the Inland Revenue on our behalf.'

'Thank you for approaching me,' said Fay sincerely. 'I'll talk it over with Don, and let you know.'

'Naturally we appreciate that you won't be able to give us a final decision until you're well again,' said the Reverend. 'But there's plenty of time before we need to know. The end of the summer would do.' He paused for a minute or two and then said, 'By the way, you might be interested to know that I've been digging around in recent months trying to get together some information about the history of the vicarage. I'm letting everyone know just in case there are people who have access to records I haven't yet seen.'

'I don't know of anything myself,' said Fay thoughtfully, 'but I'll certainly pass the word round, although I'm not in contact with as many people as usual at the moment. I'll tell Don. He might be able to help. Is there any particular reason why you decided to start these researches?'

'It's not an unusual thing for someone in my position to be doing,' the Reverend began, 'but there was something in particular that prompted me to make a start.'

'What was that?' asked Fay eagerly.

'It was one evening when I was returning home from a meeting in the church hall. It was dusk. I was crossing the road to the garden gate when I realised that the vicarage looked different from usual. At first I thought it was something to do with the way I was seeing it in the poor light, but it definitely wasn't that.'

'What was different about it?' asked Fay, as she concentrated intently on what he was saying.

'The windows were not the same as they are now. Although the overall sizes were the same, the panes in them were very small, and the single-storeyed part to the left of the house when observing it from the front garden wasn't there at all.'

'Goodness!' Fay exclaimed. 'That part is exactly the same style as the rest of the building, so no one would ever have thought that it wasn't there from the beginning. Tell me more about the windows.'

'In my mind I have an impression of them as old-fashioned leaded lights. It has often puzzled me since, because that style of window is not one that I would have thought was in keeping with the rest of the building.'

'I would agree with that,' Fay reflected. 'Have you any idea why this happened to you that evening?'

'No. I can't begin to work that out. The only thing that seems to have any bearing on this is what happened to my brother when he began to research into our family history.'

'I didn't know you had a brother.'

'I don't see him very often, although we do keep in touch by letter and phone. He lectures in physiology and biochemistry. Like me, he's a very busy man, but he began to look back into our ancestry some years ago.'

'How does that relate to what happened to you that evening?' asked Fay, intrigued.

'Not only did he look for records of our ancestors, but also he spent time going to find the places where they had lived,' the Reverend replied. 'It was during that time that he discovered he could actually see buildings that were no longer there.'

'How could that be?' asked Fay, astonished at what she was hearing.

'We don't know how it came about, but he could verify what he saw in several instances, as he found old photographs in books that confirmed that what he had "seen" was true.'

'That's absolutely amazing!' Fay could not hide her reaction.

'In a way it astonished me,' the Reverend agreed, 'but in another way it didn't.'

'Why was that?' asked Fay.

'Ever since he was a young man, he has known exactly which direction to take without looking at a map.'

'I'm speechless,' said Fay, leaning back in her chair. 'I just can't think of anything to say… although there is one thing,' she added.

'What's that?'

'Had you had any unusual experiences before you saw the vicarage in that way?'

'No, I hadn't. It had always been my brother who had experiences outside what one would normally expect.'

Fay's mind was whirling. She had always known the Reverend to be a very well-grounded person, and she had no reason to disbelieve anything he was telling her, but it was totally outside her own experience. She had occasionally read articles in magazines about people who had unusual gifts, and she had never come to any conclusion about what she had read. But here was someone she had known for a very long time telling her something that challenged how she thought the world was. And there was his brother too... All that was surely quite out of the ordinary.

Reverend Howard noticed her silence and asked, 'I hope I haven't disturbed you in any way?'

'Oh… no…' Fay replied. 'I was just thinking…' Here her voice trailed off as she remembered the ruin in her dream, and the picture of the mansion house in the book, and the feelings of 'home'.

The Reverend glanced at his watch. 'I'm sorry, I've stayed much longer than I had intended,' he apologised. 'I must go and let you rest.'

He stood up, and Fay led the way to the door.

As he left he said, 'Now remember, there's no pressure on you to make a decision straight away.'

Fay felt quite disorientated, and the all too familiar dizziness threatened to overwhelm her. She made her way back to the sitting room and lay down on the couch. The phone rang, but she made no move to answer it. Anyone who knew her well would realise that she was resting, and would leave a message. Anyone else would just assume that she was out.

As she lay there she felt profoundly grateful that Don would be back soon. She felt in need of a long conversation with him. Although their time on the phone together was not necessarily limited, when there were deeper things to talk through she much preferred them both to be in the same room. The phone was a welcome substitute while he was away, and it was invaluable when there was information to be passed on; but it could never stand in place of an exchange of thoughts, ideas and news that could evolve when they were together. There were two things she was always aware of about the phone. The first of these was the fact that it was not natural to have someone speaking into one's ear for an entire conversation, and the second was that it did not lend itself to natural breaks in a dialogue.

There was a chance that Don would be back late that evening, but it was more likely that he would not return until some time tomorrow. She would find out when he rang later.

She lay on the sofa for some time, resting and steadying herself as she sifted through what she had learned from Reverend Howard's visit. After this she stood up cautiously and then went to the window to examine the garden once more. As she stood there, she allowed herself to look forward to the time when she would be planting seeds again.

'Even if I can only plant a few,' she pronounced aloud. 'But of course, what I really want is to be well again, and then I can plant as many as I would like to!'

It was after seven by the time Don rang. Fay had just finished eating more of the store of fruit that Joan and Jim had brought. She learned from Don that he would be home by about lunchtime the following day. She told him that Reverend Howard had visited, but said that she would say more about it once he was back. It was a short call. Don had papers to read through, and they both agreed it was best that he worked on them that evening so that he did not have to work over the weekend.

Chapter Four

Fay heard Don's car draw up outside the house just after noon. She was very pleased to see him, and threw her arms round him as he came into the hall.

'What a relief to be home again,' Don said with obvious feeling.

He dumped his large heavy briefcase into the cupboard under the stairs, and slammed the door shut with a look of determination on his face.

'I'd like to forget all about that for the next twenty-four hours if I can. Let's have a proper hug without that encumbrance,' he said.

A little later they were sitting together at the table in the dining room eating lunch.

'It's a relief to see you eating something other than oatcakes,' said Don, smiling.

'Yes, it's a bit of a relief to me too,' Fay replied as she slowly worked her way through some pieces of fruit. 'Tell me a bit about how the inquiry's going.'

'I don't want to say much about it. As always it's important that I don't talk about it outside that context, and I want our time to be our own. There are times when my job is tedious, and there are times when it's very stressful.' He laughed, and then said, 'I often wish I had a better seat to sit on! I must look round for some sort of flattish cushion to take with me.'

'Perhaps we can find one together,' Fay said, laughing.

'And now, I'd rather be hearing about Reverend Howard's visit. What exactly was he after?'

'What do you mean "What was he after"?' Fay asked.

'He's a good enough guy, but I've heard that when he visits it's usually for more than one reason.'

Fay was glad that Don had guessed something. She had always respected his assessment of people. It was never exactly the same as her own, and she viewed that as a good thing. She had learned a lot from his perceptions over the years.

'I'm glad you've spotted that,' she said, and added playfully, 'where would I be without you?'

'You'd be fine,' Don replied firmly. 'I've learned a lot from the things that you can see. So, we learn from each other, and that's how it should be.'

When Fay told him about the church accounts, Don groaned. 'Oh no!' he said, pulling a mournful face. 'Not that!'

'It's not as bad as you think,' said Fay. 'Apparently I'd just be presented with all the papers. It's someone else who has the responsibility of filing them all as they come in. I'd only be involved about twice a year. I must say I'm tempted. I'd like to be a bit more involved with that church. There's a good community of people there, and you never know where that might lead.'

'It might lead to your being sucked into a lot more and wearing yourself out,' Don said matter-of-factly. 'And since I think the length of your present illness has something to do with your having done more than you have the energy for, I don't feel particularly enthusiastic about the proposal.'

'I take your point,' Fay acceded, 'but I don't want it necessarily to stop me from doing the accounts. There's no pressure on me to get back to him quickly on this, and I'd like to keep thinking about it.'

'Okay, it's your decision.'

'I know it is, but it's *our* life, and so your views are important to me. I'll certainly bear in mind what you've said about my getting sucked into things. We've spoken about it before, and I know I do. What happens is that I'm in a situation where I can see exactly how to help, and I just find myself offering that. It seems logical at the time.'

'I know. I've seen you doing it so many times.'

'I've an idea,' said Fay thoughtfully. 'I could try to make a habit of saying something about how I'd like to help out, but need to think it through for a day or so. That way I'd have time to talk it over with you, or someone else if you weren't around at the time.'

'That sounds an excellent plan.' Don was enthusiastic.

Fay felt excited. There had been innumerable occasions in her life where she had pushed herself to help, when she did not really have the resources at the time.

'I wonder why neither of us has thought of this before?' Fay asked.

'Can I be honest?'

'All right.'

'When I've seen you like that in the past, you've looked completely unstoppable, and I've just watched and let it happen. But now I see that I should have tried to talk to you about it in between the times you were doing it.'

'So in a way it's been something that we've been colluding in,' mused Fay, half to herself.

'Yes, I can see that now. I should have spoken to you about it before.'

'So it's obviously time to turn over a new leaf,' said Fay. 'Here am I, not able to do much for myself, let alone anyone else. Now is definitely the time to start to behave differently. And this offer from Reverend Howard is a good example to focus on.'

'That's right. But there's one thing you're doing already.'

'What's that? I'm not doing anything these days except feeling ill.'

'That's not entirely true,' Don reminded her. 'You've been working on Danny's book.'

'But that's just something I'm doing to help…' Fay's hand flew to her mouth.

'Precisely. And I think the question that we have to ask ourselves is whether or not your act of helping him is at the same time giving you some help too. But let's leave that for now. I want to take you out for a bit this afternoon. The sun's shining and the air is warmer than it has been. We could go for a drive and then sit somewhere.'

Fay felt cheered by this suggestion. 'Perhaps we could go and look at that new garden centre.'

'Okay, garden centre it is.' Don jumped up from the table.

'But there's something else I want to tell you about the Reverend's visit,' said Fay.

'Let's leave that for this evening,' Don replied.

The trip to the garden centre turned out to be very pleasant. There was a partially covered area with seats that overlooked a fountain, where they sat for some time watching people with young children selecting items for their gardens, and older people planning their summer displays of flowering plants.

Fay decided to choose some packets of seeds, together with several peat-free growbags. She had wisely chosen seeds for plants she could grow in the house as well as some for the greenhouse and the garden, deciding that if the worst came to the worst and she couldn't work in the garden this year, she could save them for the following season. The herb seeds could easily be grown in pots along the windowsills.

As they sat and relaxed after their evening meal, Don said, 'Now tell me about the rest of Reverend Howard's visit.'

'It was so strange,' Fay began. She went on to tell him what had prompted the Reverend to begin to research the history of the vicarage, and about what he'd said about his brother.

'That's fascinating,' said Don when she had finished. 'I've heard of things like this, but I've never known anyone personally who had these experiences.'

'Where have you heard things?' asked Fay, surprised.

'I expect the most likely source would be the radio. As you know I often listen when I'm on my own in the car, and I pick up all kinds of snippets of information. I wish now that I could remember the details.'

'So do I,' said Fay. She felt encouraged by Don's response to what she had told him, and she went on to talk to him about her reaction to the photograph of the mansion house in the book.

'Why on earth didn't you tell me this before?' he asked when she had finished. 'Let's get the book and you can show me the photograph now. I want to have a look at it.'

Fay collected the book from the top of the record cabinet and soon found the place. 'Here it is,' she said as she handed it across.

'Wait a minute. You said that this is the house that was demolished just after the war, and that the farm that belonged to it was where you lived some time before we met?'

'That's right.'

'We went together to look at the farm buildings, and I took a series of photographs of them. The whole place was deserted by then, of course. Wasn't it about to be demolished?'

'Yes. And I was telling Joan and Jim about it when they came round this week. I showed them this book and the photographs you took.'

'Do you have them handy?'

'They're upstairs on the chest in our room. I haven't put them away yet. I'll go and get them.'

'No. You stay here. I'll back in a minute.'

She heard Don run upstairs. He soon returned carrying the pack of photos.

'Yes, I remember,' he said slowly as he examined each of them in turn. 'I thought the farm buildings were rather unusual. I hadn't seen a layout before where there was a large stone-built shed in the middle of a central courtyard.'

He picked up the book again and studied the mansion house intently.

'It's very interesting to compare this with the buildings in my photos,' he said. 'They're obviously from the same period, and the details of the building style certainly suggest that they were built by the same people and belong together. Perhaps that's the reason why you got the feeling of "home" when you saw the mansion house in this book.'

Fay heaved a sigh. 'What a relief to hear a logical and sensible explanation of my reaction. Thanks, Don. It's been bothering me, and now I can put it to rest.'

She relaxed back in her chair while he continued to scrutinise the photos. 'There's a rather unusual carving in the stonework over the front door of the mansion house that matches some that appears over the archway here,' he said, handing the book and the photo across to Fay.

'That's the stone archway that led into the courtyard,' mused Fay. 'Yes, I see what you mean. It's funny, but I never noticed that when I lived there.'

'The eye of the camera can be quite revealing at times,' said Don.

As she sat staring at the mansion house once more, Fay's mind began to fill with the memory of the dream image of the ruined stone building surrounded by trees.

'There's something else, Don.'

'What have I missed?'

'Not on the pictures. It's something else I told Joan and Jim about.'

'Go on then.'

'It's about a dream I had years ago. It came into my mind earlier this week, after I'd been relaxing with a book I was reading. Well… actually… although I was relaxed when I put the book down, I was almost instantly overwhelmed with fear about being ill like this. I struggled with the feelings, and then I began to think about what I should do next to help myself to get well again. It was then that the dream came into my mind.'

'I wish you'd told me before.'

Fay thought for a few minutes. Then she said, a little defensively, 'It's not been in my mind when we've been talking to each other.'

'I'm not getting at you,' Don reassured her. 'I just want to know about it. Tell me everything you remember about the dream.'

Fay told him all that she had told Joan and Jim, and then finished by saying, 'That's everything. Jim was keen to look for more clues, but I couldn't think of anything.'

'That's Jim for you. But you can be sure that I'm just as interested. Is there anything else you can remember now?'

'Nothing,' Fay assured him.

'Do you remember when you originally had the dream?'

'All I can remember is that it was a number of years ago, but exactly when I can't say.'

In the middle of the night, Fay woke with a start. She was struggling for breath and grappling with the duvet. She heard Don's voice saying, 'What is it, Fay?' and she felt the familiar touch of his hand on her arm.

She relaxed back on the pillows and took a deep breath. 'What's the time?' she asked.

Don looked at the luminous dial on his watch. 'It's nearly two. What's the matter? You were in quite a state.'

'I was convinced that I was in a long low narrow tunnel,' said Fay, grateful for his persistence. 'I was struggling along on my front. It was all earth, with a few stones and rocks here and there. I was sure I was going to get stuck. I felt I couldn't go forward any more, and the possibility of wriggling backwards seemed non-existent. What a relief to wake up and discover it was only a dream!'

'I'm glad I was here,' said Don. 'Let's try to get some more sleep now, and we can talk about it again in the morning.' He linked his arm through hers, and soon she found herself dozing off.

The following morning, they decided to lie on for a while. The phone rang about nine, and Don answered to find it was Jim.

'I'm phoning to let Fay know that the reading group is definitely on for Thursday,' said Jim. 'Has she decided whether she's coming or not?'

'I don't know,' Don replied. 'I'll hand you over to her.'

'I still don't know if I'll be up to it,' said Fay as she took the phone.

'Well,' said Jim. 'I've promised Joan that I'll go along this time anyway, so you can tell me when I see you on Wednesday what you've decided. By the way, I've managed to borrow a copy of *Russian Voices* from the library. I'll be passing your way on Monday, so I'll drop it off for you to look through.'

'That's very kind of you, Jim,' Fay replied. 'But don't put yourself out.'

'Don't worry about that,' said Jim. 'It's up to me. And in any case, I might just decide that I want to put myself out for you sometimes.'

'In that case, I'll accept gracefully,' said Fay. 'Do you want another word with Don while I go and clean my teeth?'

'That would be fine.'

Fay handed the phone back to Don, and made her way to the bathroom.

When she returned, he said, 'Jim was telling me what an impact it had had on him when you told him about your dream, so I told him what had happened last night, and he was very interested.'

'It was terrible,' said Fay ruefully.

'Is there any more you can tell me about it?'

'I don't think so.'

'Have you any idea how you got into the tunnel in the first place?'

'Of course not,' said Fay in a snappy voice.

'Hey, you don't need to bite my head off.'

Just then the phone rang again, and Don picked it up.

'Oh, Helen,' he said. 'It's great to hear you. Yes, I'm here until mid-afternoon. You want to speak to your mum? I'll hand you over.'

Fay took the phone. 'Hello, Helen. If I sound a bit odd, it's because I've just had a funny night. I woke up from a nightmare that gave me a fright, and your dad was in the middle of asking me if I could remember anything more about it.'

Fay and Helen talked for a while and then arranged to speak again on Wednesday evening after Fay had been to see her GP.

'I'll hand you back to your dad now,' said Fay as she said goodbye to Helen. 'Speak to you soon.'

When Don replaced the phone, Fay turned to him and said, 'When you were speaking to Helen, I had a flash in my mind of where the entrance to the tunnel was.'

'Tell me what you saw.'

'You remember that yesterday evening I spoke about the ruined building in the dream? Well, I had a clear sense that the tunnel began at one end of that building – the end on the far left when looking at the front – and that the tunnel led underneath the full length of it. I don't know the point at which I felt I got stuck in the dream, but I have a vague sense that somewhere, about half way along the tunnel, it opened out into a kind of underground hallway, and then continued on in its low narrow form again. It was all very dark, and I could see almost nothing.'

'What you're telling me just leaves me with more questions,' said Don. 'I'd love to know if that ruin really exists somewhere.'

'That hadn't occurred to me,' said Fay, surprised. 'I'd just assumed it was something that my mind had created. But why should I get a feeling of home about a ruin?'

'You didn't say before that you had,' remarked Don. 'Was it the same feeling that you'd had about the mansion house in the book?'

'I didn't manage to work that out,' replied Fay. 'And I expect the whole thing will remain a mystery.' Here she stopped, and then said, 'Except…'

'Except what?'

'It might sound a bit unlikely, but it feels now as if that tunnel has something to do with why my chest is in this odd state. Don't ask me why, because I haven't a clue. It's just something that came into my head.'

'I don't know what to say,' said Don, 'except that I believe you.'

Fay reached across and gave him a hug.

'Thanks. That really helps. Now, hadn't we better be getting up?

We haven't got all that much time before you'll be getting ready to leave again.'

Chapter Five

It was Wednesday morning, and Jim arrived at the door just after half past nine.

'Sorry I'm a few minutes late,' he said. 'The traffic was very heavy. But we'll be there in plenty of time.'

'Thanks for dropping that book off on Monday,' said Fay, settling herself in the passenger seat. 'I've dipped into it and read one or two of the interviews. They're fascinating. I haven't got very far with it yet, though.'

'Don't worry about that,' Jim reassured her. 'You've got a couple of weeks, and after that I can phone the library to renew it. Have you decided about tomorrow evening yet?'

'I think I'll have to wait and see how I feel after today. A visit to the GP can be very exhausting, and I might need to rest.'

'So long as you let me know by about six tomorrow.'

As promised, Jim delivered her to the surgery promptly, and she was glad to find that her doctor was not running late that morning. She returned to Jim's car clutching the yellow card the GP had handed to her.

'How did you get on?' he asked.

'He wants me to go and get a chest X-ray, and he's going to refer me to the hospital for some more tests,' Fay replied.

'When do you have to go for the X-ray?'

'Apparently I can turn up any time between ten and four on a weekday.'

'Why don't I take you up now? I kept the morning free in case anything like this cropped up.'

'Thanks. I must admit I was wondering how I was going to manage.'

Jim grinned. 'And by the way, well done for agreeing straight away to my suggestion. I thought I might encounter some resistance. Hospital here we come!' He swung his car out of the car park.

The hospital was only about three miles away, so it was not long before he was dropping Fay off at the front entrance.

'I'll park the car and then come and find you. Don't worry. If you're finished before I arrive, just stay where you are.'

Fay made her way towards the archway that led into the courtyard from which the main doors were accessed. It was a new hospital, and she had never been there before. She felt shocked when she passed several people drawing desperately on cigarettes as if their lives depended on it. But the exact reverse is true, she said to herself. Their lives depend on them *not* doing it. She knew a considerable amount about the nature of addictive processes, but she still marvelled at the power of them. 'Some of the most powerful addictions are a result of deprivation in childhood,' she murmured as she passed through the automatic doors. Her thoughts ran on… 'Of course it's not surprising, since a young child is entirely dependent.'

By this time she had entered a large open area with a reception desk in the middle. She asked the way to the X-ray department, and following the instructions she made her way past shops selling flowers, newspapers and sweets, and a hairdressing area that was full of older women patients. Further down the wide corridor she took the signed turn to the left and handed her card to a woman behind a desk. The waiting area had few people in it, and it was not long before she was taken by a woman in a pale blue uniform to a row of changing cubicles. The woman handed her a wire basket containing a pale blue cotton gown, and instructed her to strip to the waist, put on the gown, and wait where there was a row of seats. Fay noticed her reflection in the mirror as she undressed. The sight always surprised her. It was familiar, yet often it did not look anything like the image she had of herself. She looked away again, and concentrated on her task.

At the row of chairs she sat next to a man already wearing a gown, and asked him about himself. She learned that he was having a series of tests and screenings that day, as he was soon to have a quadruple bypass operation. He explained that a recent angiogram had revealed that he required urgent surgery, and that he was to be given an admission date very soon. He further explained that he had made many lifestyle changes since suffering a heart attack some years ago, but that genetic traits were against him, since all the male members of his family had had this kind of problem.

Fay heard her name called. She wished her companion well, was shown to the X-ray room, and was soon positioned in the way she remembered from her young days. Her mind went back to secondary school. A classmate of hers had contracted TB, and the whole class had been sent to have chest X-rays.

The radiographer told her that she could go, and she returned with her basket of clothes to the cubicle to dress. She found Jim waiting for her by the desk where she had booked in, and they walked together back along the corridor to the front doors, through the courtyard and past the smokers to the car park.

'How was it?' he asked as they drove off.

'They were very efficient. I was braced for a long wait, but it was amazingly quick. I spoke to a man who's just about to have a quadruple bypass. It gave me something else to think about for a while.'

'Is there anywhere else you'd like to go before I take you back home?' asked Jim.

'To tell you the truth, I'd love to be out for longer, but my body isn't up to it. I need to get back now and lie down for a bit.'

Back home, she let herself into the house, and waved to Jim. 'Thanks for everything,' she called.

'I'll hear from you tomorrow,' Jim answered cheerfully before driving away.

Fay felt weary and lonely. She had spoken with more people than she had on any day since she had been ill, and it had been exhausting. She was relieved that she was having more help, but she had to face the fact that there was no quick solution to her illness. Yes, she felt lonely, but the presence of people tired her. There were people she could invite round, but she knew she did not have the energy to sustain a conversation at the moment.

She had just settled herself on the sofa when she heard the doorbell. At first she felt too exhausted to go and open the door, but then she thought better of it, and slowly made her way there. She found the relief postman standing waiting with a packet for her.

'How are you?' he asked conversationally, as she signed the sheet he handed to her.

Mechanically Fay started to say 'Fine thanks…', but she broke off, and instead said, 'Actually I've been more or less housebound for three months.'

'You too?' replied the postman. 'I was ill for more than two months.'

Fay stared at him.

'But I'm fine now,' he added.

'That's good news,' said Fay, with heartfelt gratitude to be speaking to someone who had recovered. 'Tell me what happened.'

'I went off sick, and soon I had three courses of antibiotics, which made no difference whatsoever. Then I was given steroids for a while.'

Fay shuddered involuntarily. She had heard such bad reports of problems in the use of steroids that she wasn't sure she would be keen to take them. She felt profoundly grateful that her own GP had not suggested that course of action.

'The steroids didn't seem to help, but afterwards I gradually got better. The whole illness was awful. I've never been ill like that before – ever. My *head…*'

Fay looked at him with understanding. 'Yes,' she said. 'I think I know what you mean. My head felt so poisoned and for so long. I couldn't get through to anyone what it was like. The GP thought I was just talking about tension in my head as a result of feeling very dizzy, but it wasn't like that at all.'

The postman squeezed her elbow. 'You'll get well again,' he said, as he dashed off to deliver the rest of the parcels.

Sustained by this conversation Fay went into the kitchen, took the strong scissors out of the drawer, and cut open her parcel. Ah! It was that powdered food supplement that a friend had recently recommended. I might be able to face using something like this now, she thought. She cut open the top of the sachet, dipped her finger in, and tasted the powder. Not bad. She took a small spoonful and decided that it was in fact surprisingly pleasant. She found a large glass storage jar in one of the cupboards, poured the powder into it and then left the jar in a convenient position on the worktop, intending to use the contents every day as indicated in the instructions.

After this, she lay down on the sofa and fell asleep.

She woke to the sound of the phone ringing. At first she couldn't work out what the sound was or where she was. She struggled to reach the extension that was placed on the top of the bookshelves.

'Hello?' she said.

'Hello, Mum. It's me.' Fay heard Helen's voice at the other end.

'What time is it?' asked Fay, confused.

'It's about four,' said Helen. 'I know I was going to phone this evening, but I couldn't wait. I wanted to hear how you got on. Are you all right?'

'I'm just a bit muddled. That's all. I lay down after Jim brought me back. Then the postman came, and after that I fell asleep. I must have been asleep for hours. Aren't you at work?'

'Yes, I am, but there was a cancellation, so I'm phoning you from my mobile in the car. Tell me what happened this morning, and I'll ring you for a proper chat this evening like we said before.'

After Helen rang off, Fay perched on the edge of the sofa with her head swimming. It had been lovely to hear Helen's voice, but she still felt disorientated. Although the visit to the GP and the hospital had been very straightforward, she realised that the morning had left her feeling stressed and upset.

Eventually she decided to eat some of her fruit, and then to spend time reading more of *Russian Voices*. When she had dipped into it the day before, she had been deeply touched by the eye-witness accounts of the explosions at Chernobyl. This time she chose a section about the education system. Having exhausted that, she opened the book at random, and found that it fell open at the account of an interview with a linguist who was fluent in many languages, and who could pick up the basis of a language in only three weeks. That is amazing, she thought, remembering her struggles with French and German at secondary school. Surely that woman must have some particular gift? She read on and discovered how the woman believed that Portuguese was her favourite language because she had been a young Portuguese woodcutter in a past life.

Fay looked up from the book. Could that be true? She wanted to discount what she had just read, but it was difficult because everything that woman had said sounded so authentic and well grounded. A past life? She didn't know what to make of this. She read on to the end of the account. The woman had apparently lost her job in a government office because of her psychic capabilities, but had since become a healer who was known and respected internationally.

Fay sat and contemplated. She remembered how, some years ago, a friend of hers had become involved with a practitioner who claimed to be able to regress people into past lives. She recalled with distaste the mess her friend had got into as a result. 'But I think I've been wrong to let myself discount the whole subject of past lives just on the basis of what happened to my friend,' she said aloud. 'I must be more open-minded.' She returned to her book and reread the relevant pages.

At six o'clock the phone rang. It was Don. He asked how she had fared today, and she told him about the GP, the hospital and the postman.

'That's good news,' he said enthusiastically. 'But I bet you're worn out after all that.'

'You're right,' replied Fay, grateful that he understood. 'How did the inquiry go today?'

'There was a bit of a hiatus at the beginning. Although it was quite challenging, the fact that it was a little out of the ordinary livened things up a bit. I'll tell you about it when I'm home at the weekend. What time's Helen phoning this evening?'

'Actually she rang briefly this afternoon and it woke me up, but it was good to hear her. She'll be phoning again soon.'

'Well, I think I'll get off the line then. I've got a large stack of papers to go through this evening, and the sooner I make a start the better.'

Not long after Fay had replaced the phone it rang again.

'Hello again, Mum.' Fay heard the familiar sound of Helen's voice once more.

'How was your day today?' asked Fay.

'I'm glad you asked,' Helen replied. 'It's been quite gruelling. I've seen an unusual number of people with the beginnings of serious problems. There was a woman with signs of glaucoma, a girl in her teens with retinitis pigmentosa, a man with advanced cataracts and a woman with signs of macular degeneration. I wish there was more we could do for patients like this,' she finished sadly.

'I'm glad you told me. It's always better to share these things.'

'I know. That's what you've always taught me. But since you've been ill, I've wondered about the wisdom of it.'

'Don't ever hold back,' Fay assured her. 'I'd been thinking you were a bit distant recently. Has that been why?'

'Yes, I think it has. I didn't know I was being distant. I just thought I was being careful about what I was saying.'

'Well, it's good we've got that sorted out,' Fay said, relieved that there was such a simple explanation for Helen's slight detachment from her.

Helen continued: 'At least the cataracts can be dealt with at the hospital. He'll soon have replacement lenses. And we've caught the glaucoma early. But the rest…' Here her voice trailed off.

'It's very hard, isn't it?' said Fay sympathetically. Then she heard Helen begin to cry.

'I'm so worried about you, Mum,' she sobbed.

'To be truthful, I'm worried about myself,' Fay admitted. 'I try to tell myself that it's all happened for some good reason. That works for part of the time, but at times I can feel quite panicky.'

'I think sometimes I pick up on that,' said Helen.

'That's not surprising, I suppose,' said Fay reflectively. 'When you were a child you seemed to know instinctively quite a bit about me that I wasn't actually saying.'

'Oh, yes. That's right.'

'Helen, do you mind if I talk to you about a dream I once had?'

'Not at all.'

Fay went on to tell her of the dream of the ruined building with the trees round it, and of her recent nightmare of being trapped in a tunnel which she later thought was underneath it.

'You said you had that nightmare on Saturday night?' Helen asked.

'Yes.'

'Well, why on earth didn't you tell me when I phoned on Sunday morning?'

'I didn't want to worry you.'

'Worry me?' Helen echoed. 'What on earth are you saying? You've just been reminding me how I must tell you about things!'

'When you phoned I was still in quite a state about it,' Fay confessed.

'I'm not surprised,' replied Helen. 'It sounds horrible. Now,' she said in businesslike tones, 'is there anything else you've not told me about? And is there anything else about that building in the dream and your nightmare that I should know?'

'There's nothing concrete, but there are a few things I think I'd like to say…' Fay's voice trailed off. 'Perhaps they're not relevant, though.'

'I think you should tell me,' said Helen firmly. 'If they're in your mind, then they're important to you, and that's all that matters.'

Fay smiled as she recognised the exact words that she had used in the past to encourage Helen to speak about things that were troubling her.

'It feels like a muddle of bits and pieces,' she began. 'And I don't know if any of it's true.' She became agitated and flustered.

'Come on, Mum,' Helen urged.

'You know how I've got this funny sensation in the upper part of my right lung?'

'Yes, of course I do.'

'Well, it was just after I was feeling panicky about it one day that I remembered the dream about the ruined house. And since I had that nightmare about being stuck in the tunnel, I've felt there's a link between the tunnel and the state of my lung.' She paused.

'There's more, isn't there?' said Helen.

'I've been reading a short account of the life of a perfectly ordinary sane Russian woman who refers to a past life as a Portuguese woodcutter. I used to discount any thought about past lives after what happened to Lily. Do you remember her?'

'Only vaguely.'

'I don't suppose I ever told you, but she got tangled up with someone who claimed to be able to regress people into past lives, and I have to admit that her experience soon led me to view the whole subject with suspicion. After reading about this Russian woman today I'm beginning to revise my attitude, and I even began to wonder if the dream and the nightmare are something to do with a past life of mine.'

'It isn't impossible,' said Helen slowly.

'But it's highly unlikely, isn't it?'

'I can't say. I can see you could associate feeling trapped in a tunnel with concerns about your breathing, but couldn't that just be a way of seeing your worry in dream form?'

'Yes, but there's another thing about the ruined house I haven't mentioned yet,' Fay added. 'I got some kind of feeling that it was home.'

'Home? But you've never lived in a house of that size.'

'Precisely. And that's why I've started to wonder if it could have been my home in a past life. Oh, I know it all sounds completely far-fetched,' Fay said wearily, 'but you did tell me to say what was in my mind.'

'Look, I'm very interested in everything you're telling me,' Helen assured her, 'and I wish I had something useful to add. But one thing's certain.'

'What's that?'

'You *must* tell me if anything else occurs to you, or if you have more dreams.'

'Actually, there are a couple of other things I should say,' Fay admitted. 'You may remember how I once told you about a place I lived in before I met your dad?'

'Yes, I do. You showed me some photos of it that Dad took later.'

'It was the farm for a mansion house that had been demolished just after the war. I found a book last year that had a photo of the mansion house in it. I haven't shown it to you yet, but I must remember to next time you're here. When I saw that photo I was so excited, and I had such a strong feeling of it being my home, although I hadn't a clue why. Your dad and I were looking at it at the weekend, together with the photos he took of the farm buildings, and he pointed out some unusual carving in the stonework of both the archway into the farm courtyard and the stonework above the main door of the mansion. We came to the conclusion that it was this, together with the similarity in building styles, that had led me to feel that way about it.'

'That's fascinating!' exclaimed Helen. 'Peter and I are hoping to come and see you both at Easter, so you can show me then. I'll look forward to that.'

Fay brightened. 'You're coming at Easter? That's wonderful news! Just wait until I tell your dad. How long do you think you can come for?'

'We hope it'll be a week. We can't be certain yet, but we'll let you know as soon as we can. At the very least it'll be a long weekend. We want to fit in a meeting with Reverend Howard too.'

'He'll be very busy over Easter.'

'Yes, I know. But I'll phone him soon to see if he can fit us in.'

'Now you've mentioned him, there's something else I should tell you which may or may not be related to the things I've been talking to you about. He came round last week to ask me if I would consider doing the accounts for the church when the current accountant leaves around the end of the year.'

Helen groaned. 'Now don't take on something that's going to drown you.'

'There's no pressure. I've got plenty of time to decide,' Fay reassured her. She went on. 'Reverend Howard told me of his researches into the history of the vicarage, and when I asked him what had prompted him to look into it, he told me of a strange experience he'd had.'

When she had finished telling Helen everything the Reverend had said, Helen said nothing. 'Are you still there?' asked Fay.

'Yes, but I'm sitting here in stunned silence. I don't know what to say. You've certainly given me plenty of food for thought! There I was thinking I was phoning up to find out more about your trip to the hospital and have a chat, and instead I've heard enough puzzling things to last me for a long time. But don't hear that as a reason for not telling me any more. Remember you've promised to let me know if anything else comes up.'

'Yes, and I'll keep my promise,' Fay assured her. 'Shall we ring off for now? I've got to eat something and then get to bed early. I don't know if I told you, but I hope to go to a meeting of a reader's group tomorrow evening with Joan and Jim. I've still to say whether I'm going or not, but I'd like to try. Jim promised he'd leave early with me if I need to come home before it finishes. The book they're discussing this week is the one where I read about the linguist with the past life in Portugal.'

'I hope you make it,' said Helen. 'Before I ring off, I must tell you that I was speaking to Diana earlier this week, and she's hoping to be around at Easter too. I wonder if she'll have a visible bump by then?'

'It'll still be a bit early,' Fay replied. 'Bye for now, then. Speak to you soon.'

Chapter Six

The next day Fay felt a little better, and she phoned Jim to arrange a lift. He and Joan appeared at seven o'clock. She locked up the house and got into the back of their car.

'What's all this about nightmares?' asked Jim bluntly. And without waiting for a reply he added, 'Have you had any more?'

'Not since that one,' Fay replied. 'I spoke to Don at the weekend, and I had a long talk with Helen about everything when she phoned yesterday evening. It helped to discuss the dreams, and to tell her some of the things I'd been thinking.'

'That sounds interesting,' said Jim encouragingly. 'How about telling the rest of us?'

'Wait a minute,' Joan interrupted. 'I haven't had time to ask you how you are. Has there been any news about the results of the X-ray yet?'

'No, it's too soon. The GP said he'd phone me if there was anything serious, but it's a bit soon even for that. I was pretty wiped out for the rest of the day yesterday, but I didn't feel too bad when I woke this morning, so I thought I'd take a chance on it and say I would come along this evening. I've rested as much as I can today to give myself the best chance.'

'Remember you can leave whenever you want,' Jim reminded her. 'My offer stands.'

'Thanks, I'm banking on it,' Fay replied. 'I couldn't have risked coming without that. And now for the update…'

The rest of the journey was taken up by Fay telling her friends about the section she had read concerning the linguist in *Russian Voices*, her thoughts to date about past life regressions, and her uncertain sense that the ruined house in the dream and the tunnel that featured in the nightmare belonged not to the here and now, but to a former life.

'I'm fascinated with the idea that your present illness – especially the problem with your lung – might have some link with a past life!'

exclaimed Joan.

'You don't think it's too fanciful then?' asked Fay tentatively.

'Fanciful or not, it could be just as valid as any other explanation that anyone might come up with,' said Joan with determination. 'And at the very least anyone can see that someone who feels that they are trapped in a narrow tunnel might be having difficulty in breathing. Jim and I haven't talked about what we think about past life regressions, have we Jim?'

'No, but it doesn't mean I haven't heard the subject mentioned,' said Jim. 'But quite where I can't remember.'

'Don said he thought he'd probably heard something on one of those magazine programmes on the radio while he was driving,' said Fay.

'Maybe that's where I heard something too,' Jim replied.

'I think I've probably seen a magazine article – maybe in the dentist's waiting room,' said Joan. 'You know how there are usually heaps of them lying on a table. I end up reading all sorts of things I wouldn't usually come across.'

'We're here,' said Jim, as he drew up in front of a house at the edge of a modern housing estate.

The door was opened by a dumpy woman dressed in jeans and a baggy jumper. 'Come on in,' she called. 'It's a bit of a squeeze, but everyone's welcome.'

As Fay went in, the woman introduced herself. 'Hi! You must be Fay. I'm Fiona. Glad you could make it. I've saved you a proper chair so you won't feel squashed.'

'Thanks very much,' said Fay appreciatively. She put her head round the door of the living room. 'Hello everyone. I know we haven't met, but I'm joining you for part of the evening at least. However, I must confess I haven't been able to read much of the book so far.'

'That doesn't matter,' a thin bald man sitting on a beanbag at the other side of the room reassured her. 'By the way, my name's Kevin.'

There were several other people seated in the room. Fay took a mental count and reached five. That meant that there were ten people so far.

'That's everyone now,' she heard Fiona say as she shut the door.

The time seemed to pass quickly. Fay said very little, as she was absorbed in the contributions of those who had read most of the book. It was nearly nine thirty when she began to feel tired, and she looked at her watch.

'It's time for some refreshments,' declared Fiona, standing up and moving towards the kitchen.

'I think I'll have to go now, Jim,' said Fay quietly.

'Okay,' he responded immediately. 'Just lead the way.' He turned to Joan. 'I expect I'll be back by the time everyone's ready to leave.'

Fay thanked the group, and then said goodbye to Fiona. 'We'll let ourselves out. Many thanks for having me.'

'Join us whenever you can,' Fiona replied warmly. 'You'll be welcome.'

'I hope I'll see you again,' said Fay.

On the drive home Fay said, 'Thank you for making it easy for me, Jim. I enjoyed being out, but I do need to be back home now, and I can stay in bed for a while in the morning.'

Jim waited in the car while she let herself into her house. Fay realised how grateful she was for such acts of kindness and concern. She made her way upstairs straight away, as she knew it was important to get to bed now.

She felt quite wakeful, and her mind seemed to be full of many thoughts, most of which were apparently unrelated. She tried to discount them by engaging in a relaxation routine that she used instead of counting sheep. However, as she went through the instructions and observations, her body only became more and more tense. She went back to the beginning and tried again.

'My right arm is heavy,' she said, concentrating on the connection between her thoughts and her arm, with every intention of noticing that it felt heavy. But it didn't feel heavy. It felt tense and agitated. Never mind, she thought, I'll just go through the routine again, and perhaps something will shift along the way.

By the time she had been through each of her limbs and all of her limbs together, and was about to notice that her neck and shoulders were heavy, she was aware that her head was feeling more and more painful.

'Oh no!' she exclaimed irritably. 'This has never happened before. I should be feeling more and more relaxed. Sometimes I don't, but I've *never* ended up feeling worse. Perhaps I'll just concentrate on my breathing instead.'

She exhaled slowly, and observed herself inhaling without effort. 'That's better,' she murmured to herself. 'I'll just go on with this.'

She was relieved to find that she was calmed quite quickly by this simple expedient. One useful thing that I learned from those antenatal classes, she thought. It's useful for this, and it's useful when I go to the dentist too. She smiled fleetingly as she remembered how impressed the dentist was by her ability to welcome his needle into her gums. She felt herself begin to doze.

A second later she found herself jolted into full consciousness once more. But why was that? What had happened? She searched her mind, but found nothing. Lying wide awake she tried to think about what to do. 'But I don't have to do anything,' she reminded herself. 'All I have to do is lie here and rest. It's a pity I can't sleep, but it's not the end of the world.' Having decided this, she felt content to lie staring into the dark of her room.

As she lay there, she found that her mind drifted back to her visit to the hospital for the X-ray. What was it that the GP had said about phoning for the result?

'Never mind,' she said aloud. 'I can phone the surgery in the morning and ask them what the usual procedure is. They're bound to know.' She saw once again in her mind's eye the image of the smokers, and then on to the courtyard beyond the archway. 'Cobbles,' she said. But then she felt uncertain. This was after all an entirely modern hospital complex. How could there be cobbles in the courtyard beyond the archway? Added to that, cobbles would not be a wise choice, since many people with difficulties in walking would pass that way, and people in wheelchairs too. She felt muddled. Perhaps there was a wide path of concrete or slabs between the archway and the main doors, she decided. And perhaps there were cobbles on either side to give a decorative effect.

Satisfied with this explanation, Fay found herself beginning to doze once more.

'Cobbles,' she murmured sleepily. And now her mind suddenly filled with a clear picture of the archway leading to the courtyard of the farm buildings where she had lived. She felt agitated again. Perhaps I got the two places muddled up, she thought, in an attempt to settle herself.

But Fay was now wide awake, and she could not stop her mind dwelling on the question of whether or not there were really cobbles at the hospital. I'll settle it once and for all when Don is back at the weekend, she promised herself. I'm sure he'll be willing to take me up to see. She felt content with that decision, and began to doze.

Chapter Seven

It's not long now before Easter will be here, Fay thought. Several weeks had passed. She felt very happy thinking of Helen and Peter coming for a whole week, and it had been confirmed that Diana and Paul would be staying with Joan and Jim at the same time. Only Jack would be away this year, and that was fine, since Fay knew he was pursuing the career he really wanted for himself.

The X-ray had been clear, which was a great relief to both Fay and Don, and although she still felt unwell, her health was better than it had been. It was hard that improvement was so slow, but at least now she could believe that one day she would be well again, whereas for a long time she had thought that would never be the case. She had no more discomfort in her lung. There were times when she felt able to make brief trips to the local shops, and on her best days she could drive the car.

She had completed her work on Danny's book. At first she had intended to edit the whole of it, but in the end she limited her input to a few chapters, realising that it was best to give Danny some encouragement to use as a basis from which to continue through the book himself. It had been a big step forward for her to realise that this was better not only for herself but also for him.

She felt frustrated by her lack of ability to go out as much as she would have done if she were well, but the better weather was on its way and she hoped this might help her. Don had been firm with her about her plans for getting the house ready for Easter. 'Don't do more than you can really manage,' he had said. 'We can do it together at the weekend when I'm back. That way you won't end up not being able to enjoy yourself when Helen and Peter are here.' She knew he was right, and she had done nothing except look after herself. Tomorrow evening he would be home, and on Saturday they could prepare everything. Helen and Peter were planning to arrive on Monday, so there would be plenty of time.

The morning's post had brought an appointment card from the

hospital, which informed her that she was to attend the outpatient department. Good, she thought, as she noted the date. That's about ten days after Helen and Peter leave here. She fervently hoped that she would be completely well by then, but she was glad to have the appointment just in case. This illness had been such a shock. Time after time she had searched her mind for reasons why she had been so ill for so long, but each time she tried she came up with nothing. For many years she had enjoyed a lifestyle generally recognised as one that led to good health and not to illness. The only foods she liked were ones that were consistently listed as being healthy choices; she had never smoked, she didn't like alcohol and she had never enjoyed coffee or even tea. She went for a walk most days, worked in the garden through the growing season, and in the winter months she usually attended yoga or Tai Chi classes. She had never advanced beyond the starter groups of these, and this was because she enjoyed the calming effect that the repetition of familiar postures or moves had on her. After all, she went to the classes for pleasure and relaxation. There was no need to push herself.

She picked up the appointment card in its envelope and took it out again. 'Dr Grayling's clinic,' she read aloud. She had no idea whether Dr Grayling was a man or a woman, but it hardly mattered. All she needed was someone who was pleasant and competent. She stared at the card, but it told her nothing other than the date and time when she was to meet this person. Still she stared at it. Feeling a little irritated, she asked herself firmly why she was sitting concentrating on a piece of white card. The answer was almost instant, and it came in the form of an image of the courtyard space she had crossed to reach the main entrance door of the hospital the day she had gone for the X-ray.

'Cobbles!' she exclaimed. 'I wish I'd asked Don to take me back to look, as I'd planned.' She remembered how disturbed she had been when she went to bed after her evening at the book group, but she realised how the following day it had gone out of her mind, together with her plan to ask Don to take her to examine the courtyard that weekend. She glanced at her watch. It was three o'clock. 'Why not drive there now?' she asked herself impulsively. But then she felt foolish. It seemed such an unnecessary journey. 'But it's something I really want to do,' she said firmly, startling herself with the sound of her determined tones. 'I can drive now, so I can take myself.'

The sun was shining and the weather was mild. Fay picked up her handbag and selected her light jacket from the coat cupboard in the hall. Her movements were unhurried, but deliberate. She let herself out of the front door and locked it carefully behind her. Next she opened the garage and drove her car on to the drive so that she could secure the door before she left. She had always liked the silver-grey colour of her Nissan Micra. It must be at least six years old now, she reflected.

She was about to drive away when a thought occurred to her, and she went back into the house, returning soon afterwards with her camera, which she put on the passenger seat beside her. Driving in the direction of the hospital she thought how good it felt to be able to use her car. Although she could only drive on the days when she felt well enough, it meant that she could sometimes go to the supermarket for things she needed, and was no longer so reliant on Don, Joan and Jim for her shopping. And today she was able to follow her impulse instead of having to wait until Don was at home.

She was glad to find that there were several empty spaces in the large hospital car park, and she chose one that was on the end of a row, so that she had a little more room to manoeuvre. She picked up her bag and her camera, locked her car and made her way across to the main entrance. Having reached the archway she stopped and stared at the cobbles in the courtyard. She had been right after all. But the cobbles were a modern imitation of the old kind. They were larger and somehow flattened, thus allowing people and wheels to move across them without difficulty.

Fay took several shots of the courtyard, and then turned to go back to her car; but as an afterthought she inspected the brickwork above the archway as if she expected to see an inscription. Finding nothing, she smiled, shook her head, and left.

When she arrived back at her house, she felt very tired indeed, and having garaged her car and hung up her jacket, she lay down on the sofa and fell asleep almost straight away.

It was dark when she woke again. At first she wondered where she was. Having established that she was in the sitting room, she switched on the lamp that stood on a table by the arm of the sofa; and realising that she felt cold, she turned on the gas fire. She put her hand on the radiator under the window before drawing the curtains, and was surprised to find that it was quite hot. Of course, she thought, it will have come on automatically while I was asleep, but it's odd that I'm feeling so cold.

'Ow!' she exclaimed, grabbing involuntarily at the thumb of her left hand. 'There must be a needle in this curtain,' she muttered, annoyed. She began to search the seam for one, but could find nothing. 'That's funny,' she continued aloud. 'I could have sworn something stuck itself into my thumb.' She scrutinised it carefully, but could see no puncture in the skin. 'How very strange.' She shivered. 'Cobbles, pins, and no inscriptions...' she said as she made her way upstairs to look for a thick jumper. Her head began to whirl and she had to sit down before she got to the top. 'There are inscriptions above the entrance to the farm courtyard and the front door of the mansion in the photograph in that book,' she reminded herself.

She sat trying to breathe deeply until she felt steadier, and then she went to the chest in her bedroom and selected a winter-weight jumper. It was navy, with a cable pattern down the front, together with a few paint splashes that had been added while she was doing some decorating one winter.

Then in the kitchen she filled the kettle to make a hot drink, and put some yoghurt and a banana in a bowl. She didn't feel hungry, but thought she ought to eat something. The clock on the wall told her that it was nine already. Don wouldn't be phoning tonight, as he was coming back tomorrow.

Sitting in front of the fire sipping her drink, Fay puzzled about the pain in her thumb, and then put it out of her mind. But other dilemmas soon replaced it. There was that ruin in her dream, and the tunnel underneath it. Why had there been a connection in her mind between that tunnel and the problems she had had with her lung until only recently? She had no further thoughts on the matter, but still it lingered in her mind. Another image joined it, and she smiled fleetingly when she realised where it had come from. Surely it was an illustration from one of the 'Rupert' stories she had known as a child? Rupert had reached the edge of a forest, and his way was blocked by two large planks of wood crossed to bar him from following the path...

'*Russian Voices*. I must ask Jim if he'll get that copy from the library again for me,' Fay heard herself say. She suddenly knew that she wanted to reread the section about the woman who had spoken about past lives. And there was something else niggling at the back of her mind. She finished her drink and began to toy with her bowl of yoghurt. She was feeling a lot warmer now, but did not want to turn down the fire yet.

She sat gazing into its warmth for a few minutes. Then she took a spoonful of yoghurt and was about to put it in her mouth when she had the answer. 'Got it!' she exclaimed. It must have been years ago. Helen and Diana were only babies. She remembered how one day when she had been out with them both in the twin buggy she and Joan had shared, she had bumped into an old friend who told her a story that she found hard to believe. Her friend said that when her daughter was three, she had pointed to a specific place in the town where they lived at the time, and had said, 'Mummy, when I lived here before, there was a bridge there.' She went on to explain how, because her daughter had been so insistent about this, she went and checked old records of the town and discovered that there had indeed been a bridge in exactly that position.

Fay desperately wished that she wasn't alone. There was now so much she needed to talk over with someone. It was too late to phone anyone now, and in any case it wouldn't be all that long before Don came back. Surely she could wait until tomorrow evening. Although she had slept for a long time when she came in, she felt very tired again, and decided that the best thing was to finish her yoghurt and go to bed.

After cleaning her teeth she caught sight of herself in the bathroom mirror. Those eyebrows... Determinedly she opened the small cabinet that was mounted on the wall and took out a pair of tweezers. Why hadn't she thought of this before? Slowly and deftly she removed hair after hair until she had taken away all those that were so like her mother's. What a relief! More than satisfied with the result, she stared at her reflection for a few minutes and then went to her bedroom. Although she knew that pulling out a few hairs from her eyebrows was not in itself likely to result in a significant change in her life, she sensed that the impulse that had led to it might.

Once in bed she lay awake for a while with the light on.

Something had begun to change, but exactly what she did not know. Her mother… Her mother's death had been simple and straightforward, but not her life. Fay began to realise that the impact of her mother's problems upon her had been much greater than she had ever before imagined.

She switched off the light, promising herself that she would spend the following day quietly, allowing plenty of time for reflection. She could make a start on the knitting that she had intended to do for Diana's baby, and this would keep her hands busy while she thought about her mother, and indeed the many other things that were now puzzling her.

The following morning Fay woke with a feeling that she recognised – one that had been unfamiliar throughout the months of her illness. She felt refreshed. Yes, that was it – refreshed. She had an impulse to get out of bed immediately and start the day; but caution prevailed, and she decided instead that she would lie in bed for a while enjoying the sense of feeling brighter. As she lay there she promised herself that she would follow her original plan to have a quiet day.

She got up about an hour later. The mirror in the bathroom reminded her of the new shape of her eyebrows, and this strengthened her resolve to think about her mother. After this she ate breakfast, and then installed herself on the sofa with a simple knitting pattern, needles and yarn. But before she began to study the pattern she leaned back and shut her eyes.

Her mother had died when Jack was learning to walk. He must have been barely one year old, and Helen and Diana were only just past three. Joan had had to take time off work, and she had looked after the three children until after the funeral. The news had come late one evening. Fortunately, Martin had been visiting their mother at the time. He had been out for a walk before going to bed, and when he returned he found her slumped in a chair, and he could not rouse her. He had phoned for an ambulance, but she was dead.

She recalled the unbearable pain she had felt at the funeral, and how she had made a conscious decision to bury it as deeply as possible and get on with her life. She had thrown herself into the care of the three children, and managed to numb her feelings of loss.

Her mother had been a harsh, unyielding woman who appeared to be incapable of showing her any love. By contrast, she had been quite affectionate towards Martin. As the years had gone by, Fay had asked Martin about his life when he was a child, and was surprised to find that he had not felt comfortable around their mother either. This was a revelation to Fay, and she had said as much, telling Martin how she had been sure that he was the favoured one. Martin had never married, as he found close contact with women brought with it a sense of claustrophobia. Although he owned a pleasant house in a small village about an hour's drive away, he rarely spent time there, preferring instead to travel. He had a series of jobs – each of which involved moving about, both in the UK and abroad. This arrangement suited him well, and Fay saw little of him, although he did send an occasional cheerful postcard. They had seen very little of their father, who had been in the Merchant Navy. He died at sea when they were young. Fay remembered how she used to keep forgetting that he was dead.

Her thoughts went back to her mother – that grim-faced woman with a hand all too ready to deal a slap for the slightest misdemeanour, or indeed just for the purpose of venting her own inexplicable rages. Fay could see how frightened she had been in the face of this, and she was astonished that she had not been aware of it before. The memory of that fear, now conscious, overwhelmed her, and she felt herself break out in a cold sweat. The familiar support of the sofa provided only a distant sense of comfort as she slipped back into the pain of the beatings she had endured. In an attempt to steady herself she grasped the arm of the sofa, but she found herself assailed by a growing feeling of nausea, and her head was swimming as she staggered to the kitchen to splash cold water on her face and neck. To her relief, this seemed to bring her back from her child state, and she filled a glass and sipped slowly.

A word came into her mind – 'control'. Surely that was the word that had come to her some weeks ago when she was thinking about how much she physically resembled her mother. Now things started to fall into place in her mind. There was a world of difference between the containment she had provided in the care of her own children and the control that had been exerted upon her by her mother. People had always remarked upon how well behaved and helpful she had been as a child, but now she could see that this was born of fear of the consequences if she did not comply. She had never been free to express the full range of child behaviour that she had enabled and encouraged Helen, Diana and Jack to do.

Slowly she became aware that she was clutching the edge of the sink to hold herself steady, that the hand that was holding the glass was trembling, and that her head was swimming in an alarming way. Cautiously she made her way back to the sofa, leaning on the wall on the way, her legs shaking.

Once safely back, she attempted to divert herself by studying the knitting pattern, but she could not focus on the instructions. In fact, she could hardly read the print, and she put it to one side. A thought brought her up with a jolt. Don had been entirely right when he advised her to think very carefully about whether or not to take up Reverend Howard's invitation to become the accountant for the church. Her immediate impulse had been to agree to the offer, and it had only been her illness and Reverend Howard's insistence that there was no hurry to decide that had allowed her to delay. She could see now why she needed plenty of time to think it through, and that in reality she had no idea if the post would be suitable for her. She knew now that she was perfectly capable of behaving towards herself and everyone else as if the job was entirely right for her, when all the while it might be an enormous unrecognised stress.

'How awful,' she heard herself say. She shuddered, and as before, a feeling of intense cold pervaded her whole being. Mechanically she made her way to the foot of the stairs, slowly climbed them on all fours, found the thick jumper once more, and having put it on, collapsed on her bed. Her mind filled with thoughts and images at a speed which prevented any hope of pondering on any of them. Flash after flash of memory from all the years of her life came and went. She had no way of telling how these memories related to each other, how they related to the past and how they related to the present. She had some faint grasp of the fact that this state was a consequence of having seen the link between her mother's treatment of her and her current predicament, but she was unable to even begin to examine any of the details. She wrapped the duvet around herself and accepted that there was nothing else she could do but endure what was happening to her.

Fay had no idea of the passage of time, but at length the intensity and speed at which her memories emerged began to decrease. She noticed that she was clutching the edge of the duvet so hard that her knuckles were white, and she eased her hands open and massaged her stiff fingers. To her astonishment the bedside clock indicated that several hours had passed since she had come upstairs.

Experimentally she slowly peeled the duvet away, and she was relieved to find that she felt all right lying on the bed without it. After ten minutes or so she rolled over and moved one leg gingerly over the side of the bed. So far so good. She sat up, swinging the other leg to join the first. To her surprise, her head felt clearer than it had done for some time, and at first she wondered if she was imagining this. But no, it definitely felt clearer. Not wanting to risk taking this for granted, she moved carefully towards the bedroom door, across the landing and then down the stairs.

When she reached the hallway she noticed something else – her breathing was deep and measured. Throughout her long illness she had often noticed that it had been tense and shallow, and every day she had spent time trying to correct this. But now it had corrected itself without any conscious intervention from her.

Feeling tired, she returned to her favourite position on the sofa. Then she realised that the tiredness she felt was just that, and not the perpetual extreme exhaustion she had been experiencing for so long. She found herself picking up the knitting pattern again, and this time she read it without any difficulty. She selected the first pair of needles and cast on the stitches for the back of the little jacket she planned to make. It felt entirely right to be knitting something for the baby that Diana was carrying. In fact she had knitted several things for Diana when she was a baby. After she and Don had met Joan and Jim at the antenatal classes, she had made a few things for Joan to add to her layette; and once the girls were born and they had made the agreement that she would be caring for Diana several days a week, she had often made two of each garment she produced – one for Helen and one for Diana.

As she worked, she thought about how deeply she had bonded with Diana – it was almost as if she had been her own child. This had never led to any problems for either Joan or Diana, but now Fay began to realise that her own situation had been unusual, and at times very hard for her, especially when Diana was tiny. Referring to Helen and

Diana as 'the twins' had had a much deeper meaning for her than was apparent at the time. In fact, if she were honest with herself, she felt a tearing feeling inside on many of the days when Diana was at home with Joan. This eased once Diana was no longer a baby, but it had been hard at the time. It had not been that she wanted Diana to herself. It was that she had longed to see her, touch her and hold her – just for a few moments each day. Of course she and Joan would speak to each other on the phone nearly every day; and although this was an important part of their friendship, it did nothing to reach the ache that Fay felt inside – an ache that had no words and no expression.

'I must find a way of speaking to Joan and Diana about this,' she said decisively. 'When Don comes home this evening, I'll tell him about it, and he'll remind me that we must talk about it.' She put her knitting down, reached across for the small notepad she usually kept by the phone, and jotted a reminder.

About an hour later, Fay heard the sound of Don's car in the drive, followed by his key in the lock. She jumped up and rushed to the hall to greet him.

'Hello,' he said as they hugged each other. 'Hey, there's something different about you. You've got some colour in your cheeks and…' He put his hands on her shoulders and studied her face intently. 'Your eyebrows are different,' he pronounced triumphantly.

Fay spluttered with sudden mirth. 'You're right,' she replied. 'I never thought you'd notice. Actually, something else is different too, but I don't think you'll find that out by looking at me.'

'That sounds very intriguing,' said Don. 'Are you going to keep me guessing, or are you going to tell me?'

'Why don't you put your things away, and we'll have something to eat first?' Fay suggested. 'I thought I'd wait until you came. And by the way, I stuck to the rules and did nothing to the house, so we've plenty to do over the weekend to get ready for Helen and Peter coming.'

Having put his things in the cupboard in the hall, Don took a chair from the dining table and positioned it in the kitchen.

'You sit there,' he ordered. 'Just because you're looking a bit better, I'm not going to assume that you're all that well. If you sit here we can chat while I make something, and you can join in if you feel like it.'

'You're right,' Fay agreed. 'I feel quite a bit better at the moment, but I do feel very tired. It's as if I've been through some kind of crisis.'

'Crisis?' said Don. 'What's happened?'

'Nothing really,' Fay reassured him. 'Look, let's make the food, and then I'll tell you what I mean over dinner. How about telling me about your last two days?'

'Actually, there's not much to tell,' said Don as he put some rice on to boil. 'I've got a very sore behind from far too much sitting.' He massaged himself ruefully before looking in the fridge and selecting the vegetables. 'Shall I chop these up and do a stirfry?'

'I'd like that,' Fay replied. 'There's a pack of tofu at the back of the fridge that you could use.'

'Sounds great,' said Don enthusiastically. 'I haven't enjoyed much of the food I've been eating this week – it's all been a bit soggy and overdone.'

Fay nodded sympathetically. 'I wish there were some way we could get round that.'

'Never mind,' said Don cheerfully. 'I'm here now for a whole two weeks, and we can enjoy some good things together.' He paused and then went on. 'Actually, there *is* a bit of news – there was quite a hiatus yesterday morning when I arrived at the hall where the hearing was being held.'

'What was it?' asked Fay, immediately interested.

'There was a small demonstration. I thought for a while that we might have to get the police to come, but actually the people were quite peaceful. They just wanted to have their say, albeit in loud voices, and then they joined us quietly in the hall.'

'I don't remember you ever having anything like that before,' Fay remarked.

'You're right, I haven't.' Don looked thoughtful for a moment and then added, 'When I think about it there was something unusual about the people who did it.'

'What do you mean exactly?'

'I don't know. I can't quite put my finger on it. It only occurred to me now when I was telling you about it. At the time when it happened I was too concerned about whether or not I would need to contact the police, and after that my mind was taken up with the hearing. At the moment all I've got to go on is a gut instinct.'

'I'm intrigued,' said Fay. 'I wonder what it can be. Can I ask you some questions? Perhaps that would help.'

'Good idea,' said Don, checking the rice and then reaching for the wok. 'If you don't mind I'll get on with the chopping while we talk.'

'Was it something they were wearing?'

'No, I don't think so. I can't remember anything of note.'

'How many people were there?'

'About ten I should say.'

'What ages were they?'

Don stopped with the large knife poised above the vegetables. 'How silly of me,' he said. 'It's so simple. If I hadn't been stressed with my responsibilities I would have been able to see straight away.'

'See what straight away?'

'They were all older people. I would say they were all in their seventies or older – except for one young couple.'

'What exactly were they saying?' asked Fay curiously.

'Now that you ask, I'm very aware that what they said was entirely unexpected when coming from a group of demonstrators. It was more like a religious march. No… no, that's not right either.'

'Tell me what you can remember of what they said,' Fay repeated.

'They said that they sincerely hoped that only something good would come from the hearing. They said that it was the rightness that was important to them, whatever the final decision. I have to say that this surprised me, because I'm usually in a situation where people are desperate to know whether the decision is for or against. These people were clearly not saying anything about that.'

'That's fascinating!' Fay exclaimed. 'And it's very encouraging too.'

'It was,' replied Don. 'And I have to say I wouldn't mind encountering a few more people like that.' He tossed the chopped vegetables deftly into the wok and stirred them carefully. 'Can you pass me a couple of plates from the cupboard and I'll warm them under the grill?'

Fay handed them across, and then asked, 'Is there anything else you can remember?'

'Not at the moment, but I'll tell you if anything comes to mind.'

'Shall we have a few fresh chives?' asked Fay. 'I saw some coming up in the garden yesterday.'

'That's a good idea,' replied Don. 'I'll go and get some.'

'No. I'd like to go,' Fay insisted.

Not long afterwards they were both seated at the dining table enjoying their meal.

'Now, what is it that you were going to tell me?' Don reminded her.

Fay proceeded to tell him what had happened that day.

He listened quietly and intently to everything she had to say. His only movement was his slow chewing of his food. It was almost as if the rhythmical motion of his jaw aided his concentration.

When he was sure Fay had finished her account, he said, 'I'm lost for words.'

'Actually, so am I,' Fay confessed. 'It's one thing telling you what happened, and it's quite another trying to say something about its effect on me. I think anything I might say at the moment would sound inadequate and superficial.'

'That's why I was thinking about what *I* could say,' said Don. 'Would you mind if I try a couple of things?'

'Go ahead.'

'I knew that your mother was a very, very difficult woman, but I had no idea of the extent of what she did to you when you were young. I wish you'd said something to me before. Maybe I would have been able to be of more useful support to you while she was still alive… and since her death.'

'*I* wish I'd been able to say something to you, but actually I wasn't even able to say it to myself.'

'I can see that,' Don replied. 'But one thing that can come from this is that it might be easier for us to work together. For instance, we can help you to stop and think when you're just about to agree to something that isn't going to be right for you. We'd already decided we were going to be careful about that, and I feel certain that what you've been talking about is going to help us.'

Fay nodded. 'But the habit of agreeing to things and being helpful is so deeply entrenched in me that I'm still likely to be right into something without realising.'

'I understand that,' said Don sympathetically, 'but I think we'll be more able to stick to our earlier plan – the one where you say to people that although you'd really like to help, you'll think it through and then get back to them. That way you can be sure of talking things over with me before you agree to anything.'

'Mm,' said Fay uncertainly.

'What's the matter?' asked Don.

'To be scrupulously honest, I think that once I'm well again it's still likely that I'll agree to things without realising it.'

'We'll see about that,' said Don. He thought for a while in silence before continuing. 'I think it might help if you were wearing something that was a constant reminder to you that we're together in this – something that helps you to know that you aren't alone with your mother's problems any more.'

'That's a good idea, Don,' Fay replied. 'But what do you think would work?'

'I've an idea of what I'd like you to try,' said Don confidently. And before Fay had time to say anything, he said, 'A ring.'

'A ring?' echoed Fay.

'Yes, a ring.'

'But I can't think of any I have that would do.'

'Precisely,' said Don, staring meaningfully at her across the table. 'So, while I'm here over the next two weeks we're going to go shopping to see what we can find.'

'That's such a good idea,' said Fay sincerely. 'Don, I think you're right. And I'm not going to worry about whether we'll find something suitable or not. If it's the right idea, the right ring will be found, I'm sure. And I think that even if we don't find one, the very fact that we've been looking will change things for me.'

'That's what I was thinking too,' said Don, reaching across the table and squeezing her hand. 'Now, there's one other thing.'

'What's that?'

'When you were telling me about today, you asked me to remind you to talk to Joan and Diana.'

'That's right.'

'I won't forget.'

'Thanks, Don.'

It was when they were lying in bed later that evening, discussing how they would go about getting things ready for Helen and Peter's arrival, that Don brought up the subject of Fay's eyebrows again.

'What made you change them?' he asked. 'I've never known you to bother doing anything to your face before.'

'I think it's been on my mind for a very long time, and it was only last night that I realised I could do something about it. I hate the way I look like my mother, and I suddenly realised that I could easily do something about those few hairs in my eyebrows that are like hers.'

Don looked at her with understanding dawning on his face. 'No wonder you felt like you did today then,' he said.

'Yes,' said Fay. 'I hadn't made that connection myself.'

'It's hardly surprising,' said Don as he smiled across at her. 'Fay,' he added suddenly, 'did you do anything in particular during the day yesterday?'

Fay stared at him blankly. 'No. I don't think so,' she said. 'I can't really remember. I expect I was resting. Why do you ask?'

'It's just a hunch I had. Never mind. Shall I put out the light?'

'No!' gasped Fay, clutching at him. 'No! Don't make it dark.'

Don saw the colour drain from her cheeks. He tried to soothe her. 'Don't worry. I'll leave it on. Can you tell me what's the matter?'

'I feel I can't breathe,' said Fay anxiously. 'And all I can think about is that tunnel.'

'You mean the one under that ruined house in your dream?'

'Yes.' Fay was thankful that Don had remembered.

'Fay, are you *sure* you were just resting yesterday?' asked Don gently.

It was then that Fay remembered, and she felt herself grow colder and colder. Why had she forgotten? There was no reason why she should have done so. And why had she become so cold?

'Don,' she began, 'I've just remembered that I went to the hospital yesterday.'

'The hospital? I didn't know you had an appointment. What happened?'

Fay shook her head. 'I didn't have an appointment.' Don looked puzzled. He didn't say anything, and she continued. 'I wanted to see if there were cobbles in the courtyard,' she explained simply. 'I was going to get you to take me there but I forgot, and I remembered about it again yesterday. Now I can drive, I decided to go there and then. I took my camera with me and I've got some pictures.'

'I'm not sure that I quite understand yet,' said Don patiently.

'An appointment card arrived that morning from the hospital…'

Here Don interrupted. 'What did it say?'

'It said I've to see someone called Dr Grayling. The appointment is a few days after Helen and Peter go back home.'

'Good,' said Don. 'That means I'll be here to go with you.'

'I was sitting there looking at the card when I remembered that after I'd had the X-ray I'd been confused about whether or not there were cobbles in the courtyard that led to the main entrance door of the hospital. It was important to me because of the cobbles in the courtyard of the farm where I used to live. I'd felt muddled, and I wanted to know one way or the other. But by the time you came home the following weekend it had gone out of my mind, so I couldn't ask you to take me.'

'And it was only when you got the appointment card yesterday that it came back to you?' Don finished for her.

'Yes. That's right.'

'Did you find any cobbles?'

'Yes. But they were modern fakes.' Fay smiled.

'That's better,' said Don. 'You don't look so strung out any more. We can survey the cobbles together when we go for your appointment. It looks to me as if you're trying to sort out a whole lot of things in your mind – dreams of a ruin and a tunnel, courtyards with cobbles and…'

'And inscriptions on stones,' added Fay. 'When I was at the hospital taking the photos I felt a bit silly when I looked above the archway that led to the courtyard to see if there was anything carved there. Of course there wasn't.'

'I can guess why you wanted to know though,' said Don. 'You were thinking about the carving above the archway in those photos I took for you, weren't you?'

'Yes. And the one above the main door of the mansion in the picture in that book.'

'Of course,' said Don. 'Why don't we get those pictures out in the morning and take a closer look at them? If you want we could go down to the hospital together. It isn't all that far. It won't take us all weekend to get things ready for Helen and Peter coming. In fact, if we wanted we could have the day to ourselves tomorrow. Yes, let's do that,' he finished firmly.

'Good,' said Fay. 'Now I think we can put out the light.'

Chapter Eight

The following morning was warm and bright. Fay could see the sun shining round the edges of the curtains, and the temperature of the room felt pleasant, despite the fact that the heating was not on. She looked at the clock and saw it was half past eight already. She had slept very well. Don was stirring.

'I'll draw the curtains,' she said, getting out of bed.

'There's no rush,' Don reminded her sleepily. 'Take things slowly, and then we'll have the best chance of you lasting the day.'

'I'll draw them and then get back into bed,' Fay bargained. 'By the way, there's one more thing I should tell you that might be part of the whole puzzle.'

Don was instantly alert. Fay was reassured because this indicated to her that she had not overburdened him last night with everything she had told him.

'I'm waiting eagerly,' he said.

'I hurt my thumb on the curtains downstairs after I'd been to see the hospital,' Fay explained.

'How did you do that?'

'I don't know. It felt exactly as if I'd stabbed my thumb on a pin that had been left in the curtain, but when I examined it I found nothing.'

'I'm not surprised you didn't find anything,' laughed Don. 'You must have made those curtains about six years ago. If you'd left a pin in them, surely we would have found it by now! But I can't begin to guess what could have caused the pain.'

'I pricked my thumb on something that wasn't there, and soon afterwards I went very cold and went to get an old jumper. After that I was thinking about past lives and wishing that there was someone to talk to.'

'Well, you've got someone to talk to now,' said Don. 'You've got me. And you've got me for a whole two weeks. And today we're going to be together all day, just the two of us. We're going to have a good time, and we're going to see what we can make of what's been happening to you. This business of past lives… I think I'll have to do some reading about it. Perhaps I could make a start with that chapter you told me about in *Russian Voices*. I expect that copy Jim got for you has gone back to the library by now.'

'Yes, it has.'

'Let's have a look on the Internet and see if we can order a copy,' Don suggested.

After breakfast, it did not take them long to track one down, and learned it would be with them in a few days.

'Let's get out the photos next,' said Don, obviously keen to study them again.

Fay found the pack and the book and laid them on the table. She found the page with the picture of the mansion, while Don sorted through the photos to find the carving above the archway. Then they laid them side by side.

'I'll just get that magnifying glass from upstairs,' said Don as he disappeared through the door into the hall. Fay heard him running up the stairs and down again, and he reappeared waving his trophy. 'Got it!' he said. 'You can have the first look.'

Fay took the glass and studied the two inscriptions. Although they were of a similar style there was definitely a difference between them. Without saying anything she handed the glass over to Don, and she watched as he scrutinised them.

'They look similar to me,' he said, 'but quite different as well.'

'That's my reaction too.'

'I can't say that they particularly remind me of anything I've seen before,' Don mused.

'I'm the same.'

'Let's leave them out on the table,' suggested Don, 'and we'll have another look at them later. For the moment I think I just want to absorb what I saw. The lens definitely helps me to see the detailing. And now I'll tell you what I'd like us to do next.'

'Go on.'

'I'd like to go on that ring hunt,' said Don. 'We may not find anything today, but I certainly want to go and look.'

'Then we'll definitely go,' replied Fay. 'But would you mind if we have a quick look at the hospital courtyard together first?' she added eagerly.

'Okay,' said Don. 'Let's get ready, and then we'll go. I'll bring the Yellow Pages in the car – it might give us some clues for our hunt.'

About half an hour later they were returning to the car after Don had seen the courtyard.

'I'm glad I've seen it, because now I know what you've been talking about,' he said. 'By the way, did you take a picture of the archway when you came?'

'No, just the courtyard.'

'In that case I'll go and take one. I'll be back in a minute.' Don opened the glove compartment and took out a small digital camera. 'This is the one I use for work, but it'll be fine,' he said.

While he was away Fay picked up the Yellow Pages. Having decided to try under 'Jewellers', she then found there were four pages to examine. She was studying them intently when Don returned, and she jumped when she heard his voice.

'Have you found something?' he asked.

'Not yet. But there are plenty to choose from.' She ran her finger down the columns of advertisements. 'By the way,' she continued, 'I was thinking that I'd prefer something that had been used before.'

'Any special reason?'

'Not as far as I know. It's just the way I feel.'

'Okay. Then we should consider looking in antique shops as well.'

Fay looked up from her task. 'That's a good idea, Don. Will you help me to pick two or three likely places – not too far away? I'm not up to a lot of travelling yet.'

Together they scrutinised the entries, marking the ones that looked promising. Then they made a list of three.

'Which shall we try first?' asked Fay.

'Let's look at the addresses and then plan an itinerary,' replied Don. 'Ah, there are two in the town and the other one is quite a way out into the countryside.'

'That's strange!' exclaimed Fay. 'I don't associate jewellers' shops with the countryside.'

'Actually this is the antique dealer that we chose,' said Don. 'Courtyard Antiques Limited.' He laughed. 'No wonder we chose it with a name like that! Let me have a look at the map and see how long it will take us to get there.' He took a map out of the glove compartment and studied it. 'It'll be about forty minutes from here, I'd say. And if we start by going into town, that'll make the journey a bit longer because we'd be travelling in the opposite direction first. It would be nearly an hour by then. Perhaps we should go there first.'

'I think I'd rather start off with the jewellers if you don't mind. I hope we'll find something suitable there. That way we'll avoid a long drive. And right now it feels a bit strange to be going to a place with a courtyard.'

'All right. I'll park in the multi-storey in town and we can walk to the two shops from there.'

It was not long before Fay and Don were standing reading a sign that said *Godwin's – Antique Jewellery and Fine Silver*. The window display included a large range of items, and Fay began to feel overwhelmed.

'Come on,' said Don, taking her hand. 'In we go.'

Inside the shop there were several tables, each of which had its own lamp. A smartly dressed woman came towards them, and when they described the kind of ring they were looking for, she ushered them to one of the tables and invited them to sit down.

'I'm afraid we haven't got a large range at the moment,' she said, 'but I'll bring you some to look at. You said you wanted something relatively plain and without any large stones?'

'That's right,' said Fay a little nervously.

Don touched her arm. 'Now remember,' he said, 'you don't have to take something just because it fits, or because I like it.'

'I'm glad you reminded me,' said Fay. 'I needed to hear that.'

The assistant returned with a box, which she opened and laid on the table.

'This is all we have at the moment, madam,' she said. 'However, we are expecting more in at the end of the month.'

'Thank you,' said Fay, and she began to examine each ring closely.

'Of course, we can usually adjust the size,' the assistant added.

Fay turned to Don and said in a low voice, 'I need to choose something that is certain of reminding me of our pact.' She thought the assistant must have overheard because she smiled approvingly, and Fay flushed slightly with embarrassment.

Although she tried on a couple of rings that caught her eye, Fay was not convinced that either of them was exactly what she wanted, so they thanked the assistant and left the shop.

Outside on the pavement Don said 'Well done' and gave her a hug.

'But I haven't bought a ring,' Fay protested.

'Of course,' said Don. 'Well done for not buying one. If you had it would have been for the wrong reasons.'

Fay's face lit up. '*Now* I follow you,' she said. 'Right,' she continued confidently, 'where's the next shop?'

But when they arrived at Hall's, it was shut. There was a notice in the window that apologised, saying that the shop would be closed for a week due to unforeseen circumstances.

'It looks as if we'll be going to the *Courtyard Antiques*,' said Don cheerfully as they made their way back to the car. 'I think you might enjoy a run in the countryside, and if you're tired when we get home, you can go to bed and I'll bring you something up on a tray. Is that a deal?'

'Done!' agreed Fay readily. Don was right. A run might be a good idea.

The Courtyard turned out to be situated next to a rather dilapidated farmhouse. It was a group of buildings arranged on three sides of a quadrangle, with space for parking in the middle. Fay noticed with relief that there were no cobbles or archways anywhere to be seen. The sensitively restored buildings housed various shop units. There was one that sold old-fashioned linen, another displayed replicas of household equipment of bygone times, the next had toys that Fay had only seen in museums, and the one along from that sold jewellery. There were several more shops, but Fay was not interested in them at the moment. She took Don's hand and went inside the jeweller's.

In contrast to Godwin's, the shop was brightly lit throughout. A young man dressed in a smart grey suit approached them and greeted them courteously. Having ascertained what they had come for, he showed them to some comfortable chairs arranged round a low table in a corner of the shop floor.

'I'll bring you something to try,' he said, and he disappeared behind a heavy curtain at the back of the shop.

When he reappeared he was carrying a number of boxes – the kind in which small sets of cutlery are often kept. He placed the stack on the table, took the one on the top and opened it out next to Fay, before taking a seat nearby.

'Just take your time,' he said pleasantly.

Fay looked at her watch. It was nearly lunchtime. 'Do you close for lunch?' she asked nervously.

'Please don't worry about the time,' the young man reassured her. 'You must take as long as you need.'

Fay relaxed and began to examine the rings. There were several that drew her attention, and she pointed them out to Don.

As she explored the contents of each box in turn she became completely absorbed in her search. The only thing that mattered was to find the ring she needed – the one that would remind her of her pact with Don. There were many beautiful and attractive pieces. A large number of them included stones of very striking appearance, which she was interested to examine. She noticed that she was drawn to the colour of sapphires. The intense blue was more than just appealing, but she could not define the exact effect upon her. One of the boxes included a very handsome signet ring, which she showed to Don.

'Why don't *you* have this one?' she joked.

He took it from her and tried to work out what letters were combined to make the intricate design.

'I can't work this out,' he said with some exasperation.

'Perhaps I can help, sir,' said the assistant, reaching across to take the ring. He scrutinised it for a few minutes, and then said, 'I have to admit that it defeats me too. I'll go and get the catalogue. Excuse me one moment.'

He disappeared behind the curtain again, and when he returned he was carrying an old leather-bound ledger. Fay was surprised to see such a large old book being used for this purpose, but she made no comment, and waited patiently while the assistant carefully turned its pages. Having identified a particular one, he checked the number on the small white tag that was attached to the ring and consulted the corresponding entry.

'The details I have here say that this signet ring was made around 1830 and that the letters on it are DLB. Of course, they are a mirror image, and interwoven with one another on the face of the ring. I should also say that someone who has made a study of such rings made this assessment, so I'm sure it's as accurate as possible.'

Don and Fay stared at each other in astonishment. 'DLB,' Fay repeated. 'But those are *your* initials, Don.'

Don looked a little uncomfortable. 'This is certainly a strange coincidence,' he managed to say. He picked up the ring from where the assistant had laid it on the table and examined the inscription once more. 'Now that I know what the letters are I can just about make them out,' he said. 'But it's difficult.'

'I think it has something to do with the unusual style of the lettering, sir,' said the young man helpfully. 'I was surprised that I couldn't make it out myself. I usually have no difficulty. Incidentally, there's another part to the entry in this ledger. The report of the assessor included the view that the ring had been made by someone who was a skilled goldsmith, but who produced very little work because we know of no other pieces of the same style and quality.'

'That's one possibility,' said Fay slowly, 'but it could be that most of the other work has been destroyed, lost or hidden away.'

'You're correct, madam,' the assistant replied.

Don consulted the reverse side of the white tag on the ring. 'Two hundred and seventy-five pounds,' he mused.

Fay addressed him directly. 'Don,' she said. 'I'm very keen that we buy this ring for you. In fact, I'm going to insist.'

Don looked at her in surprise. He realised that he was about to protest, but then he allowed himself to be infected by her determination and enthusiasm. She looked almost joyful, he noticed, and it was so good to see her eager and excited after so many months of illness, when she had appeared grey and low.

'It's all right,' he reassured her. 'I'm not going to argue. Of course we'll buy it. I was only hesitating because we'd come here to buy a ring for *you*, and instead we're buying one for *me*.'

'Maybe that's what was meant to happen,' Fay replied gaily, reaching in her bag for her cheque book. 'And I don't want to look at any more rings at the moment. I'd like to go home.'

She wrote a cheque and handed it to the assistant together with her cheque card.

'Perhaps you would like to try the ring for size, sir,' the young man suggested.

'That won't be necessary, thank you,' Don replied.

The assistant looked surprised, and Don smiled at Fay conspiratorially. They both knew that the size was of no consequence.

Minutes later they were leaving the shop. As soon as they were in the car, Fay took the box out of the small plastic carrier bag and opened the lid. She was pleased to see that the box was of very good quality – a kind she associated with bygone times. The hinged lid was lined with white cotton satin, and the deep velvet which held the ring was an intense purple colour.

'I want to see which of your fingers it fits,' she said suddenly.

Don held out his hands and Fay tried the ring – finger by finger.

'That's the one!' they said together as she tried the ring finger of his right hand.

'It's perfect,' said Don. 'It's as if it had been made for me.' He stopped and struggled for a moment. 'Fay, when I said that I felt a bit odd,' he confided.

'What do you mean exactly?' Fay asked.

'I suddenly felt as if it really *had* been made for me,' he confessed.

Fay laughed.

'Why are you laughing?' asked Don in hurt tones. 'I don't feel it's funny at all.'

'It isn't,' Fay agreed. 'But there's something I have to tell you.'

'What's that?'

'When we were sitting in the shop looking at this ring, I had such a strong feeling that we had to buy it for you. It was almost as if I had been *told* to do it.'

Don stared at her, first in disbelief, and then with a dawning admiration.

'You're really special,' he said.

'Well… thanks… and so are you,' Fay replied.

'And now I'll take you home,' Don said briskly.

They said very little on the journey back to the house. Once inside, Fay went to lie down upstairs, and when Don went up to speak to her he found she was asleep.

It was evening by the time she came downstairs, where she found

Don immersed in a book.

'What's that?' she asked with interest.

'Just something I picked up to dip into in the evenings when I was away,' he said, a little defensively. 'It was in a second-hand bookshop.'

'Let me see,' Fay persisted.

'In a minute,' Don replied. 'First tell me how you're feeling.'

Fay considered for a moment. 'Actually, I don't feel too bad,' she said. 'How long have I been asleep?'

'Nearly four hours.'

'Oh! I had no idea it was so late!' exclaimed Fay looking at the clock. 'It always makes me feel so disorientated when this kind of thing happens. But I do feel better for the rest.'

'You certainly look quite good – better than you have been for a long time,' said Don. He handed his book across to her and she read the back of the cover.

'This looks interesting…' she said immediately. 'An ex-CIA spy in search of a peaceful mind. Let me know how you get on with it.'

'Well, as I said, I've only been dipping into it, but it's certainly unusual to read about a hard-bitten spy looking for something completely different – something he hasn't known before.'

Fay looked at Don's hand. 'Where's the ring?' she asked.

'In its box, of course.'

'But you should be wearing it,' she protested.

'In that case, you'd better put it on for me,' said Don, laughing. 'No. Wait a minute.' He stood up.

'Where are you going?'

'I'll be back soon. I'm off to look for something.'

There were rumbling sounds from upstairs, and Fay realised that Don was going up into the loft. He returned later with a triumphant look on his face.

'I knew I had some somewhere,' he said, waving a packet above his head. 'I'll get the matches and then we'll be ready.' He smiled at Fay's puzzled face. 'Don't look so worried,' he teased.

Fay watched as Don produced a stick of gold-coloured sealing wax, lit it, dripped some on to the back of an envelope, and then pressed the inscription on the ring into it.

'Hey presto!' he said as he passed the imprint across to her for her to see.

'It's really clear,' Fay said with obvious delight. 'It's such an old ring, but this is very clear.'

'I had the impression right from the outset that the ring had hardly been used,' said Don. 'I'll give you my hand lens, and you can see if there are any scratches on it.' He reached into his pocket and passed it across to her.

Fay looked at the ring carefully. 'You're right,' she pronounced. 'It would be fascinating to know its history, wouldn't it?'

Just then the phone rang, and Don reached across to pick it up.

'Helen. It's great to hear you... Yes, I've been away every time you've phoned recently. Of course your mum keeps me up to date with your news, but it isn't the same as talking to you myself... Yes, and I'm looking forward to seeing you soon, too... Monday, isn't it? No... That's good news... You mean you're arriving tomorrow instead? Supper time... Do you want a word with your mum? Okay, I'll hand you over.' He passed the phone to Fay.

'Hello, love... Of course it's all right... We might not be completely organised... No, I promise I won't. See you tomorrow then. Bye.' She put the phone down.

'Now don't you start getting in a flap about the spare room,' Don instructed her with mock severity.

'I've already promised Helen that I won't,' said Fay. 'And in any case I'm glad to say that it was already in my mind when I heard you speaking to her,' she added proudly. 'It looks as if perhaps something is starting to change already.'

'It certainly is,' Don replied. 'This is the first time you haven't leapt out of your chair and started to rush around when something like this happens.'

Fay smiled. 'For one thing I can't do any leaping, and for another I'm sure I don't have to, even if I could. And I can see that's a big step forward. What I want is a quiet evening with you, talking about the ring and anything else that comes to mind. Tomorrow we'll do what we can with the house and the shopping.'

Chapter Nine

The following day Don organised the spare room, and then he and Fay went to the supermarket together. Don had been insistent that it should be he who did the work in the house, since most of the clutter that had accumulated was his.

Just after seven there was a ring at the door. 'Hello!' Helen shouted through the letterbox. It was an old trick of hers from her school days, which she often liked to repeat when she came home.

After they had greeted each other in the hallway, Peter offered to take the bags upstairs while Helen joined her parents in the sitting room.

'Something to drink?' asked Don when Peter appeared.

'Some of your elderflower cordial would be nice,' said Helen.

'I'm afraid we haven't got any of last year's batch left now,' Fay replied, 'but we brought some from the supermarket in case you asked.'

Don soon appeared with a tray with four glasses and jug of cordial. He filled the glasses and handed them round.

'I managed to get through to Reverend Howard last week,' Helen said. 'As we thought, he's very tied up with services in the run-up to Easter Sunday, but he said he can spare an hour on Monday afternoon. We decided in the end that it was best to rearrange things so that we arrived here today instead of setting off early tomorrow morning.'

'I'm keen that we have some time to prepare for the meeting,' added Peter. 'I don't want it to be only a business meeting about the ceremony. I want to do all I can to familiarise myself with the church, its background and its vicar before the wedding. It's only right.'

'I'm very glad you feel that way,' said Don. 'That's important to us too, isn't it, Fay?'

Fay nodded.

'Mum, have you spoken to Joan recently?' asked Helen.

'Not in the last few days,' Fay replied. 'Why?'

'Then you won't know yet that Diana and Paul are arriving

tomorrow morning, and they're staying over until Easter Monday,' Helen explained.

Fay flushed with pleasure. 'That means it's certain that we can all spend some time together. It'll be the first time for ages.' She turned to Don. 'I'd like to arrange a meal out for all of us one evening this week,' she said impulsively.

Don grinned across at her and said, 'Surprise! Jim got in touch with me on my mobile as soon as he knew the exact dates, and we've fixed up a secret rendezvous for Wednesday evening at seven thirty. And there's no chance that you'll get me to say where we're going.'

'All right, I won't try,' said Fay good-naturedly. 'But there's something we should tell Helen and Peter before they see Joan and Jim... Isn't there?' she added meaningfully.

'I'll leave it up to you to say,' said Don.

Fay turned to Helen and Peter and said, 'Joan and Jim have offered to buy you a digital piano as a wedding present.'

'That's extremely generous of them,' said Peter.

Helen looked simultaneously excited and anxious. 'What do you think, Mum?' she asked. 'We'd love to accept it, wouldn't we Peter? But isn't it over-generous?'

'I spoke to them about that when they raised it with me at first,' Fay reassured her. 'They were adamant that their relationship with you meant that this is what they want to do.'

'I'm glad we've had a chance to talk about it first,' said Helen. 'It took me completely by surprise.'

'That's it settled then,' said Don. 'Now I think I'll get the food on the table.'

'Can I give you a hand?' asked Peter.

'Thanks. It should all be ready in the oven, but I'd appreciate a hand to carry it through.'

'The ladies will lay the table,' said Fay with a chuckle.

Helen opened the drawer in the chest in the dining room where Fay kept the table mats, and as she did so she caught sight of Fay's knitting.

'Hey, Mum!' she exclaimed. 'What's this? I haven't seen you knitting for years.'

'Oh… it's just something I started for Diana's baby,' Fay said as casually as she could.

Helen looked at her suspiciously. 'There's more to it than that, isn't there,' she said deliberately. 'Diana's baby isn't due for months. But you can tell me later if you want.' She began spreading table mats.

Despite the fact that she had spent most of her time away from home in recent years, Helen had never lost her intuitive understanding of her mother, and this was further proof of it, Fay thought. It was both a delight and a burden to her. To be so close that this was part of the relationship was a treasure beyond price, but Fay could not help fearing that at times it might be a stress on Helen to know about her struggles. However, Helen had often had to remind her mother that it was a stress on her if Fay didn't tell her things because she was mistakenly trying to protect her.

Peter appeared wearing a pair of bright orange oven gloves he had found in a cupboard in the kitchen, and everyone laughed as he waved them in the air while dancing a mini solo.

'Is that a traditional clog dance?' Don asked from the kitchen.

'No, just instant entertainment,' Peter replied. 'Are you ready for the hot dishes, ladies?'

Over a dinner of chicken with roast vegetables, they entertained each other with local news and amusing anecdotes. It was only when Don was serving out the sweet of fruit salad and yoghurt that Helen first caught sight of the signet ring.

'Dad!' she exclaimed. 'You've got a new ring. Where did it come from?'

Don smiled. 'I wondered when you would notice. Just to speed the discovery I twisted it round before I served your fruit salad so that you could see the front of it with the design on it.'

'It's a signet ring, isn't it?' asked Peter with interest. 'Do you mind if I have a closer look?'

Don took the ring off and handed it to him. 'There's a lens over on the fire shelf you can use if you want,' he offered.

'You haven't told me how you got it,' said Helen accusingly. 'Come on, Dad. Don't keep us in suspense.'

'Well, actually your mother and I bought it yesterday.'

'Yesterday,' echoed Helen. 'Only yesterday? Was it some sort of anniversary that I don't know about? So now there are two mysteries – the knitting and this ring.'

Fay explained. 'Don had the idea of buying me a special ring to remind me of our new pact. We went to look for something and found this.'

'More mysteries,' said Helen. 'You'll have to tell us about this pact now as well.'

Peter was quietly studying the ring with the aid of Don's lens.

'There seem to be three letters on it,' he said slowly and rather uncertainly.

'That's correct,' said Don encouragingly, smiling across at Fay and winking. 'But can you see what they are?'

'I can't be sure, but I think that one of them is D,' Peter said at last.

'Let me see,' said Helen, taking it from him.

Fay could see that Peter was not entirely willing to hand it over, but he did so, saying nothing.

'Oh!' exclaimed Helen as she looked at the inscription through the lens. 'The letters are beautifully done, and they're very clean cut, as if new.'

'That's what we found when we pressed it into sealing wax,' Don agreed.

Helen continued. 'Yes, I can see what looks like a D. But it would be easier to read from the seal you made. Can I see it?' She went on studying the ring while Don went to get the seal.

When he returned she handed the ring back to Peter and looked at the seal through the lens. 'I think one of the other letters is a B,' she said triumphantly. She looked across at her father. 'No wonder you bought it,' she proclaimed. 'It's got your initials on it.'

'Look a bit harder, and you might make out the L as well,' Don advised her. 'The whole thing defeated your mother and me in the shop, but when the assistant went and got the details and told us what the letters were, your mother insisted that we bought it. Peter, you did well to see the D from the ring itself. We didn't even get that far.'

'I suppose it's a lot less tricky reading it from the seal,' said Helen grudgingly.

'Do you know anything else about the ring?' asked Peter.

'Very little,' replied Don. 'Apparently the style is unusual and it can only be assumed that the maker, although skilled, made only a few pieces, or…'

Here Helen butted in. 'Or whatever else he made was lost or hidden,' she finished for him. 'This is really exciting,' she continued. 'I wonder how we could find out more about it. But apart from that, there's one mystery that you can solve for me straight away. Mum and Dad, tell me what your pact is.'

Fay explained, and added that she was to wear a special ring as a reminder.

'Mum, it's great to hear your plan,' said Helen. 'Actually it's a big relief to me. I've often worried about you with that sort of thing, and to be honest, sometimes I've found myself behaving like you – agreeing to things that aren't right for me.'

'I suppose it's not surprising that you've copied some of my bad habits,' said Fay ruefully, 'and that's all the more reason for me to stick to the pact.'

'Now, Mum,' said Helen with mock sternness, 'you must concentrate on changing things for yourself, and not on trying to improve things for me.'

'She's absolutely right,' Don agreed, 'and of course we have this little problem of having bought a ring for me instead of for you. What are we going to do about that?'

Fay drew herself up confidently. 'I know it was exactly the right ring to buy, not only for our pact but also…' Here she trailed off and began to look confused.

The others waited patiently while she struggled for words and found none.

'What is it, Mum?' asked Helen gently. 'What were you going to say?'

'I don't know,' said Fay. 'I was quite clear that there were two things to say, but when I got to the second one, my head went blank.'

'Well, you can tell us later,' Helen encouraged.

Don spoke next. 'Fay, I didn't know you felt we had got the right ring for our pact. Can you tell me why?'

'No, I can't,' Fay replied. 'I just know.'

'I noticed that you were wearing it on the ring finger of your right hand,' said Peter. 'Is that for any special reason?'

'Not really,' Don replied. Then he laughed. 'That's the finger it fitted – quite unexpectedly.'

'Almost as if it had been made for you,' Peter observed.

Don looked perplexed. 'Well… actually…' he said, 'that's what came into my own mind.'

There was a long silence during which everyone appeared lost in thought.

When eventually Don spoke he said, 'In any case, I shall go ahead and wear it, and I sincerely hope that it will help Fay to keep in close contact with me about anything she's thinking of taking on.'

Perhaps it's a kind of marriage,' said Peter reflectively.

'What do you mean exactly?' asked Don with interest.

'As you know, I've been thinking a lot about marriage recently,' said Peter, smiling at Helen. 'We've got the wedding day in September, and after that we have to discover what our marriage means to us as we live it and breathe it. What you and Fay are talking about could be a very important part of a married relationship – one which few people mention, either to each other or with others. The pact you have made you have sealed with a ring, and that ring fits the ring finger of your right hand – the finger that's used for a wedding band in some other countries.'

'Peter, I'm deeply impressed by what you say,' said Don. 'Thank you.'

'Yes. Thank you,' said Fay.

'Now we've sorted all that out,' said Helen, 'you can tell me about the knitting.'

'First, would anyone like anything else to drink?' asked Don.

More elderflower cordial was passed round, and Fay began.

'There's not much to tell,' she said.

'Oh yes there is,' said Helen. 'I know.'

'Shall I explain now, Don?' asked Fay.

He chuckled. 'I think you'd better.'

Fay carefully explained the background to her relationship with Diana, and then spoke of the depth of her attachment to her when she was small.

When she had finished Helen said, 'Mum, that's all really interesting. I knew a lot of it before – about how you'd met Joan and Jim, and about Joan's depression – but you've told me a lot more this time, and I had no idea about the difficulty you had about being separated from Diana.'

'To tell you the truth,' Fay replied, 'I'm not sure that I knew it as clearly as I can describe it now. I've been thinking about it a lot over the last couple of days.'

'So you haven't ever spoken to Joan and Diana about it?' asked Helen.

'No, the only person I've told is your dad, and that was yesterday,' Fay replied.

'I've been thinking about it,' said Don reflectively, 'and I think it's just as important that Jim knows about it too.'

'Oh, I wasn't going to leave him out,' Fay hurried to reassure him. Then she stopped and thought for a minute. 'But you're right to say what you did, because my mind was fixed on talking to Joan and Diana.'

'I'm glad you've told us,' said Peter, taking hold of Helen's hand. 'It's very important that we know about it. So, I'm going to have a wife who's got a special kind of twin sister!'

Fay looked at Helen. 'And there's something else to tell you,' she said.

'More?' exclaimed Helen. 'Carry on.'

'I think we should get everything tidied away and settle ourselves in the sitting room first,' said Don. 'You two ladies go and sit down, and Peter and I will make short work of this.' He winked at Peter.

'All right. We won't resist,' said Helen as she and Fay disappeared into the hall.

It was not long afterwards that Don and Peter joined them. Don was carrying a tray bearing four mugs full of steaming liquid.

'Surprise!' he said. 'You don't have to drink it if you don't like it, but I thought I'd give some of this acorn coffee a bash. Did you know that there's a tribe somewhere that relies on acorns as a staple crop?'

'No, I didn't,' said Helen, surprised. 'Do you know any more about them?'

'Unfortunately not,' Don replied. 'It's yet another subject I must research sometime.'

Helen sipped tentatively at the hot liquid. 'Mmm… This is quite nice. It's got a really distinctive flavour.' She turned to Peter. 'Try it, Peter.'

'I already have,' he replied. 'I had some in the kitchen before I committed myself to a whole mug full. I think it's fine.'

'I'd like to show you the photos next,' said Fay, and she handed the photos of the farm buildings to Helen, and the book to Peter. 'I think the one I want you to look at is on page nine.'

'I'll swop with you when I've finished looking through these,' Helen said to Peter, and she began to work her way through the photos. 'So Dad took these before I was born,' she mused. 'That explains why they're black and white. Mum, show me the bit where you lived.'

Fay selected two pictures and showed the windows of her former home to Helen. 'And I want to point out some carving to you,' she added, searching for the photograph of the archway. 'Here it is. Have a look with the lens. You can see it a bit more clearly, although of course when it's enlarged like that it looks a little fuzzy.'

Helen examined it with interest. 'I can't say it reminds me of anything, but I'm glad you showed it to me,' she said.

'Take a look at the picture that Peter has,' Fay urged.

Peter passed the book across and Helen handed the photos to him. 'Ah!' she exclaimed as she looked at the picture. 'I know why you wanted me to see this now. There's a carving on the stonework above the main door of this mansion house.' She looked at it through the magnifier. 'It's a similar style to the one over the archway of the farm buildings, but it's not the same.'

'That's right,' said Don. 'Now let Peter have a look.'

Peter took the lens. 'I haven't quite finished looking through all these photos yet,' he said. 'Fay, would you mind explaining more about what they are?'

'This is a place where I lived for a while before I met Don,' she replied as she pointed out the windows of the part of the buildings that had been her home. 'I feel a bit silly because this carving you can see on the stonework above this archway is something I never noticed while I was living there. Don and I went back years later and he took these photos for me.'

Peter studied the carving and then looked at the one in the book. 'Do you know how far away from the farm the mansion house was?' he asked.

'I think it was about a quarter of a mile, if that,' Fay explained. 'Why do you ask?'

'No particular reason,' said Peter.

'I must say it had quite an effect on me when I found that the new hospital had an archway and a cobbled courtyard,' said Fay. 'In fact, only the other day I felt I had to go back to check, and I took photographs, but they're still in the camera.'

'Is there a carving above the archway?' asked Helen playfully.

Fay nudged her in mock irritation. 'What do you think?' she asked.

'I suppose not,' Helen replied.

'Can we have a change of topic?' asked Fay. 'I think we've concentrated on me for quite long enough, and I've got some things to ask you.'

'Are you trying to avoid something?' asked Helen suspiciously.

'Not really,' Fay replied. 'I do have other things I'd like to talk over, but I'd rather leave it until another day.'

'All right,' said Helen, 'but I won't forget.'

'What time are you due to see Reverend Howard tomorrow?' Fay asked.

'He said to come for three o'clock,' Peter replied.

'It would be good not to feel rushed,' said Helen, 'but we know he's busy.'

'Is there anything about it that you want to talk over this evening?' asked Don.

'I don't think so, thanks, Don,' replied Peter. 'Helen and I started a notebook, and we've kept adding things to it whenever they occur to us.'

'That's a good idea,' Fay remarked. 'Don and I will look forward to hearing how you get on, won't we Don?'

'Yes, of course. And if there's anything we're needed for at this stage, let us know.'

'I'm afraid I'm beginning to feel a bit tired,' said Fay apologetically. 'I think I'm going to have to go to bed.'

'I don't think we'll be long behind you,' said Don. 'Off you go. I'll see you upstairs. And don't worry about anything. I'll make sure Helen and Peter have got everything they need.'

'I'll see you tomorrow,' said Fay, and she made her way into the hall and up the stairs. Her legs felt very heavy and she was struggling against some of the old dizziness. She was soon ready to get into bed, and gratefully drew the duvet up over herself. She was dozing by the time she heard the others coming up the stairs, and was barely aware of Don as he climbed into bed beside her.

She woke only once in the night, convinced that there was someone moving around on the landing. She strained her ears, but could hear nothing...

Chapter Ten

When Fay woke she could hear the sound of voices floating up the stairs, together with the chink of cutlery. There was a space in the bed where Don should be, and she looked at the clock. It was nine thirty already, and she still felt tired. She heard Helen's footsteps on the stairs, then her head appeared round the door.

'You're awake at last,' she said cheerfully. 'I've made you a tray of breakfast, and I insist that you have it in bed.' She disappeared again, but soon returned carrying a tray with a glass of fruit juice, a bowl of grapes and some oatcakes. 'Dad told me what you like,' she said as she put it on a chair beside the bed and perched next to it. 'I think you should stay there as long as you really need to,' she advised. 'I'd like to chat, but I can go away if you want to be on your own.'

'Don't go. I'd love you to stay,' said Fay, sipping the fruit juice. 'I'll just pop to the bathroom and then lie down again.'

When she came back she found that Helen had piled a few pillows in a wedge shape.

'There!' said Helen. 'Now you can eat your breakfast but still be lying down. Did you sleep all right last night?'

'Yes. I woke only once. I thought I could hear someone moving about, but there wasn't anyone there. I must have been dreaming.'

'That's funny,' said Helen.

'Why?'

'The same thing happened to me. I woke up convinced that someone was there, but I couldn't hear anything and I went back to sleep. I haven't a clue what time it was. It was dark – that's all I know.'

The two women stared at each other.

'Have you said anything to Don and Peter?' asked Fay.

'Yes. I told them at breakfast. Of course, they had both slept like logs, and hadn't got anything to contribute.'

'There's something odd going on,' said Fay, half to herself.

'What do you mean?' asked Helen.

Fay jumped involuntarily. 'Did I say something?' she asked.

'Yes, you did. You said "there's something odd going on", and now you're looking a bit pale. What's the matter?'

Fay took Helen's hand. 'Helen,' she said. 'Something really strange happened to me a few days ago. I thought I'd pricked my thumb on a pin in the curtains in the sitting room, but there aren't any pins in it, and there was no blood. I'd been back to the hospital to look at the courtyard. I was really tired afterwards and fell asleep on the sofa. After that I drew the curtains and I could have sworn I had stabbed my thumb on a pin. Then I went very cold. And before I went to bed I plucked my eyebrows.'

'I thought they looked a bit different,' said Helen. 'Why did you do that?'

'I didn't like the way the bushy bits reminded me of my mother.'

'I don't remember much about Granny, but I don't think I liked her.'

'You didn't see much of her, and I never left you alone with her.'

'I'm glad you didn't. But why was that?' asked Helen.

Fay's voice sank to a whisper. 'She was very cruel to me, and I didn't want to risk her doing anything to you too,' she said as a tear slid down her cheek.

'Oh, Mum!' exclaimed Helen, and she gave Fay a hug. 'I sensed that something had been wrong, but you never said.'

'I think I didn't admit to myself just how bad it had been,' said Fay. 'But the day after I plucked those hairs out of my eyebrows it all hit me.'

'Have you told Dad about it?'

'Yes, of course. I told him soon after he came home.'

'Was Granny cruel to Uncle Martin too?' asked Helen.

'Not that I knew of.'

'But there must have been something wrong,' said Helen shrewdly, 'because he's always avoided being close to people.'

'I thought about that as well,' admitted Fay. She squeezed Helen's hand. 'I'm so glad that Reverend Howard could make time to see you and Peter today. Have you had any more ideas about your dress?'

Helen smiled. She knew her mother so well. Although this question was entirely authentic, it also signalled the fact that Fay wasn't able to go on talking about her mother at the moment. Helen made a mental note to talk to her father about the whole subject.

'I'm looking around,' she said. 'But I keep changing my mind.'

'Don't leave it much longer before you decide,' Fay warned her. 'It can take a while to order things up, or to get them made.'

'I know,' replied Helen. 'Don't worry, I'll make my final decision soon. I seem to be oscillating between something very simple and something old-fashioned that has some special embroidery on it.'

'Special embroidery sounds lovely. I wish I was better and that I could look around with you this week,' Fay said longingly. 'Even if you had quite a simple dress, it might suit. Do you have a picture in your mind of what it might look like?'

'Not really,' replied Helen. 'And I know it probably sounds silly, but it's more of a feeling than an image.'

'Helen, I've just thought of something,' Fay said suddenly. 'Will you call your dad up for a minute?'

Helen called down the stairs and Don soon appeared.

'It's nice to see you having a lie-in,' he said. 'What is it you want?'

'Don, remember how there was a whole courtyard of shop units where we bought your ring?'

'Yes, of course.'

'There was one that sold all kinds of old-fashioned linen, wasn't there?'

'Yes, that's right.'

'Did you notice any shops with old-fashioned clothes?'

'I'm afraid not. Once we found the jewellery shop, I didn't notice anything else. Why do you ask?'

'I'd like to go and look,' said Fay determinedly. 'I know we can't go today, but can we go tomorrow?'

'We could phone the jewellery shop and ask them to tell us what other shops are there,' Don suggested.

'No. I want to go and look myself,' said Fay urgently.

'I'm certainly willing to take a drive out there tomorrow,' Don reassured her.

Fay looked relieved. 'You will come, Helen, won't you?' she said. 'I've a strong feeling that we might find something there for you.'

Don looked puzzled. 'What have you two been plotting?' he asked good-naturedly.

'I was telling Mum my thoughts so far about what I might wear on my big day,' Helen explained.

'I can't promise there will be that kind of shop, but I'm more than willing to take everyone,' said Don. 'I'll go back down now and leave you two to chat while I finish my conversation with Peter. Just call out if there's anything else.'

Fay got up about midday, and after a late lunch Helen and Peter set off to walk the short distance to the vicarage. The air was cool but pleasant as they made their way along the road hand in hand. They were soon there, and Peter rang the bell. Helen found herself scanning the stone lintel above the door in search of an inscription, but of course none was apparent.

Reverend Howard opened the door and showed them into his study, which was a small room to the rear of the large sitting room, immediately to the left of the entrance. He invited them to sit down in two rather tattered armchairs, while he used an upright chair with a curved back.

'It's very good to see you both again,' he said warmly. 'Tell me what's on your agenda and I'll add anything I think you've missed out.'

Peter produced his notebook and opened it at the list he and Helen had made.

'Oh, good man!' exclaimed the Reverend. 'How very sensible. I wish everyone was as organised as you are. It would make life so much simpler.' He sighed, and Helen let herself imagine for a minute how complicated his life must be.

Peter read out all the headings. The Reverend shut his eyes and leaned back in his seat. At first Helen feared that they had offended him in some way, but when he opened his eyes again he said, 'Good. I think you've got it all there. I haven't anything in particular to add. Let's work through it.'

The time sped by, and two hours later Helen and Peter were standing at the front door once more, shaking Reverend Howard's hand and thanking him for his time.

'Do you mind if we go into the church before we leave?' Peter asked.

'Not at all. The door isn't locked at this time of day,' the Reverend replied. 'I would say you've probably got about an hour before the verger comes with the keys.'

He stood at the door watching Helen and Peter walk down the path, nodded to them as they turned into the road and glanced back towards him, and then went back into the vicarage and shut the door.

'He's exactly the kind of person I want to conduct the service,' said Peter. 'We're very fortunate that he's the vicar of your local church.'

'I know,' said Helen. 'He's a deeply religious man, and it means a lot to me that he's known me since I was small.'

By this time they were entering the church by the small side door nearest to the vicarage. They stood together quietly at the back, looking towards the altar.

'This church reminds me of one I saw when I was just a boy,' said Peter in a low voice. 'I think it was at a place called Deerhurst. I'll tell you about it on the way back to the house.'

They stood in silence for a long time, before leaving through the same door.

'What were you going to tell me about that other church?' asked Helen, as they walked back together.

'I think I must have been about twelve when I went there with my parents,' Peter began. 'There isn't all that much to tell, except that when I walked in front of the altar I became aware of a very strong sensation of alcohol in my mouth. The only alcohol I had ever tasted was a teaspoonful of whatever my mother put in the Christmas puddings, and the taste was much like that.'

'How strange,' said Helen.

'Yes. I've thought about it from time to time since then, but I can't make any sense of it.'

When they got back to the house Don let them in.

'Fay's on the phone to Joan,' he explained. 'She rang a few minutes ago. Diana and Paul arrived earlier today, but Diana's had a bit of a bleed since then. She's resting, but Joan wanted to let Fay know straight away. I'm pleased to say that after Joan told her, and Fay had let me know what was happening, she went straight on to tell Joan about her bond with Diana when she was small. I'd like to leave them to it for the moment. Shall we go and sit in the dining room and have something to drink?'

'Yes, let's do that,' Helen agreed in a low voice.

As they sat sipping elderflower cordial, Peter asked Don what he knew of the history of the church.

'I think I've got a book about it in the small room,' said Don. 'I'll go up and have a look.'

Fay and Don had turned the small room upstairs into their library some years ago. It was shelved from floor to ceiling on two walls. Don searched for a few minutes, found what he was looking for, and returned.

'Here you are, Peter,' he said. 'You can study it at your leisure. We've had it for a long time, but these things hardly go out of date. Sometimes there are additions, but it's rare for existing information to be changed.'

'Thanks, Don. I'll make a start on it in bed tonight.' Despite having said this, Peter began to turn the pages, and was soon absorbed in the text.

A little while later Fay joined them. Her face was flushed. 'Thanks for leaving me to get on with that,' she said.

'How did it go?' asked Don and Helen together.

'I think it went very well,' Fay replied. 'But I feel quite shaky. I'll have to sit down.'

'Why don't we all go to the sitting room,' Don suggested. 'You can relax on the sofa. We want to hear all about it.'

'But I want to hear how Peter and Helen got on with Reverend Howard,' Fay protested, trying to steady herself by holding on to the back of Helen's chair.

'One thing at a time, Mum,' said Helen firmly. She took her mother by the arm and led her back to her place on the sofa. 'Now tell us a bit about it,' she demanded kindly.

'My head's in a whirl,' said Fay. 'But I do feel certain I managed to say everything I needed to for now.'

'That's great, Mum,' said Helen. 'And what did she say?'

Fay's face began to tremble and she clutched Helen's hand. 'I can't remember exactly, but I could tell she understood, and she apologised for not realising at the time. She said that she had been so tied up with her own emotional state then, and that she can now see she had little or no awareness of what anyone else might be feeling. And then later on when she felt okay, she thought everyone else was okay too. She could see straight away that we should all talk about it, and that it was long overdue.'

Helen hugged her mother, and Fay began to cry. Tears poured down her cheeks. Helen went and got the kitchen roll and sat patiently tearing pieces off and handing them to her.

When Fay was able to speak again she said, 'There's one more thing I remember her saying, and that was that she thinks it might even be a part of the reason why I have been ill for such a long time. I must say I was astonished at that, and I'm not sure that I agree, but I was deeply affected by her thought.'

'We ought to talk about that some more, Mum,' said Helen. 'We don't have to just now – not if you don't want to – but I think we should come back to it sometime. She may have a point.'

'Helen's right, Fay,' Don added. 'Close trusting relationships are very important, and I can see that must be especially so after what you suffered at the hands of your mother.'

'I have a feeling that you're both trying to tell me something very important,' said Fay, 'but my head's too muddled to take it in at the moment. Can we leave it for now and talk about Helen and Peter's news?'

Here Peter took over. 'Yes, of course, Fay,' he said. 'Helen and I spent nearly two hours with Reverend Howard, and then we went and stood in the church together for a while.'

'Yes. It was a very special time for me, Peter – standing there with you. And in only six months we will be in that church waiting to be married.'

Peter went on. 'Reverend Howard was very helpful. We talked about practical things for a while, and then he encouraged us to raise any questions or anxieties we had. I found I was able to talk freely about some things I had been thinking of raising with Helen, but hadn't yet managed to put into words.'

'I found that too,' said Helen. 'It all seemed to come quite naturally for both of us.'

'I'm so glad to hear that,' said Fay. 'Just tell us any details you want. But first shall we decide what to eat tonight?'

'It's all under control,' said Don. 'I got most of it ready this afternoon while you were dozing in the chair.'

The evening was spent pleasantly, sharing the meal that Don had prepared, and talking over some of Helen and Peter's plans and ideas about their future. Before Fay went to bed, slightly ahead of the others, they agreed what to do the following day. Helen would phone Joan to see how Diana was, and if all was well, she hoped to be able to go round to see her. After lunch, they would all go to the Courtyard. Peter had offered to drive. At first Don had resisted, but had later agreed, saying that he could then enjoy the scenery.

Chapter Eleven

Helen was able to spend much of the morning with Diana. The bleeding had stopped late the previous evening, and she was taking things quietly, but was cheerful and positive. She was clearly looking forward to the evening out with the two families the following day. She was intrigued to hear about the trip to the Courtyard, and insisted that Helen should phone her that evening to let her know how it had gone. They had talked about what they knew of the phone conversation between Fay and Joan, and before Helen left, Diana had handed her a letter to give to Fay, telling her that she and her parents had written it together.

When Helen arrived back at the house, she handed the envelope to Fay straight away, but did not mention whom it was from.

Fay looked puzzled. 'I wonder what it is?' she said as she opened it.

Inside she found a photograph of Diana as a very small baby, and there was also a handwritten letter which looked rather odd, as it appeared to be made up of three different kinds of handwriting. Studying it more closely, she found that she recognised the writing of Joan, Jim and Diana, and that each had taken it in turn to write a word in each sentence. She turned the photograph over and read out what was on the back of it.

To a very special Mum, with love from Diana, Jim and Joan

Then she read out the letter in a voice which was so wobbly that she found it hard to sustain.

Dear Fay,

Please accept our very sincere apologies for not realising until now that we should all be talking about this very important subject. We would like to talk about it soon, but want you to be the one who decides when that will be.

Very much love from Joan, Jim and Diana

'I don't know what to say,' she said between sobs.

'I don't think there's anything else at the moment,' said Don wisely, putting his arm round her. 'I think that just about sums it up. It's a good job I persuaded you to stay on in bed again this morning, because it looks as if this is likely to be another big day. You might not feel like eating any lunch at the moment, but don't worry, I can pack some for you.'

'Thanks, Don,' said Fay gratefully. 'I think I'll lie down for half an hour while you eat.'

'I'll come up and get you when we're ready to leave,' Helen reassured her.

When she went upstairs later, she found Fay propped up on her pillows reading a paperback.

'It's one that Don picked up when he was away,' Fay explained. 'I'm finding it very interesting.'

'What's it about?' asked Helen.

'It's written by an ex-CIA spy,' replied Fay.

'Goodness!' exclaimed Helen. 'I wouldn't have expected anything like that. You must tell me about it sometime.'

'I haven't got very far into it yet,' Fay said.

'Never mind,' replied Helen. 'We're off to the Courtyard now, so come and get ready.'

Just over an hour later Peter drew up in the car park at the Courtyard.

'Hey, Mum. This looks a really interesting place!' exclaimed Helen. 'It was a good idea of yours to come here. Even if it hasn't got any clothes, it's the kind of place to look round and enjoy.'

Fay pointed to the jewellery shop. 'There's the shop where we got your dad's signet ring,' she said, 'and over there is the linen shop.'

'Can we go there first?' asked Helen. Without waiting for an answer, she walked across to the shop and stood gazing into the window. 'Oh, there are some lovely things here,' she breathed.

Fay joined her, while Peter and Don wandered off in the opposite direction to a unit that appeared to stock memorabilia from the early days of motoring.

'Let's go in,' Fay suggested.

Helen opened the door eagerly and went inside. The shop was quite small, but almost the whole of the wall space was covered with linen items hanging over wooden straps that had obviously been put there for the purpose of display. Many of the items were edged with intricate patterns of lace, while others, such as pillowcases, were decorated with beautifully embroidered flowers.

A plainly dressed woman, who looked as if she might be in her forties, asked them if they needed any help. Helen hardly seemed to notice her, so Fay spoke.

'We'd like to look round if we may,' she said politely. 'We don't have anything particular in mind at the moment, although we might well see something. My daughter is getting married in the autumn,' she explained.

'That's nice,' the woman commented. 'I hope everything goes well.'

'We aren't familiar with this place, so perhaps you could tell me if there's anywhere that sells clothes of old-fashioned styles here.'

'I'm afraid not,' the woman replied. 'There used to be a shop like that, but it closed down only last week.'

Fay felt a stab of disappointment, and something must have showed on her face, because the woman went into the back of the shop and returned with a card, which she handed to her.

'This is one of their old business cards,' she explained. 'It has a contact phone number on it as well as the shop details. You could try phoning.'

'Thank you very much,' said Fay, and put the card in her bag. She touched Helen's arm. 'Have you seen anything you particularly like?' she asked.

'I seem to have fallen in love with that pair of pillow cases up there,' said Helen, pointing half way up one of the walls.

'I'm not surprised,' said Fay with a smile. 'I had my eye on them too, and I'd like to buy them for you.'

Helen offered no resistance, and soon the assistant was wrapping them up in tissue paper that she described as 'acid free'.

Outside the shop Helen asked, 'What were you two talking about?'

Fay explained, and showed her the card. 'I want to phone that number now,' she said determinedly.

Helen looked at her mother with surprise, but said nothing. Instead she took her mobile phone out of her bag and keyed in the number.

After a few rings, a man with a slightly foreign accent replied. Helen could not place it immediately. She told the man that she was looking for old-fashioned clothing of a particular kind, and that she had been given his number by one of the shops at the Courtyard.

'Ah yes,' said the voice. 'I had to close down my unit there, but I do have a few interesting items here. It is for yourself?'

'Yes, that's right,' said Helen. 'Actually I'm looking for something slightly out of the ordinary that might form part of a wedding outfit for me. I'm getting married in September. I'm here at the Courtyard with my family and my fiancé at the moment.'

'I shall be here for most of the afternoon,' said the man. 'I do have a few things you may care to look at.'

'Thank you,' said Helen. 'But can you tell me where you are. I don't have an address.'

The man gave directions, and added that it would take about forty minutes to get there.

'I'm fairly certain we'll be coming,' said Helen, 'but I'll give you another ring if we find we can't.' She rang off. 'Right. Let's get Dad and Peter,' she said. 'I really do want to go.'

Fay smiled. It looked as if Helen was now infected with the same hunch as she herself had had. They managed to extricate Don and Peter, explain the situation, and persuade them to set off to find the address that Helen had written down. Fortunately, the directions she had been given were very clear, and it took almost exactly the predicted time to reach their destination.

'This must be it,' said Peter as he drew the car up outside what appeared to be a large converted barn.

'It looks rather impressive,' said Helen. 'Can anyone see the house name? It should say Cotfield somewhere if this is the right place.'

'I can see there's some kind of a sign on the side gate over there,' said Don, pointing across to what he had noticed. 'Hang on a minute. I'll go and check.'

He was back in a short time, confirming that the name was indeed on the gate.

Just then, a tall man with short dark hair, dressed in smart casual clothes appeared round the other side of the building. He must be in his thirties, thought Fay. He can't be much older than Peter.

'Good afternoon,' he said politely, inclining his head slightly. 'I believe I spoke to one of your party earlier this afternoon.'

'That's right,' said Helen, stepping forward and holding out her hand. 'I phoned you, and I was keen to come and see if you had anything suitable for my wedding outfit.'

'Then please come this way, mademoiselle,' he said, motioning for her to go in the direction from which he had come.

Fay walked along beside her, and Peter and Don started to follow behind, but the young man held up his hand. 'Is either of these gentlemen to be the bridegroom?' he asked.

'I am,' said Peter.

'I am afraid it is not possible for you to come, monsieur,' said the young man.

'Why not?' asked Peter, who was clearly puzzled.

'It is not appropriate for the groom to see the bridal attire until the wedding day,' the young man insisted.

Don turned to Peter. 'We can take a walk down the road together while the ladies are busy.' Then he said to Helen, 'I've got my mobile. Give us a ring when you're ready.' They turned and started to stroll down the road, deep in conversation.

Helen and Fay followed the young man round the back of the building, where he let them in through a glass door into a large hallway from which many doors opened.

'Please take the third door on the left,' he instructed them. 'You will see a flight of stairs. Follow it to the top landing and wait for me there. I won't be a moment.' After that he disappeared through one of the other doors.

'What a beautiful place this is,' said Fay as she noticed the fine wallpaper and the striking light fittings.

They made their way up the stairs, admiring the paintings that were hung at intervals on the walls. Fay noticed that there was a mixture of portraits and rural scenes of past times, and she commented on this to Helen. When they reached the landing, the young man was already there, waiting for them.

'I'm sorry, we were rather slow,' Fay apologised.

'Please do not worry, madame.' He opened a narrow door that was just behind him, and motioned Helen and Fay through it.

Helen could not contain a gasp as she saw what was in the room beyond. It was so unexpected that she found it difficult to take in. The whole of one wall of the room was lined with mirrors as in a ballet practice room, but the room itself was not at all like a practice room. It had a moderately low ceiling, two of the walls consisted almost entirely of very large windows, and along the remaining wall was a row of free-standing racks of clothing.

'I will show you the two racks on which you might find something suitable,' the man said. 'Then I will leave you. There is a bell here.' He pointed to a bell push. 'Please ring for me when you are sure you are ready to leave. As you will see, this room is entirely private. There is no possibility of being overlooked.'

After that he indicated the appropriate racks, and then disappeared through the door by which they had entered.

Helen looked at her mother with a stunned expression. 'I don't know what to say,' she said. 'I feel completely overwhelmed.'

'I'm the same,' Fay replied. 'But I think that since we're here we should at least make a start on looking through some of the clothes. There's no way of telling what we might find. Let's take one rack each and work our way down,' she suggested. 'If either of us sees something that catches our eye, we can stop and look at it together.'

'That's a good idea,' Helen replied, grateful that her mother was taking charge of the situation. She began to work her way slowly through the clothes, feeling relieved that they were not tightly packed. She soon became aware that she was not concentrating on her task; instead she was merely going through a mechanical exercise. She went back to the beginning of the rail and started again. This time she was able to take in more of what she was seeing, and she was entranced by the quality and variety of garments she encountered. She realised quite quickly that some of the styles were unusual, while others were unique in her experience.

'Mum,' she said. 'I think you should look through all of these too. I don't think I want to try any of them on, but they are so amazing that I want you to see them.'

'That's what I was thinking about these,' Fay replied. Her voice was a little muffled as she bent down slightly to examine the cuffs of a jacket she had found.

'Actually, there are one or two things I've seen that you may well want to try on. Are you any clearer about what you're looking for?'

'Not really,' said Helen. 'Well… er…'

'What is it?'

'Um… er…'

'Is something the matter?'

Helen regained some of her equilibrium and found herself able to speak again.

'Mum, can you come and look at this?' she said.

'Of course,' said Fay. She put the garment she had been examining back on the rail and went to join Helen. There she stopped in her tracks. 'Oh!' she exclaimed.

'What do you think?' asked Helen unnecessarily.

'I think you should try it on,' said Fay urgently, gazing transfixed at the garment that Helen was holding out towards her.

It was a slightly padded fitted jacket made out of cream satin that was completely covered with fine embroidery worked in pale gold thread. Helen slipped off her own lightweight jacket, revealing the plain blouse she had put on that morning. Carefully she took the embroidered jacket off its hanger and began to put it on. She hardly dared to breathe as she put first one arm and then the other through the sleeves.

'I think it must have been made for you,' said Fay quietly as she watched. 'Go and look at yourself in the mirrors.'

Helen looked across at the wall of mirrors and then walked towards them. The jacket was certainly for her. Its close-fitting sleeves opened out a little at her wrists, matching the curve of the jacket below her waist. It had no collar; instead it finished in a scalloped edge, bound in the same gold thread as in the embroidery, and matching the edge of the sleeves.

'I've no idea what I would be wearing apart from this,' said Helen, 'but I'm quite certain I want to wear it on my wedding day.' She stopped, looking worried. 'Mum,' she said, 'I haven't a clue how much any of this costs. Have you?'

'No,' replied Fay. 'I haven't seen any indication of price on anything I've looked at so far.'

'What shall we do?' Helen asked anxiously.

'I think we should ring the bell and speak to the young man,' replied Fay. She pressed the bell and a few minutes later he appeared.

'You rang?' he observed.

'Yes,' said Fay. 'We need your help. My daughter has found something here that she's very drawn to. Can you give us some indication of the price? We can't find a tag or a price list anywhere.'

The man smiled. 'Ah,' he said. 'The price depends very much on the buyer.'

'What do you mean?' asked Helen, staring at him in a puzzled way.

'The buyer, and the purpose for which the garment is required,' he added.

'I'm sorry, but I don't understand what you're saying,' said Helen with as much dignity as she could muster. In fact, she was beginning to feel as if the man might be making fun of her, and she started to take the jacket off.

He put up a hand towards her. 'No. Please, mademoiselle. It is very important that you keep the jacket on while we negotiate the price.'

He sounded so sincere that Helen was convinced that he had no intention of making her appear foolish, and she waited to hear what he had to say.

'This garment is a copy of one that was made specially for a young bride who was a descendant of a royal family. Her husband was a good man. She bore many children and lived with good health into old age. More than that I am not permitted to tell you. You have chosen this jacket because it is part of your destiny to do so, and the price must reflect that.' Here he paused, before continuing in slow deliberate tones. 'At some time in the future you and your mother have a task to complete together. It is one of crucial importance, and you must be sure to recognise it when it manifests itself to you. Your mother will guide you, and your husband will support you through your part in it. Take the jacket now, and return only if you learn later that you must leave money here.'

Helen opened her mouth, but shut it again. She looked at her mother, and noticed that for the first time since her illness began she appeared to have some vitality.

'Do you have any guidance about the care of the garment?' asked Fay a little anxiously. 'I'm particularly concerned, not only because it's very special, but also because I have a sense that it will not always be in our possession. Another person may have need of it later.'

The young man shut his eyes for a few moments, and then said, 'It must be hung in your home, madame. That is all I can say.' He turned, opened a false door in the wall behind the rails, and produced a substantial bag into which he zipped the jacket with great care and handed it to Helen. 'What is the date of your wedding?' he asked.

'September the twenty-first,' Helen replied.

'Ah, yes. That is right,' he said, half to himself. 'And now I must show you to your car.'

He led the way back down the stairs and out through the glass door at the back of the building.

'I'll just phone Dad,' said Helen, switching on her mobile.

'There is no need,' the young man said. 'They are waiting for you.'

They went round the corner of the building and saw Don and Peter waiting in the car. When they turned to say goodbye to the young man, he had gone.

'You were in there for a long time,' Don remarked. 'We were beginning to get worried.'

Helen glanced at her watch to find that three hours had passed since they had parted. 'No wonder you were worried!' she exclaimed. 'We had no idea how late it was. We got so absorbed in what we were doing. It was an amazing place.'

'I see you got something,' said Peter curiously. 'I know I'm not allowed to look at it, but you must tell us as much as you can while we're driving back.'

In the car Helen turned to Fay and said, 'I think we can at least tell them about the inside of the house and the room where the clothes were, can't we, Mum?'

'Yes, I'm sure we can, but I'm not certain about the rest. I think we both need time to think it through before we try to talk to Don and Peter about any of it, and even then we might have to agree that it must wait until your wedding day or afterwards.'

Helen nodded. 'You're absolutely right, Mum. Something very

profound happened there, and I need time to take it in.'

Peter glanced across at Don, who was sitting in the front passenger seat. 'I'm finding all this quite hard, Don. How about you?'

'Me too,' Don agreed readily. 'It's as if Helen and Fay are talking in riddles. But I'm not about to push them to say anything they're not ready to divulge.'

'Neither am I,' Peter agreed.

Don turned and looked at Fay and Helen. 'There's one thing that's very reassuring,' he said. 'Fay looks better than she's looked for months, and Helen looks somehow more complete in herself.'

'Yes, and I'm glad of that,' said Peter. 'And now perhaps they'll tell us what they saw of the interior of the house.'

After Fay and Helen had described as much as they could, the conversation lapsed as Peter drove back along the country lanes. There was a long silence, at the end of which Helen and Fay began a guessing game about where they were to be taken the following evening, and Don and Peter discussed the best route to take, while exchanging stories of what they had admired most at the Courtyard shop.

Having exhausted the names of all the venues she could think of, Fay turned to Helen and said, 'There's something on my mind that I want to tell you.'

'What is it?' asked Helen.

'You remember that conversation we had some time ago about my nightmare?'

'Of course I do.'

'… and how I was thinking about the subject of past lives?'

'Go on,' Helen encouraged.

'… and I mentioned Lily?'

'Yes. Since then I've been trying to see if I could remember anything about her myself. Her name was Lily Anthony, wasn't it?'

'That's right.'

'I'd like to tell you the whole story of how she became involved with that so-called past life therapist,' Fay said tentatively.

Helen waited patiently for Fay to begin.

'Are you sure it's all right?' asked Fay worriedly.

'Of course it is,' Helen reassured her.

Fay began. At first her voice faltered from time to time, but as she went on it became stronger.

'I first met Lily when she became a neighbour of ours. It was a few years before you were born, I think. I got to know her better when I gave up going out to work after I was first pregnant with you. I was very tired and was sick a lot, and Don and I agreed that the best thing was for me to stop work, as we had already decided that I would be a full-time mum once you were born.

'Lily's husband was often away. I never knew what he did for a living, but she didn't need to work for money, and she did a number of voluntary jobs. We used to meet from time to time for a cup of tea. One day she confided that she had been having quite a lot of strange experiences. I wish now that I could remember more of what she told me. There are a few things that stuck in my mind, though. They happened mainly in her house, which was about a hundred years old. Much later she discovered that the house had been built on the site of another building, and when I last saw her she was researching into that.

'For quite a while, whenever she went to bed she found that a man's head would come and hover above her, staring into her eyes. She used to shout out in panic, and the head would disappear, only to reappear the following night. At other times she would smell things that weren't there. Wood smoke was a common one, but others included rose petals and new-mown hay.

'She couldn't understand why these things kept happening, and that troubled her a lot. She kept trying to find someone who might be able to explain it all to her, and that's how she first encountered Roy. Roy was a healer. Lily had heard of him from some unexpected source, and she contacted him and made an appointment to see him. I remember I had some misgivings about the whole thing, and said so, but she was determined to go ahead. When she saw him, he said that he was certain that these experiences were to do with past lives she'd had, and that he could help her to enter full memories of these. She agreed to this straight away, and was very excited as she went off to the first session. After that she became very secretive, and I stopped asking her anything about it. As the months went by she grew thinner and thinner, and she looked pale.

'It eventually transpired that Roy had behaved inappropriately with her, and it took her a long time to recover from this. Fortunately she bumped into an old school friend who had become an architect. This woman was a breezy no-nonsense kind of person, and she helped Lily to begin to research the history of her house and the site in general. Some interesting information came to light that helped Lily enormously, and she became stronger again, albeit slowly.

'I'd never heard of past lives before, so this was my first encounter with the whole subject. It left me with a very bad impression, and it wasn't until I read the section in *Russian Voices* about the woman who knew a lot about her own past lives that I began to reassess my views.'

'I'm not surprised you felt the way you did,' said Helen. 'Poor Lily. It was really horrible what happened to her, even if it did work out all right in the end. Does she still live nearby?'

'No. She and her husband moved away when you and Diana were at primary school, and unfortunately I lost touch with her. We used to exchange Christmas cards at first, but I think she must have moved again, and didn't give me her new address. I kept getting cards from her, but mine were always returned "addressee unknown", and after a few more years her cards stopped.'

'How strange,' mused Helen. 'You'd think she would have realised and sent you her new address.'

'Yes. So I've no idea what happened.'

'I'd like to read *Russian Voices*,' said Helen suddenly.

'I'll soon have a copy,' replied Fay. 'Your dad and I ordered one on the Internet only a few days ago. With luck it'll come while you're here.'

By this time Peter was turning into the road that led to their home and was soon parking outside.

'I'm glad you told me about Lily,' said Helen as they got out of the car and went into the house, carrying her jacket carefully by its hanger. 'Where shall I put this?' she asked anxiously.

'If you put it on the rail in the cupboard on the landing I'll make sure no harm comes to it,' Fay assured her.

Helen's face cleared. 'Thanks, Mum,' she said. 'And by the way, I've got an idea.'

'Tell me what it is.'

'Wait a minute while I put this away,' Helen replied, and she ran upstairs with the precious jacket. When she returned she said, 'We've been looking at the photos of the farm buildings and that one of the mansion house in your book, but we don't have a picture of the ruin in your dream. How about spending some time this evening trying to paint one?'

Fay burst out laughing. 'But you know I'm hopeless with any sort of artwork!' she exclaimed. 'It would just be a messy blob.'

'I'm not so sure,' replied Helen, 'and in any case if you get stuck we can all help you. Have you got any paints?'

'I think there are some in a box in the loft,' said Don, who had overheard their conversation. 'I'll go up and look around after we've eaten something.'

'Thanks, Dad,' said Helen cheerfully. 'I can give you a hand if you want. In any case I wouldn't mind having a look up there. I'm sure some of my things must still be there.'

'It's a date,' said Don with a smile. 'Come on Peter, let's get to work in the kitchen, and we'll leave Helen to talk her mother round in the sitting room.'

Their meal finished, Peter offered to clear up while Don and Helen had a look in the loft. It was not long before Helen appeared, carrying a medium-sized cardboard box. She found Fay still sitting at the dining table, and she put the box on a chair beside her.

'Here we are,' she said. 'There's everything we need – paper, various kinds of paints, crayons, charcoal, pencils…'

'Goodness!' exclaimed Fay. 'I'd forgotten we had all this.'

'Dad seemed to know exactly where it was,' said Helen. 'In fact he's got the loft really well organised. There are just a couple of boxes of my things. He wasn't sure who they belonged to, but they're definitely mine. I had a look in them, and I've left them for now. He doesn't mind.'

'It's ages since I was last up there myself,' said Fay wistfully. 'I wouldn't mind having a look sometime to refresh my memory.'

'I think we should get started on the project now,' said Helen briskly.

Fay hesitated. 'I don't think I can do it,' she said.

'I can do it for you if you describe it to me,' Helen offered. 'I'm not all that good myself, but I can usually manage something.'

Fay suddenly realised how much she wanted to have some kind of picture of the ruin and its environs. 'Would you really?' she asked eagerly.

'Of course I will. Let's make a start and see how we go,' replied Helen. 'What medium should we use?'

'Can we begin with a pencil sketch?' Fay suggested. 'Pass me some sheets of paper and I'll draw some rough diagrams you can work from.'

They were soon absorbed, and did not notice Don putting his head round the door before disappearing again. He and Peter went quietly to the sitting room, leaving Helen and Fay undisturbed.

'Here's an idea of the façade of the building,' said Fay, struggling to get the proportions right. 'As you can see, it has almost totally collapsed in places, but in others there's quite a height of wall left. You can't see the end walls in this sketch. I'm sure they're almost complete, although the stonework is quite eroded in places.'

'Mm… I've got a much better idea of it now than when you told me about it before,' said Helen.

'Next I'll do a sketch as if from above,' said Fay. 'Most of the partition walls are gone. Only the foundations remain, and you can see them at ground level.'

Helen watched her mother as she worked. She had lost all her uncertainty. Helen made no comment about this, as she did not want to risk disturbing her flow. Instead she asked a question from time to time to help to clarify exactly what Fay was trying to portray.

'There,' said Fay at length. 'That's about as much as I can remember.'

'And you think it's about a hundred and fifty metres long and fifty deep?' Helen said. 'That's huge. It must have been very imposing when it was still intact. Now, how are the trees around it positioned?'

Fay did not answer. Instead she was staring at the rough drawings.

'What is it, Mum?' Helen asked urgently.

Fay shook her head as if in an attempt to clear it. 'I suddenly had a very clear picture in my mind of the house before it became derelict. It didn't last for long, but it was so real.'

'That's amazing!' exclaimed Helen. 'Tell me everything you can remember.'

'There were people – servants, I think – in old-fashioned clothing. Some of them had unusual head covers – not scarves and not hats – and they were made out of coarse off-white material.' She stopped and considered for a moment before saying, 'That's all.'

'This is astonishing,' said Helen. 'I'm going to go and find Peter and Dad.'

She went into the hallway and called them, and soon they were all sitting round the dining table. Fay sat quietly while Helen spoke to the others about her drawings. Then Fay heard her say, 'And you'll never guess what happened then.'

Peter and Don looked across the table blankly, and Fay said, 'I had a very brief flash in my mind of how the house and some of its occupants looked a long time ago.'

'Really?' said Peter and Don in unison.

'Yes. There were people in old-fashioned clothing with strange linen head covers, and the house was in good condition.'

'What era do you think it was, Fay?' asked Don curiously.

Fay looked worried. 'I don't know... I can't guess,' she stumbled.

'Don't worry, Mum,' said Helen. 'Dad was just interested.'

'Yes... yes... of course,' Fay blundered.

'Fay, I wasn't trying to test you out,' said Don. 'You know that, don't you?'

'Well... yes... um... I do,' said Fay nervously.

Helen put her arm round Fay and said, 'Mum, it was great that image came into your mind, and it's perfectly okay if you don't know everything about it.'

This approach seemed to steady Fay, who said, 'Yes, I know. I just feel frustrated that I can't give you any more detail.'

Peter, who until now had been sitting quietly, spoke next. 'Perhaps we could put these things away for now. There's plenty of time over the next few days to try again if Fay wants to. It's getting late, and we've had quite a long day. I think I'll turn in soon.'

'Good idea,' said Don, taking the lead. 'Fay, let's go up to bed. We could read for a while before we put the light out.'

'I made a start on that book about the church last night,' said Peter, 'and I've already learned quite a bit.'

Fay was glad to be in bed with Don beside her. She hadn't

realised how tired she was until she lay down. It certainly had been an eventful day.

'There's just one thing I want to say about your ruin,' said Don. 'Do you remember when you spoke about it before, I began to wonder if it exists somewhere?'

'Yes, I do.'

'That thought came back into my mind this evening, but that's as far as it went. It's perfectly possible that it's a real place. And even if it no longer exists, there may well be illustrations of it somewhere.'

Fay sat bolt upright in bed. 'You're right!' she exclaimed. 'Maybe I'll start doing some research when I'm able to get out and about a bit more.'

'I want to give you a hand when I'm around,' Don said emphatically.

'I'd like that,' Fay said quietly.

Chapter Twelve

In anticipation of the evening out, Fay rested for most of the following afternoon. She felt quite drained after the events of the previous day, and was glad to stay quietly while the others went out for a walk. The venue was still being kept secret, and she and Helen joked about where it might be. Their increasingly wild guesses only provoked secretive smiles from Don, and eventually they gave up. The copy of *Russian Voices* had arrived in the post that morning, and Fay dipped into it while she relaxed on her bed. She was to hand it over to Helen that night so that she could read the chapter about the woman and her past lives.

When evening came she chose a long warm blue dress and a plain navy jacket to match, and then sat downstairs waiting for the others to finish getting ready.

'I think I ought to be handing out blindfolds,' said Don cheerfully as he came into the sitting room. 'Then none of you will know where you're going until you arrive.'

'You definitely have a twinkle in your eye,' Fay observed as she scrutinised his face for clues. 'I have to admit I'm stumped.'

Don looked at his watch. 'We'd better get off,' he said. 'It's quite a drive.'

After nearly an hour's driving Helen suddenly shouted out, 'Got it! We're going to the place where Diana and Paul's wedding reception was, aren't we Dad? Do I get a prize now?'

Don laughed. 'Well done! Do you know why we chose it?'

'Go on, tell me.'

'Jim and I wanted to see if it was still up to the same standard. And if it is, we were going to suggest that you and Peter might like to use it for *your* wedding. I checked if they're available on September 21st and we've made a provisional booking.'

'Oh Dad!' Helen exclaimed. She reached round the driving seat to give him a squeeze.

When they arrived, the others were waiting for them inside the entrance door.

'We didn't want to go in without you,' Jim explained. 'Let's leave our coats and sit in the lounge. It's a bit nippy now, and it'll be good to be in the warmth.'

The evening was a great success. Fay was so happy to be with her two families, and the service was excellent. She found herself relaxing in a way that she rarely experienced. At dinner they had been allocated a circular table, which meant that it was easy to converse with each other individually and as a group. Helen and Diana sat together almost directly across the table from her, and she loved to observe their close relationship. The time slipped by imperceptibly, interwoven with pleasant conversation that had an ease born of decades of close sharing and understanding.

Joan was sitting to Fay's left, and as the evening progressed she said, 'I don't want you to feel I'm putting any pressure on you, Fay, but I wanted to ask if you've an idea yet of when you'd like to talk about your relationship with Diana.'

'I've been thinking about it a lot since I got the photograph and the note,' Fay replied. 'It meant so much that you sent them to me.'

'Personally, I was hoping that we might get together while Diana and Paul are here this week,' said Joan, 'but don't let that dictate what you decide. You might want to leave it for a bit, or you might want to talk to Jim and me first. After all, that's where it all started.'

Fay could feel tears welling up in her eyes, and she fumbled in her bag for a tissue. Her friend was being so caring and sensitive, and she found it overwhelming.

Joan squeezed her arm. 'Just phone and tell us what you decide,' she said, 'and we'll fit round it.'

'Thanks,' Fay replied gratefully.

'No, it's we who are thanking you,' Joan reminded her. 'We have no idea what Diana's life would have been like at the beginning if it hadn't been for you. But one thing's certain, she couldn't have been more loved whoever had been caring for her.'

Fay said very little during the rest of the evening. Instead, she enjoyed watching the others and listening to their conversations. Although she was largely silent, she felt deeply involved. When the evening ended and it was time to leave, she and Joan hugged each other tightly, and Fay said, 'I'll phone you sometime tomorrow. It'll probably be afternoon or evening.'

'Good,' replied Joan. 'I'll look forward to that. If I'm out, I won't be far away, so just keep trying.'

On the way home in the car, Helen asked, 'Are you all right, Mum? You've not said much for ages.'

'I'm fine thanks. I'm thinking, that's all.'

Helen persisted. 'What are you thinking about?'

'I'm thinking about the lovely evening we've had, and what I'll be saying to Joan when I phone her tomorrow. I think I'm ready to fix a time for that talk.'

Helen linked her arm through Fay's affectionately. 'I hope it'll be soon. Tell me as soon as you know.'

'I know now,' said Fay. 'I'd like to meet on Friday – afternoon or evening.'

'That's Good Friday.'

'Yes,' said Fay, 'and that feels right for me. I don't know why exactly, but it just feels right.'

Later, as she was getting ready for bed, Fay remarked to Don, 'I don't feel so tired tonight.'

'It's a good thing you rested today,' he replied.

'I don't think that's the only reason.'

'You certainly looked more yourself over the meal,' Don observed. 'And I think your secret purchase with Helen has had quite an effect on you.'

'But…' Fay began, and then stopped herself as she thought about the terms under which she and Helen had been given the jacket.

'What is it?' asked Don.

'I'm not sure that it's the right thing to tell you what happened,' said Fay uncertainly.

'I've wanted to know, but I haven't pressed you. I've thought about it from time to time, but since that young man was so insistent about Peter not seeing anything Helen bought until their wedding day, I wondered if that should be the same for me.'

'It isn't just the j… the garment itself,' said Fay. 'It's the terms under which we were handed it.'

Don looked puzzled. 'That's very intriguing,' he said. Then he added, 'No, it's more than intriguing. It's fascinating and tantalising… and it involves a whole lot of other things as well. My daughter's getting married in about six months' time, my wife and she disappeared into a rather grand conversion of a barn, while I accompanied the prospective groom down the road, since his presence was barred. My wife and daughter reappeared much later bearing a mysterious parcel which they guarded all the way home and haven't mentioned since. And now you're saying something entirely inexplicable about the terms under which you took whatever it is. And there's one more thing… The way we heard about that place was unusual in the extreme. We only heard about it because we returned to the place where we had gone to buy you a ring – the place where we ended up buying one for me instead. And of course there's the fact that the ring we bought mysteriously fitted the ring finger of my right hand. Incidentally, I don't know if you noticed during the meal that Jim was taking quite an interest in it. Of course, I told him the story of how we'd come by it and how we'd really gone to get something for you.'

'No, I hadn't noticed,' Fay replied, 'but I'm glad you got a chance to tell him. I'd like to hear what he and Joan have to say about it.' She stopped and considered for a moment before going on. 'Don, I wish I felt free to tell you everything that happened when Helen and I went into that place, and to tell you what's in that parcel, but I don't. You'll be seeing the garment on September 21st, that's without doubt, but everything else…' Here her voice trailed off.

Don waited patiently before prompting her. 'You were going to say something about the rest,' he said gently.

'I don't know. I must talk it over with Helen and see what she thinks. There's been so much going on.'

'Why not have some time together in the morning?' Don suggested. 'There's shopping to be done, and Peter and I could go to the supermarket. I'm sure he and I could find other things to do to give you a few hours without interruption.'

'Thanks, Don. I'd like that,' Fay replied.

Don and Peter departed at about ten the following morning, leaving Fay and Helen with the house to themselves.

'I'd like a cup of green tea. How about you, Mum?' asked Helen, going into the kitchen to put the kettle on.

'Yes, I'd like one too,' Fay replied. 'Then we can make ourselves comfortable in the sitting room.'

'I've been desperate to talk to you about the jacket,' said Helen as she poured the hot water into the cups, 'but we haven't been on our own since we got it.'

'The thing I'm struggling with at the moment is how much to say to Don,' Fay confided.

'I hadn't thought about that,' Helen admitted. 'I've been so busy stopping myself saying anything to Peter.'

They both burst out laughing.

'What did you think of the young man?' Helen asked.

'He was very polite and courteous,' Fay began. 'He had a slight accent.'

'I assumed he was French,' said Helen.

Fay considered for a minute. 'I think you're right. His English was entirely accurate, but I think that he was French.'

Helen jumped out of her seat. 'I'm going to get the jacket. I'll be back in a minute. I can't wait to have another look at it and put it on again,' she said as she went out of the room.

She was soon back, carrying the bag, which she unzipped carefully before lifting the jacket out. She laid it on the sofa beside her mother and stroked the satin material tenderly. 'It's so beautiful,' she said quietly.

Fay took hold of her other hand and squeezed it. 'Yes, it is,' she agreed, 'and it's as if it had been made specially for you. The material is exquisite, the style suits you perfectly, and the size is exactly right. You looked lovely in it.'

'I wonder what to wear with it,' Helen mused. 'Perhaps I could have some trousers made out of cream satin… with the legs slightly flared to match the cut of the jacket. What do you think, Mum?'

'That sounds ideal,' Fay replied, 'and I'm wondering if it would be best not to wear a blouse under it.'

'I hadn't thought of that,' said Helen, surprised. 'Let me try it on like that and see what it looks like.'

She took off her jumper and blouse, and then slipped the jacket on once more.

'That looks absolutely stunning!' exclaimed Fay delightedly. 'Go and look in the mirror in the hall and you'll see what I mean.'

'Oh, yes,' Helen marvelled as she saw her reflection in the mirror.

Fay followed her into the hall and encouraged her to turn round so that she could see how the back of the jacket fitted. 'It's perfect, isn't it?' she said. 'Wait here a minute while I go up for my pearls. I think you need something at your neck.'

She soon returned with a box, which she opened to reveal a string of pearls of high quality.

'Aren't these the ones you wore on *your* wedding day?' asked Helen as Fay fixed the clasp at the back of her neck.

'That's right,' replied Fay, turning Helen round to face her. 'Wonderful!' she said happily. 'What do you think?'

'Mum, I think they're beautiful, and they go so well with my jacket.'

'That's it settled then. That will be your "something borrowed" item on the big day.'

Helen gave her mother a hug and said, 'I'll be proud to wear them. Perhaps I'll be a mother at least half as good as you one day.'

Fay was astonished. 'What do you mean "at least half as good"? That makes me sound like something better than I've been.'

'Nonsense,' said Helen firmly. 'The problem here is that you don't recognise your own value.'

'But there are things I would have done differently when you and Diana and Jack were young, if only I'd known more at the time.'

'Precisely,' Helen said triumphantly. 'That proves what a good mother you are.' Fay stared at her with incomprehension and Helen went on. 'If you weren't, you wouldn't have realised any of those things, and you wouldn't be thinking about the subject at all. The very fact that you think about them and talk to us about them means that all the time you're considering what might be best for us, and that shows what a good mother you are.'

Fay was silent, but it was clear that she was trying to take in what Helen was saying. However, before she had a chance to find something to contribute to the discussion, Helen continued.

'I've been thinking recently that one of your problems is that you've got to stop being a mother, and think more about being Fay. You're always considering other people more than yourself, and I don't think that's a good thing, especially now that you're not well. In fact, it might even be something to do with why you've been unwell for such a long time.'

'I'm trying to take in what you're saying,' said Fay slowly, 'but can you tell me more about what you mean?'

'Just think of one huge glaring example of you putting everyone else before yourself.'

Fay stared at Helen blankly, and then said, 'But I haven't rushed to take on the job of church accountant.'

'Yes, I know,' replied Helen, 'and we're all trying to encourage you to think about it very carefully before you make your decision.'

'Don and I bought that ring…' Fay's voice trailed off.

'Yes. The ring was to remind you to talk things over with Dad before agreeing to anything new. But look what happened – you ended up buying one for him instead of for yourself.'

'But it had his initials on it and it fitted him,' Fay protested weakly, beginning to realise what Helen was getting at. Helen looked at her meaningfully, and Fay added, 'All right. I think I'm starting to see something. Let me tell you what I'm thinking. I was pleased and excited when Don and I found the ring, but you're right, we'd gone to get one for me and we came back without one. I must talk to him and fix a time when we can go and have another look. If we can't find a ring, then I'll choose some other piece of jewellery – a brooch perhaps.' Her face brightened as she thought about planning another outing with Don.

'That's better,' Helen encouraged. 'What else?'

'What's coming into my mind next is this talk we're going to have with Jim and Joan and Diana,' Fay said. 'I think I'm beginning to see something important.'

'Go on, Mum. Tell me,' Helen said eagerly. 'What is it?'

'When Joan felt so bad and I offered to mind Diana so that she could work part time, it seemed such an obvious solution.'

Helen opened her mouth as if to say something, but then thought better of it and shut it again.

Fay continued. 'And when Jack came along there were three of us for half of each week.' Her face softened as she went on to talk about how the girls had loved helping her to change Jack's nappy and to feed him once he could eat from a spoon. 'Then your granny died…'

'That was when I was three, wasn't it?' Helen asked.

'Yes, that's right. It was a few months after your third birthday, so Jack was not much past his first.'

'I remember vaguely that Joan took time off work to help out for a while,' said Helen.

'It was for two or three weeks. I knew I was struggling, but I coped somehow. I threw myself into looking after you all. I loved you all dearly, and we enjoyed so many things together.'

'But that meant you didn't have time to think about what Granny's death meant to you,' Helen commented wisely.

'I can see that more and more now,' Fay admitted. 'As you know, I've started thinking about her quite a lot recently, and I've got a feeling that there's plenty more to come.'

'If Granny wasn't able to be a proper mum to you, how was it that you managed to be such a good mum to us?' asked Helen.

'I just did everything I could to respond to you all in the ways you needed.'

'And that was before anyone had responded to you in the way that *you* needed,' Helen reminded her. 'So now it's your turn. I think we must all get together to help to make sure that you always take yourself into account. That's what you need now.'

'But I don't want to be unpleasant and self-centred,' Fay protested.

'You couldn't be unpleasant even if you tried,' Helen reassured her. 'And if you could practise being self-centred, I think that would be a very good thing.'

'Will you keep reminding me?' Fay asked uncertainly. 'I want to try to do what you say, but I think I'm going to need some prompting.'

'Don't worry about that. I'll make sure we all take it in turns to get you to try it out,' said Helen. 'Now I think we should phone Joan to fix a time to go round tomorrow.' Without waiting for an answer she picked up the phone and keyed in the number. 'Hello… Joan?' she said when she heard a voice at the other end. 'I've got Mum here for you.'

'That's it fixed,' said Fay when she came off the phone. 'We're going round for eight tomorrow.'

'Well done, Mum. That's a good start.'

'I think we should talk now about how much we can say to Don and Peter about the jacket,' said Fay decisively. 'And…'

'And what?' said Helen quickly.

'And then please will you help me with that picture,' said Fay, almost in a whisper. 'It's so important to me.'

'Of course I will. I was wondering whether to say anything about it myself. We'll decide what to say about the jacket, and then get the picture out again.'

'I don't know about you,' Fay began, 'but I think we shouldn't say anything about the jacket itself. Don and Peter know we found something that's going to be part of your outfit, and we should leave it at that. What do you think?'

'I agree,' said Helen. 'And we can't tell them about the story behind it either. But personally I'd like to tell Dad and Peter what the man said about the task we're to accomplish, and what he said about payment.'

'That's exactly how I feel too,' Fay said eagerly. 'After all, he said that Peter will be supporting you during your part in the task.'

'He called him my husband, so that must mean the task won't become apparent until after we're married,' said Helen. 'We must get you well again so you'll be ready for your part in it.'

'I wonder what it'll be,' said Fay. 'At the moment I haven't a clue, and I wouldn't even know where to look.'

'I don't think he was saying that we had to look for the task,' Helen mused. 'I think he was saying that we should keep alert so that we'll recognise it when it comes.' She stood up. 'I'm off to get the things out on to the dining table. Come on, let's get started on that picture again.'

When Don and Peter returned, they found Fay and Helen deep in concentration over the picture of the ruin.

'That's very good,' Don remarked, looking at it over Helen's shoulder as she filled in more of the details under Fay's direction. 'When your mum described it to me I had an idea of what she meant, but this gives me a much clearer image.'

'It means so much to me to have this,' said Fay. 'It's such a relief to have something down in this kind of detail, and Helen's made such a good job of it.'

'I've got a suggestion,' said Don. 'I noticed a couple of frames in the loft when I went up there. I'm sure that one of them is about the right size for this. I'll go up and get it if you want. Then we could frame the picture and hang it up.'

'We could have it in the bedroom,' said Fay confidently. Then she added hurriedly, 'If you don't mind, Don.'

Helen nudged her gently. 'You can have it in your room if that's what you want, Mum,' she said.

'Yes, you don't need to have my approval,' Don added with a twinkle in his eye. 'But I'd like you to know that I'd like it there too.'

He disappeared, and soon Fay could hear him opening the hatch into the loft. He returned after a while carrying a frame, which he put on the table beside her picture.

'I didn't know we had that one!' exclaimed Fay delightedly. 'It's lovely.' She picked up the picture and held it over the frame. 'It's almost an exact fit. It's as if it could have been made specially.'

'I've got some good card here too that I can use for a mount,' said Don. He opened a large brown envelope and produced some thick pale grey card. 'I'll do it this evening after our meal.'

'Thanks, Don. And I should tell you that we're going round to Joan's tomorrow evening. She said to come any time after eight and stay as long as we wanted.'

'That's great,' said Don enthusiastically. 'I'm glad you've got that fixed up.'

'And there's something else,' Fay continued. 'Helen and I have got something to tell you both.'

'Yes,' said Helen. 'Mum wants to hunt for a brooch or something to have instead of the ring you were going to get for her.'

'That's not what I was going to say,' Fay protested.

'Exactly,' said Helen, looking at her mother meaningfully. 'But I was so determined that it wasn't going to be forgotten that I thought we'd better say that first. I suppose I should have got you to say it.'

'What's this?' asked Peter. 'Don't keep us in suspense.' He scrutinised her face and then said, 'It's about what happened in that converted barn, isn't it?'

'You're spot on,' said Helen. 'How did you know?'

Don burst out laughing. 'Peter and I have been trying our best to guess what you bought. It's been on both our minds.'

'We're definitely not telling you, of course,' said Helen. 'It's against the rules. You'll both have to wait until September.' She looked across at Fay. 'But we've agreed that there is something we can tell you about it.'

'Actually, it's something I think we *ought* to tell you about,' Fay added.

Don and Peter sat down at the table and Don said, 'Fire away then. Don't keep us in suspense any longer.'

When Helen and Fay had finished, there was a stunned silence from Don and Peter. They both sat almost motionless, staring across the table, until Peter said, 'That's totally amazing, and even that is a complete understatement.'

'The question in my mind is "What will the task be?"' said Don. 'Fay, I hope that you'll be a lot better before it sees the light of day. I don't want you having to push yourself. The most important thing is for you to get well again. That's a big task in its own right.'

'Are you sure this man wasn't off his chump?' asked Peter carefully.

'I can't think of anything at all that would lead me to think that,' said Fay.

'At first I thought he might be trying to make fun of me,' said Helen. 'You remember, Mum? It was when I still had the j… er … the garment on. But he definitely wasn't. To tell you the truth I'm still reeling from the impact of it all. I hardly know what to think.'

'Me too,' Fay agreed. 'I'm so glad we've told you two – it helps to make it more real.' She turned to Helen and asked, 'Do you think we should discuss it with the others when we go across tomorrow evening?'

'Mm,' said Helen. 'I think in principle it would be a good idea, but in practice I'm not so sure.'

'Why's that?' asked Fay.

'I don't want anything to get in the way of the original reason for going,' said Helen passionately. 'Nothing at all, however important it might be.'

'You're right to keep your mother on track,' said Don. 'It's all too easy to get swept away by something as exciting as what you've described. The most important thing now is to get Fay well again, and that means going ahead with what we'd planned.'

'We could let them know there's something else,' Fay suggested. 'Perhaps they'll have time to come round here before Diana and Paul leave, and we could tell them then.'

‘I’ll be the one to remember to ask them,’ Helen offered. ‘And if I forget, Peter will remind me.’

‘I’m your man,’ Peter replied without hesitation.

The meal over, Don carefully prepared the mount, fixed Fay’s picture in the frame and hung it on the wall near the foot of the bed, so that Fay could see it easily. They left the light on and lay awake talking about it, and about the strange predictions of the young man in the converted barn.

Before Don switched off the light he said, ‘Fay, I’ve got something to tell you.’

‘What is it?’

‘Last week I was told that the central office is changing its location.’

‘Where’s it moving to?’

‘Apparently it will be about six months before it happens,’ Don began, ‘and the new address will be…’ Here he paused dramatically.

‘I know,’ said Fay, with sudden certainty, ‘The Courtyard.’

‘You’ve got it,’ Don replied without a trace of surprise. ‘It’s going to be number 4. It’s not the same location as the ring shop. It’s an office complex that’s being developed on the site of an old…’

‘… mansion house,’ Fay finished for him.

‘Yes, of course. After all that’s been happening recently we could almost have expected it. I haven’t been out there yet, but I heard that some of the original park area still surrounds the site, so it should be very pleasant.’

‘I wonder if there are going to be any cobbles?’ asked Fay sleepily.

‘We’ll have to wait and see.’

Chapter Thirteen

The following evening Don drew up at eight fifteen outside Jim and Joan's house. Fay could see Joan standing waiting for them in the doorway.

'There's not enough room in the hall for eight people to say hello to one another at once,' Joan said practically. 'Just go to the sitting room. The others are there.'

Paul approached Fay as soon as he saw her. 'You don't know me very well yet,' he said, 'so I'm not sure how you feel about me being here while you're talking things over. I do feel very involved because you're so important in Diana's life, but please be honest with me if you'd rather I wasn't in on this.'

Fay considered for a moment, and then said, 'Thank you for saying that, Paul. If I have any difficulty I'll let you know, but I'd rather you were here because you're part of the family. That's why Peter's here too.'

'The men can sit on the dining chairs I've brought through,' said Jim cheerfully, 'and the ladies can have the comfortable seats.'

When they were all settled Fay turned to Diana and said, 'It was a very special moment for me when I heard that you were pregnant. In my heart you're one of my little girls, and you always will be.'

'I know that, Fay,' Diana replied. 'I'm lucky to have two mums who both care about me, especially at a time like this.'

Here Joan took over. 'Diana and I have been doing a lot of talking, Fay,' she said seriously. 'We're worried about you.'

Fay made as if to protest, but Joan put a hand on her arm.

'You've been ill for such a long time,' said Diana worriedly, 'and we want to do everything we can to help you to get well again.'

'I've been talking to Mum about how she must concentrate now on putting herself first,' said Helen, 'but I know she's going to need a lot of reminding.'

'I accept that Helen's right,' Fay admitted.

Here Jim interrupted. 'We're going to help. I know you don't find it easy, Fay, but we can help you to think of ways you can try. For instance, you can practise phoning us to ask for help – even if there's nothing you need at the time.'

Fay laughed. She was grateful for Jim's suggestion. It was a good one, and it had lightened the atmosphere in the room. It was so difficult being the centre of attention, she reflected.

'I'd like to do that, Jim,' she said, 'but do you think you could phone me from time to time to remind me?'

'That's no problem,' he said with alacrity. 'Now let's get down to the real business of this evening. Fay, I'm very very sorry that we hadn't realised how difficult it was for you to be separated from Diana when she was small. We should have realised at the time.'

Fay began to cry. Joan put her arm round her and Diana brought a box of tissues. 'Just take your time, Fay,' Joan encouraged her. 'There's a lot to come out.'

When Fay became calmer, Joan continued. 'When Diana was a baby, and I was in such a state, you rescued us all by taking her under your wing.'

'Yes,' Jim agreed. 'I was off my head with worry about Joan, and I couldn't see a way ahead at all. Then you stepped in with your offer. It meant that not only could we cope, but also we began to have a life again.'

'Fay,' said Joan gently, 'looking back I can see that for a long time we all used you as a mother – someone who was unfailingly there for the children and interested in how we were. I feel embarrassed and guilty now that I realise what a strain this must have been on you.'

'But I loved the children,' Fay insisted.

'That's not the point,' said Jim firmly. 'We were *all* relying on you, and you must have been exhausted. From what little I've heard, you never got much care from your own mother, and her death was traumatic for you, but you kept on going. And on top of that you were coping with all your distress each time you were separated from Diana.'

'It's your turn to be cared for now, Fay,' Joan insisted. 'We all want you to enjoy your life and find interests of your own which you would have developed if you hadn't been so busy looking after everyone else.'

'But I was always interested in the children,' said Fay weakly.

'We know that,' said Jim. 'That has been all too easy to see. It's the things you haven't seen about yourself that we want to help you with now.'

'We've been looking through our photograph albums,' said Joan, 'and I'm going to duplicate a lot of the pictures of Diana and make them into a special album for you. I'm going to photocopy all her school reports and put them in a file for you. I expect there are other things I'll think of as well, but we want to give you as much as we can so you can have your rightful place in her life. We can't ever take away the pain you had to feel, but we can try to put things right, and we can help you with your life now.'

Don, who had been silent throughout this conversation, began to speak. 'I can see that I've been at fault too. I thought that Fay was fulfilled by the children, as indeed she was, but I didn't see anything of what she was coping with underneath. I'm sorry for my part in this, Fay,' he finished, reaching over and taking her hand.

'Please can we all talk about something different?' begged Fay. 'I promise I won't forget what you've all said.'

'We'll make sure of that,' said Don, patting her hand.

'We'll all remind you,' said Diana. 'By the way, since you're a kind of granny, I've had a copy made of the scan photograph of my baby for you. I'll go and get it. It's in my bag.' When she returned she was carrying an envelope which she handed to Fay. 'Here it is. And I'll keep in touch to let you know how the baby's getting on.'

'Thank you so much, Diana,' said Fay. 'It means a lot to me.'

'Shall we tell them about our trip to the barn now, Mum?' asked Helen.

Fay nodded. 'Where shall we start?'

'I think we'd better begin with the ring,' said Don.

Fay looked across at his hand. 'But you haven't got it on.'

'It's all right. I've brought it with me,' Don reassured her. He reached into his pocket and took out his handkerchief, the corner of which was knotted round the ring. He undid it and slipped it on to his finger.

'Yes, Don,' said Jim. 'I think you should tell the others about it.'

Over the next hour, Fay and Don recounted the story of how they came by the ring, and how they later returned to the Courtyard in search of a garment for Helen's wedding outfit. After this, Helen took over the story and described their trip to the converted barn.

'I'm sorry we can't divulge the whole story until my wedding day,' she apologised.

'I can't wait to hear the rest,' said Joan, 'but I see I'll have to be patient.'

'Can I see the ring again, Don?' asked Jim.

Don took it off his finger and passed it across.

Jim studied it. 'The style of the lettering is certainly very unusual. Not that I know much about these things, of course.'

'How about passing it round to the others?' said Don comfortably. 'I'd like you all to have a close look at it.'

While Paul was looking at the ring, Fay said to Joan, 'Helen has helped me to produce a picture of the ruin I saw in that dream I told you about. It's very good. Don's framed it for me, and it's up on our bedroom wall now. It was strange… I can hardly believe it now, but the first time we worked on it I had a flash of what it must have looked like when it was still inhabited, and there were people around it with unusual head covers.'

'That's astonishing!' exclaimed Joan. 'You must tell me if anything else like that happens.'

'Don told me you've got a copy of *Russian Voices* via the Internet,' said Jim. 'Have you read much more of it?'

'I've got it at the moment,' said Helen. 'I've just read the section about the woman who was very psychic and could see into some of her past lives.'

'I want to get my hands on that chapter,' said Don amiably, 'but I think I'll probably have to wait until Helen and Peter have left.'

'When's the book group starting up again after Easter?' Fay asked Joan.

'It's off for a month, I think,' Joan replied. 'I'll get my diary before you go, and check the dates.'

Fay went on. 'I had an idea about it. I wondered if they'd be interested in meeting Danny. You know, he's the son of a neighbour of mine. He wrote a horror story, and I did a bit of editing for him.'

'That's an interesting idea, Fay,' said Joan. 'I'll be sure to ask the others at the next meeting, and I'll let you know what they think.'

'I wish I knew why I get that feeling of home about the ruin and about the mansion house in the photograph in the book,' said Fay suddenly. 'Oh!' she exclaimed. 'I'm sorry. I didn't mean to burst out like that.'

'That's all to the good,' Jim encouraged her. 'It isn't very often that you say something without thinking it through first. Don't ever hold back around us. You never know what might come out.'

'That's what I'm worried about,' said Fay with embarrassment.

'You don't need to worry with us,' Joan insisted. 'And after what you've told us tonight, I've got a hunch that there are some very interesting things just round the corner.'

'My next project is to go with Don to look for a brooch or some other piece of jewellery, instead of the ring I was going to have,' said Fay. 'Perhaps we'll have another adventure,' she added with apparent flippancy.

Diana stood up. 'Everyone stay here,' she said. 'I've been baking this afternoon, and I'm going to bring through the results, together with something to drink.'

'I'll give you a hand,' said Helen.

The rest of the evening was very relaxed, and by the time they were ready to leave, Fay felt much better than she had for a long time.

Before she left, Paul spoke. 'I know I haven't said much this evening, but I didn't want to interrupt. Now I want to thank you for including me.'

'I'm so glad you were here, Paul,' replied Fay sincerely.

On the way home Helen said, 'That went really well, Mum. You were great.'

'Thanks, Helen,' Fay replied. 'It was very hard at first and I was worried, but I must say that I ended up feeling very relaxed.'

'I could see that,' said Don. 'You looked more yourself again. There have been a couple of times recently that you've looked better, but this time you looked well.'

'By the way,' said Helen, 'I told Diana we hoped to see them again before they go back. We've half arranged that we'll go to church together on Sunday, and we thought we could come back to our house afterwards. She'll phone in the morning when she's spoken to the others. You did so well this evening, Mum. In the past you wouldn't have been able to concentrate on what was bothering you. You would have been rushing to talk about the exciting news of how we'd found something for my wedding outfit.'

'But that's important,' Fay protested.

'Of course it is,' Helen agreed, 'but it was even more important to concentrate on your relationship with Diana. It's something that's been stressing you underneath ever since she was a baby, and that's a long time. Although our news is exciting and intriguing, it had to wait.'

'I see what you're trying to tell me,' Fay acknowledged, 'but I must admit it's going to be hard for me to keep this sort of thing in mind.'

'We know,' said Don, 'and that's why we're all going to keep reminding you.'

'I might not have much opportunity to be involved directly,' said Peter, 'but I certainly want to help where I can. At the very least, Helen and I will be talking it over.'

'Thank you all so much,' said Fay warmly.

'No,' said Helen, giving her mother a nudge. 'Thank *you*.'

Chapter Fourteen

Fay spent Saturday quietly. She opted to stay at home while the others went out shopping and then for a walk. Before they left, Helen had phoned Diana, who confirmed that she and her parents would be at church the following day and would call round afterwards.

Fay did not feel as tired as she had been, and considered spending part of the day going out with Helen, Don and Peter; but she knew that she needed time alone to think through the events of the previous evening and everything else that had been happening. She tried to do some of her knitting, but found she could not follow the pattern because her mind was so preoccupied. After a while she found herself going to get the paints, and she sat at the dining table with them, staring at a blank sheet of paper; but she found she could not settle, and instead went into the kitchen to make a drink.

'What shall I paint?' she murmured to herself.

Her mind went back to memories of sitting round that table with Diana, Helen and Jack, encouraging them to enjoy themselves with pots of paint and a variety of brushes. It had all seemed so easy then. She would paint green leaves and stems on her sheet of paper, and then put blobs of different colours at the tops of the stems to make flowers. It was a simple device, through which she could involve herself in their fun, making herself available to assist whenever help was needed. But now was very different. If she painted something it would be for herself, and that felt uncomfortable and almost strange. She thought about the paintings that had been hanging on the walls of the staircase at the converted barn, and wished fleetingly that she could paint rural scenes like those she had seen there.

'It's no use thinking like that,' she said firmly, and then she jumped at the sound of her voice. That's odd, she thought. There had been something unusual about it. It didn't sound like her, and it wasn't the sort of thing she would say to anyone. 'How funny,' she mused aloud, 'I hardly recognised my own voice.'

She pondered for a few minutes, sipping meditatively from the glass of water she had in her hand, before returning to the table where she picked up a narrow brush, dipped it in a pot of yellow paint, and attempted to paint some flower heads shaped like stars. Pleased with the effect, she continued. Somewhere at the back of her mind she could hear that voice again saying, 'It's no use'; but she paid no heed to it, and carried on slowly filling up the small white sheet with her yellow flowers.

'That's so nice,' she commented to herself as she worked.

When she had finished, she put the sheet to one side to dry, and tore another from the pad. 'Now what?' she questioned aloud. Then she heard a voice so clearly inside her head that the words might have been spoken. 'Fay,' it said, 'there's no use you trying to paint. You'll never make anything worthwhile. You're not artistic at all.'

Then she realised she was remembering her mother's words. Her mother had been quite artistic, and had enjoyed painting pictures of still life. Martin had inherited her skill, and had gone on to paint interesting objects such as old clocks and antique ornaments. Fay had never been allowed to be a part of this. Her early attempts at painting had resulted in blotches and mess, and her mother had banned her from using paints and brushes. That must have been before Martin was born.

Feeling very sad, she put her brush down and rested her head on her hands for a while. 'What a waste,' she said aloud. 'Even if I was limited in what I could do, I could have had some pleasure from it. After all, look what fun I had with the children!' It was then she realised that she had needed to be caring for children before she could give herself permission to paint, and when they no longer needed her for that she had given it up.

So now I must paint just for me, she thought. She considered the memories she had of the blobs and mess she had produced as a child, and then burst out, 'No wonder! It was because I felt lumpy and useless around my mother.'

She picked up the brush once more and began to experiment with the yellow paint. 'It's all right,' she reassured herself. 'You can do exactly what you feel like doing. You don't have to be a Van Gogh. All you have to do is enjoy yourself.' At that her mood lightened, and she soon became absorbed in experimenting with each colour in turn. She lost all track of time, and filled sheet after sheet from the small pad.

'Purple plums,' she pronounced cheerfully as she carefully devised four in a row. 'Brown stalks,' she said as she added one to each plum, before laying the sheet on one side and tearing another from the pad.

'Green now. Green ferns...' Carefully she began to paint several fronds, and added shaggy brown scales down the back of each. She was pleased with the effect. 'Not perfect by any stretch of the imagination, but not bad,' she pronounced. On impulse she stood up and went upstairs to her bedroom, where she stood and looked at the picture of the ruin again before taking it off the wall. Then she returned to the dining room and propped it up on the seat of one of the chairs on the opposite side of the table.

'The mystery of the ruined mansion...' she murmured, '... the mansion in my dream.' Suddenly she clutched at her chest. 'I can't breathe properly,' she whispered. 'Help me. Please, somebody help me.' She began to shiver uncontrollably. It was as if there was something heavy pressing down on her and everywhere seemed to be dark. 'Where am I?' She choked. 'The tunnel... it's the tunnel again...'

When Fay came round, she found that she was slumped across the table. She gradually became aware of a dripping sound, and realised she had knocked over the water she had for her brushes. It had soaked everything on the table and run on to the carpet. It was dripping into a puddle. The wetness on the table had soaked into her clothing, producing a large stain of a muddy colour. She felt panicky as she surveyed the mess. What will become of me? she wondered in her distress. She slowly began to grasp that it was her own table and her own house, and no one was going to be angry with her.

Having established that there was no imminent threat, she began to wonder where to start with the clearing up. Me first, she thought as she tried to stand up from her chair. But her knees felt like jelly and she abandoned the attempt. What's happening to me...? She noticed that her breathing was coming in short gasps, and she tried to steady herself by breathing out as far as she could.

Persisting determinedly in trying to stabilise her breathing, Fay noticed eventually that she was feeling a little less agitated, and she started to plan what to do next. A few more breaths and then I'll go and get changed, she promised herself. Despite the warmth of the sun through the window, she felt chilled.

She felt somewhat better with dry clothes on, and she put the stained ones into the washing machine and considered the task of cleaning the carpet. Perhaps I'd better do the table first, she thought, as she surveyed the mess. Luckily the picture of the ruin had not been affected, as the chair on which it stood was far enough back from the table to have avoided the spill. She collected a dustbin liner from the kitchen, and put all the wet paper into it before wiping the dirty water up with a cloth. It was fortunate that the colour of the carpet was not too dissimilar to that of the dirty water, and once she had soaked up the puddle it did not look too bad. Using a clean cloth and a bucket of cold water she worked to remove the remaining stain, and was content with the result. After that she cleaned the brushes and put the paints away.

It was then that she noticed she felt hungry. 'Goodness!' she exclaimed as she glanced at her watch. 'It's four already. I knew I lost track of time while I was painting, but I'd no idea it had got so late. No wonder I'm hungry.'

She emptied the bucket into the sink and put it away. Then she made a snack and moved one of the dining chairs up to the window, put her plate on the sill, and sat looking out at the birds busily pecking on the lawn. She could see they were mainly sparrows, but one or two blackbirds came and went.

She was still at the window when she heard the others coming in.

'Hello, Mum,' called Helen. 'We're back.'

'I'm in the dining room.'

Helen appeared with her cheeks glowing. 'We had a lovely walk. Dad took us round just about all the paths we used before I moved away.' She stopped, looked closely at Fay, and then said, 'Something's happened, hasn't it?'

'I suppose it has,' said Fay, reluctant to deflect Helen from her enthusiastic description of the afternoon's outing. 'I decided to try to do some painting.'

'That was a good idea,' said Don, putting his head round the door. 'Do you want a cup of something? I'm just putting the kettle on for the rest of us.'

'No thanks. I'm fine for now,' Fay replied. She stood up and moved the picture of the ruin on to the shelf near the table to clear the seat for Peter.

When Don appeared with three steaming mugs, Fay told the story of how she had tried painting, had struggled with memories of her mother's discouragement, and had ended up engrossed in what she was doing.

'What were you painting?' asked Don.

'Yellow flowers, then more flowers in different colours, then plums, then ferns... Oh... ferns...'

'What about the ferns?' asked Helen. 'And where are the pictures? I'd like to see them.'

'I'm afraid I had to throw them away,' Fay explained. 'They got wet when... when I knocked over the water.'

'That's a shame,' said Helen.

'Do you do any painting, Peter?' asked Fay, struggling to appear normal.

'I don't think you've told us the whole story yet, Mum,' said Helen perceptively.

'Actually, I think I passed out for a moment, and that must be how I knocked the water over,' Fay admitted uncertainly.

'You passed out!' exclaimed Helen. 'Why didn't you tell us straight away? How are you feeling now?'

'Er... my chest felt...' Fay faltered, and then to her embarrassment she started to cry. 'Here I am crying again,' she gasped miserably through her sobs.

'It's all right to cry, Mum,' Helen encouraged. 'You can tell us the rest when you're ready.'

Fay took a deep breath. 'I think it was that tunnel under the house,' she said. 'Only this time it wasn't in a dream. It happened just after I'd painted the ferns and brought the picture downstairs. I felt as if I couldn't breathe, and everywhere was dark. I tried to call for help, and then I must have passed out.'

Don looked concerned. 'I don't like the sound of this. Perhaps we should get you looked over,' he said.

'But I'm all right now,' said Fay anxiously.

'Don's right,' said Peter. 'You should really be checked by a doctor.'

'No!' shouted Fay, and then put her hand to her mouth. 'I... I mean I'd rather not at the moment,' she said in as normal a voice as she could muster. 'After all, it's Saturday, and I don't think it counts as an emergency.'

Helen looked at her mother sharply, but said nothing. Instead she turned to Don and said, 'Dad, perhaps it would be okay so long as Mum has someone with her all the time for a couple of days.' She stared at him meaningfully. 'I don't think she's up to any examinations at the moment.'

'That's a good idea,' Don agreed. 'I'll be here until Tuesday morning. We'll see how things go tomorrow and Monday.'

Fay relaxed visibly. 'I promise I'll be good,' she said meekly.

'You don't have to be good,' Helen reminded her. 'All you have to do is tell one of us if you don't feel right.'

'Oh... yes...' Fay replied. 'Yes, I'll do that.'

'Helen,' said Don suddenly. 'Do you mind letting me have *Russian Voices* tonight? I want to read about the woman with the past lives.'

Helen jumped up from her chair. 'I'll get it for you,' she said. She returned promptly and handed it to him saying, 'You could read it straight away if you want. Peter and I can make the meal.'

'Yes, I'll do that,' Don agreed. He made no move away from where Fay was sitting. He opened the book to find the section, and soon he was engrossed.

Fay went back to watching the birds, and felt comforted by their activity and by the presence of the others in the house. She could hear the clatter of utensils in the kitchen together with the voices of Helen and Peter, and these familiar sounds soothed her.

'Don,' she said suddenly. 'Will you be going to church with Helen and Peter in the morning?'

'I don't think so,' Don replied. 'Well, not unless you're going too.'

'I'd like to, but I don't feel up to it yet,' said Fay. 'If you want to go I'm sure I'll be all right for an hour or so.'

Don looked at Fay. There was something slightly odd about her, but he couldn't put his finger on it. She looked normal enough, but there was something about the way she was speaking that led him to sense that all was not well. Mechanical – yes, that was the word – there was something very slightly mechanical about the way she was speaking, and it meant that she came across as being detached. It was almost imperceptible, and Don questioned himself about it. The main feeling he had was a sense of intangible unease, a stirring in his gut, but all the while doubting his perceptions, as Fay appeared so ordinary and so plausible. There was something that just didn't ring true.

'I'd rather stay at home with you,' Don said firmly. 'I don't want you to be on your own at all over the next couple of days. And I think we should speak to Joan and Jim tomorrow about the possibility that you might need a hand on Tuesday when I go off again.'

'I'm sure I'll be all right,' Fay insisted. 'I feel fine already.'

'If I'm to be truthful,' said Don bluntly, 'I would say that you are not fine. You look okay, but you're not fine. Something's not right, but I don't know what it is.'

Tears welled up in Fay's eyes. 'You're right, Don. There's something, but I haven't a clue what it is either.'

Don put down the book and stroked Fay's arm. 'When you think about it, it's not surprising. After all, there's so much going on at the moment.' He paused before continuing. 'I've an idea,' he said.

Fay wiped her eyes and waited.

'I'm going to get something to write on,' said Don. 'At the very least it'll get some order into my own thoughts, and you might find it helpful too.' He went to the cupboard in the hall, and Fay could hear him rummaging about before he returned carrying an A4 pad. 'I'm not sure where to start,' he said, 'but I don't suppose it matters. I can organise it later if necessary.'

Fay could not help smiling as she watched Don write a heading on the page. His mind seemed to work best like that. She wasn't sure if it was a product of his working life, or if it was his natural way.

'What have you written?' she asked.

'Mysteries and possible past lives. I know that's imprecise, but it'll do. After all, I'm not at work now,' he joked. 'What shall I put down first? You should be the one to start, because you're at the centre of it.'

Fay nodded. 'Write "strange illness".'

'Done that,' Don replied. 'What's next?'

'My mother and my children – including Diana, of course,' said Fay as she warmed to his idea. 'The meeting with the others yesterday evening – it went so well, didn't it?'

‘I’m glad you think that,’ Don commented as he wrote down what Fay was saying. ‘As you know I have a very good feeling about it. I’m sure it’s one of the things that’s going to help you.’

Fay went on. ‘Then there are the photos you took for me of the farm where I lived, and the picture of the mansion house in that book.’

Don wrote rapidly, and then added, ‘And the painting of the dream ruin that Helen helped you with.’

‘That leads on to courtyards,’ said Fay, almost excitedly.

Just then, Helen put her head round the door. ‘It won’t be long now,’ she said. ‘What are you two up to?’

When Don and Fay had explained, she said, ‘I can’t wait. Let’s get the meal over, and then Peter and I can join in.’ She went back to the kitchen, and the clattering increased until she and Peter appeared, laden with plates and a large dish. ‘Come on you two,’ she ordered with mock severity. ‘It’s time to clear the table.’

The meal over, Don and Helen returned to their list, while Helen and Peter cleared the kitchen. Although Fay was aware of Helen’s eagerness not to miss anything, this did not prevent her from continuing.

‘The courtyards,’ she said to Don. ‘There’s the one at the farm and the one at the hospital.’

‘And there’s the name of the place where we bought this ring, and there’s the address of my new office,’ Don added.

‘You’d better make a note that the Courtyard at the ring shop led us to the converted barn and all that happened there,’ said Fay.

‘Okay,’ said Don, writing quickly.

‘Carvings and inscriptions,’ said Fay. ‘There are two carvings in stone.’

‘And of course there’s this lettering on my ring,’ Don added. ‘I’ll make a note of that.’

‘Reverend Howard’s researches,’ said Fay slowly. ‘I know it isn’t strictly to do with us, but I feel it could be a part of the picture.’

‘How about *Russian Voices*?’ asked Don.

‘I’m not sure, but you can put it in if you want.’

At this point Helen and Peter joined them.

‘Helen’s been telling me what you’ve been doing,’ said Peter. ‘How far have you got?’

‘I think we’ve got all the main headings down,’ Don replied.

'Whatever you've been doing it's obviously been the right thing,' Peter observed.

'Why do you say that?' asked Fay.

'You're much more yourself again, Fay. I could see that Don was concerned about you, and to be honest, so was I.'

Fay stared at him. Peter was not a person who spoke unnecessarily.

'Thank you for your concern, Peter,' she said sincerely, as she began to realise that he was far more involved in everything than she had previously given him credit for. She had always known that he was a very pleasant and hardworking young man, and she was delighted that he was to be Helen's husband, but until now she had not been able to take in the fact that behind his quiet exterior he was concerned about her.

'Tell us what you've written so far, Dad,' urged Helen.

Don read out the headings and then added, 'We've got a bit of padding to put in. I need to make some notes about what the young man told you when you got that whatever-it-is for your wedding, and we must put a heading about the task, although none of us has a clue what it might be.'

'After that you should write something more about the ring,' Peter said unexpectedly. 'It's quite a puzzle, isn't it? And at this stage there's no way of telling whether it's a single piece or not.'

'That's a thought,' mused Fay.

Don wrote a note beside the entry about the ring. 'Do you think there's anything else I should include?' he asked.

'Put something about that stab I felt in my thumb,' said Fay suddenly. 'It's important, I know.'

'It's such a strange thing,' Helen reflected. 'A definite stab – like a pin digging into you – but there was nothing there, and no blood. Tell me again what happened after that.'

'I went very cold, so I got a jumper from upstairs. Later I had something to eat.'

'Wasn't that the night before I came home?' asked Don.

'That's right.'

'So that's the night you plucked the hairs out of your eyebrows?'

'Yes,' Fay said, 'and before you arrived home I felt very peculiar, and had that long bout of bad memories of when I was a child.'

‘Fay, can you remember what you were doing before you felt the stab in your thumb?’ asked Peter.

‘Let me think.’ Fay shut her eyes, and instantly her mind was filled with an image of cobbles. ‘Cobbles,’ she said, as if to herself.

‘Where were the cobbles?’ asked Peter quietly.

‘In the farmyard,’ replied Fay, her eyes still shut. ‘No. How silly of me!’ she exclaimed, looking across at him. ‘I went to the hospital and photographed the courtyard there. It had rather odd-shaped modern cobbles.’

‘And that was the day you got your appointment card through the post,’ Don finished for her. ‘So the sequence was that your appointment came, you went and took photos, you felt a stab on your thumb but there was nothing there, and then you felt very cold. That night you plucked some hairs out of your eyebrows, and the following day you had a blast of bad memories. I’ll write all of that down. I don’t know if these things are connected, but I feel they might be.’

‘When’s your appointment at the hospital?’ asked Peter.

‘I’m pretty sure it’s just over a week after you go back home,’ Fay replied. ‘I’ve been wondering about cancelling it though, because I’m beginning to feel a bit better at last.’

‘There’s no way you’re cancelling that appointment, Mum,’ said Helen vehemently. ‘You’ve got to promise me that you won’t.’

Fay looked at her with surprise. ‘But it’s not a good idea to take up hospital time if you don’t really need it,’ she said.

‘But you *do* really need it,’ Helen insisted. ‘You might be feeling a bit better now, but you’ve been ill for ages, and we’ve all been worried about you. Added to that, you passed out when you were on your own today. You *have* to go.’

‘Helen’s right,’ said Don quietly, and Peter nodded. Don continued. ‘And there’s the more immediate problem of whether or not it’s going to be okay to leave you on your own from Tuesday onwards. I’m glad Joan and Jim will be round tomorrow morning. We can talk it over with them and decide what to do.’

‘But I do feel quite a bit better in general,’ Fay protested.

‘In general, yes,’ agreed Don. ‘You certainly look a lot better some of the time, but there’s still a long way to go before you’re back to full strength, and I’m concerned about what happened when we were out.’

‘Put it this way, Mum,’ said Helen in practical tones. ‘How would you feel if one of us hadn’t been well for a long time and had just passed out?’

‘I’d be very worried, of course,’ said Fay without hesitation.

‘Precisely,’ said Helen meaningfully. ‘So this is an example of the sort of thing we’re trying to get you to see. Your life doesn’t consist of making sure that everyone’s okay and not doing the same for yourself.’

‘It’s so obvious when you spell it out to me,’ sighed Fay. ‘Yet when I’m thinking about it on my own I can’t see it.’ She turned to Don and said decisively, ‘When Joan and Jim come round I want to be the one who raises the question of next week. You can remind me if I forget.’

‘Of course I will,’ Don replied.

‘And in the very unlikely event that Dad forgets, Peter and I will remind you both,’ added Helen with a smile. ‘By the way, you two, when are you going on that hunt for a brooch or something to remind Mum about all this?’

‘That’s a good point, Helen,’ said Don. ‘Fay, let’s make a date.’

‘Would you…’ Fay began and then laughed. ‘I was going to ask if you would have some time next weekend, but I managed to stop myself. I’ll start again. Let’s go out on Monday afternoon – after Helen and Peter have left.’

‘Well done, Mum!’ Helen congratulated her. ‘Peter and I will phone in the evening to see if you’ve found anything.’

Chapter Fifteen

'Mum, the church was completely packed!' exclaimed Helen as she burst through the front door, with the others following close behind.

'There were even people standing outside the doors, I believe,' said Jim as he came into the house. 'It's a good thing we all went early.'

'The sermon was so good that I was disappointed when it finished,' said Paul. 'I don't think I've ever had that experience before. It was impressive the way he spoke about hope and renewal in life in a general sense, as well as the specific Christian beliefs about Easter and its meaning.'

'Yes,' agreed Peter, 'it was outstanding. I feel very lucky that he'll be conducting our wedding ceremony.'

'All the time he was speaking I had in my mind the hope that what's happening in Fay's life now will mean a renewal for her,' said Joan sincerely. 'Fay, I've been going over in my mind the conversation we had on Friday evening. I know it might sound a bit way out, but I did wonder if all you've been going through is some kind of preparation for the task the young man told you about.'

There was silence.

'I don't know what to say,' said Fay at length.

'I don't think you have to say anything,' said Don quietly. 'Joan has given us all something to think about, and we should leave it at that for now. I'd like to offer everyone a drink, and by the way I assure you it's not an attempt to provide a distraction.'

'Some of your amazing elderflower cordial would be welcome,' said Joan. 'It's simple, straightforward and delicious.'

Don was soon filling eight glasses from a large jug, which he replenished several times.

As they sat round sipping the cool liquid, Don said, 'Fay's got something else to talk to you about while you're here.'

Fay took a deep breath and began. She told her friends about her attempts at painting, and what that had revealed about the negating effects of her past with her mother. After that she described the sequence of the paintings she had done, and how much she had enjoyed herself. She finished with her account of how she got the picture of the ruin from upstairs.

'That's interesting, Fay,' said Joan. 'You must do some more painting soon. Can I see what you've done so far?'

'I had to throw them out,' Fay explained. 'You see, soon after I brought the picture downstairs I felt I couldn't breathe properly. It seemed as if I was in the tunnel under the ruin, and I tried to call out for help. Then I must have passed out, and when I came to, the water I had for washing the brushes had spilled all over the table and on to the floor. The paintings were completely ruined. I had to clean everything up, which included changing my clothes.'

'What a shame!' exclaimed Diana spontaneously. 'I remember how much I loved painting with you when Helen and I were small. It was such good fun.'

'I remember that too,' Fay said. 'In fact, I was thinking about it when I took the paints out. It seemed pleasant and easy when we used to do it together, but trying to do it on my own, just for me, was quite a different matter.'

'Tell us about the sensation of being in the tunnel, Fay,' Joan urged.

'The first thing that happened was that I felt I couldn't breathe properly, and I called out for someone to help me. I realised that it was totally dark everywhere, and there was something pressing on my chest. Then I knew I was in the tunnel.' Her voice dropped to a whisper. 'It was horrible.'

'So you were lying down in the tunnel?' asked Jim.

'I must have been,' said Fay with surprise. She shut her eyes and tried to picture her experience. 'Yes.'

'Were you on your back, your front or one side?' Jim asked casually.

Again Fay shut her eyes. 'It's very difficult to say,' she said hesitantly. 'It was completely dark… I couldn't see anything.'

'Try and think which surface of you had the greatest pressure on it,' Jim suggested.

With her eyes still shut, Fay tried to think about it. Suddenly, she clutched her chest. 'My chest, my chest,' she gasped. 'Someone help me. Please help me!'

Don took hold of her by the shoulders. 'It's all right, Fay,' he said slowly and firmly. 'You're in your own sitting room, and everyone is here to help you. Breathe out slowly and you'll be fine.'

Fay opened her eyes, held on to Don's arms, and exhaled slowly.

'Again,' Don instructed after she had taken a breath.

This steadied her to the point where she said, 'I'm sorry everyone.'

'That's all right, Fay,' said Joan. 'There's obviously something going on here that you need help with, and we must get to the bottom of it.'

'I don't think I can do any more today,' said Fay in a voice that was filled with anxiety. 'It's terrifying.'

'I can see that,' said Joan, 'and I wasn't trying to suggest that we do any more about it now.'

'I'm feeling concerned,' said Jim. 'When do you leave for work again, Don?'

'Tuesday morning.'

'From what I've just seen and heard, I think you shouldn't be on your own, Fay,' Jim advised.

'That was the other thing we wanted to talk to you about while you were here,' said Don.

'I've made my decision,' said Joan determinedly.

The others looked at her in astonishment.

'What decision, and about what?' asked Jim.

'From Tuesday to Friday either Fay's going to be living with us, or else I'm moving in here,' said Joan in a voice that did not invite discussion. 'As it happens, I've got this week off work, but if I hadn't, I would have arranged it.'

The expression on Fay's face was a mixture of relief and anxiety. 'But… you can't,' she burst out.

'Why not?' Joan challenged.

'It's your holiday…' Fay stuttered.

'That's right,' Joan agreed, 'and I'm going to do what I want with it. I'm going to care for my friend, my daughter's other mother. How better could I spend my time?'

'I was so worried about how I would cope,' Fay admitted in a wobbly voice.

'I guessed you were,' said Joan, 'and I knew there was no point in asking, because you would have denied it. We can have a good time. Even with your limited energy we can get out and about, and there are plenty of things we can do in the house apart from chatting. We could have a couple of nights at my house and the other two at yours. What do you think?'

'That sounds wonderful,' said Fay, who was quickly regaining her composure.

'The three of us could go out for a meal one evening,' Jim suggested. 'I'll be based at home on Thursday. Let's make a date for then.'

'That's settled,' said Helen. 'Diana and I can take it in turns to phone in the evenings to find out how you two have been enjoying yourselves, and hear about any developments.'

Diana reached down and picked up her bag. 'I've got something here for you, Fay. It's fragile,' she warned, as she passed over a small parcel wrapped in tissue paper.

Fay opened it very carefully to reveal an egg with a delicate design painted all over it. 'It's beautiful!' she exclaimed. 'Where is it from?'

'I made it specially for you,' Diana explained.

'But it must have taken you hours to paint it.'

'Yes, it did. And I was thinking of you the whole time.'

'Thank you so much,' said Fay, admiring its detail.

'I'll go and get you an egg cup, and then you can have it on the mantelshelf,' Don suggested. The beautiful egg was soon placed in a prominent position.

'Fay, there's one more thing I'd like to ask,' said Jim. 'Would you mind showing us the picture of the ruin?'

'Of course not,' Fay answered, standing up. Then she caught sight of the signet ring on Don's finger. 'No,' she said firmly. 'I don't want to look at it again at the moment.' She sat down.

There was a moment's pause in the room, and then Helen began to clap. 'Well done, Mum!' she said.

Fay looked puzzled. 'I haven't done anything.'

'That's it in a nutshell,' Don pronounced. 'Doing nothing was what you really wanted, but you did something as well. You told Jim that you didn't want to do what he was suggesting.'

Fay's expression changed from its perplexed state into one of dawning understanding. 'I thought that Jim should see the picture because he wanted to, and I forgot that I didn't want to think any more about the tunnel for now. The picture of the ruin is so evocative of the tunnel that looking at it isn't right for me at the moment. Somehow I must have known that because I stopped myself from getting it, and said "no". That's really good, isn't it?' she finished almost to herself. Then she added triumphantly, 'Actually, what I really want to do is talk about what Joan and I might do together this week!'

'Hooray!' cheered Diana, reaching across and giving Fay a hug.

This was followed by lively conversation about what the following week meant for everyone. Don and Peter served a simple impromptu lunch, allowing the gathering to go on until late in the afternoon, when with much reluctance Joan, Jim, Diana and Paul left, so that Diana and Paul could prepare for their journey the following day.

'It won't be long now before you'll be moving back,' Don said to them as they parted at the front door.

'Yes,' Paul replied. 'It's only another eight weeks before I start my new job. As we told you earlier, we think we've got a buyer for the house, and as soon as we're sure about that, we'll be able to redouble our efforts in searching up here. However, at this rate it looks as if we'll be with Joan and Jim at first, for a few weeks at least.'

Later, Helen noticed that Fay seemed withdrawn.

'I think I'd like to have another look at the picture now, Helen,' she said eventually. Her voice was quiet. 'Would you mind bringing it?'

'What are you thinking, Mum?' asked Helen as she returned carrying it.

'I've been thinking of how I was lying in the tunnel. I've worked out that I felt there was pressure on my back and my front, both at the same time.'

'That's interesting,' said Helen.

'But somehow that doesn't seem quite right.'

Fay looked at the picture and then closed her eyes. Helen sat quietly beside her and waited. She could hear noises from the kitchen where Don and Peter were clearing things away and preparing a meal for the evening.

After a little while, Fay began to speak. 'I'd gone into the tunnel from the end of the building that is to the left of this picture. There was a door there. I think the lower part was made of oak and the upper part was an iron grille. It wasn't locked, and I pushed it open. Inside the tunnel was pitch black, but I felt compelled go into it. At that stage I felt apprehensive, but not frightened. Somehow I knew I was doing the right thing, and this spurred me on. At first there was plenty of room and I could stand upright without difficulty, but as I worked my way along I had to bend my head forward, and then I had to crouch slightly as I walked. Not long after this I noticed that the tunnel began to narrow, although there was still space for me to move forward without turning to my side. The walls of the tunnel felt quite rocky, with little or no earth, and the ground under my feet seemed dry.

'As I worked my way carefully further and further along the tunnel I had to crouch more and more, until I reached a point where I could only move forward if I was on my hands and knees. I didn't hesitate. I knelt down and crawled along, and proceeded in this way for what seemed to be a long time. At no stage had I any thought of turning back. I wanted only to continue, but I had no idea where I was going, or why.

'Then it became apparent to me that I could only move forward if I was lying flat, dragging myself forward slowly on my front. I found this very tiring, and had to rest frequently. I had an idea that perhaps I could sometimes move along on my back, and I rolled over.' Here Fay sighed, and she leaned back limply in her chair. 'It was then that I heard a noise above me, and I felt a crushing weight on my chest. I was terrified.'

Helen noticed that her mother was looking very pale, and her skin appeared damp. She wondered what to do.

'I can't remember anything after that,' Fay finished. She was now clearly exhausted.

Helen left the room for a moment, and returned carrying a lightweight travelling rug which she tucked round her mother. Fay seemed hardly to notice. Her eyes were still shut.

'It was good you remembered all that, Mum,' said Helen. 'Of

course my mind is full of questions.'

Unexpectedly, Fay opened her eyes immediately and said, 'Tell me what they are. It might help.'

'For a start, I wanted to know if you had any idea of what you were wearing,' Helen said.

Fay shut her eyes again. 'I have on a garment with long sleeves. I think it must be a dress… with quite a long skirt. But I'm not wearing any shoes,' she added, surprised.

Helen continued. 'And I wanted to know how old you were.'

Fay sat upright for a moment, before sinking back again, saying, 'I was going to tell you that was a silly question, but then I realised I was much younger than I am now. I would say I was in my early twenties.'

'This is amazing, Mum!' exclaimed Helen. 'I wonder what on earth it all means.'

'Have you got any more questions?' asked Fay hurriedly. 'The whole thing seems to be fading now.'

Helen's mind seemed to scramble, and she searched feverishly for another question. 'Your name. What's your name?' she asked urgently.

Fay looked at her blankly.

Helen persisted. 'Who are you? What are you called?'

'Morna.'

Just then Don came into the room. 'What are you two up to then?' he asked. 'And I don't think you've mentioned Morna to me before, Fay. Who is she? It's an unusual name.'

Helen looked at him and said deliberately, 'This is Morna.'

'What do you mean?' asked Don. Then he laughed. 'Ah, you've been playing a game. Can I join in? The food's cooking, and Peter's in charge.'

'It isn't a game,' Helen informed him seriously. 'But you can join in. Sit down and we'll explain.' She turned to Fay and asked, 'Shall I tell him, or do you want to?'

'I'd like you to tell him,' Fay replied, 'and if I think of anything else along the way, I'll say.'

Helen began. 'Morna is in her early twenties. She was wearing a dress that had long sleeves and a longish skirt. She had nothing on her feet. She went through a gate at this end of the building…' – here she pointed to the picture – '…and she was making her way along the tunnel. It was completely dark, and the tunnel kept getting lower and narrower. She ended up having to crawl, and then wriggle on her front. At one point she turned over, and the roof of the tunnel caved in on her chest. That's about it so far,' she finished.

'Phew!' exclaimed Don. 'But what on earth was she doing in that tunnel?'

'I don't know,' said Fay, 'but it seemed exactly the right thing to be doing. Of course, she'd been through it before…'

'She'd been through it before?' Helen echoed.

'Yes. That's right,' Fay replied. 'The tunnel goes right under the building and out at the other end. About half way along is a shaft which leads up into the great hallway. There are special gaps in the stonework to allow a person to climb up the shaft and into the hall.'

'Wow!' Don expostulated. 'How many people lived there?' he asked, fascinated.

'About fifty, I think,' said Fay.

'I wish we knew where this building was,' said Don emphatically. 'It's been on my mind since you first told me about it.'

'I suppose we can't be certain it ever existed,' said Fay. 'After all, all we've got to go on is my dream.'

'I've had a feeling all along that it does exist somewhere,' said Don. 'I don't know why I'm so sure about it, but I am.'

'I'm glad you are,' said Fay, relief showing in her voice. 'It's so real to me I think I'd find it very hard if you doubted it.'

Don went on. 'And now you've had this experience as if you were Morna.'

'It seems it could well fit with this problem I've had with my lung,' Fay reflected. 'And if you remember, weeks ago when the dream came back into my mind, I did think it was linked to my illness in some way.'

'While you've been telling me about all of this, I've been thinking about the account I read in *Russian Voices*,' said Helen. 'If what the woman said there is anything to go by, it would be easy to believe that you were Morna in a past life and that you've just been remembering how, as Morna, you died.'

Fay considered this, and then said, 'If that's right, then I should think about why I am remembering it now, and whether being ill was something that had to happen first.'

Don spoke slowly. 'There are some staggering possibilities here, and I think all we can do is make a mental note of them and see what happens.'

'I'd prefer it if we made more than a mental note,' said Fay worriedly. 'Can we add all of this to the things we were writing down yesterday? I don't want to forget anything.'

'Of course,' Don replied. Soon he was recording everything he had heard about Morna, and their discussion so far.

Over the meal that evening they told Peter what had happened. He listened intently to everything before adding, 'I know it's a bit of a wild idea, but I wonder if Don's signet ring has anything to do with this.'

'It hadn't crossed my mind,' said Don. 'None of us know what's really going on, and all we can do is stay alert, so that we miss nothing. And it's important not to discount things just because we don't understand them, or because they seem unlikely.'

'Dad's starting to talk a bit like the young man when I got my er… isn't he, Mum?' Helen observed.

'You're right, Helen,' replied Fay. 'What was it he said about the task?'

'Mm… I think it was something like "you must be sure to recognise it when it manifests itself to you",' said Helen.

'That sounds like it,' Fay agreed. 'And taking into account what Don's saying, if we discounted things just because we didn't understand them, we'd be running the risk of not recognising our task when it presents itself.'

'Fay, we should also remember what Joan was saying,' said Don thoughtfully. 'Her idea that your illness might be a preparation for the task is one we should consider carefully.'

Fay groaned. 'I hope it doesn't mean that I'm going to be ill until after the wedding. It's months away.'

'Why should you think that?' asked Don.

'Don't you remember?' said Fay. 'The young man referred to Helen's husband supporting her through her part in the task. Peter won't be a husband until after the wedding.'

'I don't think it means you've got to be ill that long,' Helen objected. 'Maybe just for long enough to learn certain things.'

'That's plausible,' Fay agreed. 'Of course, I'm already aware of something I have to learn – and that is how I have to take myself into account. I can see very well how that could fit with preparing for a task. If I'm not able to listen to myself and take myself into account, I might not be able to play my part in the task.'

'I wonder what's going to happen at the hospital appointment,' said Helen suddenly.

'Why has that come into your mind just now?' asked Fay. 'I must say that in the middle of all this I'd almost forgotten about it.'

'Well,' Helen began, 'they'll be able to rule out any known diseases, and in a way that might help us.'

Here Peter interrupted. 'Apart from that, there's this business of courtyards to consider. You told us there's one at the hospital entrance, Fay, and although it's only a modern imitation, it could have some effect on you.'

Fay agreed. 'I think you're right, Peter. If I was sufficiently affected by it that I had to go back and photograph it, then it must be important to me.'

'We should go and have a look at it together again some time before your appointment,' suggested Don. 'And I must get the film developed.'

'But it's not finished yet,' Fay protested.

'Never mind about that. I think it's important to have the prints so that you can look at them alongside the picture in the book and the photos I took of the farm.'

'And the picture of the ruin,' Helen added.

'Yes, I'd like that, Don,' Fay admitted. 'Can we go to one of those while-you-wait photography places tomorrow, after Helen and Peter have left?'

'Yes, of course.'

Chapter Sixteen

Joan arrived at Fay's house on Tuesday morning just as Don was leaving.

'I promise I'll take good care of her,' she said as they waved him off.

'You didn't have to come straight away,' said Fay.

'Of course I did,' Joan replied. 'When you phoned to let me know what had happened after I left yesterday, I was doubly glad I'd planned this time with you. And you've got to remember I've been looking forward to it.'

'So have I,' Fay admitted.

'I'll tell you something else,' Joan added. 'I've been thinking a lot about our conversation about you and Diana. We always knew that you were like a second mother to her, but we had no idea about the real depth of that relationship.'

'It wasn't something I could put into words until recently,' said Fay.

'Yes, I understand that,' Joan replied. 'What I wanted to convey is that everything you said has set me thinking – not just about your situation, but about mine too.'

'What do you mean exactly?'

Joan went on. 'I was struggling so much when the girls were babies that I wasn't aware of my own depth of attachment to them. But it must have been there, because since you've been talking about how painful it was to be separated from Diana, I've been having some very painful feelings myself about being separated from her, and from Helen too. I'd been all too conscious of the loss of my womb, and that meant I was unaware of the pain of the separations until now, just after you were talking about it yourself.'

Fay gave her a hug and said, 'Two mothers sharing the same twin pair. That must be quite an unusual thing, and it makes our relationship even more special than our close friendship.'

'And we're soon going to have our first grandchild,' said Joan, smiling.

'I must show you my knitting,' Fay said spontaneously.

'Have you got spare needles and yarn?'

'Yes, plenty. And I've collected a few patterns from various sources. You can choose something.' Fay began to cast off the back of the little jacket she was working on. Then she said, 'I've an idea. Why don't we phone Jim and see if he wants to join us for the evening meal? In fact, he could stay the night. We can change the sheets on the spare bed.'

'I'll give him a ring,' agreed Joan. She put down her needles, and was soon discussing the plan with him. 'That's it fixed,' she said as she finished the call, 'but he says not to cook because he'll bring a surprise for us.'

Fay smiled. She liked Jim's surprises. 'Perhaps he'll want to come tomorrow evening as well.'

'I think that would fit, and I'm sure he'd like to,' Joan replied. 'After that it'll be Thursday, and we'll move up to our house until Don's back on Friday evening. And don't forget we're eating out on Thursday.'

'Have you any thoughts about where we might go?'

'I think Jim has,' Joan replied with an air of mystery, 'and I think it's quite safe to leave it to him.'

The rest of the week passed pleasantly and uneventfully. Jim had indeed thought up some unusual menus, and his surprise venue for Thursday's meal was an enormous success. As promised, Helen and Diana had taken it in turns to phone in the evenings, and Fay and Joan had enjoyed hearing their news. Fay was grateful for the lull in the series of intense events in her life, and welcomed this relatively quiet time. When Don returned, she and Joan were sad that their four days together were over, and made a pledge to arrange more time soon. Fay's hospital appointment was to be at ten the following Tuesday morning, and Jim had insisted on taking time away from his work to drive her there and bring her back.

When Tuesday came, Fay was aware of feeling uncomfortable and anxious. She rose early, and was ready long before Jim was due to collect her. As she sat and waited, she took out the photos of the hospital courtyard that she and Don had had developed the afternoon after Peter and Helen had departed. They had delayed looking for a brooch for Fay until they felt they had more time.

It's a good idea to have another look at these before I go, she thought as she spread the photos on the table. This is one part of the hospital that will seem familiar to me when I arrive, and that might help me.

There were five shots – one of the archway through which the courtyard was visible, one of the courtyard while standing under the archway, and the other three were of sections of the courtyard area. The artificial cobbles had come out quite clearly.

As she sat and stared at them her head began to swim a little, and she shut her eyes. She could see a courtyard, but it wasn't the one she had just been looking at – it was the one where she used to live, and she was particularly aware of the carving on the stonework above the archway.

'That's funny,' she said aloud. 'The carving is much clearer than it appears on the early photos Don took.' She shook her head. 'Maybe I studied it when I lived there. Yes, that must be the explanation.' But try as she might she had no memory of having done so. 'Silly me!' she pronounced. 'I didn't even notice it when I lived there, so how could I have studied it?'

She shook her head again, and began to gather up the photos from the table. But something made her stop and spread them out again. She stared at them once more, and then shut her eyes. Again she felt disorientated, again she saw the carving, and again it appeared clearer than on Don's photos. In an attempt to reduce her confusion, she went and collected the photos of the farm and searched through them to find the ones with the carving. Then she put them on the table beside the photos of the hospital archway. That felt better. Now she was sure she was right. The carving she had seen when her eyes were shut was certainly much clearer than it appeared in these photographs.

She shut her eyes once more. Yes, there it was again, and this time she didn't feel any unsteadiness. How very strange this is, she thought. It's almost as if I'm seeing the carving as it used to be when it was first put there... As she concentrated on it in her mind's eye she could see that it consisted of a long snake woven into a complex knot, and that the end of the tail was in the snake's mouth. That the carving depicted a snake had not been apparent from the photos, even when examined with a lens.

She glanced at her watch. Jim would be arriving shortly. She left the photos on the table and went to collect her jacket from the cupboard in the hall. The doorbell rang, and soon she and Jim left for the hospital.

'Do you want me to come in with you?' he asked as they approached the car park.

'No thanks. I should be fine,' Fay replied.

'I've got a couple of things to do,' said Jim. 'I'll be away for about an hour. So if you're finished before then, stay in the waiting area and I'll come and find you.'

He drew up near the archway, and Fay showed him her appointment card together with the sketch map the hospital had provided.

He studied them for a moment. 'Dr Grayling's clinic. I'll make a note of that in case I get lost.' Then he drove off.

Fay made her way slowly across the artificial cobbles and through the automatic doors into the extensive reception area. There she showed her card to a thin middle-aged man behind the desk who directed her down a corridor opposite, and told her to follow the signs.

The clinic was easy to locate, and Fay showed her card to the cheerful young woman who was sitting next to a computer.

'Could you take a seat over there please?' said the woman, pointing to a row of chairs by the window. 'Someone will be with you soon.'

Fay picked up a magazine from a table nearby and sat down, but she could not concentrate, and put it back. A few minutes later a nurse who looked like a schoolgirl came to collect her.

'Can you come this way, please?' she said. 'I have to weigh and measure you. After that we need a specimen of urine.'

'I would prefer not to be weighed, thank you,' said Fay.

'That's fine,' the nurse replied.

Inwardly Fay heaved a sigh of relief. She had dreaded that moment – a situation that she had guessed was inevitable – and she had negotiated it surprisingly easily. If her weight had been a problem, she would have agreed to the request without hesitation; but it was not, and she did not want to run the risk of evoking memories of being judged adversely about her weight during her childhood.

Back in the waiting area again, Fay sat observing the people who came and went. There was a tall, striking-looking woman with darkish skin and a formal hairstyle. She appeared to be very competent in the way she communicated with others. An older woman, long past retiring age, was being helped along by someone who Fay thought must be her daughter. They seemed to know where they were going, although their progress was painfully slow.

At last a tall man, possibly in his late thirties, appeared and introduced himself as Dr Grayling. Fay followed him into a large airy room, and he motioned to her to sit down at the side of his desk. He proceeded to ask her a series of questions about her illness, and she did her best to respond as accurately as she could.

When he was satisfied that he had covered all the necessary ground, he took her across to an examination couch.

'Can you sit on the edge of the couch first, please?' he said.

Fay obediently positioned herself as he had indicated.

'I have to come behind you now so that I can examine your neck,' he explained.

A voice inside Fay's head said, 'That's amazing. He told you what he was going to do, instead of just grabbing you.' A sense of safety and warmth spread through her.

When he had finished he said, 'That's fine. Now please lie down.'

Fay bent to loosen her laces. 'Don't take your shoes off,' he directed.

She felt very anxious as she placed her feet carefully on the sheet of disposable paper that was across the bottom of the couch. It seemed wrong to be wearing shoes, and she felt worried about getting into some kind of trouble. Childhood again, she thought to herself, and tried to relax.

He examined her carefully and took an interest in the remains of the rash she showed him on her chest and in her groin.

'It first appeared about five weeks ago,' she explained. 'It was very itchy at first, but it hardly bothers me now.'

He unhooked a device attached to the wall and fitted it on her arm. 'Blood pressure on the low side of normal,' he observed. 'That's good. Now I'll take some blood samples.'

Expertly he slipped a needle into a vein near her wrist, just below her thumb. It seemed quite painless, Fay reflected with surprise, and was quite unlike the stabs she had felt in her thumb – the phantom stabs from the non-existent pin in the curtain at home.

After he had finished, he took her over to the desk again and explained that he would write to her GP. He also said that since she had been unwell for so long and appeared to him to look depressed, it might help to take a short course of medication for this. Fay was startled, and he explained that a high proportion of people who had been unwell for a long time showed some benefit from taking an antidepressant, whatever the origin of the original illness.

Before she left she thanked him for his time, and said that she would consider everything he had said. She was relieved to see Jim waiting for her, and they walked together, back along the corridor, across the courtyard, through the archway, past the desperate smokers, and to his car.

'How long did you have to wait?' asked Fay from the safety of the inside of the car.

'About five minutes,' Jim replied as he started the engine. 'How did you get on?'

'I was anxious, but I think I managed all right,' said Fay. 'There are a few things I want to think over. The doctor has taken some tests. He'll write to my GP, and I'll get the results from there.'

'Is there anywhere else you want to go?' asked Jim.

'Not particularly, thanks. Actually, I feel terribly tired now. I'd like to go straight home.'

A little while later Jim dropped her off at the end of the drive.

'Is there anything you need?' he asked.

'I'll be fine, thanks,' Fay replied.

'Phone if you think of anything later,' Jim reassured her before driving off.

Fay was glad to be inside the house and completely on her own. Her head felt as if it was spinning, but it was her thoughts that were in turmoil. She hung her jacket in the cupboard and collapsed on the sofa in the sitting room, where she remained motionless for a long time, with images of the hospital, its staff and the patients whirling round in her mind. She knew that she had again felt profoundly disturbed by the sight of the smokers, but she could not yet identify what was affecting her about the rest of the visit. It was as if in her mind she was scanning everything she had seen and experienced in an attempt to pinpoint some crucial event.

At length she became aware of feeling thirsty, and she went to the kitchen to get a glass of water. She found that sipping the water slowed down the speed at which her mind was working, and she was able to sort more calmly through what had happened. She then returned to the photographs that still lay on the dining table.

'A snake,' she mused to herself.

She put down her glass, and went to get the book containing the picture of the mansion house to which the farm had belonged. 'I wonder if the carving over the main door is a snake too?' she asked aloud. As she toyed with this notion, she wished that she had the ability to visualise it in the same way as the carving over the archway. That had happened quite easily and entirely unexpectedly. I looked at the hospital photographs, then at the farm archway and courtyard, shut my eyes, and there it was, she remembered. The most obvious feature of that sequence is the new followed by the old. I wonder if I could do an experiment by finding a picture of a new mansion house? I'd look at that, then the picture in the book, and then shut my eyes.

Fay laughed. How fanciful! Surely there was more to it than a simple procedure like that? But as far as she knew, nothing else had happened before she visualised the carving over the archway, and there was no harm in trying the same kind of sequence for the mansion house. Then a thought struck her – the Ideal Homes magazine that she and Joan had bought last week. It had been purchased for fun, and had given them both a great deal of pleasure. Surely she had seen a picture of a modern mansion in it? She searched rapidly through the heap of magazines and newspapers that lay in the corner, and about half way down she located it. She put it on the table and began to scan the pages.

'Ah! Here it is,' she exclaimed. Although the building was not as large as the one shown in the book, its general style was at least similar.

She cleared everything away from the table apart from the magazine and the book, each open at the relevant page. Then she stared at the house in the magazine, the house in the book, and shut her eyes. To her utter astonishment she could see the carving over the front door with great clarity, and it was definitely another snake. The complexities of this knot were different. What does this mean? she wondered. It's so strange, yet so real.

It was then that she remembered Reverend Howard's vision and what he had told her of the vicarage in an earlier state, and how his brother had been able to see buildings that were no longer there. Her head began to swim again, and she became preoccupied with the memory of the doctor's needle in her wrist, and of the stabbing in her thumb. She suddenly felt completely exhausted and stumbled to the sofa in the sitting room, where she lay down and fell asleep almost immediately.

When she came to, she was on the floor beside the sofa.

Her mind was filled with images of snakes, twined together in complex knots, and she was saying something... What was it? She tried to recall the words... 'A monk?' Yes. 'A monk was buried here...' Then... something about a curse... the curse of the two kinds of happenings... 'The curse of the two kinds of happenings was laid to rest.' There was something else... a name... 'Lily Anthony'.

Fay shut her eyes again. She did not want to risk trying to move yet, as she felt unsteady even in her prone position. She wished that her glass of water was within reach, but it was still in the dining room where she had left it hours ago. Yes, hours ago. Her watch told her that at least four hours had passed since she fell asleep, and she had no memory of falling from the sofa on to the floor, yet that must have been what happened.

Lily. She wondered where Lily was now. Past lives... 'At least I've been able to rethink the subject because of that book *Russian Voices*,' she said aloud.

She looked at her left thumb as if expecting to see a series of punctures in it, but could see nothing. Looking at her other hand, she noted that her wrist appeared unblemished, although there had been a needle in it only that morning. She reached up to a cushion that was at the end of the sofa, pulled it to the floor and put it under her head. That felt a little better.

A monk? Where had that come from? A monk was buried here... A curse? Two kinds of happenings? None of this made sense. And what did it have to do with the knotted snakes? If indeed it did.

Fay shut her eyes once more in an attempt to still the tumbling of her thoughts. But this made no difference at all, and she turned to her trusted technique of concentrating on her breathing. This certainly produced the familiar calming effect, but her mind was still full of unanswered questions, and she could not even attempt to count them. At least I don't feel stirred up by them any more, she reflected. She was glad to note that she was not worried about lying on the floor, and any sense of urgency she had had about finding a way of getting up had dissipated.

Her calmer state must have allowed her to doze off, because the next thing she knew was that the phone was ringing. Without taking time to consider what to do, she rolled over on to all fours and crawled to the extension on the coffee table, which was not far from where she had been lying.

'Hello... Oh! It's you, Don,' she exclaimed, as she heard his familiar voice. 'Why are you ringing so early? Is something wrong?'

'Fay,' said Don, his voice full of concern, 'I'm phoning at the usual time. It's half past eight.'

Fay propped her back against the side of the sofa and looked up at the clock. Don was right.

'Don, I feel rather odd,' she admitted.

'I can tell that. Shall I phone Joan and Jim and ask one of them to come round?'

'No, don't do that,' said Fay urgently. 'Please don't do that.'

'Why on earth not?' asked Don reasonably.

'I want to be alone!' said Fay desperately. 'I *must* be alone.'

There was silence while Don digested this, and then he said, 'Fay, there's obviously something, and I feel worried. But perhaps if you can talk to me about your day I'll be able to understand why you want to be on your own, and then we can take it from there.'

'I haven't been feeling too good this afternoon,' said Fay almost truculently. 'That's all.'

Don tried again. 'Fay, you were at the hospital this morning. How did you get on?'

Fay shivered. 'Hospital?' she queried.

'Yes, hospital. You had an appointment to see Dr Grayling this morning, and Jim took you,' Don reminded her carefully.

'Dr Grayling... yes... I saw Dr Grayling,' said Fay slowly.

'Yes... Jim dropped me off and then came and waited. He brought me straight home... because I wanted to be here.'

'How did it go?'

'The doctor talked to me, examined me and took some tests,' said Fay. 'I'll get the results later.'

Don relaxed a little. Fay sounded much more herself now, but he had to find out what had distracted her. 'Have you been doing some more painting?' he asked astutely.

'No, no painting,' said Fay. 'I've been too tired... far too tired. In fact, I'm exhausted. I was just resting on the floor when you phoned.'

'On the floor?' Don repeated.

'Yes, I lay down on the sofa, and I must have fallen off while I was asleep,' Fay added casually.

'Fay,' said Don deliberately. 'Were you doing anything else today?'

'No, not really,' she replied. 'Except I was looking at the photos we had developed last week. I thought I'd have another look at them before I went to the hospital. Then I got out the ones of the farm, shut my eyes, and seemed to see the carving over the archway in fine detail. It was amazing. Do you know it's actually a snake in a complex knot, and it's swallowing its own tail?'

'No wonder you've been feeling odd,' said Don sympathetically. 'Did that happen before or after the hospital visit?'

'Before it,' Fay replied. 'Actually, I think I was keen to come back and be on my own so that I could think about it. I'd left the pictures out on the table. Maybe it hadn't been a good idea to look at them before I went, because I think it all got muddled in my mind with the trip to the hospital. And then before I had time to sort it out, something else happened.'

'Something else?' echoed Don.

Fay explained. 'I did an experiment. I found a picture of a modern mansion house in a magazine Joan and I bought last week. I looked at it, looked at the picture of that old mansion in the book, and then shut my eyes. To my utter amazement I got a clear image of the carving over the main door of the mansion. It was just as clear as the image I'd seen earlier of the carving over the archway. Again I could see it was a snake, and this snake is swallowing its tail too. You'll remember the knot is different. It's amazing Don, I could see the scales on the snakes so clearly – just as they must have appeared when they were first carved.'

'Why did you look for a picture of a new mansion?' Don began. But then he answered his own question. 'The hospital is new, so you wanted a new mansion to begin with. That's the explanation, isn't it?'

'Yes, and after I'd seen the other carving so clearly my head started to swim, and all I could think of was those stabs I had in my thumb, and the doctor putting the needle in my wrist this morning. Then I felt completely exhausted and lay on the sofa.'

'From what you say, you must have been lying down for a long time,' Don observed.

'I suppose I must have been,' Fay agreed. 'But I'm sure I was asleep for nearly all of it.'

'Fay,' said Don gently. 'You didn't sound yourself when I was speaking to you at first. Can you remember anything else that might have happened?'

'No, I can't think of anything.'

'Anything you've eaten, or anything you might have been thinking about?' Don probed.

'I haven't eaten anything today at all,' Fay told him. 'I didn't feel like having anything before I went to the hospital, and I haven't had anything since I came back.' She felt mystified. Why was Don pressing her like this? 'What made you think I wasn't myself?'

'It's difficult to describe,' Don replied. 'It reminds me of the evening before Easter Sunday, when you were trying to convince me you'd be all right on your own if I went to church. That was after we'd all agreed that we shouldn't leave you on your own!'

'I've a vague memory of that,' Fay admitted. 'It seemed so important to get some time entirely alone.'

'Why do you think that was?'

'I don't know.'

'It could be important,' said Don. 'If you think about it, today you wanted Jim to bring you straight back to the house, and that was because you wanted to be on your own. Then, when I suggested phoning to get one of them to come round and sit with you, you were adamant that I mustn't. In fact, you sounded in quite a panic about the idea.'

'You're right,' agreed Fay. 'I don't know what's going on. Easter Sunday… A monk.'

'A monk?' asked Don, clearly not understanding.

'Yes, a monk,' Fay confirmed. 'There's something important about a monk.'

She was quiet for a while, and Don did not attempt to interrupt her thoughts. Instead, he waited patiently, slightly reassured by the steady rhythm of her breathing.

'Don,' she said at last. 'When I came round on the floor here, there was a collection of what seemed to be entirely unrelated thoughts in my mind.'

'Tell me what they were,' Don encouraged.

'I could see the two snake carvings,' Fay began. 'Then I heard what seemed to be a voice in my head that said "a monk was buried here", and this was followed by something about two kinds of happenings, and that the curse of them would be laid to rest. Then I thought about Lily Anthony, and after that all I could think of was the stabs in my thumb, and the one in my wrist from this morning. I felt I had so much in my head that I couldn't think about anything, and in the end I did my breathing exercises and must have fallen asleep again. Then you phoned and woke me up.'

'I've been making a note of what you've just told me,' said Don. 'I'm sure it's important, but I haven't a clue what it all means. I wish I could come home. I want to see you,' he finished bluntly.

'I feel a lot better now,' Fay reassured him. 'I could hardly move before, and now I feel hungry and I want to stand up and walk around a bit. Do you think you could phone me again in about an hour?'

'I like that idea,' Don replied with relief in his voice. 'I'll do that.'

Fay said goodbye and put down the phone before standing up and walking confidently to the kitchen, where she collected some pieces of fruit and began to eat them slowly. Afterwards, as arranged, she spoke again briefly to Don, and then made her way to bed.

The following day Jim called round at lunchtime bearing some mixed salads that he had bought at the supermarket on the way.

'Don phoned me early this morning,' he informed her cheerfully. 'He said he was a bit worried, and I offered to pop round to see you.

You can tell me to go away again if you want.' He winked. 'But I wouldn't if I were you. These salads are excellent, I promise you.'

Fay smiled and let him in. 'Did Don tell you anything about yesterday?' she asked.

'As a matter of fact, he did,' Jim admitted lightly. 'He told me everything. After that *I* was worried about you too, so I had to come round. Want to talk about it?'

Fay laughed. 'I'm fine today, but as you've heard there was something very odd going on yesterday. Have you any thoughts about it?'

'If you want my considered opinion,' said Jim grandly, 'I think you need some pretty close supervision for the duration.'

Fay laughed again.

'It's not funny,' Jim admonished her. 'We're all worried about you. I know you're supposed to be concentrating on yourself, but you've got to take our feelings into account too.' He wagged his finger playfully at her.

'Oh, Jim. You're so funny,' gasped Fay.

'You've got to take this seriously, Fay. If you want I'll get down on bended knee and implore you. But we've got to get something sorted out so we can be sure that you're safe.'

Fay studied his face. Although Jim appeared to be fooling about, she could see he was really serious underneath, and that he was very concerned for her.

'Jim,' she began, and then stopped. 'Jim, I think Joan was right.'

'What about?'

'I think she was right about all this being a preparation for this task I've to accomplish with Helen.'

'What makes you think that? And what's it got to do with keeping you safe?'

'Today I'm sure she's right. When she spoke of it at first I couldn't be sure one way or the other, but now I am. That's all I can say. And about safety… I've got a sense that anything that happens that's to do with this preparation will be all right, and although I might feel very strange at times, even to the point of losing consciousness, all will be well.'

Jim groaned. 'I wish I had the same conviction as you,' he said. 'What am I going to do about my worries meantime?'

'I'm afraid that's something you'll have to cope with,' Fay said confidently, but not unkindly.

Jim stared at her. 'You really are changing, Fay. You would never have said anything like that before. I must say this gives me a bit of confidence that everything must be going in the right direction, even if I can't understand any of it.' He looked at the empty salad containers. 'I haven't got any more excuses to stay, so I'd better go back to work,' he said reluctantly. 'I'll give you a ring about six, and if you don't answer, I'll be back straight away.'

As Fay let him out of the front door she said, 'I do appreciate your coming round, Jim.'

He squeezed her arm, gave her a quick peck on the cheek, and was gone.

Fay spent most of the afternoon in the loft. She didn't want to go out, but she wanted to do something different, and she felt well enough now to make the trip up and down the ladder. It was an absorbing journey back into the past, and she enjoyed reacquainting herself with what had been stored. She made a list of everything so that in future she could find anything she thought she might be able to use. It was almost six by the time she closed the hatch and made her way downstairs again.

The phone rang at exactly six o'clock, and when she lifted it she heard Jim's familiar voice.

'This is your friendly neighbourhood checking man,' he joked. 'How've you been? I've been thinking about you.'

'Fine thanks. I've been investigating the loft. It was an absorbing pastime.'

'Sounds healthy to me,' said Jim. 'I can tell I don't need to bother you for long, but expect one of us to phone at lunchtime tomorrow if we haven't heard from you. I think you'll be well covered this evening, because Diana's phoning you soon and Don will be speaking to you later on.'

'You've been doing some research then,' said Fay gaily.

After she had eaten, she had a long and enjoyable conversation with Diana, and then she got ready for bed before Don phoned.

'You've been doing some work behind the scenes,' she challenged him when she heard his voice.

'Too right. I'd have been off my head with worry if I hadn't activated the network. How did you think I'd be able to concentrate on my work without that?'

'It was very nice, and I'm glad you did. And of course I understand why you did it when you spell it out.'

'Now tell me if anything else has come up since we last spoke,' Don demanded.

'Nothing that I'm aware of. After Jim had gone I spent a pleasant afternoon in the loft, cataloguing everything.'

'The loft!' exclaimed Don in horror. 'What if you'd passed out up there?'

'Well I didn't. I was fine,' Fay said firmly. 'Don't let your imagination run riot.'

'Are you surprised?' Don asked quietly.

'I suppose not. But you've got to accept that I can't just sit in a chair while you're away, and I don't want to be supervised the whole time. I've been thinking quite a lot about it all, and I think what I said to Jim is right.'

'What's that?'

'If all these strange things that are happening to me are part of the preparation for the task that Helen and I have to do, then I believe that whatever happens to me won't harm me.'

'That sounds not unlikely,' Don agreed, 'but on a practical front, you've got to admit that some of it's quite alarming.'

'Yes. I suppose it's okay talking about it like this, but it doesn't feel quite the same when I'm in one of the funny states,' Fay acknowledged. 'But I do think I'm getting more used to it now. When I was lying on the floor yesterday I didn't panic about not being able to move.'

'Oh good,' said Don unenthusiastically. 'Incidentally, you hadn't told me that you spent some time not being able to move at all.'

'It didn't seem as important as the other things I was saying.'

'It's rather important to me.'

'Don,' Fay said emphatically. 'I think we've both got to trust what's happening. I know it doesn't fit with ordinary life as we know it, but it's something we've got to learn about and accept. There's no way out of it.'

Don could hear the strength and determination in Fay's voice. 'I agree with you,' he said. 'It's just that I feel very responsible for you.'

'I appreciate that,' Fay replied, 'but I think we've got to accept the situation. Now, can we talk about your work for a bit? I'd like to have some idea of what's happening.'

The next twenty minutes passed pleasantly, with Don giving her an amusing account of some of the difficulties that had arisen over the last couple of days. Afterwards Fay turned off the light, and fell asleep almost straight away.

Chapter Seventeen

It was almost lunchtime the following day when Fay heard someone at the door. Jim, she thought to herself as she hurried to open it; but when she did so she saw Reverend Howard standing smiling at her.

'Mrs Bowden... Fay,' he said. 'I was passing in this direction and thought I'd call to see how you are.'

'That's kind of you,' Fay replied. 'Would you like to come in for a cup of something?'

'Thank you.'

Fay showed him into the sitting room and went to the kitchen. Moments later she returned carrying two glasses of elderflower cordial.

'I hope this is all right for you,' she said as she passed him a glass.

He took a sip and declared, 'Ah! Elderflower cordial. I used to make some every year before I took up this charge. There was a piece of waste ground near where I lived, and it was covered in *Sambucus* bushes.'

'How interesting. Do you have a recipe you could give me?'

'Of course. I'll write it out and drop it off when I'm next passing.'

'I'm glad you had time to see Peter and Helen when they were here at Easter,' said Fay conversationally.

'A fine young couple. Peter is a deep thinking young man. You'll be pleased to have him as a son-in-law.'

'How are your researches progressing?' asked Fay.

'I've had hardly any time to devote to anything other than church responsibilities since I last saw you, but my brother sent me some material recently, and I'm looking forward to being able to study it.'

Fay had an impulse to confide some of what had been happening to her, particularly about the jacket for Helen's wedding attire, but she did not feel completely confident about this, and decided to limit what she told him to the bare minimum.

'Helen has quite a good idea now of what she'll be wearing on her wedding day,' she said.

'I'm glad to hear that,' the Reverend replied sincerely. 'It usually means a great deal to a young woman to feel confident about what she's wearing. Now tell me how you are.'

'I'm better than I was, thank you,' Fay answered truthfully. 'I was at the hospital on Tuesday, and the doctor there examined me and took some tests, but I don't think they'll show anything. I still get very tired, so I have to rest a lot. I'm afraid I haven't been able to make a decision about the accounting for the church yet.'

'Don't worry about that. There's plenty of time. The main thing at the moment is your health.'

When the Reverend left, Fay felt somewhat guilty for giving him very little information about her true situation. Why had she not said more? She had certainly felt tempted to confide in him, but something had held her back. She wondered what his brother had sent, and where he had collected the information. Maybe she could ask him about that another time, as it might help her and Don in their search for records about the building that had become the ruin in her nightmare. That project was potentially so huge that she could not at the moment imagine embarking on it without some clues.

She sat at the dining room table staring out into the garden, and drifted into a kind of reverie. 'When I had that flash of the house before it was ruined…' she murmured to herself. 'Was there any kind of carving on the front of the building?'

No answer came to her, but she knew it was important that the question had arisen in her mind, and she went upstairs to get the painting from her bedroom wall. On her way back downstairs the phone rang and she found it was Jim.

'Just checking,' he admitted cheerfully.

'I'm fine, thanks,' said Fay. 'At the moment I'm wondering whether or not Don is right in his belief that the ruin was once a real building somewhere, and if so where that might be.'

'That's something that's been on my mind too,' Jim confided. 'And I've been fantasising about hoards of treasure made by the same craftsman who made Don's ring.'

'That's exciting!' exclaimed Fay delightedly. 'Shall we split the proceeds when we find it?'

'Good idea,' agreed Jim.

'On a more serious note,' Fay continued, 'Reverend Howard was round this morning. I asked him how his research on the vicarage was progressing. He hasn't got any further, but he did say he had some material from his brother. I half wanted to ask him if I could see some of it, but in the end I left it.'

'He's bound to be round again some time,' mused Jim. 'You could ask him then. By the way, is there anything you want?'

'No... well yes, there is, but it isn't anything you can get for me,' answered Fay. 'I want to know more about that ruin. It's very important to Morna... I mean me.' She suddenly felt flustered.

'We'll all keep thinking about it,' Jim reassured her. 'You never know what might come up. Helen's phoning you tonight, isn't she?'

'Mm.' Fay suddenly wanted to be alone. The sound of Jim's voice was stressing her and she wanted him off the phone. 'I think I'll go and get some lunch now, Jim. Thanks for calling.'

'Bye then,' he said.

Fay put the phone down, thankful that he had not lingered.

I'm so tired, she said to herself, and went to lie down on the sofa. Her thumb was hurting once more, as if it had been stabbed in several places. 'A monk,' she muttered, and then she felt asleep.

When she woke she had a strong impression that she had been dreaming about a monk who devised snake patterns. She tried to dismiss this as a convenient fantasy, but the impression persisted as she got up to make herself something to eat.

Both Helen and Don phoned in the evening, and she told them about the dream as an amusing incident, but neither of them encouraged her to take it as lightly as she was presenting it. Before Don rang off she suggested to him that they could spend some time that weekend looking for a brooch for her. He had agreed with alacrity, saying that he had been thinking about it himself.

Tomorrow is Friday, Fay thought. Don will be home in the evening, and then we can plan the weekend. There were times now when she felt able to do more, and she hoped that her new energy would allow her to be out with him for much of the time. A quiet day tomorrow would be sensible.

When Fay woke the following morning, the sun was streaming in through the gaps at the edges of the curtains, and she had a strong desire to put the greenhouse in some kind of order and plant some seeds. I never thought I would be well enough this spring to do anything in the garden, she thought happily as she put on some old clothes, ate a quick breakfast, and was soon absorbed in the task of chasing spiders out of a stack of plant pots. She worked slowly and methodically, and had soon cleared a large area of the main shelving and was filling a few pots with the intention of germinating some courgette seeds. My favourite, she reflected as she placed each seed in an upright position in the fibre.

Having achieved this much, her mind turned to the row of pots of herbs on the concrete slab just outside the doorway. Several of them were overgrown with weeds.

'I'll sort these out next,' she said aloud. She began by emptying the pots one by one, freeing the roots from the restricting weeds. When she had accomplished this, she carefully put each herb back in its pot, together with new fibre. The result was very satisfying, and she was aware that her ability to do this much was deeply rewarding, helping her to believe that she would eventually regain her familiar pleasures.

Time for a rest now, she told herself. She put her things away, dusted herself down, and went into the kitchen to wash her hands. She sat down on the sofa with a magazine and must have dozed off for a while, because the next thing she was aware of was the sound of the magazine landing on the floor.

As she ate her lunch she became aware of a strong impulse to go round to the vicarage to see if Reverend Howard was in; but being aware that he was a busy man, she decided instead to write him a note that she could either post or deliver by hand. If she went round she could call into the church afterwards. It had been a long time since she had been able to go there.

She found her writing pad, addressed the first sheet, and then began.

Dear Reverend Howard,

Thank you for calling round. I was interested to hear that your brother had sent some material he thought might help with your research. Would it be possible for me to have a look through it sometime? I will understand if you don't feel that is appropriate. My interest stems not only from having heard how your interests in the subject originated, but also because I myself have been having some rather unusual experiences of late which I am trying to understand and come to terms with.

Yours sincerely,

Fay Bowden

'I'm definitely going to take it now,' said Fay decisively. She liked hearing the note of determination and confidence in her voice as she spoke. The morning in the garden had helped to clear and focus her mind, and she was sure this was exactly what she wanted to do.

On foot or by car? she questioned herself silently as she changed her clothes. I'd like to walk round, but maybe it would be a bit too ambitious at the moment, she wondered. Erring on the side of caution, she reluctantly took her car out of the garage. As an afterthought she went back into the house, phoned Joan and Jim's number and left a message to say that she was fine. Then she locked all the doors and drove off in the direction of the vicarage.

A few minutes later she drew up in the layby outside the church, picked up the letter and went down the path to post it through the letterbox. The door opened almost immediately.

'I saw you coming,' said the Reverend. 'I see you have a letter for me. Would you like to come in for a few minutes? I'm rather tied up at the moment, but please feel welcome.'

'I think I'd rather leave the letter with you and spend a few minutes in the church,' said Fay hurriedly. She noticed that she felt agitated, and desperately wanted to be alone in the peace of that ancient building.

'That's fine. You'll find the side door is open. Take as long as you want.'

Fay thanked him and retreated down the path. Her heart was beating rapidly and her chest felt constricted, but all this eased considerably as she entered the cool stillness of the church.

She sat in the pew right at the back, and stared towards the altar.

What was it that Helen and Peter had told her about Peter's experience at the church at Deerhurst? She searched her mind. Wasn't it something about alcohol? Yes, that was it. Peter had had an inexplicable taste of it in his mouth when he visited that church. How odd. And he said that this church reminded him of the one at Deerhurst. She could not draw any conclusions from this train of thought, and she moved away from it.

She began to think of the brooch she and Don would be searching for the following day. Gradually she became convinced that it had to be something she could wear at Helen's wedding, although no image came into her mind of a suitable design. I'm sure I'll know when I see the right kind of thing, she thought. Helen and I both knew straight away when we found the jacket. If we don't see anything tomorrow, Don and I can keep searching.

Fay felt calmed and rested by her time in the church. Her mind was clear, and she felt restored. She made her way back to her car and drove home. Not long afterwards she heard Don's car in the drive. She was pleased that he had come back earlier than expected. That would mean they had plenty of time that evening to turn over the events of the week.

That night Fay was very restless. She woke several times, convinced that there was someone on the landing. She even woke Don on one occasion to see if he could hear anything.

'What exactly do you hear?' he asked sleepily.

Fay thought for a moment and then said, 'I don't hear anything. I just have a sense that someone is there.'

'Have you any idea who it might be?'

Fay pondered and then said slowly, 'It's not a child. That's all I know.'

'Can we talk about it in the morning?' asked Don wearily.

'Yes, and remind me to talk to Helen about it when we speak to her on the phone in the evening. Remember how she thought there was something one night when she was here with Peter?' She smiled a little as she heard a quiet snoring sound coming from Don.

They discussed it over breakfast the following day, but nothing more came into Fay's mind, and they agreed to leave it until the evening, when perhaps Helen would be able to contribute something.

'We must concentrate on the brooch hunt today,' Don reminded her as he cleared away the breakfast things. 'I'm keen to get off as soon as we're ready. We can take the Yellow Pages with us as we did before, and we can come home if and when you get tired.'

'I don't know where to start,' Fay began.

'It doesn't matter. Just get ready and we'll go. If you want to leave it up to me, I'd like to suggest we go somewhere out of the ordinary. We've had such good luck at the Courtyard, and at that place where you and Helen disappeared. I don't want to spend any time at the usual kind of high street jewellers.'

'Don, something's just come into my mind,' said Fay excitedly. 'I want to go to the museum.'

'The museum?' Don queried. 'I don't think you'll be able to get a brooch there. But perhaps I'm wrong, there might be something in the gift shop.'

'I want to look in the museum itself,' Fay insisted. 'That's where I want to start.'

'Okay then,' Don agreed. 'I can't say I think it'll take us very far, but let's follow your instinct for now.'

The museum was a huge Victorian building near the centre of a local town about ten miles away. It was fortunate to have its own car park, and because Don and Fay arrived relatively early in the day, it was by no means full. Fay enquired at the reception desk about the pottery and jewellery, and was told to go to the second floor – rooms A and B. They soon found themselves engrossed in examining the collections on display.

'All of this is amazing,' breathed Fay as she studied each item. 'We did the right thing to come here.'

'But this is all pottery,' Don pointed out. 'You haven't seen any jewellery yet. It's certainly interesting though.' He read out the details on a large display board that was fixed to the wall beside one of the glass cases. 'I see some of these pieces are on loan from other collections,' he mused. 'Lawerlocke Hall – surely that's only about fifty miles from here.'

'It's one of the few places we haven't visited yet that's reachable on a day trip,' Fay commented. 'Let's go into the other room and see the jewellery now.'

Room B revealed a vast array of fine jewellery securely stored in glass cases.

'I expect this glass is unbreakable,' Fay observed.

'It would have to be,' Don agreed. 'Some of this must be very valuable, and possibly priceless.'

They spent some time working their way slowly along the cases that lined the wall on the left hand side of the room.

'Oh look!' exclaimed Fay as she reached the corner of the large room. 'Here's a catalogue.'

Don saw that there was a wooden chest with innumerable small drawers. Fay had pulled one of them open, and had discovered that it was full of photographs of pieces of jewellery.

Instantly a uniformed attendant appeared. 'Can I help you?' he asked politely.

'Could you demonstrate this catalogue to us, please?' asked Fay.

'I'll tell you what I can about it,' he replied, 'but I don't know much. It was delivered only yesterday. We put it here to be out of the way until someone has time to go through it.'

'That's interesting,' Fay commented. 'Do you know where it came from?'

'It was brought down from Lawerlocke Hall,' the man replied. 'Apparently it has been sitting in the basement for years. It seemed to be a hobby of one of the past owners to collect photographs of jewellery that caught his eye. He looked in museums and collections in many different countries. The British ones are in these three drawers.' He indicated some on the bottom row. 'You're welcome to have a look through them if you wish,' he added. 'I know you will take good care of them. I'll bring a chair for you.' He pulled out a small table that was stored under the chest, and put a low chair beside it for Fay to use. He checked the time. 'You have about an hour. After that I'll have to lock this room for the weekend. We can't afford to supervise it all the time.'

Fay sat down, and Don brought a stool across to join her. She began to sort through the pictures in one of the drawers. Don watched her face as she concentrated closely on each of them and then turned over those that interested her so that she could read any details that were written there.

'This is so helpful, Don,' she said in a voice that could only be described as passionate.

Don said nothing, but sat and waited patiently, convinced that Fay was involved in a process that would eventually lead her to know what she was looking for in the search for a brooch. He looked at his watch from time to time.

About fifty minutes had passed when Fay stopped quite suddenly and exclaimed, 'I can't believe this, but it's true because I can see it here in front of my own eyes. Look, Don!' She passed the photograph to him.

Don stared at it in disbelief. 'It's a similar design to the carvings!'

'That's right,' said Fay. 'Now turn it over and tell me what it says on the back.'

Don did as Fay asked and read out the words 'Morna's brooch'.

'Are you sure?' gasped Fay.

'Of course I am.'

'What else does it say?' Fay demanded urgently.

'That's all.'

'Maybe there's something in this chest that will tell us more about it,' said Fay. But although she looked in all the drawers, she could see nothing in them but photographs. 'I've *got* to know more,' said Fay desperately. She turned to the attendant who was now approaching her. 'Can you help?' she asked.

'I'm afraid there's nothing further that I can contribute,' he replied, 'and I have to leave shortly.'

Fay began to tremble. 'Don, I can't leave without finding out more,' she stuttered.

Don put his hand on her arm to steady her. 'We'll have to leave now, but we can come back again soon.' He addressed the attendant. 'When is this room open again?'

'Tuesday morning at ten.'

Fay grew very pale, and she was shaking visibly.

'Could you possibly put us in touch with whoever is responsible for the museum today?' enquired Don politely.

'I'll go with you to the front desk, and someone will phone from there,' the attendant replied.

Fay was still clutching the photograph.

'I think we'd better put that back in the drawer for now,' said Don.

Fay nodded and did as he suggested.

Don took her arm while they followed the attendant to the central area. A phone call was made, and about five minutes later a young woman dressed in a smart suit approached them.

'Is there some problem?' she enquired.

'We wondered if you might be able to help us,' Don began. 'My wife found a photograph of great interest to her while she was looking through a chest in the jewellery room. I believe the chest and its contents have only just arrived at the museum.'

'That is correct.'

Don continued. 'I wanted to ask if we could have copy of the photograph.'

To Fay's utter relief the young woman said, 'Certainly. Please follow me.'

She led the way back to the room, where she unlocked the door using a master key. Then she asked Fay to find the photograph again.

'If you wait in the front hall, I'll send someone down with the copy in about an hour. Would that be all right?'

'That's fine,' said Don.

'What's the name?'

'Bowden,' Fay replied. 'Fay Bowden. And thank you so much,' she added with heartfelt gratitude.

The young woman was disappearing round a corner when Fay remembered the writing on the back. 'Excuse me!' she called anxiously.

The young woman stopped, turned and smiled.

'Please could you copy both sides?' asked Fay with desperation in her voice.

'Surely,' the woman replied, and then she was gone.

Fay was grateful to be able to relax sitting next to Don on a row of chairs inside the entrance hall.

'I wish we knew more about it,' she said, 'but at least we'll have our own copy.'

'That should help,' Don agreed.

As promised by the young woman, an envelope was delivered to the desk, and someone called out 'Bowden'.

Fay had to try hard not to run to collect it. She saw straight away that the envelope had 'no charge' written on it. 'Thank you,' she said.

She opened it, checked the contents, and then carefully stowed it in a section of her handbag. 'Don, I'd like to go back to the car now, please,' she said.

In the privacy of the car she added, 'Don, I want to find someone who can make a reproduction of this brooch, and I want to wear it at Helen's wedding.'

'Let's get on with trying to find someone to do it then. It's certainly a very striking design, and I'd like to know how it fits with the carvings in the photographs we have at home.'

'I want to go straight home now,' said Fay suddenly. 'I want to compare this with the other designs. One of the things that excited me so much when I saw this photograph was that there's no doubt that the knot is formed from a snake, and that the snake's tail is in its mouth – just like the close up images of the carvings that came into my mind the day I went to the hospital.'

The drive back was uneventful. Don did not hurry. As they left the town Fay watched the trees at the sides of the road, her mind in turmoil. She saw the buds were bursting on many of them, although the oaks and ashes were still dormant.

Back at the house Fay opened the front door to find a hand-delivered letter on the mat inside. She picked it up, but did not recognise the writing on the envelope. She tore it open and found a note from Reverend Howard.

'Don,' she called as he disappeared through the door into the kitchen.

'What is it?'

'I've a note here from Reverend Howard.'

'What does it say?' he asked, as he came and peered over her shoulder.

Fay read it out.

Thank you for your note. I hope to be looking through some of the material on Monday morning. If you are free, please do join me.

Rev Howard

'What's this about?' asked Don curiously.

'Didn't I tell you last night?' said Fay in surprise. 'When he came round to see me again I asked him about his researches. He said he hadn't got any further, but that his brother had sent some material that might be helpful. I realised later that I wanted to look at it, so I went to put a note through his door. He saw me and I handed it to him, and then I went and sat in the church.'

'You certainly didn't tell me any of that before,' said Don emphatically. 'You said you'd been to the church, but the rest is new to me.'

'I can hardly believe that,' said Fay, astonished.

'Do you think you'll go round on Monday?' asked Don.

'I hope so,' replied Fay. 'To be honest, I thought it might give us some leads, however small, on how to identify the building that's the ruin in my dream – the building with the tunnel underneath where Morna died.'

'It's a long shot,' said Don slowly, 'but you never know what might turn up. I'll be eager to hear all about it when I phone you that evening.'

'I can't wait to tell Helen and Peter about my brooch,' said Fay.

'I think you should phone them now,' suggested Don.

There was no answer when Fay tried the number, but she left a message on the answering service for Helen to phone her as soon as she could because she had some exciting news.

'I'll make something for us to eat,' said Don, 'and you can assemble all the photos on the dining table.'

By the time Don joined her, Fay had not only arranged them on a tray that she had put on the table, but she had also taken out the paints and pencils and the drawing pad.

'I'm going to try to draw them,' she said determinedly. She chose a soft pencil and was soon engrossed in her task.

Don watched her for a while and then said, 'I think I'll get my book.' He went upstairs and collected his paperback about the ex-CIA spy.

Fay glanced up when he returned, and when she saw his book she said, 'I thought you'd have finished that by now.'

'No, I'm about half way through,' Don replied. 'I've got other things I'm reading, so I only pick this up from time to time. How are you getting on?'

'I've been trying to copy the three patterns. What do you think?'

She passed the pad across for Don to see. 'I did the carving over the archway first, then the one over the main door of the mansion, and then I did Morna's brooch. They're just rough. As I was copying them I began to realise that what I really wanted to do was to start at the snake's head in each, and then follow the body round the pattern and into the mouth. I'm going to try that now.'

'What you've done so far looks good,' Don commented. 'Tell me when you've finished the next lot because I'd like to see them. I like your idea.' He passed the pad back to her and returned to his book.

Fay was totally absorbed in what she was doing. She spent some time making sketches in an attempt to work out how the pattern must have been devised. Once she was as sure as she could be about this, she began to fill a fresh page with the archway carving. It was a slow process, because she wanted to make this as exact a replica as possible of what she remembered seeing just before she went for the hospital appointment. She was pleased to discover that she could remember the details of the snake's head quite clearly. It was different from the head on the other carving she remembered, and from the one on Morna's brooch.

As she worked her way along the length of the snake, she wished that she could see the clear version of the carving again. She tried the sequence of staring at Don's photo of the archway and then shutting her eyes, but she could see nothing.

'I'm sure there was some faint pattern down the upper part of the snake's back,' she mused.

'There are four diamond shapes,' said Don, not looking up from his book.

'Thanks,' said Fay, and she began to draw one just behind the snake's head.

When she was about to draw the third one she said, 'I'm not sure if this one was on the curve here or just beyond it. Would you have a look, Don?'

Don looked across at her drawing. 'That's very good, Fay,' he said admiringly. He picked up a paintbrush, and using the end as a pointer he said, 'The second diamond goes here, and the fourth one here.'

Fay thanked him and resumed her task. When she had completed the drawing, she leaned back in her chair and viewed it with satisfaction.

'I'm glad I did that,' she said. 'It looks right.'

'Yes, that's excellent. Are you going to do the carving from above the door of the mansion house next?'

'I'd like to,' Fay replied. She tore the sheet from her pad and handed it to Don.

'Perhaps I should frame this,' he said, before putting it on the seat of a chair on the other side of the table.

Fay set to work once more. Again she could see the snake's head quite clearly in her mind's eye, and worked to reproduce it on the sheet in front of her. Again she had a sense that this snake had a pattern on the upper section of its body, but could not remember what it was.

She turned to Don. 'What's the pattern on this one?' she asked conversationally. It was only then that she realised what had been happening. 'What on earth's going on?' she exclaimed.

'Steady on,' said Don. 'You gave me quite a start. Here I was absorbed in my book, and the next minute you're shouting. What's the matter?''

'Don,' said Fay as calmly as she could. 'How did you know there were diamonds on that snake? There isn't any sign of them on the photograph. I shut my eyes hoping that I'd be able to see the carving clearly as I'd done before. I said something about how I was sure there was a faint pattern, and you supplied the details. I never thought for a moment there was anything strange about that until I was about the do the same thing again. How did you know about the diamond pattern?'

'I… I don't know,' he said, puzzled. 'I had no doubt. Maybe when I took the photograph I could see the carving more clearly than the camera was able to record it, and I've remembered it unconsciously since then.'

'I suppose that's possible,' Fay conceded, 'but can you tell me about the pattern on this one before you go back to your book?'

'It's a series of four double circles,' said Don confidently.

'That settles it,' said Fay triumphantly. 'You never saw this carving, but you know what it looks like!'

'Has the snake that is Morna's brooch got a pattern on it?' asked Don. 'Perhaps I was remembering that.'

'It has, and it's a series of four crosses,' Fay told him. She passed the photograph of the brooch across and pointed to them.

Don shifted in his seat. 'Perhaps it's got something to do with the book I'm reading,' he said uncomfortably.

'How can that be?'

'I read a section earlier about how one person took out a pack of cards and held one up while the ex-spy was supposed to guess which one it was. He got quite a lot of them right.'

'That's not the same as this,' Fay protested.

'I know, but to me it's the same kind of thing – knowing something that you can't know. You've been having experiences of that kind, but this is the first time I've been aware of anything myself, and I admit I feel rattled.'

'It can be quite disorientating,' said Fay. 'I've experienced a number of unusual things, but I can't say it gets any easier. I suppose I'm more used to it though.'

'Would you mind doing some more of that second drawing?' asked Don. 'I think I'd like to walk about outside for a bit.'

'I'll see you later then.' Fay picked up her pencil and continued her work.

By the time Don returned she had completed the carving from the mansion, and had almost finished her copy of the photograph of Morna's brooch.

'How are you feeling now?' she asked.

'Excited,' Don replied. 'I felt very strange at first, but that shifted as I walked. I feel excited because I know I'm more a part of what's happening instead of being just an interested bystander. I've been trying to work out what might happen next, but of course I didn't get anywhere with it. I know that's the way it has to be, but it doesn't stop me from trying to predict the next stage. And now I'm going to add all this to what we've written down already.'

He went off to get the notepad, and Fay returned to her work on the final snake.

'I wish I had three more picture frames,' said Don impatiently when Fay had finished. He checked the time. 'I thought so,' he said. 'The shops will be shut now.'

'When I was in the loft last week I saw a poster-sized clip frame,' said Fay. 'I wonder if that would do? Perhaps we could put all three in it?'

'Perfect! I'll get it down after we've eaten something.'

They had just finished their meal when the phone rang. Don picked up the extension in the sitting room.

'Hello, Don. It's Peter here.'

'Good to hear you, Peter. We've been looking forward to your call. I think Fay's got a few things she wants to ask Helen about. How are things at your end?'

'We're fine thanks,' Peter began. 'Naturally, Helen and I have been talking a lot about everything that's been going on recently. It's difficult to keep up with it all.'

'I find that too,' Don agreed.

'We both found it quite hard to come back here,' Peter continued. 'It can be awkward being far away when we're so involved.'

'It's like that for me during the week,' said Don, 'but of course I'm back at weekends.'

'Helen worries about her mother… and actually so do I,' Peter admitted.

'She's much better than she was,' said Don, 'although she's still got quite a way to go.'

Fay picked up the extension in the hall. 'Hello, Peter,' she said. 'I've put a chair in the hall.'

'Hello, Fay. What a good idea. I'll get Helen to go to the phone in our bedroom.'

Fay heard the click as Helen joined them. 'There's quite a bit of news,' Fay began. 'I've got a brooch in mind now.'

'That's great, Mum,' said Helen. 'What's it like?'

'The first thing I should tell you is that it's for me to wear at your wedding. I took a note round to Reverend Howard yesterday, and after that I sat in the church for a while. It was then I knew.'

During the following hour Don and Fay recounted everything that had happened since, while Peter and Helen listened silently.

When they had finished, Helen burst out, 'That's absolutely amazing! Do you think it's the same Morna that you are… I mean were?' Without waiting for Fay to answer, she rushed on, 'Dad, when are you going to find someone to make the brooch? And have you decided what metal it'll be made of?'

'I can imagine it in either steel or copper,' said Fay slowly. 'We'll have to ask around to find someone who's competent to do the work.'

'We could try round here,' Peter suggested. 'I can think of one or two people I could approach who might know.'

'We'd appreciate that, Peter,' said Fay.

'Next time we come to see you I'd like to visit Lawerlocke Hall,' said Helen. 'Maybe it's somewhere we're meant to go. You never know, we might get some clues there about our task.'

'I'll find out when it's open,' said Don.

'I think I saw a poster when we were out somewhere last summer,' Fay reflected. 'I can't be certain, but I think it said it's only open for a few days each year. If so, it might be quite tricky to organise a trip there.' She paused for a moment and then said, 'Helen, there's something I must remember to ask you.'

'What's that?'

'The night we both thought there was someone on the landing…'

'Yes.'

'What kind of person did you think it was?'

'I haven't a clue,' replied Helen. 'It certainly wasn't a child, but apart from that I don't know. Why do you ask?'

'It happened again last night. Like you, I was sure it wasn't a child. I didn't hear anything, I just had a sense that someone was there.'

'So this is another mystery to add to the ever-increasing list,' said Don.

Peter broke in, 'And you'd better keep it handy. At this rate, it'll be me who has the next experience to add,' he joked. 'I'm the only one left out of the four of us.'

'I've been hoping I might get some clues from the material that Reverend Howard's brother sent him,' said Fay. 'He says I can go round and join him on Monday when he'll be looking through some of it.'

'It's a long shot,' said Don, 'but you're right to follow it up.'

'Yes,' Peter agreed. 'None of us know what's happening or exactly what we're looking for, and all we can do is stay as alert as possible.'

At the end of the call they all expressed their reluctance to part, and Helen made Fay promise to phone her on Monday to let her know about her visit to the vicarage.

Before they went to bed, Don retrieved the clip frame from the loft and mounted Fay's drawings in it.

'I'd like to hang it on the bedroom wall next to the ruin,' he said, 'but perhaps that wouldn't be sensible.'

'I think we should put it there,' said Fay firmly.

Chapter Eighteen

'We must get a copy of Mum's photo of Morna's brooch,' Helen told Peter over breakfast the following morning. 'Remind me to ask her when I speak to her tomorrow.'

'Why not phone her now?'

Helen reached out to pick up the phone, but then stopped. 'No,' she said. 'I think I'll leave myself a note. There's no rush, and I want to think through some of what we learned last night before our next conversation.'

'It's been on my mind most of the night,' Peter admitted, stifling a yawn. 'You were sound asleep, but I seemed to wake about every hour.'

Helen looked at him in surprise. This was a departure from what was familiar to her. Peter was invariably the least affected by events. Even in emotionally charged situations, his comments were objective and were delivered in matter-of-fact tones. As she studied his appearance she could detect that in addition to his obvious tiredness he looked slightly agitated.

'You should have woken me,' she said.

'It didn't occur to me,' Peter replied. 'Why should I interrupt your sleep just because I'm awake?'

'If you had something on your mind it might have helped to tell me,' Helen pointed out. 'You might have slept after that.'

'I can see the logic in that,' Peter agreed.

'Try and remember to wake me if something like that happens again.'

'Okay.'

'Anyway,' Helen went on, 'was there any particular part of it that was on your mind?'

Peter thought in silence, and Helen sipped her drink to give him time.

'Most of the time my mind jumped around – logging up all the strange things that have been happening since your mother's been ill.'

He fell silent again, and again Helen gave him time to reflect. After a while he continued uncertainly. 'There was something…'

Once more Helen was struck by Peter's demeanour. If anything his agitation had increased a little and he seemed unsure of himself. Peter was never patronising or overbearing, but he normally exuded an air of calm confidence, even when he was not entirely clear about a subject. He never pretended to know more than he did, and he always researched everything carefully and thoroughly, to enhance already well-grounded contributions. This morning he was in a state of inner confusion, which he did not understand or find easy to describe. Helen continued to sip her drink while she waited patiently.

At last Peter spoke. 'I think the main issue here is a sense of responsibility that I don't entirely understand.' He seemed to be more certain of himself now.

'Can we talk about it now, or would you rather leave it until later?' Helen asked.

He continued, almost as if she had not spoken. 'It's something to do with that task you and your mother have to accomplish. I have to support you through your part in it. It's impossible to know how to prepare for that.'

Helen looked straight at him with a serious expression on her face. 'Peter,' she said. 'It's difficult for all of us. Mum and I don't know what the task is yet, and we don't know when and how we're going to find out.'

'That isn't what I mean,' said Peter. 'I know we're all in the same boat, but what if my supporting you is going to involve my having to rescue you from a sudden life-threatening situation?'

'I hadn't thought about that,' Helen said uneasily. 'I can see now why you feel stressed. I hope it won't come to that, but we don't know.'

'At worst, it could be something that happens very suddenly and without any warning,' said Peter, not attempting to conceal his anxiety.

'Perhaps you and Dad should get together and talk this through,' Helen advised. 'We know he's been worried about Mum, so I expect the whole thing's on his mind too.'

'I think you're right,' Peter agreed. 'This is one of the occasions when I wish my dad was still alive. It isn't the sort of thing I could approach my mother or sister about.'

Helen squeezed his hand. Peter rarely referred to his father, who had been killed in a climbing accident just after Peter had left home at eighteen. His mother had never recovered from the shock, and had eventually gone to live with her daughter, Marjory. Marjory was considerably older than Peter, and lived in a large rambling house with her husband. They had no children, and were immersed in their work and their interests. It had been easy to make a small flat in the house for Peter's mother, and the result had been a success, allowing her to live a relatively independent life.

Helen watched Peter thoughtfully as he got up from his chair and went into the kitchen for another drink. He must be feeling very stressed indeed to be thinking like this, she thought. But it made sense, and she felt guilty for not realising the effect that all of this was having on him.

When he returned with a glass in his hand she said, 'I'm sorry.'

'What for?' Peter asked with surprise.

'I know I've been alarmed by some of the things that have been happening, but my main feeling has been excitement. I can see now that I should have realised that has put a lot of responsibility on you. In some ways I've been behaving like a child.'

Peter opened his mouth as if to say something, but Helen stopped him. 'No, don't say anything,' she said. 'I know I'm right, and I want to apologise. We're in this together as two adults, and I shouldn't lean on you unless it's about something we've agreed in advance. You couldn't wake me up because you felt on your own with this, and that's got to stop. I'm embarrassed to say that I've been thinking about this task I have to do with Mum in the wrong way.'

'What do you mean?'

'It's hard to admit, but I'd better get on with it. I've had a fantasy of me and Mum doing some high profile task – possibly involving some exciting drama – with you and Dad hovering around to pick up the pieces if anything went wrong. That's no good, is it? I think I'll have to revise my ideas.'

A look of relief spread across Peter's face. 'Maybe that's what was wrong,' he said. 'Maybe I was picking up that we weren't all thinking about this in the same way.' He groaned. 'That's my weak point, of course. I should have said something, but I find it hard to spot these things. I just end up like I felt when Dad was killed – with a huge feeling of responsibility for everyone, and not being able to talk about it.'

'I've got an idea,' said Helen. 'Let's go for a walk and talk through everything that's been happening, and this time I'll try very hard to be realistic about my position in it.'

It was not long before they were strolling along the path that led through the local woods.

'I don't know why,' said Peter suddenly, 'but I'm keen to be the one who finds a craftsperson to make the replica of Morna's brooch for your mother.'

'I don't think we have to know why. I think we should just tell Mum and Dad that's how you feel, and then get on with finding someone. You can tell Mum tomorrow evening.'

'I'd rather phone this evening – when your dad will still be there,' Peter said decisively. 'I'd rather speak to them both about it.'

'That's decided then.'

Peter went on. 'How would you feel about going back to see them one weekend in a few weeks' time?'

'I've no doubts about that,' Helen said with enthusiasm. 'In fact, it's been on my mind too. But I thought we wouldn't be going until the summer, so I didn't mention it.'

Peter stopped, took her by the shoulders and shook her gently. 'Silly,' he said. 'You're just like me – not saying anything.' They walked on together hand in hand. 'Lawerlocke Hall,' he mused. 'I think we should look it up on the Internet when we get back to the house. I should have thought of that before.'

'Let's go back now,' said Helen excitedly. 'I want to know if it'll be open when we see Mum and Dad again.'

'Don't get carried away. Let's finish our walk. There are a few more things I've got to talk about first.'

'Sorry.'

'I want to go back to the brooch for a minute,' Peter began. 'I'd like to find someone to make it, and I'd like to give it to your mum. That's important to me if she's going to be wearing it at our wedding.'

'Okay,' said Helen. 'I'll do my bit in getting them to agree. What's next?'

'I want to talk about the task.'

'I don't think there's anything else to say at the moment,' Helen said.

'But I want to go through the little we know so far.'

'All we have is what that man told Mum and me,' Helen objected.

Peter persisted. 'I want to think about what he might have meant. For instance, we can't be sure when he referred to me as "your husband" if he meant that the task wouldn't come to your notice until after we're married.'

'We've talked about that already,' Helen reminded him irritably. 'Why do you have to go on about it?'

Peter squeezed her hand. 'Please try to remember that I've got some responsibility here,' he said.

'Oh no!' exclaimed Helen. 'There I go again. I'm so sorry Peter.' She fell silent, and when she spoke again she said in a flat voice, 'I hope it isn't until after we're married.'

'I've a hunch it won't be until then,' Peter replied, 'but why did you say that?'

'I don't think I'll be ready for quite a while,' Helen admitted miserably. 'I get carried away too easily. All I want to do is to rush to Lawerlocke Hall to search for clues. Oh, I know it's impetuous, but it doesn't stop me wanting to get on with it as quickly as possible.'

'That's perfectly understandable.' Peter was sympathetic. 'I want to go to Lawerlocke Hall as soon as we can, but I'm trying to think things through first in case there's anything else we should do in advance.'

Helen gave him a hug. 'That makes it much easier for me,' she said. 'Now I don't feel like an impulsive teenager.'

'You think you're not ready for the task yet,' said Peter. 'Well, to be perfectly honest I don't think I am either.'

'I think each of us is preparing,' said Helen reflectively. 'There's Mum with her illness, and us with what we've been talking about this morning. I'm sure there's plenty going through Dad's head, and then there's Joan and Jim and Paul and Diana. I'm sure they're going to be involved, even if only indirectly. We're really all one family anyway.'

'Do you have any ideas about what the task might be?' asked Peter.

'No, I don't. As I said, I have fantasies about it being something grand, but I don't see anything specific. Do you?' Peter shook his head, and Helen continued. 'If I could choose, it would be something that brings a lot of good to many people. How about you?'

'The same. The only thing I'd add is that it could be some small thing, but one that starts off a train of events leading to as much good for as many people as possible.'

'I hadn't thought of that,' Helen murmured, almost to herself. 'Some small thing,' she repeated. 'I like that. I wouldn't want anything grandiose. Peter, I think you could have put your finger on something very important.'

They finished their walk in comparative silence, and returned to the house about lunchtime.

'I'm going to look on the Net before I have anything,' said Peter as he switched on his laptop. He was soon typing 'Lawerlocke+Hall' into the search engine.

Helen leaned over his shoulder. 'Oh no!' she exclaimed. 'Nothing.'

'Wait a minute,' Peter said. 'I want to try something else.'

Helen watched as he worked his way through other routes.

'Here we are,' he said. He clicked on a web address and a picture of the Hall began to form on the screen. 'It looks to me as if the website has just been set up,' he commented. 'There's only one page here so far, but it should give us some information.'

Helen stared at the relatively modest eighteenth century mansion that had appeared, and read out what was written beneath it.

Lawerlocke Hall was built in 1721 by a merchant who had fallen on good times. He was a philanthropist – a man well ahead of his time. He treated all his servants and employees in an exemplary way, and was well loved by all who knew him. He did not live a lavish life, instead preferring to share his accommodation with those less fortunate than he.

The Hall will be open to the public for several weekends this season. It is closed throughout the winter.

'This place is the same style of building as the one your mum showed us in that book of hers,' Peter commented.

'You're right. Peter, it says "several weekends", but it doesn't tell us which they are.'

'Perhaps they haven't decided yet. There's a number to ring, so we could phone and ask. It's Sunday, so there may not be anyone there, but I'll come offline and you can try now if you want.'

When Helen got through, she heard some clicking noises and was about to put the phone down when she heard a recorded message.

'This is Lawerlocke Hall,' it said. 'We are open the first weekend in every month from June to September, from ten until five each day. We look forward to seeing you.'

'Peter, it opens the first weekend in June,' Helen burst out excitedly.

'Is it open any other time?' he asked.

Helen explained, and then waited, watching the expression on Peter's face intently.

'Shall we try and go to your parents' house that first weekend?' said Peter.

Helen grabbed the diary, and searched feverishly through its pages. 'It's clear!' she announced. 'Why don't we phone Mum and Dad straight away?'

'Perhaps we should check our work diaries first,' Peter suggested.

'Why?' demanded Helen impetuously. Then she covered her mouth with her hand and apologised through her fingers. 'Oh! I'm getting worse, not better,' she said worriedly.

'Look,' said Peter firmly. 'I'm just as eager as you are, and I thought we might be able to get Friday or Monday off so that we can go for a long weekend. But let's phone your parents now.'

Helen keyed in the number. Don answered, and without saying anything she handed the phone to Peter and then sat quietly, listening to Peter's side of the conversation.

'That's it fixed,' he told her when he had finished the call. 'Your dad says that's fine, and they're looking forward to seeing us. They are as excited as we are at the prospect of visiting Lawerlocke Hall, and there's no problem about sending me a copy of the photograph of Morna's brooch and letting me go ahead with getting a reproduction. You'll have gathered that I said I'd like a chat with him about the task and our worries about you and your mum, and he was as keen as I am. Of course your mum's looking forward to speaking to you tomorrow evening. By that time we'll know if we can get the extra day off.'

'Only a few weeks to go,' said Helen excitedly. 'I've just thought of something else,' she added. 'Isn't that around the time Diana and Paul are moving back?'

'I think they're due back a bit later than that,' Peter replied, 'but we can phone and check. If they're going to be there we could meet up.'

Chapter Nineteen

Fay arrived at the gate of the vicarage at five past ten. She did not have to ring the bell, as Reverend Howard appeared at the door.

'It's good to see you,' he said, holding out his hand. 'I'm looking forward to your companionship while I look through the stack of papers. Come in and make yourself comfortable.'

He led the way to his study.

'Do sit down,' he said. He pointed to a pile of documents. 'This is what my brother sent.'

Fay contemplated the size of it. There were several large files, each bulging with papers.

'As far as I could see at a glance,' said the Reverend, 'there's a mixture of photocopies from books and journals of all kinds, there are newspaper cuttings, photographs, and even some diary entries. However, it may be that a lot of it is irrelevant.'

'Perhaps I could make a start on one of the files, and maybe sort out the contents into different categories,' Fay suggested.

'That sounds helpful,' the Reverend agreed.

They worked together in silence for about an hour, after which he offered Fay something to drink.

'Just a glass of water for me, thank you,' said Fay. She was so engrossed in what she was doing that she had barely heard him speak.

It was fascinating. Although much of what she was looking at did not appear at all relevant to this church and vicarage, it covered unusual aspects of the history of many religious and ecclesiastical buildings up and down the country she had never before been aware existed. She dimly sensed that the Reverend was placing a glass at the far end of the table at which she was seated, but she did not look up, as she had just come across a packet of photographs of gargoyles and misericords.

She made a space on the table and spread them out before examining them in detail. It would have been easy enough to photograph the misericords, she reflected, although perhaps the lighting could be a problem. However, the gargoyles were another matter. She supposed that some of the photographs had been taken using scaffolding. That would have been an expensive solution, but one that allowed the best access. Perhaps the photographer had chanced upon some buildings that were being repaired. She put the photos in the packet and continued to search through the file.

When she had finished, she carefully replaced everything. Although the material had been fascinating, there had been nothing that appeared to be directly relevant to the Reverend's researches into this vicarage.

She took the next file off the pile and opened it. Again she found the contents fascinating, but again there was nothing of particular relevance to Reverend Howard's current interests. The third file she opened was full of packets of photographs. More photographs... Looking through these reminds me of the museum, she said to herself as she opened the first packet. This was a collection showing carving around the doorways of several churches. Having studied them all, she put them away and opened the second packet.

She was immediately arrested by what she saw on the first photograph. It was a monk. His tonsure was obvious, and he wore a habit. He was standing with his back to the stone wall of what must once have been a building. The photograph was in black and white, so she could not tell the colour of his clothing. She was immediately struck by the fact that this man did not look unlike Reverend Howard, and for a moment she thought of drawing it to his attention, but she thought better of it, and continued to study it herself. The monk had a rope girdle – but no, it wasn't a rope. Fay stared closely at what was tied around his waist, and to her utter astonishment could just make out the head of a snake at one end of it.

She was vaguely aware of holding her breath as she slowly turned the photograph over to see if there was anything written on the back of it. There were several lines of handwriting, but Fay found it almost impossible to read, as it was of a style that she had never before encountered. At first glance she had thought it was written in a foreign language, but as she studied it more closely she was sure it was not. As she struggled to make sense of the script, she became aware of Reverend Howard looking over her shoulder.

'Are you having trouble with that handwriting?' he asked.

'I'm afraid it's defeating me,' Fay admitted.

'I'm not surprised.' He chuckled, and Fay felt startled. 'It's my brother's writing. If he wants other people to read what he's written he prints it,' the Reverend explained. 'If not, he writes it.'

Fay did not know what to say. She was in a dilemma, as she was eager to know what the writing said, since it might throw some light on the snake belt.

'I'll read it out for you,' said the Reverend.

Brother M. Chapel in the grounds of Lawerlocke Hall.
Unusual snake girdle – origin unknown.

'Is this of interest to you?' he asked.

Fay could not speak. Every time she tried to say something she found the words stuck in her throat. To cover her discomfort she reached for her glass of water and took several small sips from it before once again trying to reply.

'I'm hoping to visit Lawerlocke Hall next month,' she said at last. 'Er... Do you happen to know if any monks are buried anywhere near here?' she blundered.

'You mean near Lawerlocke Hall, or near our church?'

'Either,' Fay managed to say, although her voice did not sound right.

'Actually,' he said, 'I believe that there was once a small monastery not far from Lawerlocke Hall. From what little I know, it fell into disrepair a long time ago. There have been plans to excavate a few likely sites, but no one ever got beyond that.' At this point he turned the photograph over and saw the picture of the monk. 'Goodness!' he exclaimed. 'He looks quite like me. How very strange.' He turned to Fay. 'Is this why you were asking?'

'Not exactly.' Fay was almost stuttering. She swallowed hard and gathered herself. She desperately wanted to tell the Reverend about the stabbing in her thumb and about the curse, but she held back, uncertain as to whether it would be the right thing to do.

At this point he glanced at the clock. 'I'm afraid we're going to have to finish for today,' he said. 'I'm due at a meeting elsewhere soon, and I had no idea it had got so late. Perhaps we can arrange another time.'

Fay stood up and started to reassemble the contents of the file.

'Of course,' she said.

'Would you like to take that file with you?' she heard the Reverend ask.

'I would love to,' she replied. 'Are you absolutely sure?'

'I know you'll take good care of it, and I'll know where it is if I think I need it before you come back again.'

'Would you mind if I get copies made of any of these?' asked Fay tentatively.

The Reverend considered her request and then said, 'I'd rather do that myself, but by all means make a list of anything that interests you, and I'll see to it when I have time. Would you like a bag to put the file in?'

'Thank you. That would help.'

He produced a strong polythene bag from a drawer in his desk and handed it to her. Fay put the file carefully into it, picked up her own bag, and the Reverend showed her out.

'I'll be in touch about arranging another time,' he assured her.

Fay could not wait to get home to examine the rest of the contents of the file. As soon as she was back she laid it on the dining table, hurriedly ate some oatcakes in the kitchen and set to work.

There were seven packets of photographs in the file. She put them in a row at the far edge of the table and then opened each in turn, laying out the photographs one by one across the table towards her. When she had finished, most of the surface of the table was covered. However, to her great disappointment, although she scrutinised the front and back of each photo, there was nothing else that particularly caught her attention. The pictures were a mixture of buildings of varying ages, each of which she guessed was no more than a hundred years old. Each bore an address on the reverse side, but all of these were meaningless as far as she was concerned. She packed them away again.

At least there is the one of the monk, she thought. She was looking forward to her phone call with Helen that evening, and she wondered what Helen would make of it.

She sat and took stock of her situation. The hospital tests had revealed nothing sinister, and in general she was feeling considerably better.

'But I haven't got much energy, and there's still an odd sensation in my right lung,' she said aloud.

Having decided that there was no point in worrying, she opted to listen to some music. Searching through Don's collection of CDs in the sitting room, she came across some Mozart chamber music, and without bothering to discover exactly what was on the disc, she loaded it into the player. She sat down on the sofa, leaned back, and closed her eyes. To her delight she realised that it was being played on original instruments, or at least on reproductions. She felt soothed by the sound and soon fell asleep.

Fay was sure there was ringing coming from somewhere, but how could that be? She opened her eyes and stared with incomprehension at the gas fire in front of her. Where was she? The ringing sound continued and she turned her head towards its source, but she could not make any sense of what was happening and she closed her eyes again. Much to her relief the sound stopped and she gradually drifted off once more.

'Fay! What's the matter?' said a voice near her head.

What did that mean? Fay wondered.

'Fay, it's Jim here,' said the voice. 'I let myself in. Helen phoned me. She was worried when she couldn't get an answer from you.'

Fay sat up. 'Helen?' she said. 'Where is she?' She could see a man's face looking at her, and she was aware of feeling very uncomfortable.

'Fay,' said the face. 'There's something wrong, isn't there?'

'Where's Helen?' asked Fay urgently, and then she began to cry. But it wasn't really crying. It was more like wailing.

The man touched her arm. 'Joan will be here in a minute, Fay. It's all right. We won't leave you on your own again.'

She felt very frightened at first when the man touched her, and she shrank back from him, but he didn't seem to be going to hurt her after all, so she was able to ignore him. The wailing sound that was coming from her went on unchanged.

A woman came into the room and was talking to the man.

'How is she, Jim? Have you any idea what happened?' said the woman.

‘Helen. Where’s Helen?’ screamed Fay, and then slid on to the floor clutching her throat.

The ringing sound started again, and the man picked something up and spoke to it. ‘Yes, we’re both here, Don,’ he said, ‘but she doesn’t seem to recognise us. She keeps calling out for Helen though… Yes… yes… of course. I’ll go and get it straight away.’

Fay was writhing on the floor still clutching her throat. The woman knelt down beside her and stroked her head. ‘It’s all right, Fay,’ she said. ‘Jim and I are both here, and Jim’s just gone to get something to show you. He’ll be back in a minute.’

Jim reappeared carrying a large photograph of Helen at her graduation ceremony, together with a smaller one of when she first started school, which he handed to Joan.

‘Here are some pictures of Helen,’ the man and the woman said together.

Fay stared at the pictures. Her hands fell away from her throat and she said, ‘Helen!’ and clutched the pictures to her.

She looked at Joan and Jim. ‘It’s nice to see you,’ she said. ‘But why have you come?’

Jim picked up the phone again. ‘It’s all right, Don. I think she’s coming round a bit. Would you like to speak to her now?’

‘Hello, Fay,’ said Don. ‘We’ve all been worried about you. Helen couldn’t get a reply when she rang this evening, so she wisely called me and then phoned Joan and Jim.’

‘That’s funny,’ said Fay. ‘I’ve been here all day. I was at the vicarage this morning, and I got back here around twelve. What time is it now?’

‘It’s about eight thirty,’ Don informed her.

‘That’s strange,’ said Fay, puzzled. ‘Where has all that time gone? And I seem to be sitting on the floor. Can you hang on a minute while I get up on to the sofa?’

‘I think I’ll just call Helen on my mobile,’ Joan said quietly to Jim, and she went into the hall.

‘Fay,’ said Don. ‘I think it’s important that you aren’t on your own at the moment.’

‘Why do you say that, Don?’ she asked. ‘I’ll be fine until the weekend.’

‘Can you please accept that I need you to be with Joan and Jim at the moment?' asked Don. 'I'll explain why when I see you. Will you just do it for me?'

Fay started to protest, but then thought better of it and said, 'Of course, Don. If it'll make you feel any easier. We'll either be here or at their house, so you'll know where to get me.'

'I'll be back at lunchtime on Friday, Fay,' said Don. 'And I'll ring you every evening as usual.'

'That's fine. Shall we say goodbye for now?'

They made a time to speak the following evening, and then she put the phone down.

'Don wants me to be with you until he's back,' Fay began.

'Yes, we want that too,' said Jim immediately. 'Joan's going to spend tonight with you here, and then she's hoping you'll move in with us until Don comes home.'

'All right,' Fay replied. 'Where is Joan at the moment?'

'She'll be back in a minute,' Jim reassured her.

'I'm here, Fay,' said Joan as she came into the room. 'How about phoning Helen now? She'd like to hear from you.'

'I'll slip away, Fay,' said Jim. 'I've got things at home I've got to finish tonight, but I'll see you tomorrow.'

'Bye, Jim,' said Fay, as she picked up the phone again.

'Hello, Mum.' She heard Helen's familiar voice.

'It's good to hear you, Helen,' Fay replied. 'We were going to talk about my visit to the vicarage, weren't we? It was very interesting. There was quite a big stack of files, so I didn't get very far. Reverend Howard lent me one.'

'That was good of him. What's in it?'

'It's full of photographs. I was particularly struck by one I was looking at just before I came back. It's a picture of a monk, and it was taken in the grounds of Lawerlocke Hall. The others aren't really of any interest.'

'Lawerlocke Hall!' exclaimed Helen. 'No wonder that one caught your eye.'

'I think what drew me to begin with was the fact that he looks a bit like Reverend Howard.' Helen giggled, and Fay went on. 'And I saw his girdle rope had a snake's head at one end.'

'A real snake's head?' asked Helen.

'I think it was some kind of long belt. I couldn't see what it was made of, but the end of it was fashioned as a snake's head.'

'This gets more and more curious,' said Helen. 'I can't wait until our visit to the Hall. By the way, Peter and I have booked the Friday and the Monday off work so we've got a long weekend. Can you ask Joan when Paul and Diana will be back?'

'Joan says it'll be the middle of June, so you won't see them this time,' said Fay, her tone conveying regret. 'It would have been lovely to have everyone together again. Never mind, I'm sure we'll be able to fix that in the summer.'

'Diana will have quite a bulge by then,' Helen laughed. 'I've just thought of something,' she went on. 'She'll be enormous at our wedding. We'll have to take lots of photos to remind her.'

Fay felt relaxed after her conversation with Helen. She and Joan made something to eat, and then decided to go to bed early.

The week passed pleasantly. Fay enjoyed her time at her friends' house. If Joan was at work, Jim was either sitting with her or working in the room that was his office – in the single-storeyed extension they had built when he first set up his business from home. She read a selection of short stories from their bookshelves, and found them to be the right length for the level of concentration she had.

Don came to collect her after lunch on Friday.

'That's me finished for now,' he proclaimed cheerfully.

'I thought you had another week,' said Fay.

'I've arranged that I can do the rest of what I'm responsible for from home,' Don explained.

Before they left Joan and Jim's house they promised themselves an evening out together the following week.

'I think we've got quite a lot to catch up on,' said Don on the way home, 'but there's no rush. What I'd like to do first is to leave my things at the house, pick up the picture of Morna's brooch, and go and get it copied straight away to send to Peter.'

'I'm glad you've remembered. It had gone right out of my mind,' Fay replied. 'Yes, let's do that. While you're putting your things away I'll write a note, and get an envelope with a piece of card in it to keep the picture from getting bent in the post.'

After supper that evening Don told Fay as much as he knew of what had happened to her the previous Monday.

Fay was aghast. 'Why didn't Joan and Jim tell me?' she said.

'We all discussed it, and we decided it was best to wait until I was home again,' Don explained. 'We may have been wrong to do it that way, but it was with the best of intentions.'

'Are you *sure* I didn't recognise Joan and Jim when they came round and let themselves in?' Fay questioned him.

'You can phone them and check if you want,' said Don, 'but that's definitely what they told me. Naturally they were very worried. You only came out of the state you were in when at my suggestion Jim got the photos of Helen down from our bedroom to show you.'

'I can begin to appreciate something of what you must all have been feeling,' Fay admitted, 'but I wish I could remember what happened.'

'Maybe you will when you're ready,' said Don. 'Don't try to push it.'

'At least I might be able to remember what I did when I got back to the house,' mused Fay. 'Let me see… I was eager to open up the contents of the file. I put it on the dining table, and I went into the kitchen to get something to eat…'

'What did you have?'

'I wanted something quick, so I had a few oatcakes and a drink of fruit juice. I looked through the rest of the things in the file, but they weren't of interest. I'll show you if you want.' She started to get up.

'I can see them later,' said Don. 'Finish what you were telling me.'

'I came in here and put some of your music on. Then I fell asleep. The next thing I knew I was sitting on the floor holding the photographs of Helen, and Joan and Jim were looking at me rather oddly.'

'It's a good thing they've got a key to the house,' said Don. 'Otherwise I suppose they'd have had no alternative but to break down the door.'

'Surely not!' exclaimed Fay.

'We were all extremely worried,' stated Don baldly.

Fay stared at him.

Here Don changed the subject. 'By the way, what music were you listening to?'

'It was some Mozart chamber music. It should still be in your CD player.'

'Ah yes, it's some quartets played on original instruments.'

'I thought that. But surely they're copies?'

'No. The ones they were using for that recording were loaned from a private collection.'

'Let me see the insert in the CD case.'

Don passed it to Fay, who read the details. 'Fancy that,' she said. 'Where did you hear about this recording?'

'I was listening to a concert on the radio, and I took a note of the details. It's a recent recording.'

'It's amazing how they manage to restore these very old instruments, isn't it?' said Fay. 'I was thinking… Peter said that Lawerlocke Hall was built in 1721. Mozart was born in 1756. I wonder if any of his music was played there once it became popular in this country?'

'You never know what we'll find out when we go there,' Don replied.

Chapter Twenty

Fay's health continued to improve slowly over the following weeks. She and Don saw a lot of Joan and Jim. Apart from eating out together they went to see some films and plays, and there were times when they all went to the book group. Fay arranged for Danny to go along and read some of his writing. He had been working on the rest of his book, following the guidelines Fay had suggested in the initial chapters, and by the time he was invited to the group he was quite confident about his presentation. He was warmly received, and much encouraged by this he began work on another book soon afterwards.

Reverend Howard had been very tied up with his pastoral duties, and he had not been able to offer Fay another time to look at the files with him. Consequently she had given him the photograph of Brother M to be copied, and she had added the copy to her growing collection of significant items. And all the time she was eagerly counting the days up to Helen and Peter's arrival, and their trip to Lawerlocke Hall.

When the Friday came, she could not settle to anything, so Don took a break from his work and they went out for a walk until lunchtime. They were not long back before they saw Peter draw up outside the house, and Helen rushed down the drive to play her trick with the letterbox.

Once inside the house Peter pulled a box out of his pocket and said, 'Surprise!' He had a wide grin on his face as he handed it to Fay.

'What is it, Peter?' she asked as she took it from him.

'You'll have to look inside and see,' he answered mysteriously. 'I'll get you a better box when I've got an opportunity. That one will have to do for now.'

Fay began to open it cautiously.

'It won't bite, Mum,' laughed Helen.

Fay lifted the lid off and removed the pad of tissue paper that lay beneath.

'It's amazing!' she breathed as she saw an exact replica of

Morna's brooch. 'Look, Don,' she said as she held it up for him to see.

'That's excellent,' he said. 'What's it made from, Peter?'

'It's stainless steel,' Peter replied. 'The chap I approached thought it would be best, and I went along with that.'

'Who made it?' asked Fay.

'There's a card in the bottom of the box,' Peter replied. 'It's someone called Bruce Steele. I thought you'd like to have his details in case you wanted to ask him anything.'

'Not an inappropriate name,' Don commented with amusement. 'How did you find him?'

'It was sheer luck,' Peter began. 'At first I asked around a few friends and colleagues, but I didn't get very far. When I explained I was hoping to get a brooch made that was a reproduction of one in a photograph, everyone was interested, but no one had any suggestions of where to go.'

Helen could hardly contain herself. 'Just tell them, Peter,' she urged. 'I've been dying to tell you, Mum, but Peter said we had to keep it a secret until he gave you the brooch.'

Peter turned to her and said firmly, 'You'll have to be patient, Helen. I want to do this my own way.' Then he continued his story. 'As you know, I see quite a number of people in my consulting room in the course of a week, and I began to think that I could ask some I felt I knew well – people who have been coming for a number of years. By the end of the week I struck lucky. One of the men had wanted to have something special made for his wife for their ruby wedding anniversary. He had gone round quite a number of places before he was satisfied that he had found someone who could do the job. Interestingly, he had chosen a brooch he had seen in a book, and he wanted to have it copied. He kindly invited us round to his house, and his wife showed us the brooch. It was beautifully crafted, and an excellent reproduction of the one in the illustration in the book. Of course,' he finished with a twinkle in his eye, 'it's been very difficult to persuade Helen to keep quiet this long.'

'I bet it has,' said Don, putting his arm round Helen's shoulders and giving her a hug.

'I feel I want to wear it straight away,' said Fay, 'but it's even more important to me that I keep it for your wedding day.' She took it out of its box and held it on her shoulder and then up to her neck.

'It suits you perfectly, Mum,' said Helen admiringly. 'It looks as if it was made specially for you.'

'It was!' laughed Fay.

'I mean it looks as if it was designed for you,' Helen corrected herself.

Fay took it to the small mirror that was hanging in the hall and gazed at her reflection. She held the brooch in several positions and considered each carefully.

'It has to go on my left shoulder,' she pronounced confidently.

'But it looks just as good at your neck,' said Helen. 'It'll depend a lot on what you're wearing.'

'I'm absolutely sure it has to go on my left shoulder,' said Fay firmly, 'so that's where I'll wear it.'

Helen noted the determination in Fay's voice and did not argue. Maybe her mother was sensing something, and it was important to go along with that. 'Have you decided what you'll be wearing yet?' she asked lightly. 'We've talked about my outfit, and I've been working out how to get the rest of what I need, but we haven't talked about yours yet.'

'I know,' Fay replied. 'It's funny, but I couldn't think about it at all. Every time I tried, my mind seemed to be empty, so I thought I'd leave it until later, but now I have the brooch I've got some ideas already.'

'Do you want the men to absent themselves?' asked Don with an amused expression.

'No. Helen and I can talk about it later,' Fay replied. She turned back to the mirror and tried the brooch at her shoulder again. 'It's my brooch,' she murmured almost inaudibly. 'This is me. Yet I don't look like me…'

Helen watched her worriedly; but after only a short while Fay put the brooch back in the box and shut the lid.

'Peter,' she said. 'Thank you so much. It's perfect.' She kissed his cheek affectionately. 'I'm going upstairs to put it somewhere safe, and then we can all have something to eat.'

'Can I make a suggestion?' asked Peter when she returned.

'Of course. Fire away,' Don encouraged him.

'Perhaps Fay and Helen could spend some time talking about

clothes later today, while you and I do some more talking about our support role.'

'That's a great idea,' Don agreed. 'Why don't we go out for the afternoon and leave the ladies in the house – as we did before? By the way, I should remember to tell you that Joan and Jim will be joining us on our trip to the Hall tomorrow. They weren't sure at first whether they'd be free, but Joan phoned last night to let us know. They're both very keen to see what it's like. Of course there is the deeper motive of wanting to find out if there are any clues there about what's been coming into our lives of late.'

'I think that's very good,' said Peter seriously. 'The more of us that are involved at each stage, the better.'

After lunch the two men set off for a walk, while Fay and Helen relaxed in the sitting room.

'Let's get the jacket out again,' Fay suggested as soon as Don and Peter were out of sight.

'That's exactly what I wanted to do,' Helen agreed, and she ran upstairs to collect it.

When she returned, she took it out of its cover and spread it lovingly on the back of one of the chairs. 'I've found someone who's going to make the trousers to go with it,' she said. 'She gave me a sample of the material she's hoping to use. I've brought it with me.' She rummaged in her bag and brought out a small brown envelope from which she produced a piece of satin, and she held it against the jacket.

'Look, Mum!' she exclaimed. 'It's an exact match. I thought it would be all right, but I couldn't be sure until I had it here.'

'Yes, it looks perfect, Helen,' replied Fay. 'You can get her to order it now. Have you thought about shoes and a bag yet?'

'I don't want to carry any kind of bag,' said Helen. 'Shoes? I think I'll have to find something that goes with the satin trousers – something flat I would say. I'll have a look round. So that's me,' she finished. 'What about you?'

'I want something loose, flowing and quite long,' said Fay. 'I could see it when I had the brooch in my hand. The material is a pale colour and is gathered at the left shoulder using the brooch.'

'Shall we sketch it out?' suggested Helen.

'No!'

Helen was startled and looked at her mother anxiously.

'I mean… I think it's too soon,' Fay explained. 'I've got to get used to having the brooch in my possession again first. It was a wonderful surprise to get it, but it's been quite a shock too.'

Helen noticed Fay's use of the word 'again', but decided not to question it. She made a mental note to raise it that evening when everyone was together.

'Are you going to cover your head at the ceremony?' Fay asked suddenly.

'That's a good point,' mused Helen. 'I hadn't thought about it yet.' She fell silent and shut her eyes while she tried to visualise something appropriate. 'It has to be something simple,' she said at last.

'How about a rigid hair band covered in the same satin as your trousers?' Fay suggested.

'That's a good idea, but I think I'd rather have a hair band as the frame for a kind of satin cap,' said Helen slowly. 'Once I've got material I'll think about it some more, and then I'll decide whether or not to have a veil.'

Fay hugged her. 'You'll look lovely,' she said confidently.

Don and Peter had decided to go for a walk further afield. They took the local bus to a well-known beauty spot about six miles away, and then made their way back by paths that did not follow roads. This itinerary provided plenty of opportunity for conversation and reflection.

'Helen and I haven't been aware of any other developments in Fay's experiences,' Peter began, 'so we've assumed that nothing particularly striking has happened. Can you tell me any small things that might be relevant?'

'There hasn't been anything I could put my finger on,' Don replied. 'As you know, after the last event I rearranged my work so that I could be at home. It wasn't just that I wanted to know that Fay was safe, it was because I couldn't stand the strain of worrying about her when I was too far away to come back home quickly if something happened. Things have been very quiet. Her health seems to be improving, although it's all very slow, and I'm getting on with my work in between our spending time together enjoying ourselves. We keep in close contact with Joan and Jim of course, and we speak to you and Helen on the phone. We're looking forward to Paul and Diana's return. We hear from them quite a bit. They should be arriving back soon. It's a pity you won't see them this time.'

'We spoke to them last night,' said Peter. 'If everything goes according to plan, they'll be back the weekend after next. I'm glad that things have been okay over the last few weeks, but I must admit I've been wondering if something might happen at the Hall, or in the week after our visit. I mentioned it to Helen, and she's been thinking the same way.'

'It's been on my mind too,' Don replied. 'Of course, none of us can predict what may or may not happen. All we can do is to be aware that something might.'

'I think we should talk about it to Fay this evening,' Peter suggested wisely.

'You're right,' Don agreed. 'Although the strange things that happen are usually focussed through Fay, it doesn't mean that it's all to do with her. We're all involved in some way, but it's easier to see when something's happening with her. It would be totally wrong to start treating her as if she were someone with a problem and we were all fine.'

'So far I'm the only one who doesn't appear to have experienced something unusual,' Peter reflected, 'but you never know what might happen. Have you had any thoughts about what Helen and Fay's task might be? I think about it quite a lot, and as I said to you on the phone I can feel overwhelmed at times with the responsibility for my part in supporting Helen through it.'

'I think about it too,' Don replied, 'but I'm no further forward. I'm very glad we had that conversation when we did, because it made me look at how I was feeling, and it helped me to remember to keep in touch with everyone, even when nothing in particular was happening. I realised it was important to do that so we have a feeling of cohesion in case something arises quite suddenly – as it has tended to do so far,' he added with a rueful smile.

'Yes,' agreed Peter. 'And I would say the last thing that happened to Fay was probably the most alarming, wasn't it?'

'You could say so,' said Don emphatically. 'I was sitting at the end of the phone sweating and wishing I could have a helicopter that would get me home in a few minutes!'

'I wonder what the two of them are up to at the moment?' said Peter suddenly.

'Perhaps they're talking about their worries about us,' Don joked.

'I would put my money on the conversation being to do with wedding outfits,' said Peter.

'You're probably right,' Don agreed. He checked his watch. 'We've about an hour before we'll be back. How about telling me how far you've got with the plans for changing premises at work?'

'Ah, yes. We've got a choice. A large unit at the local shopping centre is about to become vacant, and it looks as if we might have a chance at that, but there's also the option of converting a house near to it into a clinic that we would be sharing with audiologists. Personally I'm particularly interested in the second option, whereas my partners are keen to be in the precinct.'

'What's for and against each, in your view?' enquired Don.

'The precinct unit is easy for clients to locate. It has a large frontage and the floor space is generous, allowing pleasant space for working. It's available on a long lease, so there would be no worries about having to move again in the foreseeable future. As for the house, it would be owned by our practice and the audiologists jointly. On the face of it that might sound rather complicated, but we've looked into it and there are no problems that can't be overcome on the legal front. Although it's just outside the precinct, it's easy to reach. I've looked into the question of access for the disabled, and we can easily have all the consulting rooms on the ground floor, with most of the office and storage space on the first floor.'

'Have you any idea about the conversion costs?'

'I've made some preliminary enquiries, and so far the picture looks promising. I'm going to push hard for the house option at our next meeting.'

'What's your main reason for preferring it?'

'I'm keen to have both services under the same roof. I think the public deserve simplicity in getting help with their sight and hearing problems, and it's not uncommon for a person to have both difficulties. But of course, if it's going to be hard to get round the problems inherent in the choice of accommodation, I wouldn't be pushing my view so much.'

'Do keep me up to date with what's happening,' Don encouraged him.

'Thanks for your interest.'

The two men walked along in silence for a while, and then Peter asked, 'What news do you have of Jack?'

'He keeps in touch mostly by e-mail, but I do have a phone call with him from time to time,' Don replied. 'I miss him a lot, but he's trying to get himself established at the moment, and he's completely engrossed in what he's doing. Fay and I haven't told him what's going on here, apart from saying that she's gradually getting better.'

'Helen and I occasionally get a letter from him from some far-flung location,' said Peter. 'Sometimes we have to get the atlas out to see where he is. We write back and give him general news. He's adamant that he'll be back to see us getting married, and that means a lot to both of us.'

'Yes, he often refers to that in his contact with us too,' Don observed. 'He's told his employer that he needs three weeks off, and that's fixed. It means he'll get a full two weeks with us once you've taken into account the travelling time.'

'I've a feeling that he misses everyone here,' said Peter reflectively.

'I'm sure he does,' Don agreed, 'but it's one of those situations where he's got to get on with things meantime, and at the moment he prefers to cope by not talking much about how he feels. On the good side, he's learning a lot about his job, and he's made some useful contacts.'

'When's your next stint away from home, Don?' asked Peter carefully.

'August,' Don replied shortly.

Peter said nothing. He could sense the anxiety in Don's tone, and he thought it better to wait to see if he wanted to say anything else before he contributed.

After a while Don continued. 'It'll be the whole of August. I must confess that at the moment I'm trying not to think about it.'

'I can understand that,' said Peter slowly. 'It's worrying. But a lot might change before then, and it's no good basing our thoughts about it solely on what we know so far.' As an afterthought he added, 'Do you know yet where you'll be based?'

'Funny you should ask that,' Don commented. 'I got the preliminary details in the post yesterday, and it's not all that far from you. I might even manage to come over and see you one or two evenings.'

'That would be great,' said Peter enthusiastically.

There was a further silence, which was eventually broken by Peter. 'I've had an idea,' he began. 'How would you feel about Fay staying with Helen and me – at least for some of the time?'

'The thought hadn't crossed my mind.' The relief in Don's voice was almost palpable as he went on. 'I'm sure Fay would love it.'

'We can talk to her about it this evening. It might seem a long time ahead, but it's something we can all be looking forward to.'

'You're right,' said Don cheerfully. He glanced across at Peter. 'Do you fancy being joint chef with me tonight?'

'Of course,' Peter replied. 'I think we make a good team.'

They arrived back at the house to find Fay and Helen on the floor in the dining room with large sheets of white paper spread on newspaper, and squeezy bottles full of brightly coloured paints.

'Oh!' exclaimed Fay. 'You're back already. We've only just started.'

'What's all this?' asked Don jovially, as he surveyed the scene. 'Playgroup?'

'Don't put her off,' Helen admonished him. 'I managed to persuade her that it would be a good idea. We went off to the shops to get supplies.'

'Okay,' said Don. 'Peter and I will shut ourselves in the kitchen, and produce some interesting aromas to stimulate all the creativity that's happening in here.'

'Some sunshine…' Fay began as she picked up the yellow paint and began to spread it across the sheet in front of her. 'Oh! This feels wonderful… You were right when you told me not to think about trying to make shapes of anything. The colour has such a huge impact when I'm not worrying about getting anything right.' She selected the purple and began to produce a series of tulip-shaped petals.

'Mum, those look lovely,' Helen commented as she started to sketch the shapes of some fruit on her sheet. 'Here, why not make some red ones next?' she added as she handed the red container across.

'We'll surprise them with these lightly grilled aubergine slices,' Don told Peter in the privacy of the kitchen. He took the pastry brush and quickly covered them with the contents of a glass jar.

'What's that?' Peter enquired.

Don looked evasive. 'Er… it's my own special recipe.'

'Am I allowed to know the secret?'

'Not yet, but I might tell you after you've eaten some.'

By the time the meal was ready, Fay had produced a bright picture of petals and sunshine that covered most of the large sheet.

'It's stunning!' exclaimed Don as he came through with the plates. 'We'll have to decide where to hang it.'

'I'll put it in the corner to dry,' said Helen as she stood up to clear the things away. 'You should have given us some warning.'

'Didn't want to disturb you,' said Don, spreading out the tablemats with his spare hand.

When the meal was finished, Peter announced, 'Don and I have got a number of things we want to talk over this evening, so we'll get everything cleared away and make a start.'

Helen and Fay looked at each other. 'Actually, so have we,' they said.

Helen explained. 'While you were out, we were talking about private things…' She paused dramatically, and then went on. 'After that we started thinking about tomorrow's trip to the Hall, and there are a few things we'd like to say…'

'Not surprisingly, that's on our agenda too,' Don interrupted.

Not long afterwards they were seated in the comfortable chairs in the front room, and Don began. 'I think we need to have a few words about this trip, since it may or may not bring some clues to our situation. To be entirely honest, Fay, I'd rather you always had someone with you while we're there.'

'It's all right, Don,' she replied. 'I'd already worked that one out.'

'It might prove to be merely a pleasant outing for all of us,' Don continued.

'But then again, it might not,' Peter added.

'Anyway, we've decided the main thing,' Helen broke in. 'Mum's not going anywhere on her own while we're there. Now that's fixed, I want to say I've been very excited about this visit ever since we planned it.'

'I can confirm that,' said Peter, smiling. 'I've had to keep reminding her that it might not produce anything much.'

'That's unlikely though, isn't it?' Helen challenged. 'Morna's brooch *and* the photograph of the monk are associated with the Hall. That's rather an unlikely coincidence in itself. I'm *sure* something will come to light.'

'I agree,' said Fay soberly. 'I've got a feeling about it. A premonition if you like.'

'Mum,' said Helen suddenly. 'When you were admiring the brooch last night, I heard you say something about it being in your possession *again*. What did you mean by that?'

'I have no recollection of saying that,' Fay said, puzzled. 'Are you sure?'

'That's what I thought I heard you say too,' Don confirmed.

Fay swayed in her seat, and she clutched at her chest.

'Steady, Fay,' said Don, taking hold of her hand. 'Take some deep breaths.'

Fay obediently followed his instructions, and once she felt better she said, 'I had a flashback to being in that tunnel.'

'I thought so,' said Don.

'Mum, you did tell me that when you were in the tunnel your name was Morna,' said Helen.

'I haven't forgotten that,' replied Fay. 'In fact it's been on my mind a lot – especially since I found the photograph of the brooch. Oh dear, my head does feel strange. This is the first time I've had anything like this for a while.' She leaned forward with her head in her hands. 'Can we talk about something else now?' she pleaded.

'Peter was asking me when I'm next to be away from home,' Don began.

'I'm not sure I want to think about that at the moment,' said Fay irritably.

'You will when you hear what I have to say,' Don promised. 'I heard yesterday that it'll be for most of August. Peter and I have been talking about it, and we've worked out that you might like to stay with them for some or all of the time.'

Fay sat up. 'What do you mean?' she asked.

'I'll be working not far away, and we can all spend some time together,' Don explained. 'I'll be quite tied up, but it won't mean that I can't come along for some of the evenings.'

'Oh, Mum!' exclaimed Helen excitedly. 'That's great! You must come for the whole time. Mustn't she, Peter?'

'The other thing Don and I were talking about is Jack,' Peter began. 'As promised, he's fixed time off for our wedding, and he'll have a whole two weeks here.'

Helen's face glowed. 'That's wonderful news,' she said. 'We can have some time together before the day. I do miss him.'

'We all do,' Peter said quietly.

'Now I'm going to give Joan and Jim a ring,' Fay decided, lifting the phone. 'I should let them know what we've decided about tomorrow, and then tell them about the brooch and what's just happened.'

The following morning Helen and Fay reported that they had once again sensed someone on the landing in the night, but as before, they could give no further details.

'I'd like to show the brooch to Joan and Jim,' Fay told Don as they were dressing.

'It's probably best to leave it at home.'

'I know.'

'Perhaps they'll come back to the house with us afterwards for a drink,' Don suggested. 'You could show it to them then.'

The journey to Lawerlocke Hall took longer than planned. Uncharacteristically, Don had taken a wrong turning, which resulted in his having to navigate along some narrow twisting country lanes; and when they arrived, Joan and Jim were waiting for them in the car park at the rear of the building.

'I'm off to get some guide books,' Helen announced eagerly, rushing ahead in the direction of the booth at the front of the Hall.

She soon returned bearing a pile of books and a row of tickets.

'I got a book each,' she said, handing them round. 'It's such an important visit that it seemed silly to have to share.'

Fay began to walk back down the drive, and Don followed her, having told the others that he would be the one to stay with her for now.

'I wanted to study the front of it first,' she explained. 'I've already seen pictures of it, but that isn't the same as seeing the actual building. Three floors, and there's some kind of basement underneath,' she murmured as she turned the pages of the guidebook. 'Ah, here we are…' she said, as she found floor plans of the different levels. She quickly became immersed in what she saw.

Don stood beside her quietly, and she jumped when she became aware of him again.

'Oh!' she exclaimed. 'I didn't know you were there. You don't have to wait for me. I'll be fine.'

'It's okay,' Don replied lightly, 'I'll wait.' He knew that Fay was already beginning to drift into another world, and for now he decided to go along with it rather than try to bring it to her attention. The others had disappeared from view. He had no doubt that they would be looking for him and Fay in an hour or so, and he concentrated entirely upon what Fay seemed to want to do.

'I'd like to see the chapel, of course,' he heard her say, 'but let's go inside the main building first and spend some time there.' Then she strode off in the direction of the main door. She hesitated for a minute as she reached it, and glanced upwards to study the stonework above the door; but seeing nothing in particular, she went inside. 'It's frustrating,' she commented. 'This guidebook is very informative, but I haven't got the time and concentration to read all of it through at the moment. It gets in the way of looking at things. I'm wishing now that we'd found a way of getting one before we came.'

'Tell you what,' said Don in the same light tones as he had used before, 'I'll bring you back next month if you later find you've missed something important.'

'Thanks, Don,' Fay replied, 'but I'll be fine. I expect you'll be busy, and I'll just come back on my own.'

'We can talk about that nearer the time,' Don suggested carefully. 'Hey, this fireplace is a decent size,' he said as he drew her attention to it.

Fay continued to study the book. 'It gives such detail, but I see that not many of the rooms are open to the public. However, they're hoping to prepare more of them in the future, it says.'

'It might be worth coming each year then,' Don suggested.

'I'd like that,' Fay replied happily.

'Which room would you like to see first?' asked Don.

'Hold on a minute,' said Fay. 'Look, Don, there's a map of the house and grounds at the back. Let's see exactly where that chapel is.' She scrutinised the map. 'I can't see it,' she said disappointedly.

'Let me have a look,' said Don, opening his copy. 'Ah! I can see what the problem is. See this key in the corner? They've used rather an unusual symbol for it. It's a square with a "c" inside. That's pretty unconventional.'

'It must have been an inexperienced person who drew up the map,' said Fay.

'I think you're right,' Don agreed. 'It's pretty diagrammatic.'

'I've got it now,' said Fay. 'It's near the perimeter of the grounds, and as far as I can see there isn't a track up to it, only a footpath. We can go with the others before we leave.'

Don nodded.

'I wonder if there's any reference to Morna in the guidebook,' said Fay as she flicked through the pages.

'I think we should start looking round,' Don advised. 'You never know what we might see.'

They made their way to the staircase at the far end of the hall and began to ascend slowly, looking at the paintings that lined the walls.

'This reminds me of going up the stairs at the barn conversion,' said Fay. 'Of course, this is very much larger, and there are far more paintings, but the quality and variety of them is very similar.'

'Let's go and see the large upstairs sitting room that's shown in this plan,' said Don. 'It's definitely open to the public, and the description says there's some interesting furniture. If we turn to the left on the first landing we should find it.'

Fay followed Don as he left the staircase, but she looked up at the wall as she went, reluctant to miss any of the paintings.

'Don! Don! Look at this!' she gasped. 'I can hardly believe it!'

Don spun round to join her and looked at the painting she was fixed on.

'That looks familiar,' he said slowly.

'It's the building in my dream,' Fay told him emphatically.

'Are you sure? It doesn't look quite like Helen's version.'

'I know,' Fay agreed irritably. 'It's less ruined, but it's definitely the same building.'

There was no sign on the wall to indicate who had done the painting or what it depicted. Fay reached up uncertainly as if to look on the back of it.

Don took hold of her arm. 'Better not do that,' he advised. 'It might be alarmed, and in any case, it might fall down and get damaged. Let's have a look to see if there's anything in the book first. After that we'll try and find someone to ask.'

'Have you got your camera with you?' Fay asked urgently.

'Yes, I've got it in my pocket.'

'Take a photograph.'

'I can't. I mean... we'll have to get permission.'

Fay sagged. 'Please help me, Don,' she said desperately.

'Let's find somewhere to sit,' Don suggested. 'We'll have a look to see what it says in the book. After that I'll go and speak to someone about it.'

They found some wooden chairs that appeared to be for the use of visitors, settled themselves, and began to read the section about the stairway, but it revealed nothing about the origin of the paintings.

'Right,' said Don. 'You stay here and I'll go off to hunt for someone.'

Fay watched him disappear lithely down the stairs. There was no one in sight. She felt exhausted and wished she could lie down. It's astounding, she thought. I knew we'd find something, but I'd never guessed it would be this.

She decided to read the section on the chapel while she was waiting, and discovered that it was the ruin of a building that was much older than the house. Apparently some sources thought it might have been a late addition to the local monastery before it fell into disrepair. How fascinating, she mused.

Not aware of what she was doing, she lifted her right hand to her left shoulder as if to reassure herself of something. Then she put the guidebook on the chair beside her and used both hands. She felt a series of sharp stabs in the thumb of her left hand and winced. 'A monk was buried here,' she murmured.

She felt confused. 'Where am I?' she whispered. 'I'm so cold. I must get out of here...' She stood up and began to move towards the stairs, leaving her book behind as something that was irrelevant to her now. She made her way slowly down the stairway, keeping in the shadows next to the wall that bore the paintings. She was relieved not to meet anyone. There were people near the fireplace in the entrance hall. She looked at them anxiously, and then darted behind the staircase and through a small door into servants' quarters. She seemed to know exactly where she was going.

Minutes later she was out in the sun at the back. She was startled by the large coloured objects with wheels that almost filled the courtyard. 'What are they?' she muttered with fear in her voice. She started to run.

She ran towards the fields and the woods beyond. Her breath was coming in short gasps and her knees felt as if they would buckle beneath her. She had to reach the chapel and find the grave. She must. It was her only chance.

When she reached the woods she had to slow her pace to a walk. She pushed her way through the low branches on the path she was sure she could see. The branches stuck into her clothing and scratched her arms, but she hardly noticed or cared. The grave… she must find the grave. She stumbled, turned her ankle and stifled a cry. I must keep quiet, she thought desperately. No one must find me. No one must stop me. She limped as she pressed on. The pain in her ankle was severe, but she ignored it as best she could. She lost a shoe and tried to keep going, but the discomfort was too great and she went back to find it.

At length she could make out the shape of the chapel through the remaining trees. Now she would be saved. She would find the grave and then… She tripped on a root, fell forward and everything went black.

When she came round she was lying on her side next to a piece of fallen masonry. Her head hurt terribly. She put her hand to her forehead and felt something sticky. Blood… And there was blood on her cheek too. How long she had been lying there she did not know.

'Where on earth am I?' she asked aloud. She looked at her watch, but the face was smashed and the hands were broken. 'That's not any good,' she observed. She tried to stand up, but her ankle gave way beneath her and she sank back down into the vegetation. She groaned. 'Whatever's happened to me means I can't do much,' she murmured. It was then she remembered that she had gone out somewhere with Don, Helen and Peter. 'I wonder where they are?' she asked the tree next to her. 'Lawerlocke Hall… Lawerlocke Hall! That's where we went.' She felt excited that she had remembered something at least. 'Yes. I'd been looking forward to the trip.' Try not to worry, she told herself. I'm sure someone will notice I'm missing. I don't know where I am, but surely someone will find me eventually.

She began to realise how shocked she felt. I suppose I must have hit my head on this stone, and I've obviously done something to my ankle, she thought. She examined it cautiously. It hurt whichever way she tried to move it, and she certainly couldn't put any weight on it. It was quite swollen too. There was blood on her arms from the scratches she had sustained, but she could see that these were only superficial. She began to shiver. I wish I had something warm to put on, she thought. I wonder how long it will be before someone finds me?

There seemed to be some sounds in the distance. At first Fay discounted them as fantasies of her bruised head, but she gradually became sure that they were audible and distinct. Yes, something was coming closer, although she could not guess what it was. I hope it isn't something I can't cope with, she thought nervously. One thing is certain, I can't escape.

'Here it is,' said a voice.

'Let's have a good search round,' said Don.

'Don!' she shouted. 'I'm here!'

'Keep shouting, Fay,' he called. 'I'll soon find you.'

Minutes later he burst through the trees and saw her. 'Fay,' he said. 'Thank goodness!' He saw immediately that she was shivering, and he took off his jumper and put it on her.

Then Peter arrived. 'I'll phone the others and tell them we've found her,' he said quickly when he had absorbed the scene. 'Then we'll decide how we're going to get Fay back to the car.'

'I think it's best not to try to talk about anything until we get you back,' Don told Fay. 'You've got a nasty gash on your head, and we'll need to get it seen to.'

'My ankle…' Fay managed to say, pointing to her injury.

'It looks as if we'll need to keep you off that,' Peter observed.

'We're going to have to carry you, Fay,' said Don. 'The first bit will be the worst. It's about twenty yards to the path.'

'The path?' Fay echoed weakly.

‘You’ll soon see,’ said Peter. ‘If you put an arm round my shoulders and the other round Don’s we’ll lift you up and get you there. Just say if you are uncomfortable and need a rest.’

When they reached the path, Fay could see it was quite wide and was covered with woodchips – the kind that were used to keep public paths dry and easy to walk on. Don and Peter made their way along it without much difficulty, with Fay in between them, resting only once or twice before they reached a Range Rover that was waiting for them near the edge of the woods. The driver introduced himself as Jake, and he helped to lift Fay into the back and make her comfortable, before driving very slowly back to the Hall.

‘Oh, Mum!’ said Helen aghast, when she saw her. ‘What happened?’

‘I don’t seem to know,’ Fay replied apologetically.

‘Never mind. The main thing is that you’re safe,’ Helen said reassuringly.

‘I think we ought to take you up to the hospital,’ Peter advised. ‘You might need a stitch in your head, and your ankle certainly needs to be X-rayed.’

‘Thanks very much for your help, Jake,’ said Don, shaking the man’s hand after he had helped to get Fay into the car.

‘Give us a ring any time, Don,’ said Joan and Jim before he drove away.

The visit to the hospital was uneventful. There was quite a long wait before they saw a doctor, who decided to put a stitch in the gash in Fay’s forehead. The X-ray revealed that nothing was broken, and Fay was given instructions to rest her ankle, before embarking on a course of physiotherapy.

On the way back home, Helen began to plan how to help Fay to get cleaned up.

‘The shower would be best,’ she said, ‘but if you can’t stand up it’s going to be difficult. The last thing we want is for you to slip in the bath and hurt yourself even more.’

‘How about taking you round to Joan and Jim’s?’ Don suggested. ‘They’ve got a shower with a folding seat. You know – in the extension.’

‘That’s a brilliant idea, Dad,’ said Helen. ‘You could drop us off there, and we'll phone you when we're finished.'

Joan and Jim tried to persuade them to stay on for something to eat, but Fay was adamant that she wanted to go home. Once there she lay on the sofa, and Don boiled some rice at her request, giving her some before converting it into a vegetarian dish for the rest of them.

'You're looking a bit better now,' said Helen as she sat beside the sofa eating from a bowl. 'You looked ghastly when they brought you back to the Hall.'

'I'm not surprised,' said Fay. 'I *felt* ghastly.'

'I think you should tell us exactly what happened,' said Helen.

'There's not much to tell. I came round not knowing where I was, and gradually I remembered that it had all started off with a day out – the four of us, together with Joan and Jim. How on earth I ended up where I did, I don't know.'

'Do you remember anything about the painting?' asked Don quietly from his seat at the other side of where she was lying.

'You mean the one I did with Helen last night? Yes, of course I do.'

'No, not that painting,' said Don patiently. He waited for a while before adding, 'Do you remember leaving your handbag and your guidebook anywhere?'

'My guidebook!' exclaimed Fay. 'I wanted to read through it when we got home. Have you got it?'

'Yes. And your handbag,' said Don steadily.

'Where did I leave them?'

'On a chair near the first landing of the main staircase in Lawerlocke Hall,' said Don deliberately. 'That's where I left you when I went off to see if I could find anyone who could tell us more about that painting. Don't you remember? You wanted me to photograph it.'

Fay looked stunned. 'Yes, I remember now,' she said. 'It's amazing that I'd completely forgotten all of that.' She was silent for a few minutes, and then said urgently, 'Did you find anyone? Did you take a photograph?'

'I took a couple,' Don reassured her. 'But no one knew anything about the picture. I asked the woman in the booth at the front where I could find out, and she said if there was any information it would be on a plaque beside the picture, or in the guidebook.'

'Pass me a guidebook.'

Don passed one across, and she began to search its pages feverishly.

'It's no good,' said Helen. 'I searched through it several times to try and find some clue as to where you might be. There's nothing about the picture.'

'But you haven't seen it,' said Fay.

'I have,' said Helen simply. 'Dad showed it to us after we were sure you were lost.'

'Yes,' Don explained. 'At first I thought you'd gone to find the toilets, although I must admit I thought it odd that you'd left your things behind. I took a couple of photos of the picture, and waited. When you didn't reappear, I picked up your things and went off in search of the others, thinking that I'd find you with them.'

'We met up with Dad in the kitchens,' Helen said, continuing the story. 'Peter and I had been there for a while. I found them fascinating. Joan and Jim had just joined us when Dad appeared. I wondered why he was carrying your handbag, and then he told us he couldn't find you. I got really worried, and we went and found a member of staff, and a search party was called together.'

'It was then that I remembered you had wanted to see the chapel before we left,' said Don. 'So I took Helen to the seat where I'd left you and pointed out the painting, and then Peter and I followed the signs to the path to the chapel. That's how we got to you.'

'There weren't any signs the way I went,' said Fay suddenly. 'I went along the path through the trees.'

Don stared at her. 'But there isn't a path through the trees,' he said.

'Perhaps that's why you're so badly scratched,' Helen suggested. 'Perhaps you thought there was a path and forced your way through.'

'Now that you say that, I do have a vague memory of pushing at twigs…' said Fay. 'I was trying to get to the grave.' She reached up to her left shoulder. 'My thumb…' she said. 'I've got to get to the grave…' She struggled to sit up, but fell back exhausted on the sofa.

'What is it, Mum?' asked Helen, her voice full of sympathy. 'You've had a really rough time. Just take it slowly. What are you trying to tell us about a grave? It seems to be something to do with that stabbing you had before in your thumb.'

'My brooch…' Fay muttered.

'Fay seemed to be fumbling at her shoulder,' Peter pointed out. 'Fay, did you think you stabbed your thumb on the pin of the brooch?'

Fay looked across at him gratefully. 'Peter, you're right,' she said. 'After that I knew I had to go to the monk's grave.'

'Which monk?' asked Don gently.

Fay stared at him blankly for a moment, and then her face took on a look of certainty. 'The curse of the two kinds of happenings. I've got to lay the curse to rest. Helen, that's the task… *our* task.'

There was complete silence in the room. No one spoke and no one wanted to speak. What Fay had said was complete in itself. There were many unanswered questions surrounding it, but now she had revealed the task to them, and there seemed to be nothing to add.

A considerable length of time passed without any sound. The room was entirely still until Fay herself spoke. 'Don,' she said, 'you asked about the monk. I'm afraid I don't know the answer yet, but please will you pass me the photograph of Brother M.'

Don went to get it, and handed it to her.

As she lay and contemplated it she said, 'It's so strange how much it reminds me of Reverend Howard. Even he thought that. What do you all think?' she asked as she handed it to Peter.

'I think there's certainly a surprising resemblance,' Peter agreed, before handing it to Helen.

'It doesn't impact on me so much,' she said. 'The thing that affects me most is his clothing – his habit.'

'Why's that?' asked Don.

'I'm afraid I can't explain it,' Helen replied.

'I want to go to church in the morning,' said Fay determinedly.

Helen was shocked. 'But you can't go like this, Mum,' she said. 'You can't even stand up.'

Fay looked tearful. 'I've got to go,' she insisted. 'Please help me.'

'I think the church has a couple of wheelchairs in the store room at the back,' said Don. He looked at the clock. 'I'll phone Reverend Howard and ask. It's not too late.' He picked up the phone and keyed in the number. There was no reply, so he left a message on the answering service.

'I hope he'll ring back,' said Fay anxiously.

'If he doesn't I can go round to the church in the morning an hour before the service and have a good look,' suggested Peter.

Fay relaxed visibly. 'Thank you so much, Peter,' she said.

'I think I'm going to have to do some research into the history of the chapel,' said Don. 'I might not find anything, but at least I can try.'

'It was Reverend Howard who told me that it was thought there was a small monastery somewhere between here and Lawerlocke Hall,' said Fay. 'Perhaps he knows something about the chapel, or…' She stopped and considered for a moment before carrying on. '… or maybe there might be something about it in the rest of that pile of files that came from his brother.'

'It's an outside chance,' said Don, 'but we mustn't discount the possibility. Fay, when I took the photos of the painting at the Hall, it was with my digital camera. Would you like me to print them for you straight away?'

Fay's eyes shone. 'Yes… Yes, please, Don.'

He switched on the computer that stood in the alcove by the fireplace. 'Just keep on talking,' he directed. 'I'll be as quick as I can.'

'I think I should get some ice to put on your ankle,' said Helen thoughtfully. 'I should have thought of it before.'

'There are bags of ice cubes in the freezer,' said Fay. She put her hand to her forehead and winced. 'I could do with a bag to put on here as well,' she remarked wryly.

When Helen returned, she helped Fay to use the packs. 'We should keep doing this for you until we go to bed,' she decided.

The phone rang, and Peter picked it up. 'This is the Bowden household,' he said. 'Oh, Reverend Howard. Thanks for phoning back. Yes… it's Fay who's hurt her ankle, and she'd like to come to the service in the morning. Right… so if we arrive about ten minutes early we'll be fine. Thanks… I'll let her know.' He turned to Fay. 'It's all fixed,' he said. 'The chair will be in the vestibule at the back with your name pinned on it.'

'Thanks, Peter,' said Fay, wiping water off her cheek.

'It shouldn't be long now,' said Don's voice from the corner of the room.

Fay could hear the sound of the printer slowly producing the first photograph.

'Let me see,' said Helen as Don handed the finished product across with a warning about the wet ink. 'I barely glanced at it at the Hall, and as I said, there was no mention of it in the book. Gosh! No wonder it blew Mum away!' she exclaimed as she examined it. 'It's just like that ruin I painted, except that it's less ruined.' She held it up in front of Fay, who stared at it hungrily, taking in every detail.

When Don had finished printing the second one, he passed it across to Peter to see.

'I can see exactly what you mean.' Peter's usual equanimity was clearly disturbed. 'I feel quite rattled by this.'

Fay's voice projected itself calmly into the room. 'Can everyone stop talking for a while, please? I'm getting some flashes of the whole building and those people with the strange head covers again. I wish I knew more about architecture through the ages,' she said. 'It might help us.'

'Do you think it's the same era as Lawerlocke Hall, or do you think it's earlier?' asked Don.

'My guess is that it's earlier,' said Fay. 'Possibly early seventeenth century. But who am I to say?'

'I'm sure I could get hold of some illustrations of houses from that period for you,' said Don. 'That should help.'

'It's fading now,' said Fay. 'But I've got a clearer idea of it than I had before.'

'Fay,' said Don, 'that's great, but I think we ought to get you to bed soon, especially as you want to go to church in the morning. Things have been happening thick and fast today, and I don't think we're going to get any more answers if we stay up talking any later.'

'I wonder whether to sleep here on the sofa tonight, Don,' Fay began.

'I think there ought to be someone with you through the night,' Don insisted. 'But I can see it's going to be difficult getting you up the stairs, so I'll bring down the spare mattress and sleep on the floor here. By the way, I'm not going to listen to any protests, so don't make any,' he said as Fay opened her mouth to speak.

'I was only going to say I thought that was a good idea,' she said.

Chapter Twenty-one

The following morning Don rose early. Fay was sound asleep, so he went into the garden to stretch his legs, but soon returned to check that she was all right. After that he waited quietly until Helen came downstairs, before he went out for a short stroll. The events of the previous day had shaken him more than he liked to admit, and he wanted a little time to let his mind freewheel before deciding what to do next.

He returned to the house later, having resolved to phone Joan and Jim to ask them to come round in the afternoon and possibly stay through the evening. He felt an urgent need to tell them about everything, and to have them involved in any discussions that might take place that day. When he returned to the house he phoned straight away, and arranged that they would come round at about four.

Fay was very sore when she tried to move, and it took a long time to get her clothes changed ready for church. She wasn't hungry, and she sat and sipped water while the others ate breakfast. Helping her into the car was a painful process, as was unloading her outside the church. Peter went to collect the wheelchair, and pushed her carefully down the path and into the back of the church.

Reverend Howard greeted them.

'Hello, Fay,' he said. 'I'm so sorry about your accident. When you've recovered, we must arrange another time for you to come and look through the files with me. I haven't touched them since you were last here.'

'Would you mind if I come with her?' asked Don.

'Of course not,' the Reverend replied. 'You're very welcome.'

'Among other things, we're keen to find out more about that monastery that used to exist between here and Lawerlocke Hall, and about the chapel at the perimeter of its grounds,' Don explained.

'Surely,' said the Reverend, before moving on to greet another family.

Fay found the service very moving. There were several well-known hymns, but there was also a religious song from Greece, sung by a young boy. The sermon was based on appreciation of the work done all over the world by Amnesty International, and all the money from the collection was to be donated to that organisation. Reverend Howard stressed the problem of double standards in many countries, where a glossy 'shop front' belied the torture that was going on in secret. Most of the prayers were for those who suffered such torture, often in isolation, and for the enlightenment of those in power, so that they might give up cruel practices.

'I knew I had to come this morning,' Fay whispered to Don as they waited for everyone to file out. 'Despite my whole body hurting, I feel uplifted by the service.'

She found she had to lie down again as soon as they got home. Helen made her comfortable on the sofa once more, bringing extra pillows to prop her up so that she could see everyone more easily. She was able to eat some more rice for lunch, and Helen produced some bendy straws out of a drawer in the kitchen so that she could drink without having to sit up.

'I didn't know we had these,' Fay commented, as Helen let her choose a colour.

'You'd forgotten, but I hadn't,' said Helen, smiling.

'I think I'm going to read the guidebook,' Fay announced after everyone had eaten. 'I'd like to familiarise myself with it as thoroughly as I can before Joan and Jim come round.'

Helen passed her a copy, and soon she was engrossed.

The others sat round quietly. Peter was reading more of the book that Don had lent him about the church, Helen was reading another copy of the guidebook and Don had returned to his book about the CIA spy.

At four fifteen there was a ring at the door, and Helen went to let Joan and Jim in.

'Hi, Fay,' said Jim as he came into the room. 'How's your egg?'

Fay looked puzzled. 'What do you mean, Jim?' she asked.

'Your head,' he explained. 'You should have seen it yesterday. Maybe Don should have taken a photo.'

'I don't think I would have wanted to be reminded,' said Fay.

'I know. I'm just fooling,' said Jim apologetically.

'Have my seat, Joan,' said Peter politely, getting up from an easy chair. 'I'll go and get one of the dining chairs.'

'I'll come with you, Peter,' said Jim. 'I'll need one as well.'

When everyone was seated, the four brought Joan and Jim up to date. Then Don showed them the photographs he had taken of the painting at the Hall.

'It's almost too much to take in,' Joan said when they had finished.

'I'm floundering,' Jim admitted. 'How are you feeling now, Fay?' he asked. 'It's bad enough to be covered in scrapes and bruises with your ankle half wrenched off, but now you've got all this going on in your head as well.'

'But at least we have some idea of what your task is,' said Joan slowly. 'That's a huge step forward, and it's very exciting. It's a great shame that Paul and Diana aren't with us this weekend. It feels wrong without them.'

The others agreed. 'Perhaps we should give them a ring,' suggested Don. 'We really should let them know.'

He handed the phone across to Joan and Jim who were soon talking intently to Diana and Paul.

Realising that the conversation was going to take some time, Fay returned to her book with her mind still half on what Joan and Jim were saying. It took them about half an hour to update the astonished Diana and Paul. At the end of the call, Diana made them promise to phone again in the evening to let them know if there was anything new. Before they rang off, Jim handed the phone round for everyone to say hello to the others.

'Make sure and take care of yourself,' Diana said to Fay when it was her turn. 'We want to see you safe and well when we come in two weeks' time, but I'll be speaking to you again this evening. Bye for now.'

Fay rang off, and turning to the others said, 'I've just got to a strange bit in the guide. Can I read it out to you? Actually, it's very upsetting. I hadn't noticed it before, but I don't think that's surprising, because it's written in very small print underneath a picture of Sir William Trethonas.'

'What page is it on, Mum?' asked Helen.

'Thirteen,' replied Fay. 'That unpleasant looking man is Sir William.'

'Got it,' said Helen, and she waited for Fay to begin.

'*Sir William Trethonas was a close friend of Samuel Locke, the merchant who built Lawerlocke Hall, until his evil doings came to light.*'

'I wonder what he was up to?' asked Jim.

'Wait a minute and you'll find out,' replied Fay, and she read on. '*A servant maid died choking due to his bestial practices.*'

'How awful!' exclaimed Joan. 'Does it say anything else?'

'Yes, there's a bit more.' She continued. '*The Head Gardener came upon them, but he could not save her. Although he dragged Sir William off her, she was already dead. When Samuel Locke found out, Sir William was properly punished. He was chased out of the shire by the Hunt, and posters were pasted everywhere to expose what he had done. He fled abroad, and it is believed he was killed by savages.*'

'So justice was done,' said Don, 'although it took a little while.'

'It's difficult to know what to do with someone like that – even nowadays,' said Jim. 'It isn't just that he killed someone, it's the way he did it, and the fact that he was abusing his position as a local dignitary when he approached the serving maid in the first place. It must have been terrible for her. The shock of it must have been enormous.'

'That's right,' Peter agreed. 'Working for Samuel Locke, she would have been used to being treated kindly, whereas Sir William treated her worse than if she'd been an animal.'

'It's hard to think about such terrible suffering,' said Helen. 'The sermon this morning certainly opened my mind beyond what I had considered before, and now this.' She looked pale and anguished.

'I believe it's up to every one of us to do whatever we can to address cruelty and brutality in the world,' said Fay. 'What I can do on a practical level is quite limited, but I do think about it frequently.'

'So do I,' Joan agreed. 'And in my book it doesn't matter whether one calls that prayer or positive thought. I believe that both have some power to affect outcomes.'

'I'm so glad we've got someone like Reverend Howard, who isn't afraid to talk about deeper thought and concern for others in the context of a number of religious orientations,' said Helen. 'I wish I had the confidence to speak out like he does.'

'You will, Helen,' said Fay. 'Your confidence will grow, and you will be able to speak out for what you believe. You will be able to speak out with your own voice, and with the courage of your own convictions. And your convictions will be well grounded, based on proper care and concern for everybody in the world.'

Helen stared at her mother. Fay's head was badly bruised, and she was quite pallid. Lying there on the sofa she looked quite weak, yet her voice had taken on a kind of power that was arresting and deeply moving.

'You've just said something very important, Fay,' said Don.

'I know,' Fay replied. Her voice sounded completely exhausted, but she went on. 'I realise it's to do with the task.'

'That's what I thought when you were speaking,' said Joan. 'But it's taken all your strength, and you're trying to recover from your illness as well as from the shock of the fall you had yesterday. I feel very worried about you.'

There was a murmur of agreement from everyone else in the room.

'Perhaps we should leave you to rest now…' Jim began.

'No! Please don't leave me,' said Fay, almost shouting. She stopped, her mind whirling, and then corrected herself. 'Sorry, I was muddled. I don't quite know why I shouted. What I meant to say was that I want to keep talking over what's been happening. I know that will help us all, me included.'

'Joan and I could go home and get something to eat and then come back this evening,' Jim suggested reasonably. 'You can phone if there's anything urgent.'

'Mum, I think he's right,' said Helen. 'I agree we should keep on talking, and I want to do that, but you should have a break – it will help your body to recover.'

'You might be right,' Fay began uncertainly, 'but I'm not sure. I've come to understand that getting better from my illness not only means resting, but also means understanding what I need to do to free myself from the past. Whether it's past lives or my past in this life, the need is the same. I have to see what it is that's holding me back and keeping me unwell. And I have to find a way of talking about it that will bring more meaning into my life now, with my growing knowledge of our task.'

‘I understand what you’re saying about your illness, Fay,’ said Peter, ‘but I think Jim’s right about your recovery from the shock of your fall yesterday. You’ve had a nasty bang on your head, and we need to take that into account. If it were just your ankle it would be bad enough, but physically you need quiet time to let your head recover.’

‘Try not to worry, Fay,’ said Don. ‘Having a break now doesn’t mean we won’t be talking about the things that are important to us all. In fact it might help each of us to have some time to think through what we’ve learned.’

‘That’s particularly so for Jim and myself,’ said Joan.

‘Thanks, everyone,’ said Fay. ‘I can see things more clearly now, and I think it would be a good thing if I rest for a while. Can you come back around eight, unless of course we phone before that?’

‘That’s fine by us,’ Joan replied, looking across at Jim, who nodded and stood up to leave.

When they had gone, Fay said, ‘Perhaps you could draw the curtains and leave me here on my own for a while. I won’t have anything to eat, thanks. I feel a bit sick. I might have some more rice later on.’

‘I’ll leave you with some water,’ said Helen as she arranged the curtains, ‘and I’ll have another look at the guidebook while the others are working in the kitchen.’

Fay discovered that she was grateful to have time to herself. She was glad to be with the others, but she also needed time to let her thoughts freewheel; and with the assurance of knowing that she would be seeing everyone again quite soon, she was able to relax while allowing her mind to wander. She closed her eyes.

At first her mind seemed to be blank, but then she became aware of the sensation of twigs scratching her arms. I’m remembering going through the trees to the chapel, she thought. She felt exhilarated, as she longed to learn more about what it all meant. I saw the painting, Don went to find someone, I hurt my thumb again, I went down the stairs… But although she had images of running to the woods and forcing her way through the trees, she got no further.

Sir William… What a revolting man, she mused. Involuntarily she put her hand to her throat. That’s odd, she said to herself, my throat feels very strange. She picked up the glass of water from the coffee table next to her, and she sucked slowly through the straw. That was better. The cool liquid soothed the unpleasant sensation. She wondered about the serving maid. Had she been someone who had come to the Hall to work? Or was she perhaps the daughter of one of the existing servants? How old had she been when she died? The account in the book had given no indication of the answers to these questions. Fay found herself wishing that she had some way of finding out, but had no idea why it was so important to her. Surely the important thing was to feel sadness that these terrible things had happened. The picture of Sir William suggested that he was probably in his late forties, but that did not answer the question of the age of the servant.

Once again Fay's throat felt uncomfortable, and she sipped some more of the water. However, this time it did not seem to help, and the sensation became more and more intense. In fact, she started to feel as if she were choking.

She managed to call out, 'Helen… Help me!'

Immediately Helen appeared through the door. 'What is it, Mum?' she asked.

She could see Fay was struggling with something at her throat. She knelt down beside her and said firmly, 'I think you should sit up, Mum. I'll help.' She struggled to help her mother into a sitting position, and at the same time called out for Don. 'Dad, I think you should come,' she said as loudly as she possibly could without appearing to panic. Then she put cushions at Fay's back to keep her upright while she went to draw the curtains. 'I think it's probably best to have some daylight at the moment,' she said with a show of confidence.

'What is it?' asked Don as he came into the room. 'Peter said he could hear someone calling and I came straight away. What happened?'

'I don't know exactly,' said Helen. 'I heard Mum call for me, and I found her clutching at her throat. I thought it best to sit her up.'

Don could see that Fay was as white as a sheet, but he was relieved to find she seemed to be entirely lucid.

'Helen did the right thing,' she said. 'I thought I was choking, but the sensation has eased since she came and helped me to sit up…' She appeared to be about to say something else, and Don and Helen waited patiently to give her time. Then, making an obvious effort to steady herself, she told them, 'I think this has happened before.'

Don and Helen looked at each other, unable to conceal their alarm. 'When?' they asked together.

'Don, remember the day you phoned to see how I'd got on at Reverend Howard's?'

'Of course. How could I forget? I was worried out of my skull until Helen managed to get hold of Jim on his mobile and he came round with Joan.'

'You told me later that I hadn't recognised them at first.'

'That's right,' said Don. 'You screamed out for Helen and I told them to get the photos of her from upstairs. It was only after you had them in your hands that you gradually came round.'

'I want you both to listen carefully to what I'm going to say,' Fay began. 'And I don't want you to ask me anything until I've finished.'

'Okay,' said Don. 'I'll ask Peter to keep the food from burning. Hang on a minute.'

When he returned, Fay explained. 'I'm sure that when they came round that day this is what was happening to me then. The difference today was that I wasn't on my own, and, very importantly, Helen herself was here. This time I had been talking to all of you about our trip to the Hall, and when you all left me to rest I began to remember how I had run out of the Hall and through the woods. After that I'd been thinking about the poor servant who was killed by Sir William, and it was just then that my throat started to trouble me. You told me before that Jim said I was writhing on the floor clutching at my throat when he found me.'

'Is it okay for me to say something now?' asked Don.

'Yes, please do.'

'You've missed something out. When you came back from the vicarage with the photographs – including the one of Brother M beside the chapel – you looked at them, and then you listened to that CD of Mozart quartets.'

'That's right,' Fay agreed. 'But what has that to do with today?'

'The music was being played on original instruments,' Don explained, 'and that meant you were being given an idea of how it would have sounded in Mozart's lifetime. He was born around the middle of the 1700s. You never know, but perhaps some of that music was played at Lawerlocke Hall towards the end of that century.'

A shiver ran down Helen's spine. 'You mean around the time the servant was suffocated by Sir William?'

'It's not impossible,' said Don.

'But what on earth does all of this mean?' Fay's voice sounded agonised. 'Who am I?'

'You're Fay Bowden, of course,' said Don steadily. 'Apart from that, you've got some particular connection with what happened to one or possibly two other people in history.'

'And we think that it's got some link with our task,' Helen added.

Peter's head came round the door. 'I can see you're tied up,' he said, 'so I've put everything in casserole dishes in the oven on a low heat. Can I join you?'

'Yes, please,' said Fay eagerly.

After they had recounted everything to him, Peter concluded, 'And so you think you're in touch with the lives of two young women from the past?'

'I really don't know what to make of it,' Fay admitted, 'but as far as I can see there are two possible explanations. One of them is this business of past lives. If that woman in *Russian Voices* can be so sure that she can remember various past lives and how she died, then perhaps the same could be true for me.'

'Her account is very convincing,' Don acknowledged.

'I agree with that,' said Peter, while Helen nodded emphatically.

Fay continued. 'The other explanation that comes to mind is something I've thought about on and off for years.'

'What's that?' asked Helen.

'I've often wondered if the resonance of traumatic events lingers on in the atmosphere, and if someone is around who is sensitive to this, that person may pick up the emotions or even images of what happened a long time ago.'

'You haven't spoken to me about this before,' said Don.

'I didn't think you would be interested.'

'I'm very sorry I've given you that impression,' said Don, 'but I suppose my mind's never been focussed on this kind of thing before.'

'If this is to do with past lives of mine, I think there are definitely two,' said Fay.

'Which do you think came first?' asked Helen.

Fay thought carefully. 'I'm glad you asked that, Helen,' she said. 'This is something I need to put my mind to.' She looked at the clock. 'It won't be all that long before Joan and Jim come back. Do you think you could all go and eat your meal now? Leave the door ajar so that I can hear you, and I'll think about it until the others arrive.'

It wasn't long before they were all assembled in the sitting room once more.

'I'm staggered about this choking thing,' said Jim, when the others described what had happened. 'But I'm glad something's gradually taking shape about it. It was very worrying indeed, Fay, when Joan and I found you like that.'

Joan nodded and looked upset.

'After that I rearranged my work so I didn't have to leave you alone again,' said Don.

'I hadn't realised it was only because of that,' said Fay. 'But I suppose I'm not surprised now that I know a bit more about it.' She paused and then looked across at Helen. 'I've been thinking about your question,' she said. 'If I'm remembering two past lives, the first one is Morna's and the second is the servant girl's.'

'Supposing we go down that route for a while,' said Peter. 'That means that the ruined building dates from an earlier time than Lawerlocke Hall. Would that fit?'

'This is why I'm very keen to get some pictures of seventeenth and possibly sixteenth century rural estate buildings for Fay to look at,' said Don.

'Morna died in the tunnel underneath the building I first saw in my dream,' said Fay slowly, 'and the servant girl died at Lawerlocke Hall, although we don't know exactly where.'

'Maybe the chapel is the common factor here,' Peter reflected. 'We should try to find out exactly how old it is, but it must have existed throughout that period.'

'The house that became ruined might be miles away from the chapel,' Helen pointed out.

'That's true,' Peter agreed, 'but on the other hand it might not. I can't claim to be a historian, but I've quite often heard of buildings being erected on the site of a previous one that had collapsed or had fallen into disrepair, and according to the guidebook Lawerlocke Hall is one of these.'

‘Where did you read that?’ asked Helen. Then she smiled and said, ‘Peter the methodical person who never misses a detail has something important to tell us. I’ve only been skimming the book, trying to find answers to particular questions. Come on, Peter, tell us.’

‘It’s on page five,’ he said, opening a copy that was handy. ‘It doesn’t say much.’ He read it out: ‘*It is known that Lawerlocke Hall was built on the site of a substantial but smaller building, which may itself have been built on the site of previous habitation.*’

‘I must say I felt a bit odd when I saw the basement level of the Hall,’ Fay admitted. ‘If what Peter is suggesting is correct, then that would be the site of the tunnel where Morna died. I don’t want to draw definite conclusions from any of this, but can we go on and see how the chapel might link into it all? I certainly had a very intense urge to get to the chapel. It was the only thing in my mind when I was running.’

‘That’s important to remember,’ said Peter. ‘It could have been that you felt you were running away *from* something, but from what you say, you were concentrating on running *to* something – the chapel.’

‘It could have been for sanctuary,’ Joan suggested.

‘That’s possible,’ said Fay, ‘except that I wanted to find a particular grave there. That was my overwhelming desire. In fact, when I mention it now, I feel desperately upset that I didn’t get to it. Instead I hit my head and knocked myself out. It was the grave I wanted, and that was why I was heading to the chapel.’

‘You first knew about the chapel from the photograph of Brother M,’ said Don slowly. ‘When we got to the Hall, you were very keen to see where it was on the map, although you wanted to go at the end of the visit, and you were clear that you wanted everyone to be there.’

‘Brother M’s snake belt had quite an effect on me,’ said Fay.

‘You must have associated it with the carvings,’ said Peter.

‘Yes,’ said Fay, ‘but what does it mean? Let me think for a minute. I couldn’t see the snakes in the photographs of the two carvings in the stonework, but I saw them clearly in my mind’s eye when I was working on copying them, and with Don’s help we got the patterns on the upper part of the two snakes. There has never been any doubt about the snake pattern of Morna’s brooch. When I saw Brother M at first, I didn’t see that his rope was really a snake belt.’

Fay looked thoughtful. 'Mm,' she said. 'There's something here about being able to see behind what is at first apparent… isn't there?' She paused and looked at the others, who encouraged her to keep following her train of thought to see where it led.

She continued. 'Brother M reminded me of Reverend Howard, and the Reverend himself agreed. The carving on the archway of the farm where I used to live… I never noticed it when I lived there, but Don's photographs revealed it. I was excited about seeing the photograph in the book – the one of the mansion house that used to be next to the farm – and then seeing the carving above the door. There's a link between my feeling of home attached to that mansion and my feeling about the ruin in the dream – the ruin that we think might have formed the foundations for Lawerlocke Hall.' She paused for breath and then went on. 'If it hadn't been for those carvings I would never have taken particular notice of the photograph of Morna's brooch when I saw it at the museum.'

'Go on,' Don encouraged. 'You're doing fine.'

'There's the courtyard and the cobbles at the hospital, but no carving. I had an X-ray of my chest because I had a strange sensation in my lung. We now think maybe that was linked to Morna's death – when she was crushed in the tunnel. When I went for my appointment to see Dr Grayling, he stabbed my wrist when I was still lying down on the couch after he had examined me. There's something about my thumb being stabbed, and I think it's to do with my brooch – Morna's brooch. When I was Morna, I hurt my thumb on it when I was trying to do something with it. It was on my shoulder… When I felt that in the Hall yesterday I started to run.'

Fay paused again, and the others waited quietly while she gathered her next thoughts.

'The chapel. The grave. A monk was buried here… the curse of the two kinds of happenings was laid to rest.' Fay broke off and started to sob uncontrollably.

Slowly and deliberately Peter repeated the words that Fay had used earlier. '*There's something about being able to see behind what is at first apparent.*'

Fay looked at him with profound gratitude as the tears poured down her face. 'That's it,' she managed to say.

It took her some time before she was able to speak again.

Eventually she said, 'There's Don's ring, and there's Helen's wedding attire and everything that happened to us when we were searching for it.'

'Can I add something for you, Fay?' asked Don gently.

'Of course, Don.'

'I want you to think about why we went looking for a ring in the first place.'

'Oh yes. It was because my illness had helped me to see that I must start to take myself into account, and that this would be part of my getting well again.'

'That's absolutely right, Fay,' said Joan. 'And one of the things that came from thinking about that was your need for us all to talk about what your relationship with Diana had meant to you.'

Fay smiled. 'It was wonderful to talk about that.'

Joan went on. 'It was wonderful for me that I too discovered so much from that.'

'There's something else,' Helen reminded her mother.

Fay looked startled. 'Something else?'

Helen laughed. 'The clue is to be found in your eyebrows,' she said.

'Oh, *yes,*' said Fay. 'I've been thinking so much about my mother, and how my relationship with her affected me.'

'That was an excellent example of there being things to discover behind what was first apparent,' said Don seriously. 'I've learned a lot about that situation that I couldn't have guessed at.'

Here Helen interrupted. 'Mum, where do you think the person on the landing fits in with all this?'

'Perhaps it's more than one person,' Jim suggested before Fay had time to answer.

'I haven't got any further with that,' said Fay. 'It seems to be divorced from everything else, yet it would be surprising if it weren't a part of it all.'

'Maybe we'll have to leave that one for now,' said Jim. 'And I've just remembered that we promised to phone Diana and Paul. We'd better do that now because it's getting late.'

Chapter Twenty-two

It was Monday morning. Before Joan and Jim left the previous evening, they had agreed to come round again on Wednesday. Then Peter and Don had helped Fay upstairs to bed, and Helen arranged pillows at her feet to keep the weight of the duvet off her damaged ankle. Fay slept very well, and when she woke it was nearly nine o'clock. She could hear Don whistling downstairs. There were sounds on the landing and in the bathroom that she assumed were either Peter or Helen getting their things ready. I wish they could stay a bit longer, she thought sadly.

Helen's head peered round the door to see if she was awake.

'Hello, Mum,' she said brightly. 'How are you today? Dad said you hardly moved all night.'

'How did he know?' asked Fay.

'I think he was worried about you, so he kept waking up.' Helen made a sad face. 'I wish I didn't have to go back today.'

'I was thinking the same thing,' said Fay. 'Be sure to phone when you get back so we know you've arrived safely. I'll start to get up so that I can wave you off.'

'I think you should stay where you are,' Helen advised. 'A morning in bed would probably be the best thing. Peter and I will be leaving soon, and we can say goodbye to you while you're resting.'

Fay did not protest. She knew that moving around would cause her pain, and at the moment she felt comfortable and relaxed. She knew that what Helen had said was right. She dozed a little as she listened to the clattering sounds of the breakfast dishes.

Helen reappeared later, carrying a glass with another bendy straw.

'Green this time,' she announced cheerfully. 'I thought you might be thirsty. Dad says he'll bring some food up once Peter and I have gone.'

'I'm not hungry at the moment,' said Fay, sipping gratefully at the drink Helen had brought. 'I think I'll get up soon and then see how I feel.'

Peter joined them. 'I don't like leaving you, Fay,' he said, 'but I know you're in good hands, and we're just at the end of the phone. There are two things to remember – take care and look after yourself, and never hold back from telling us about anything, whatever it is.'

'Yes,' said Helen. 'If you think something's going to worry us, think how much more worried we'd be if you kept it from us, and we only found out later.'

Fay considered what Helen had just said. 'I know you're right,' she agreed, 'but sometimes I go into a state where I can't see it that way, and that's the time when I hold back – not only from you, but from everyone.'

'That's the first time I've heard you saying that, Fay,' said Peter, 'and I think it's a step forward.'

'Perhaps Dad's ring is beginning to have an effect,' said Helen, half joking, half serious.

'Whatever the reason, it's the right direction,' said Peter.

'Peter,' said Fay, 'I'm very grateful for your support and encouragement about this.'

'I hope that next time you find yourself holding back, you'll remember this conversation,' Peter replied.

Fay noticed that Helen took his hand and squeezed it. She felt very lucky to have Peter in the family. She could see that he was taking his part in the preparation for the task very seriously, and that it was not just because he had a well-developed sense of responsibility – it was part of his personality to be caring and concerned. She heard Don on the stairs, and he appeared in the doorway.

'I've come to join in with the goodbyes,' he said rather reluctantly. 'I feel like a small child who thinks that if he avoids the goodbyes, the separation won't happen!'

Peter looked at him and began to laugh. 'I like that, Don,' he said. He turned to Helen. 'Come on, we'd better get on our way.'

'We'll give you a ring this evening,' said Helen as she got up to go.

After they had left, Don came back upstairs and sat on the edge of the bed.

'I wish they didn't live so far away,' he said. 'Peter was telling me earlier that his practice is moving to new premises soon, so I suppose that's him settled for a long time.'

'We've just got to accept it,' said Fay. 'They're right for each other, and they have a home there and good jobs. We've got to concentrate on that.' Her voice fell to a whisper. 'But I do miss them. And we haven't seen Jack for such a long time now.'

'Perhaps when you're well again we could fix a trip out to see him – wherever he is at the time,' Don suggested.

Fay's face lit up. 'What a wonderful idea,' she said excitedly. 'I'd love to do that. I know he's always very busy, but we'd see where he was working and have a look at the general area. Then there'll be more to talk about when he phones.'

Don looked preoccupied.

'What is it, Don?' asked Fay anxiously.

'I've been thinking a lot about the wisdom of continuing to keep all that's going on here from him.'

'But I can't see how we can say anything to him,' said Fay. 'There's so much of it, and it isn't the kind of thing we can limit to telling only a small part.'

'That's right,' Don agreed, 'but I've been getting more and more uncomfortable about the situation. As things stand, he'll come home for the wedding without a clue about what's been happening. The thing that worries me the most is that although he's absorbed in his work, he could be sensing that there's something going on here.'

'I hadn't thought of that,' Fay acknowledged. 'And Peter has just been giving me strict instructions not to hold anything back from him and Helen, and explaining exactly why.'

'What I'm going to suggest is that we draft an e-mail to him,' said Don. 'We can send it to Peter and Helen to see what they think before we make a final decision about it.'

'With something like this I'd like to involve Joan and Jim too,' said Fay determinedly. 'We'll make a start once I'm settled downstairs. And I want to give Reverend Howard a ring as well.'

'Isn't it a bit soon for that?' asked Don.

'I want to fix a definite time,' Fay replied. 'I hope I'll be well enough for us to go across together some time next week.'

'Okay,' agreed Don. 'Now, do you want me to give you a hand?'

As Fay had predicted, moving about was quite painful, but once she was comfortably installed on the sofa she felt glad she had made the effort, and she was keen to begin work on what they might write to

Jack. It was a challenge for them both, and they spent much time in discussion about it. After more than an hour of deliberation, they were satisfied with what they had decided. It read:

Hello Jack,

It's good to keep in touch with your movements and plans. We find it fascinating, and it keeps our geography up to date!

There have been some interesting things going on here that we're just beginning to get to grips with. Sorry we didn't mention anything before, but we weren't terribly clear about it ourselves, and didn't want to give you any wrong impressions when you're a long way away. Don't worry – we're not moving house or anything like that! At the moment it's more in the nature of an unusual research project.

We're really looking forward to seeing you when you come back for the wedding, and we're sure there'll be some time then when we can sit down and tell you all about it.

We've been talking about the possibility of coming out to see you once Fay's better, and we look forward to discussing that with you nearer the time.

Look after yourself.

Speak to you soon,

Love, Mum and Dad

Fay read it aloud, and when she had finished she said, 'That sounds all right to me.'

'Me too,' Don agreed. 'Let's send it off to the others for their comments.'

After this, Fay phoned Reverend Howard and arranged a time to meet at the vicarage. 'That's it. I should be fine by next Monday,' she said.

When Joan and Jim came round on Wednesday evening they found Fay greatly improved.

'I think my ankle's going to be sore for quite a while,' said Fay, 'but I can nearly take my full weight on it already. My head stopped hurting by Monday afternoon. It's too soon to tell if there's going to be much of a scar, but it hardly matters. I'm not going in for any beauty contests, and it will be a special reminder of an exceptional day.'

'That's one way of looking at it,' Jim commented wryly. 'It was extremely worrying…'

Fay broke in. 'But look what came from it. I for one have no regrets. In fact, I feel lucky that it happened. It's moved our understanding on.'

'That's a valiant way of perceiving it,' Jim observed, 'but I can't help feeling rattled.'

Fay was surprised that Jim, who was usually resilient, had been so affected. 'The most important thing is to gather information about what's going on,' she insisted.

Jim looked her straight in the eye. 'The most important thing is to make sure you stay alive,' he stated baldly. 'When we couldn't find you I was worried out of my skull, and when I eventually saw you arriving back at the Hall in the Range Rover with that gash in your forehead and looking white as a sheet, I thought for a minute we might lose you.'

Fay struggled to absorb what Jim had said. Then she turned to Don and asked, 'Did you feel the same?'

'Yes. How on earth I could have been so stupid as to leave you on your own and go looking for someone to ask about the painting I'll never know. It had already been decided that you had to have someone with you all the time we were at the Hall, and I let myself get distracted.'

'You shouldn't blame yourself,' Fay tried to reassure him. 'I was so tired, and I expect you wanted me to rest while you went to look.'

'Yes, but I shouldn't have let that divert me,' said Don.

Fay tried again. 'But if you hadn't gone, I would never have learned what I did.'

'I know, but if I'd stayed I could have been with you in all that happened.'

Fay could understand now why Don and Jim were so upset. 'Don,' she said suddenly, 'I want to accept your offer of taking me back to the Hall. I want to go at the beginning of July. Will you all come and make sure I don't go off anywhere?'

Joan looked horrified. 'So soon?' she gasped. She collected herself and went on as calmly as she could. 'I'm very glad you've asked us, but I think we should all consider this very carefully before we decide whether or not to go through with it.'

'On Monday Don and I are going round to see Reverend Howard,' said Fay. 'Apart from looking through the rest of the files his brother sent, I'm hoping to get some leads about the chapel and the remains of the monastery. If he hasn't got anything at the vicarage he may well know the best places to start looking. I'm determined to press ahead with this. It's less than four months to the wedding, and I know there's a lot more that I have to learn to prepare myself for the task.'

'I appreciate what you're saying, Fay,' said Jim, 'and I think you're very brave, but I must remind you again that the central thing is to keep you alive, and preferably well. Perhaps preparing yourself for the task is also going to involve being careful and having plenty of rest.'

When Fay spoke it was with great dignity. 'I know that if I'm doing the right things I'll be given the energy I need,' she said.

'But who's to know what the right things are?' Jim persisted. 'I know I'm playing the Devil's Advocate here, but I think it's necessary.'

'Thanks for speaking out, Jim,' said Don. 'You're voicing a number of things that I hadn't quite put together in my mind.'

'I can see why you want to press ahead with all of this,' said Joan, 'and I'll help you all I can. I've got a lot of faith in following instincts, but I agree with Don and Jim that we mustn't rush at anything, and we should talk through as much as we can in advance of any action. We tried to do that before the last visit to the Hall, and look what happened. We've learned a hard lesson.'

'I think Joan and I should come round on Monday evening so that we can talk about what you've got from your visit to the vicarage,' said Jim. 'And I won't be put off about this. I'm serious.'

'I wasn't going to argue,' Fay reassured him. 'We'll be looking forward to turning it over with you.'

Jim nodded. Then he said, 'Now that's fixed, we should have a word about the e-mail you're planning to send to Jack. Joan and I have discussed it, and the only thing we wondered is whether or not to add a bit about us. If I were in Jack's shoes, and I had a whiff that something worrying was afoot, I'd be reassured if I was aware that other people I knew well were involved.'

'Good point,' Don agreed. 'We'll add something to cover that. Helen and Peter wondered whether to wait for another week or two before sending it off, but I don't want to delay. If he's sensing something it might affect his concentration, and that's not a good thing. The only other point I wanted to cover was that when he's in touch with any of you, I'd rather you refer any questions he might ask about the e-mail back to us. I think it's important that if he's given any details he hears them direct from us.'

'I agree,' said Joan wholeheartedly. 'The person who's most visibly affected is his mother, and anything he learns about that should come from one or both of you.'

'We could put something like "Joan and Jim are assisting" after the bit about the research project,' suggested Fay. She turned to Joan and said, 'Now we've agreed all of that I want to say how excited I am about the prospect of Paul and Diana being home soon.'

'Yes,' Joan replied. 'We've only got nine more days to go. I'm ticking them off each morning when I wake.'

'You didn't get back to us about storing any of their more fragile possessions,' Don reminded Jim. 'I take it everything's under control.'

'Yes, it's fine,' Jim replied. 'They've got every confidence in the removers, who will be storing everything. It's a firm that was recommended by friends who have moved several times, complete with a collection of expensive china!'

Chapter Twenty-three

Don and Fay arrived at the vicarage at exactly ten o'clock. Don had chuckled when Fay had tried to hurry out of bed at the sound of the alarm clock that she had set for eight in her eagerness to be ready well before time. She had left the file of photographs near their front door so that they would be sure to take them. Don had the file in a bag as he pressed the bell at the door of the vicarage.

Fay was surprised to find that several minutes elapsed before the Reverend appeared.

'I'm so sorry to keep you waiting,' he apologised as soon as he opened the door. 'I was on the phone. One of our parishioners has been taken into hospital – a heart attack as far as I can tell. I've added her to my visiting list for tomorrow and prayers for this evening.'

'Can you give us her name?' asked Fay as she followed him down the hallway to his study. 'We would like to think about her recovery too. Interestingly, I read an article recently where it was reported that people with heart attacks do better if they're prayed for.'

'I'm delighted to hear about that,' said the Reverend. 'Her name is Mrs Teresa Baker.'

Fay went on. 'The thing that really stuck in my mind was that those who did the praying didn't know the heart patients personally, and the patients who were prayed for didn't know it was happening.'

'Prayer, or caring thought, both have their value,' the Reverend remarked as he showed them into the room. 'Now, as I told you, I haven't looked at the files since you were last here.' He indicated two chairs that he had put next to the table, and they all settled down to work.

Fay and Don progressed in silence, writing notes to each other rather than speaking, since they were keen to avoid interrupting the Reverend's study time. They both found the contents of the next files of some interest, but there was nothing that particularly caught their attention until they were near the bottom of the pile.

'Look at this,' Fay whispered to Don, as she put in front of him an article that had been cut from a magazine.

Don noticed that it had nothing on it that identified when it had been written or which magazine had published it. Fay watched him read.

'I think we should ask if we can get a photocopy of this one,' said Don in a low voice. 'Is there anything else?'

'Not at the moment,' said Fay.

Don put the article at the far end of the table, and together they searched through the final file.

'I'm afraid I'll have to finish soon,' said the Reverend. 'Have you found anything of interest?'

Don indicated the article. 'We'd like a copy of this if it can be arranged,' he said.

'Ah, yes,' said the Reverend, picking it up and scanning it. 'How interesting! There are quite a few references here to the monastery. Yes, of course I'll copy it for you. I must read this myself. Benedictines… How very interesting.' He disappeared out of the room, and Fay could hear his footsteps going down the corridor in the opposite direction from the front door. He returned a few minutes later carrying several sheets of paper. 'I've run off a couple of copies,' he said. 'I'm afraid I'll have to charge you – ten pence a sheet. If you decide to do the accounting, you'll have to become acquainted with the dinosaur… I mean our photocopier. It needs a firm hand to keep it under control.' He smiled. 'Now, there's one more thing before you go.'

Don stood up, but Fay waited in her chair as her ankle was not yet strong enough for unnecessary standing.

The Reverend rummaged through a heap of papers on his desk and found a small booklet. 'Here it is!' he said. He handed it to Fay. 'I managed to find time to look through a box full of old guides that had been left here when I first moved in.'

'Thank you,' said Fay as she took the booklet from him. She felt a rising excitement when she saw the title – *The Chapel: Lawerlocke Estate.* 'May we take this with us for now?' she asked.

'Certainly. You can keep it for as long as you require.'

Don collected their things, and they left.

'I can't wait to get home and start reading,' said Fay as soon as they were in the car.

'Don't get too steamed up. I know it looks promising, but there might not be anything in it that helps us. That article on the Benedictines is quite revealing though. I'd like to go through it again. It was good of him to run off a couple of copies. He must have known we'd be fighting over it otherwise.'

'There may well be something in the booklet,' Fay said. She began to read the first page, but gave up. 'It's no good,' she said. 'I'll have to wait until we're back.'

Not long afterwards Don drew the car up in the drive, and they went straight to the sitting room.

'If I'm right,' Don said, 'the Benedictines were monks of the highest integrity, who aspired to as pure a life as they could attain.'

'That's right,' Fay agreed. 'That's what I'd always understood.'

'So it comes as a bit of a shock to us both to read that article,' Don continued. 'I had no idea of the kind of corruption that could occur. I suppose it's not uncommon that once an organisation becomes established, all kinds of unsavoury things can start happening, but I wouldn't have associated that with the Benedictine order.'

'It's very disappointing, isn't it?' said Fay. 'They must have wanted it to be kept quiet.'

'Of course,' Don replied.

'I wonder if Brother M was a Benedictine?' mused Fay, almost to herself. She picked up the booklet and began to read it, while Don went through the article again, and then went off to put the kettle on.

When he returned, he found Fay sitting staring at the thumb of her left hand, and the booklet was on the floor at her feet.

'What's the matter, Fay?' he asked, but she made no reply. 'What's the matter?' he repeated. He felt his heart sink. He tried again. 'Have you hurt your thumb?' he asked gently. Still Fay did not answer. 'One more try,' he muttered, 'then I'm phoning Jim.' He racked his brains for something else to say. 'Morna,' he said as kindly as he could. 'Morna, have you hurt your thumb?'

'Yes,' she said in a voice he didn't recognise. 'I've come to see if you can help me. See, there's a red line travelling up my arm. That means I shall soon die.'

Don thought rapidly. 'How did you hurt your thumb?' he asked in the same kindly tones.

‘My brooch,’ said Fay sadly. ‘It had been in the dirt, and then I hurt my thumb on it… not long ago.’

‘There might be something I can do,’ said Don. ‘I’ll talk to one of the other brothers who knows about cures for such things.’ He went to the phone in the hallway and spoke to Jim. ‘Something’s happening,’ he said tersely. ‘Can you come over? Bring your key and let yourself in. We’re in the sitting room.’

When he returned, Fay was lying on the sofa with her left arm hanging over the side of it, and she appeared to be in a kind of trance. Don sat down close beside her, and stroked her head. That seemed to bring her into a state of consciousness and she asked, ‘What are you using?’

‘Prayer,’ said Don uncertainly.

Fay relaxed and seemed to doze off almost immediately. He was still sitting next to her when Joan and Jim tiptoed into the room. Don put his finger to his lips and motioned for them to sit down. He pointed to Fay’s copy of the article, indicating that they should read it. Then he picked the booklet up from the floor and began to study it.

The article had confirmed that a small Benedictine monastery had existed not far from where Lawerlocke Hall now stood. It had referred to a chapel that was not attached to the original buildings, which because of that had survived. It was not unreasonable to suppose that this was the chapel that Fay had been trying to get to the day when she fell and cut her head. The article explained how the community had disbanded under a cloak of secrecy about bad practices that had brought it into disrepute; and there was some suspicion that the collapse of the buildings had been hastened by local people who were angry and disillusioned by what had happened. The article made it clear that much of this was surmise, but nevertheless it was not an improbable explanation for the end of the community.

Curiously, the first page of the booklet appeared to lead on from where the article had finished. The author seemed certain that there was a strong link between the chapel at Lawerlocke and the pre-existing monastery. He then went on to describe in some detail the life of a monk who lived there until his death in 1912, whom he referred to as ‘Brother M’. His life had been very simple and frugal, and the local people loved and respected him. They maintained that he had helped many of them, and there were copies of accounts –

written in their rough handwriting – that recorded this. Brother M had come from a family in which there had been a monk in each generation. Each time, one of the blood relatives had been carefully selected for this honour.

Don looked across to Joan and Jim. They had finished reading the article and were sitting quietly, waiting. He was sure that Fay had not had time to read any further into the booklet, so he passed it across to them and held up three fingers to indicate where they should read to. Then he sat and watched Fay's face intently while resuming a gentle stroking of her head. When Joan and Jim had finished, they put the booklet down and waited.

It was a long time before Fay started to move. At first she groaned slightly, then she opened her eyes. She looked startled when she saw Joan and Jim, but when she recognised her own curtains framing the window, she asked, 'When did you arrive? I think I must have fallen asleep.' She struggled to sit up.

'Take your time, Fay,' Don instructed.

'Oh! I didn't see you sitting there, Don,' she said. 'It's all right, I'm fine.' She swayed a little in her seat and corrected herself. 'I mean… I'm nearly fine.' She stared intently at Joan and added, 'I'm not fine, am I?'

'You're okay now,' Joan replied, 'but you haven't been all right for a little while.'

'You'd better tell me what happened, Don,' said Fay.

Don spent some time taking her slowly through what he had observed.

'When did you arrive?' Fay asked Joan and Jim.

'We've been here quite a while,' Jim replied. 'We came as quickly as we could after Don phoned, but you haven't moved since then.'

'I think we should talk about the booklet now,' Joan suggested.

'The booklet… Oh, yes,' said Fay. 'I was reading it when…'

'When what?' asked Don quietly.

'When I… hurt my thumb,' said Fay, looking confused. 'Oh… I think I'm beginning to fit some of this together now.'

'What's going on in your mind?' asked Don.

'I'll tell you exactly what I'm thinking,' said Fay. 'When I was Morna I got an infection in my thumb after accidentally stabbing it on my brooch. It quickly became worse, and I went to get help from the monks. Someone there saved my life. I don't know if you all think I'm mad, but that's what I'm thinking.'

'If you're mad, Fay, then I am too,' said Don, 'because you've just said, almost word for word, exactly what was in my mind.'

'Almost a carbon copy of mine as well,' Jim added, and Joan nodded.

'It's not surprising that you legged it to the chapel when we were visiting Lawerlocke Hall,' Jim continued. 'You were trying to get help of some kind. You knew from the photo that there had been a monk there at some time, and you made your way there as fast as you could.'

'Can we read the rest of the booklet?' said Fay urgently. 'What about the grave? Remember… a monk was buried here…'

She leaned back in her seat, exhausted, while Don carefully scrutinised the booklet, but he found only a series of diagrams of the elevations of the chapel, together with annotations and some local poetry which referred to it.

'Could I have a glass of water?' Fay asked Joan, who willingly went to get one for her. 'Thanks,' she said and took a few sips. 'Would you mind staying on for a while this evening?' she asked.

'Of course we will,' Joan replied. 'I'd like to stay until I'm sure you're okay.'

'I can rustle something up for all of us to eat,' said Don.

'I think I'd better go back to plain rice for this evening,' said Fay.

'I'll put some on for you and give Don a hand,' Joan offered, and disappeared into the kitchen.

The rest of the evening passed pleasantly and uneventfully, for which Fay was profoundly grateful. For all her eagerness to advance her knowledge of her situation and her position in relation to the task, at the moment she felt desperately in need of something that seemed ordinary and familiar.

'We can phone the others tomorrow evening,' she decided, half expecting Don to disagree, but there was no dissent from him or from Joan and Jim.

Chapter Twenty-four

Later that week Don was sitting at the computer. 'Ah! Here's Jack's reply to our e-mail,' he said.

'Good. What does he say?' asked Fay.

Don clicked on the envelope icon and looked at the message. It was quite short.

Dear Mum and Dad,

It was good to get your message. I'd sensed something was brewing, but I've got to keep my mind on the job at the moment, so I didn't ask. Glad to hear that Joan and Jim are in it with you.

Look forward to hearing all about it in September.

Will be in touch soon with some new contact details.

Best,

Jack

Don and Fay looked at each other.

'We were right to send our message,' said Fay. 'I feel bad for not thinking about it earlier. I've been so absorbed in my illness and everything else that's been going on, I've just felt glad that Jack was getting on with his life, and there seemed to be no worries there.'

'That's why it's good to have two parents thinking about you,' said Don. 'They often think of different things. That's how our relationship works at least,' he added. He went on. 'I'll forward this message to the others, and then they'll know how things stand.'

'Diana and Paul will be back today,' said Fay suddenly.

'Already?' said Don. 'I don't know where the time goes these days.'

'Diana should have a bump by now,' Fay reflected. 'She's got less than four months to go.' She fell silent for a while, and Don continued working at the computer.

When Fay spoke again it was with urgency. 'Don, I'd like to talk about the next visit to Lawerlocke Hall.' She noticed that he seemed to freeze momentarily, but when he replied his voice sounded quite normal.

'Yes, you'd been thinking of going at the beginning of the month, but I wasn't sure. What's in your mind at the moment?'

Fay was relieved that she had not met with any apparent resistance, and she spoke freely. 'I want to go,' she said emphatically. 'If we go the next time it's open, we won't have long to wait.'

Don looked worried. 'I'd rather be having this conversation with Joan and Jim as well,' he said anxiously. 'To be truthful, I'd rather hoped you'd rethought the idea of going back so soon.'

'But I want to go and see the chapel,' Fay insisted.

Don's face cleared. 'Only the chapel?' he asked.

Fay nodded. 'I'd like to go round the Hall, but I'm not in a rush. It's the chapel I want to see.' She smiled. 'If you remember,' she said deliberately, 'I didn't quite make it last time.'

Don relaxed. 'I'd like to go there with you,' he said. 'I'd like to see it myself. I wasn't concentrating the last time – for obvious reasons. But shouldn't we leave it until your ankle's properly better?'

'That's a good point,' Fay agreed, 'but we've got over two weeks. Surely it'll be better by then?'

'How would you feel about the others coming too?' Don asked.

'That would be fine. If they're free I'd certainly like them to come.'

When the first weekend in July came, Fay's ankle was almost back to normal and the trip had been arranged. Joan, Jim, Paul and Diana had been eager to join them. The two cars drew up side by side in the parking area at the back of the Hall.

'You've got a whole posse this time to make sure you're all right,' said Jim, 'and I for one am not going to let you out of my sight.'

'If this visit goes without any hitches, perhaps Paul and I could spend a little time in the Hall afterwards,' Diana suggested.

‘Good idea,’ said Fay. ‘Do you want to start now? Perhaps we could meet up in the tea room.’

‘No,’ said Diana emphatically. ‘We want to see that you’re all right first.’

Paul nodded. ‘Yes, that’s the first priority. In any case, I’m intrigued by the idea of seeing the chapel… and of course the exact spot where you had a tangle with the piece of masonry!’

It was nearly noon and the sun was quite hot. Fay wished she had brought something to cover her head, but she didn’t say anything, and she couldn’t think what she could use.

‘I’d like to see if I can find where I started forcing my way through the trees,’ she said.

‘Shall we do that first, or on the way back?’ asked Jim.

Fay thought for a moment. ‘Let’s go straight to the chapel,’ she said.

Don led the way down the track the Range Rover had used when it had come to meet them, and on to the footpath that skirted the woodland.

‘I hardly remember this path,’ Fay observed as she made her way along it, slightly ahead of the others.

‘I’m surprised you remember anything about it at all,’ Don remarked.

‘The woodchip base underfoot is very effective,’ Paul commented.

‘Yes,’ Jim agreed. ‘This kind of thing is used quite a lot these days. It certainly keeps the paths dry.’

Fay felt rising excitement as she neared the end of the woodland strip since she knew the chapel was not far ahead; but she said nothing and continued at a slow pace, enjoying the scenery. The heat of the sun continued to trouble her, but she hardly noticed because she was so focussed on her goal.

The chapel… at last, she thought as it came into view. She put her hand on the top of her head. ‘That’s strange,’ she murmured, ‘my head cover isn’t there. I wonder what’s happened to it?’

Don noticed her action and took hold of her other hand. ‘What is it, Fay?’ he asked. ‘Is your head hurting?’

‘No,’ she replied vaguely, shaking her hand loose from his grasp as she moved towards the building.

'Is something wrong, Don?' said Jim, concerned.

'I don't know,' Don replied in a low voice. 'Can you stick close by?'

'Of course,' said Jim.

They all watched as Fay approached the hole in the wall that indicated a doorway. She stumbled on the rough ground, but righted herself. It looked at first as if she was going to enter the building, but instead she stopped and leaned forward through the hole, peering first to the left and then to the right. After this she retraced her steps, muttering to herself.

'No one there,' she said. Then she repeated it more loudly so that the others had no difficulty in hearing. She appeared to be totally unaware of their presence.

She stood silently for a moment and then let out an unearthly wail that seemed to go on forever, before collapsing on the ground, sobbing as if her heart would break. Uncertain as to what course of action to take, Don hesitated. Joan started to move towards Fay, but Jim restrained her.

'I think she's going through something that doesn't belong to us,' he said. 'It might be better to wait and see what happens.'

Diana was standing staring at Fay. She was clutching Paul's arm tightly.

After what seemed to be an eternity, Fay at first became quiet and still, and then she started searching round the outside of the chapel, scrabbling through the grassy tussocks. She spent a long time examining every inch of the ground, and paying particular attention to any rocks she encountered. She looked grey and strained, and she moved in a way that appeared almost mechanical.

As she extended the area of her search, Don saw that she was moving nearer and nearer to the rock on which she had fallen on her previous visit.

When at last she encountered it, she exclaimed, 'Oh look, Don! This is where I banged my head. Now, I wonder where it was I forced my way out of the wood.' She began to look at the perimeter of the wood to find a break in the tree cover. 'Can you give me a hand, Joan?' she called.

Although they all searched carefully, no one could find a place that fitted what Fay described. In the end she gave up, saying that she would follow her original plan of looking at the other end of the wood for the place where she had entered.

'It's quite possible I tried to follow the line of a previous path,' she said. 'Is there anything else anyone wants to see here? If not, maybe we could go back. Perhaps we can get some lunch at the Hall, and Diana and Paul can have their look round.'

The change in Fay was remarkable. It was as if nothing at all untoward had happened.

'I think we've all seen enough for now,' said Jim, speaking for everyone else, and they made their way back along the path.

A careful examination of the other edge of the wood revealed a likely place where Fay might have begun her tortured journey.

'It's good to see this,' Fay commented. 'It makes the whole thing feel more real. Now that my head's back to normal and my ankle's fine, it almost seems like a dream... almost as if it had never happened.' She turned and led the way across the rough grass towards the Hall.

An external flight of stone steps led downwards into a pleasant basement area. Although it was described as a tearoom, it served simple lunch menus, and it was easy to agree to settle there for a while.

'Dad, could you get some of the open sandwiches for Paul and me?' said Diana. 'We'll have them when we get back. We'll be about an hour I should think.'

Paul took her arm, and they made their way back out and up the stone steps.

'She'll be fine,' Fay commented as she watched them leave.

Don looked puzzled, but said nothing.

Fay went on. 'She's got out safely.' She paused. 'That's what I should have done. I should have gone back out again.' She felt the right side of her chest and took a deep breath. 'But I'm all right now,' she said in puzzled tones.

'Yes, Fay, you're fine,' Don confirmed.

'Shall we go and choose something, Fay?' asked Joan.

'Bread and cheese,' said Fay mechanically.

'There's quite a variety here today,' said Joan firmly. She took Fay's hand, walked with her to the counter and handed her a tray and some cutlery. 'There's quiche,' she began, pointing to several slices that were laid out on a plate, 'or a bean salad, open sandwiches…'

'… and the soup of the day is carrot and coriander,' the woman behind the counter finished for her.

Fay froze. Joan took a quick look at her, put a piece of quiche on her plate, took a slice for herself, and guided her back to her seat.

'That looks nice,' said Jim. 'Are you coming, Don?'

The two men made their way to the counter, leaving Joan who was encouraging Fay to try the food.

'She seems to be slipping in and out of something,' said Don quietly when they were far enough away from the table.

'I can see that,' agreed Jim.

'I'm loath even to try to insist that she recognises who we are,' Don continued, 'because I think she's sorting through something, and whatever it is I don't want to disturb it.'

'I'd be more concerned if she seemed to be stuck in something,' said Jim. 'But since she's sometimes talking to us in a way that's entirely to do with the here and now, I think all we need to do is stay with her and keep our eyes open.'

By now Fay was using her hands to try to smooth down the front of her clothing. When she had finished that, she put her hands behind her back, as if trying to tie something.

'She looks as if she's just put a full-length apron on,' Jim said quietly.

'You could be right,' said Don.

He and Jim selected open sandwiches for themselves and for Paul and Diana, and Don paid for everything.

When they returned to the table Joan said, 'I'm just going to wash my hands. Can you help Fay with her quiche while I'm away?' She got up and began to walk towards the door of the Ladies toilets.

'No!' screamed Fay. 'You'll die!' She leaped out of her seat, grabbed Joan, and tried to drag her back to her chair.

The woman behind the counter looked very worried, but was reassured by the calm way in which Don, Jim and Joan spoke to Fay, and she resumed her work.

Don looked round the room. Fortunately there were no other people in sight.

'Maybe it would be a good idea to wait in the car,' he said conversationally.

'It'll be rather hot,' Joan said uncertainly.

'Stupid of me,' said Don. 'Of course. It's cool here because we're effectively underground.'

Fay looked terrified. 'Underground,' she whispered. 'Help me! Please help me. Please help me out of here!' She took hold of Don's arm with a vice-like grip.

'Of course I'll help,' said Don. With a flash of inspiration he continued, 'I think we should go for a walk in the gardens. I believe there's an interesting herb garden here.'

He stood up. 'I'll take Fay out for a breath of air,' he said. 'Can you wait here for the others? We'll be in the herb garden. If you can't find it, ask the attendant in the booth at the front of the Hall.'

He guided Fay up the steps and into the open air. He noticed that she relaxed almost immediately, and he made his way with her to the herb garden, where he drew her attention to the multitude of species that grew there.

'I wish I could have cuttings of some of these,' said Fay as she examined the plants.

'I've a feeling there's a small plant stall near the car park,' Don told her. 'Perhaps there'll be something there you'd like to buy.'

'What a good idea,' Fay agreed. 'When we've met up with the others we'll go and look before we make our way home again. I'm so grateful to everyone for wanting to come on this outing with us. It's made my day,' she finished happily.

They spent the following half hour enjoying the herbs. There was a shaded area to one side of the garden, and they stood together avoiding the heat of the sun as they waited for the others to appear. After that they visited the plant stall, where Fay bought three different varieties of basil.

'I've not seen these before,' she said as she loaded them carefully into the boot of the car. They arranged to meet up at Joan and Jim's house that evening, where they were planning a meal to celebrate Paul and Diana's return.

Fay was very pleased with her purchases. 'Perhaps I'll be able to invent an inspiring dish to surprise you,' she said cheerfully to Don as they drove homewards.

By the time they were travelling to Joan and Jim's house that evening,

Fay was aware that she was feeling quite tired. 'I think we shouldn't stay too late,' she commented to Don.

'I agree,' he replied. 'You've had a long day, and it wouldn't be a good thing to stay up late. Added to that…' he began. But he stopped in mid-sentence and said no more.

'What were you going to say?' asked Fay curiously.

'Er… we're agreed it's important that you recognise your limits and stick to them,' said Don. He felt uneasy. What he had actually said was true, and was entirely to the point, but it was different from what he had begun to say. He didn't like keeping things back from Fay, but he didn't think this was the right time to talk to her about what had been happening to her. He wrestled with his conscience. If I don't tell her, I'm treating her like a child or an invalid, and that's not right, he thought. After further deliberation he made up his mind to say something.

'There's something else, Fay,' he said.

She turned towards him, interested, and waited for him to explain.

'Fay,' he began uncomfortably. 'I want you to trust me about this.'

'What is it, Don?' Fay enquired. 'Is something the matter?'

'Fay, when we were out today there were several times when you went into a strange state.'

'Oh, no!' she exclaimed. 'Not again! I don't remember anything unusual at all.'

'I didn't want to tell you, because I think you've had enough for one day. We were out for quite a long time, and we're out this evening too.' He hesitated before going on. 'I'd like us to agree that we don't talk about it until tomorrow. I might be wrong, but I think that would be best.'

'I'm very glad you told me, Don,' said Fay sincerely. 'After all, the others would have seen it too, and it would feel very strange to me if I discovered later that you'd all been avoiding talking to me about it. I'm perfectly willing to go along with your suggestion. Let's tell the others when we arrive, and then there'll be no misunderstanding about it.'

As Joan let them in, Fay said straight away, 'Don's been telling me there are things about today that we'll need to go over.'

'That's right,' agreed Joan. 'Do you want to make a start after supper?'

Don looked at Fay, and then said to Joan, 'Actually, we've agreed we'll leave it until tomorrow.'

'Are you sure?' asked Jim, who had heard the exchange from the kitchen. 'There's no time like the present.'

'Thanks, but we're sure,' Fay replied. 'It's been a big day, and we're looking forward to relaxing with you this evening. But can we come over again some time tomorrow to talk it through?'

'Of course,' said Joan. 'I think the evening should be fine. Let's check with Diana and Paul.'

Having set a time for the following evening, the six enjoyed their meal together. Paul and Diana showed Fay and Don details of houses they intended to view the following afternoon. There was one in particular about which they felt very enthusiastic. As planned, Fay and Don did not stay late, and before they left, they wished Diana and Paul luck with their search.

'We'll hear all about it tomorrow evening,' called Fay as she got into the car.

Returning the following evening, Fay and Don were looking forward to seeing if Diana and Paul had any further news. They were not disappointed, since as they walked up to the door it swung open to reveal Diana, who had a broad smile on her face.

'Guess what?' she said. 'It's perfect.'

She took them into the sitting room and began to regale them with the story of how she and Paul had fallen in love with one of the houses straight away, and how the owners appeared to be keen to arrange a sale with them.

'Of course, we can't be entirely sure until everything's signed and sealed, so I'm not building up my hopes,' said Diana.

'Don't let our news get in the way of what you've come to talk over,' said Paul seriously.

'He's right,' agreed Diana. 'We promise we'll keep you up to date whenever we get any more information, but let's get on with the mysteries now.'

'I for one am very glad we all stuck together,' said Jim. He turned to Fay and said, 'I should warn you that it was quite hairy at the chapel.'

Fay looked worried. 'You'd all better tell me what happened.'

Together they gradually explained what had taken place.

'This is quite a lot to take in,' said Fay. 'I have to say I remember none of it. It's all news to me. You say I seemed to come out of it when I saw the stone where I hit my head? I suppose that makes sense in a way. What I want to do now is to relate back to you what I've taken in so far, and you can add anything I miss out.'

She went through it slowly, stopping from time to time to consider with them the possible implications.

When she was satisfied she understood what had happened to her, she said, 'As far as I was concerned we'd gone to the chapel, had a quick look round, found the stone, tried to see the way I'd come through the wood, and then gone back along the path.' She smiled wryly and continued. 'So I won't be surprised at anything else you tell me.'

'The rest was in the tea room,' said Don. He went on to explain in detail what had happened.

'Paul and I weren't there for part of the time, but Mum and Dad have told us about it,' Diana explained.

'Were there any other people there apart from us and the woman at the counter?' asked Fay anxiously.

'I didn't notice anyone,' Don replied. 'Did you, Jim?'

'I'm sure no one else came in,' said Jim. Joan nodded.

'That's a relief,' said Fay. 'It's one thing behaving differently when you're with people who know something of what's going on, but it's quite another when there are strangers around. Again I have no memory of anything you've described to me, except of course that we went into the tea room to get something to eat, and then Don took me to the herb garden.'

'If you ask me,' said Jim, 'both the chapel and the tearoom seemed to give you an opportunity to slip into some past state.'

The others agreed.

'When we were at the chapel we decided to stay close by and let you get on with it,' said Don, 'but we had to be more involved in the tearoom.'

'I've got nothing to add except to thank you all,' said Fay.

'You don't have to thank us,' Jim replied. 'We're all part of it.'

'I think I'd like to go back home quite soon,' said Fay suddenly.

‘Will you stay for a drink of something?’ asked Joan.

‘Yes, that would be nice,’ agreed Fay. ‘Then we must get back. Don and I will phone Helen and Peter from there, and I’ll talk everything over with them. It’ll help me to absorb it.’

Chapter Twenty-five

The rest of July passed relatively uneventfully. Diana's pregnancy became more and more obvious, and she and Paul secured the house they had wanted. They would be moving in towards the end of August, which meant that they would have several weeks for settling there before the baby was born.

As the time grew closer for Don's next trip away, Fay finally decided that she would stay with Helen and Peter at least for the first week, to see how things went. Her health had improved enough for her to have no doubts about the journey or about being away from home. Helen was delighted at the prospect of having her mother to stay, and made no attempt to conceal the fact. She began to float a number of plans, and booked a couple of days off work.

'I won't take much with me,' said Fay as she packed her things. 'I'll be out shopping with Helen, and we'll buy some clothes. She and I can look around for something that would be suitable for her to take away with her after the wedding, and I think I'd enjoy looking for something new for myself.'

'I don't know how much you'll see of me,' said Don. 'I've got a pretty tight timetable, but I'll make sure I join you for at least one of the evenings.'

'What time do you want to leave in the morning?' Fay asked. 'We don't want to risk your being late.'

'It'll have to be quite early. I start at ten, so I'll have to drop you off at nine at the latest.'

'That means we'll have to set off at around six thirty,' Fay calculated.

'Yes. That would give me a bit of leeway in case there are any unforeseen holdups.'

The journey turned out to be straightforward, and Don dropped Fay off just before nine the following morning. Fay let herself in with the key that Helen had posted to her, and saw straight away that there was a letter on the table in the hall with her name on it. She waved goodbye to Don, shut the door, and took the letter into the sitting room, where she opened it.

Dear Mum,

Make yourself at home. I've booked the afternoon off work, so put your feet up this morning and we'll go out somewhere nice when I get back. There's plenty in the kitchen – help yourself.

Love, Helen xx

Fay smiled and put the note back in the envelope. She left her bag in the hall, collected a drink and some fruit from the kitchen, and made herself comfortable. She didn't feel particularly hungry, but nibbled at an apple. As she looked forward to the afternoon she felt relaxed, and she was soon sound asleep.

She woke later to the sound of the letterbox and Helen's familiar voice.

'Hi, Mum,' she called. She came into the room. 'Oh, sorry. Did I wake you?'

'Don't worry about that,' Fay reassured her. 'It's time I got going if we're planning an outing. I don't want to miss an opportunity like this.' She smiled. 'Maybe we'll have another adventure.'

'An ordinary shopping trip would suit me very well,' Helen replied, 'but if there's something unforeseen, then I'll go along with that.'

Fay looked at her daughter knowingly, but didn't say anything.

'Shall we have lunch out?' Helen suggested. 'I know a nice place not far from here. After that I can show you where Peter's practice is likely to move to.'

'Have they made the final decision yet?'

'Almost, but it's still not definite.'

'These things can take such a long time to organise,' Fay observed. 'Yes, I'd like to see that, and then we can go on to the shops.'

It feels so good to be out together like this again, thought Fay, as they made their way from the café to the precinct.

The shopping trip was successful, and they returned home with several items – including a smart but comfortable pair of sandals for Fay.

When Peter came in he was demonstrably pleased to see Fay.

'It's great to have you staying,' he said spontaneously. 'And by the way, Helen and I have been drawing up a list of things we want to talk through while you're here. The phone's better than nothing, but it's never as good as being together.'

Fay looked intrigued. 'A list?' she asked. 'You'll have to tell me what's on it.'

'For one thing, Peter and I have been discussing the wedding ceremony,' Helen explained. 'We've got some ideas about what we'd like to include, but we'd like your view on it.'

'When do you think Don will be joining us?' asked Peter.

'Wednesday or Thursday evening I should think,' Fay replied. 'Then he'll come and pick me up on Friday afternoon. What else is on your list?'

'Helen and I often talk about the task,' said Peter. 'It's quite a while since we had the opportunity to discuss it with you.'

'I don't think I'm any further forward on that subject,' said Fay.

'You might feel you aren't,' said Peter wisely, 'but with the things that have been happening I expect you are, even if you aren't aware of it.'

'For example,' said Helen, 'you're definitely better than you were. That alone means there's been a change.'

'And there's everything that happened when you went back to the Hall and saw that chapel,' Peter added.

'I agree there's change,' said Fay. 'Some of it I can't see until it's pointed out, and there's some that's so dramatic that everyone gets worried – except me, who forgets it's happened! I hardly know what to make of it all.'

'I don't think any of us know what to make of it yet,' Peter reflected, 'but I do think we need to keep talking.'

'Why don't we get something to eat and then make a start?' suggested Fay with an enthusiasm that surprised her.

Later that evening they were settling down when Don phoned.

'Just checking,' he said cheerfully. 'How are things?'

'We're going to have a discussion about the task,' said Peter.

'Wish us luck.'

'I don't think it's luck you need, it's clarity, perception and perspicacity,' said Don seriously. 'Don't go at it for too long,' he warned. 'Fay was up early this morning, and in any case you have the whole week ahead.'

'Tell him we're about to make a start,' Fay called across the room.

Peter did what she asked, and Don said, 'Well I won't keep you now, and I'll phone again around this time tomorrow. I should be with you on Wednesday evening.'

Peter said goodbye and replaced the phone. Then he looked at Fay and Helen and said, 'According to what you two heard that young man say, we're the three people that are directly involved in the task. When I knew you were coming to stay, Fay, I felt so glad that you'd be visiting, but now you're here I'm beginning to realise that this is going to be an important opportunity for the three of us.'

Helen stared at him.

'I must admit I hadn't thought about that,' said Fay. 'My mind was focussed entirely on looking forward to seeing you both, and being glad I was well enough to make the journey.'

There was a silence, which was eventually broken by Helen. 'I can't think of anything to say,' she laughed.

'Neither can I,' admitted Fay.

'I feel a bit stuck myself,' Peter said reluctantly.

'Why don't we talk about the wedding for a while?' suggested Helen. 'It might be easier.'

'All right,' said Peter. 'Fay, we've been thinking about things we want to include, and there's something we agreed on straight away.'

'What's that?' she asked.

'It's a little unusual,' Peter began. He stopped for a minute before continuing. 'And curiously enough, we had each thought about it independently. I wasn't sure what Helen would think when I raised it with her, but when I told her I found she had exactly the same idea.'

'Don't keep me in suspense,' said Fay, laughing.

'We want some plainchant,' said Helen solemnly.

'Plainchant?' repeated Fay incredulously.

'I hope you don't mind,' Peter said. 'It's important to us both.'

'I think you're probably misunderstanding my reaction,' said Fay.

'I should tell you that this is exactly what's been on my mind too for the last few weeks.'

'Why on earth didn't you tell us?' asked Helen.

'I wasn't sure how appropriate it was,' said Fay. 'I did wonder if it had more to do with the chapel and the monastery than with your wedding, and I'm not sure enough yet about what those places signify to me.'

'If we're right in our belief that the things that have been happening are connected with your preparation for the task, then any thoughts you have are relevant,' Peter pointed out. 'In any case, we've all been thinking about plainchant and not telling each other. That fact in itself is worthy of some examination.'

'Have you any particular chant in mind?' asked Fay.

'Not yet,' Helen replied. 'But we thought we might make a start by seeing if there are any CDs we can borrow from the library.'

'If you're off work tomorrow, maybe we could go together,' suggested Fay.

'I'd like that,' said Helen. 'I'm off tomorrow and Wednesday.'

'I hope you find something,' said Peter. 'Then we can listen to it together. By the way, I've remembered a couple of other things I'd like to raise.'

Fay and Helen waited.

'You might like to take a trip to see Bruce Steele while you're here,' he said.

'You mean the man who made my brooch?' asked Fay. 'What a good idea. I'd love to do that. What else were you going to say?'

'That signet ring that you and Don bought at the Courtyard. I keep thinking about how it fitted the ring finger on Don's right hand exactly, as if it had been made specially.'

'Go on,' Fay encouraged.

'I'm sure it means something about a deeper union between you. I know we touched on this before, but I've been feeling more and more certain about it.'

'I'm glad you said that, Peter,' said Fay. 'I know it's important to me that he'll be wearing it in the church on your wedding day.'

'It's surprising how far we've got this evening,' Helen reflected. She looked at her watch. 'I suppose we should finish now,' she added reluctantly. 'It's getting late.'

'I've fixed a lift again in the morning,' said Peter, 'so you two have the use of the car.'

'I'd like to phone Mr Steele first thing tomorrow,' said Fay. 'It would be so good if we could go to see him in the afternoon.

'Let's try to fix it,' Helen agreed with enthusiasm. 'I'd like to meet him too.'

'His workshop isn't all that far away,' said Peter. 'I'll jot down some directions for you just in case.'

The following morning Fay woke early, with a feeling of eager anticipation. She stayed in bed until Peter had left, as she did not want to get in the way. Then she washed and dressed, and went downstairs.

'Do you think eight thirty would be too soon to phone?' asked Helen.

'You could give him a try,' Fay suggested. 'In any case, there'll probably be an answering service.'

Helen rang the number Peter had given her, and a deep voice replied almost immediately.

'Hello,' Fay heard Helen say. 'I'm phoning on the off chance that it would be okay for my mother and myself to come and see you at your workshop this afternoon. My mother is Fay Bowden – the person for whom you made the snake brooch.'

Fay held her breath and waited.

'Right,' said Helen. 'That would be fine for us. We'll see you at around three then.' She put the phone down and said to Fay, 'You'll gather that's it fixed.'

Fay felt as if she wanted to bounce up and down in her chair like a small child. It was wonderful that Peter had the brooch made for her, and it would be even more wonderful to meet the person who had made it. She beamed happily across at Helen.

'What time will we need to set off?' she asked.

'If we leave at two, that will give us plenty of time.'

Fay went on. 'So that means we've got the whole morning to look for plainchant.'

'The library opens at ten,' mused Helen. She thought for a while and then said, 'But let's have a look at the map. I've got an idea.' She took a road atlas from the bookshelves and studied the index. Having found the right page she pronounced, 'I thought so. Bruce

Steele's isn't all that far from a place where I'm pretty sure there's a good music shop.'

'Let's take a picnic and make a day of it,' suggested Fay.

'That's what I was thinking,' Helen agreed.

It did not take long to pack food and something to drink, and soon they were waiting at the door of the library, ready for when it opened.

Helen took Fay to the section where the CDs were displayed.

'Oh, look,' Fay whispered. 'They've got the same one that Don bought earlier this year – the Mozart.'

'I think I'll borrow that one anyway,' said Helen. 'It's the one you were listening to before…'

'Yes,' Fay replied, 'but I'd rather not talk about it just now.' She picked out another CD and studied it. 'We might be in luck,' she said. 'It's almost too good to be true – *Religious Music throughout the Ages:1 – Plainchant.*'

She handed it to Helen, who cast her eye down the list of contents.

'There's plenty here to listen to,' she said. 'It looks like an ideal starting point. Yes, let's take this one.'

Fay looked through the rest of the racks, but did not come across anything else of interest.

Out in the street Helen said, 'That didn't take long. How about going to the café for a cup of something?'

'I think I'd rather get to that music shop next,' Fay replied. 'Once we've seen it, perhaps there'll be time to look round some other shops before our appointment with Mr Steele.'

'Good idea,' replied Helen.

The mid-morning traffic was relatively light, and their journey was easy and pleasurable.

'I don't know the exact location of the shop,' said Helen, 'but we can ask around once I've parked. I'm sure someone will give us directions.'

Parking was easy, but getting a ticket was not. Helen lost most of her change in a machine that failed to produce one. Fay looked in her purse, but found only notes and some ten pence pieces.

'Drat,' said Helen, irritably. 'Everything was going so well.'

'Never mind,' said Fay. 'You can stay with the car while I go to get some change.'

'Okay,' Helen replied. But as she watched her mother cross the car park in the direction of the nearest shops she began to experience a profound unease, and she locked the car and ran after her. 'Mum,' she said when she was almost abreast of her.

Fay hurried on as if she had not heard anything.

'Mum!' Helen repeated, this time quite loudly.

Still Fay did not reply or turn towards her. Helen slipped her arm through Fay's, but Fay shook her off and increased her pace.

'Oh no,' muttered Helen under her breath. 'What shall I do now?'

She struggled to keep up with her mother, who was by now almost running, and her anxiety escalated. Then she had an inspiration. 'The jacket!' she shouted. 'Mum, what about the jacket?'

Fay stopped dead in her tracks. She stopped so suddenly that Helen shot past her and had to turn and come back. She stood and faced Fay and said insistently, 'Mum, the jacket… the man… the task. You *must* stay with me in the task.'

She saw Fay's face go deathly pale, and she feared that she might collapse. Then Fay felt her eyebrows, clawed at her left shoulder, examined her thumb as if it hurt, clutched at her throat, and then finally at her chest. After that, tears streamed down her face and she said, 'Helen, I'm sorry. I'm so sorry.'

'It's all right, Mum,' Helen comforted her. 'Let me take your arm and we'll go together and get the change. If we get a parking ticket while we're away, it's not the end of the world. The most important thing is for us to stay together. There's a lot happening and we shouldn't be apart, not even for a minute.'

Fay nodded, and they soon found a newsagent's shop where they bought a paper and got plenty of change. Back at the car park Helen put money in another machine and bought a ticket for three hours.

'That might be far longer than we need,' she said, 'but we won't be worrying about the time.'

After some deliberation they decided to return to the same shop to see if they could get directions to the music shop. This was successful since the owner was a friend of the man who owned the music shop, so he knew exactly where it was. Minutes later, Fay and Helen were standing outside it, looking in the window.

'Let's go in,' said Helen, opening the door.

Inside the shop was deliciously cool. Fay had not realised how hot she had felt until she experienced the drop in temperature. The balding middle-aged man who was sitting behind the counter greeted them, and asked them if they required any assistance.

'We'd like to have a look round,' said Helen, 'but my mother's feeling a bit tired. Do you have a seat?'

'Certainly,' he replied politely. He went through a door in the far wall of the shop and returned soon afterwards, carrying an upright chair with an upholstered seat.

Fay thanked him and then she burst out laughing.

'What is it, Mum?' asked Helen a little anxiously, from the other side of the shop.

'It's all right,' the man reassured her. 'Your mother has just noticed the Hoffnung design on the chair.'

'I must see that,' said Helen, and she went across to have a look. 'I know now why you were laughing,' she chuckled as she saw several musical cartoons on the upholstery. 'I've never seen a chair like this before.'

Although Fay had felt much restored by the cool atmosphere of the shop, she was grateful to have somewhere to sit, and she enjoyed looking through the sheet music on the stand nearby, which included a wide selection of jazz, modern songs and themes from musicals, as well as well-known classical music.

'I can carry only a small range,' said the man, who had come to speak to her, 'but I can order anything you want.'

'We're beginning to think about music for my daughter's wedding,' Fay explained, 'and we're looking for recorded music we can listen to. That might help us to make a choice.'

'Certainly,' the man replied. He glanced across the shop to where Helen was standing, and he could see she was examining his stock of CDs. He turned to Fay. 'There's a book here of piano reductions of all the old wedding favourites,' he said, searching through a pile and handing her a thick volume.

'Thank you,' said Fay. 'I'll have a look through it, but we're not looking for this kind of thing.' She hesitated and then went on. 'We were thinking of including some plainchant.'

'Plainchant!' he exclaimed. 'How very interesting, and most unusual for a wedding. Is there any particular reason?'

'Yes,' said Fay boldly, 'but the story behind that is rather long and complex.' She smiled. 'It would probably take all afternoon to explain, so I won't try.'

'That's all right,' said the man amiably. 'By the way, I happen to have a special interest in plainchant. I belong to a group who meet for an evening every two weeks, and we try out all sorts of things.'

'That's fascinating!' exclaimed Fay. 'So you'll be able to advise us.'

'I can't claim to be an expert,' said the man, 'but I'm certainly an eager amateur. Do you live locally?'

'No. I'm staying with my daughter for the week,' Fay explained. 'She lives about half an hour's drive from here. She'd heard about your shop, and we thought we'd call in on our way to see someone who recently made a brooch for me. In fact, it's something I'll be wearing at the wedding.'

'Would you like to take my home phone number?' the man enquired. 'If your daughter wants to contact me, she would be welcome. I'm sure I could arrange for her to come to one of our practice sessions if that would be of any help.'

Fay took a note of his number, thanked him and then went across to join Helen, who had found a CD that interested her.

'I'll buy that for you,' she said. She took it, and then went on to tell her what she had learned about the shop man.

'Oh wow!' said Helen. 'I'll speak to Peter about it this evening.' She looked at her watch. 'Perhaps we ought to move on soon if we're going to look round some of the other shops.'

The rest of the time passed very pleasantly, and both women made some small purchases as they searched the shops. Once back at the car, Helen consulted the map and Peter's instructions before confidently finding a direct route to Bruce Steele's workshop.

This part of their trip turned out to be disappointing, since when they arrived they found he had been called away urgently, and the workshop was shut, with a note of apology stuck to the door.

'Never mind,' said Fay. 'We've been lucky with everything else, and I'm sure I'll have a chance to meet him one day. Perhaps the best thing would be to go back now, and listen to the CDs we found.'

Most of the return journey was spent turning over the events of the day, and the memory of the Hoffnung cartoon upholstery left Fay shaking with laughter again. Once back at the house they were glad to have plenty of time to familiarise themselves with some of the music.

'Which one shall we start with?' asked Helen. 'You can choose.'

'Let's try the one we bought in the shop,' Fay suggested.

Helen put it in the CD player and pressed the start switch. The chanting began and seemed to expand to fill the room. They leaned back in their seats and listened intently.

After a while Helen commented, 'There's a lot here to absorb. I think I'd like to run these first few tracks several times. Do you mind?'

Fay smiled. 'I was about to say the same,' she said. 'I want to get a proper feel of them too, before we listen to any more.' But after the first rerun she was fast asleep, so Helen switched off the player and started to prepare the evening meal.

Fay was still asleep when Peter came home, but she woke at the sound of his voice.

'Sorry, I must have dozed off,' she said.

'I expect you needed to sleep,' said Helen cheerfully.

'Did you have any success today then?' enquired Peter.

'We'll tell you all about it over supper,' said Helen. 'After that, we'll play you some of the music we've found.'

When Peter heard what had happened to Fay at the car park he looked concerned.

'Helen's got tomorrow off, but what are we going to do after that?' he asked worriedly. 'I don't think we should leave you in the house on your own.'

Fay tried unsuccessfully to shrug off his concerns, but in the end she had to agree that there was a potential problem.

'We can discuss it with Don tomorrow evening,' she said uncertainly.

'I think we'd better not leave it until then,' Peter advised.

'You're right, of course,' she conceded. 'Have you any ideas? I don't know anyone around here.'

'I wish I could take more time off,' said Helen, 'but I've got people booked in on Thursday and Friday.'

Fay felt low and gloomy. She didn't like being the focus of concern and potential trouble. She had wanted her visit here to be pleasant and uncomplicated. She was just about to say something about the way she felt, when Peter looked animated.

'I've an idea,' he said suddenly. 'I don't know what you'll think of it, but it might be worth a try.'

'What is it?' asked Fay.

'The wife of one of the partners at work has been setting up a business selling beauty products by mail order. From what he told me she's got herself in a bit of a mess with her figures. He said she hasn't set up an accounting system yet. I know it's a bit of a long shot, but how about contacting her to see if she could do with a hand for a couple of days?'

Fay brightened. 'I'd like to do that,' she said immediately.

Peter looked at her and said slowly and deliberately, 'As far as I'm aware, you've never yet found yourself in one of your experiences when you've been working on figures.'

'You're absolutely right,' Fay replied. 'Of course, I've been doing very little over the last months, but when I've been working on accounts I've been fine. I do get tired though, so I don't think I could do a full day. But why don't we go ahead and give them a ring to see if there's anything I can do?'

Peter consulted his diary for the phone number, and was soon speaking to his colleague. When he came off the phone he said, 'They'd be more than pleased to get any help they can. Jenny could come up here for half past nine on Thursday with what she's got together so far, and she could stay on until about four, when she's got to be back for the children. As you probably gathered, I explained that you'd been ill and were taking a long time to get properly well again, so you might need to lie down from time to time.' He looked at his appointments. 'If I go in early I could finish at four that day. That would mean I'd be back here about half past.'

'That only leaves the hour after we set off in the morning,' said Helen. 'I think the best thing is if I phone you when I get into work, Mum, and if you don't answer, I'll just have to go off sick and get a taxi straight home again.'

'You don't need to bother, Helen,' Fay began, but she stopped when she saw the determined expression on her daughter's face.

'I've made my mind up,' Helen confirmed. 'After the sort of thing that's been happening to you, it wouldn't be sensible to do it any other way.'

'I suppose you're right,' said Fay slowly. 'We'll tell Don what we've arranged when he comes tomorrow evening. If Friday's going to be a problem, he could come and pick me up on Thursday evening, and then I can spend the night at his hotel and go with him to work on Friday morning. He'll be finished by lunchtime. And now we've got something sorted out, let's all listen to some of the chanting.' She turned to Peter. 'We didn't get very far with it because I fell asleep.'

They listened without speaking for while.

'It's very moving,' said Peter after Helen had switched it off. 'I have a lot to learn about this kind of music. I've been drawn to it without any real understanding of what it means. I think I'd like to take up the offer of the man you met at the music shop, Helen. We could go along and meet him, and perhaps he could guide us.'

'It might be a good idea to get in touch with Reverend Howard as well,' Fay suggested.

'We'll certainly do that,' Peter agreed.

Not long after this, Don phoned. Fay told him that there was some news, but said they would tell him about it when he was with them the following evening.

Wednesday passed quietly. Peter had to take the car because he had some home visits to make, and Fay and Helen spent time in the house, reading, listening to more of the music and talking about things that were on their minds. Towards the end of the day they took a bus to the supermarket, chose something for the evening meal and prepared it together on their return. Peter and Don arrived within minutes of one another.

Don put his arms around Fay and gave her a kiss. 'Aren't I lucky to see you midweek?' he said. 'I've been missing you. We haven't been apart like this for quite a while.' He hugged Helen. 'And it's so good to have a chance of seeing you a bit more often.' He turned to Peter. 'It's great that you're settled in your profession,' he said, 'but secretly I'm always hoping that you and Helen will end up living a bit nearer to us.'

'We sometimes talk about that ourselves,' Peter admitted, 'but I can't see anything like that happening in the near future.'

The meal over, they sat and talked about the events of the last few days, and then Fay went on to outline their plan for Thursday. 'I hope you approve, Don,' she concluded.

'Sounds good to me,' he agreed. 'I'll be able to come along in the evening and see how it went, and if need be I can take you back to the hotel with me.'

'That's what we were thinking,' said Fay, 'but we decided to take it a day at a time. Would you like to listen to some of the music now?'

Don was eager to be involved, and Helen switched on the CD player once more.

'That's really good,' Don said in the short gap between the first two tracks. 'I'm looking forward to hearing more of this.'

They listened without speaking through the rest of the disc.

Don checked the time. 'I know it's getting late, but would you mind if I stay on and we listen to the other one?'

The others agreed with alacrity, and Helen changed the discs.

About half way through it, Don put up his hand. 'I'm afraid I'll have to leave it for now,' he said reluctantly. 'Could you save the rest until I'm here tomorrow evening? There's an amazing diversity on that second disc.'

'That's the one we borrowed from the library,' said Fay.

'I think I'll order a copy when we get home,' said Don. As he kissed Fay goodbye he said, 'I hope tomorrow goes okay. I'll give you a quick ring before nine.'

'I'd like that,' Fay replied.

Jenny turned out to be a cheerful lively woman in her mid-thirties. She was also very scatty as far as figures were concerned, as Fay soon discovered. Jenny was highly appreciative of her input, and the two worked side by side all day as Fay patiently went through everything Jenny needed to know. As she packed away her things just before four, Fay told her that she might be back again the following week, and that if she were, she would be more than happy to progress what they had begun.

Jenny was almost ecstatic. 'You've saved me!' she proclaimed effusively, as she gave Fay an unexpected hug. 'Selfishly, I hope you'll be back again very soon. Please give me a ring once you know.'

When Peter arrived half an hour later he found Fay reading a book and looking very relaxed. 'Thank you so much for fixing that up,' she said. 'It was ideal.'

Peter smiled. 'That's great,' he said. 'I had a hunch it would go well. I'm going to get a drink. Would you like something?'

'A glass of water would be fine, thanks,' Fay replied. 'After that, I was wondering if you and I could plan a meal to surprise Helen and Don.'

'I'm up for that,' Peter replied.

Over supper Don said, 'It's good to get away from the files for a while. It's a great benefit to me to be off the patch for a couple of hours. I was a bit worried about how today might go for Fay, but it sounds as if it's been a success.'

'It couldn't have been better,' said Fay. She glanced at Don's signet ring and said, 'How would you feel about me giving Jenny our phone number so she can get in touch if she gets stuck?'

'That's a generous offer,' said Don, 'but maybe you should think about limiting it. It would be wrong to make it sound as if you're on tap all the time. It gives a false impression, and that wouldn't be fair to either of you.'

Peter nodded. 'Don's right, Fay.'

'Thanks, you two,' said Fay. 'I'll think it through before I decide what to do. Maybe I'll leave it as it is.'

'That might be the best thing for now,' said Helen.

The rest of the evening was spent listening to the CDs once more, after which it was decided that Fay would go back with Don.

'We'll speak to you over the weekend about next week,' Don promised as they left.

'Yes, we'll see what time off we can organise,' said Helen. 'I hope we can fix something, because we want to see you again, Mum. Don't we Peter?'

'That goes without saying,' he agreed.

Chapter Twenty-six

Back home, Don and Fay woke to the sound of the doorbell. Don glanced at the clock beside the bed. It said nine thirty.

'What the heck can that be?' he said irritably. 'I know we've slept in, but who on earth can be at the door at this time on a Saturday morning?'

'Perhaps it's the postman,' said Fay, struggling to get out of bed.

'I'll get it,' said Don, pulling on a pair of trousers.

The bell rang again. It rang for several seconds this time, as if the person who was standing there was running out of patience. Don ran lightly down the stairs and opened the front door. He was confronted by a huge bouquet of flowers, and he could not see who was trying to deliver it. A van in the street had 'e-flora' written on its side.

He addressed the flowers. 'Hello,' he said. 'Who are you trying to deliver to?'

'Mrs Fay Bowden,' replied the flowers in muffled tones.

'Ah, yes,' said Don. 'This is certainly her address. Shall I take them in?'

The flowers lurched towards him, and he felt a little overwhelmed by their pungent scent, but he took them into his arms. He could now see a diminutive person who thrust a pad at him to sign. He was not sure whether this was a young man or a young woman. It hardly mattered. He took the proffered pen and scribbled something on the pad. The person seemed satisfied, disappeared back into the van and drove away.

He struggled upstairs with his burden and collided with Fay on the landing because he could not see where he was going. She yelped as he stood on her toe.

'Where have these come from?' she asked in astonishment. 'Could you take them downstairs and put them in a bucket of cold water? I'll get dressed and come and do something with them.'

It did not take her long to get ready, and soon she was examining the bouquet.

'Here's a card,' she said, as she retrieved it from between the densely packed flower heads. She opened it and read:

To my saviour, with a million thanks,

Jenny Green

Fay started to laugh. 'It's from Jenny,' she said. 'I told you she's quite dramatic.'

'You could say so,' said Don, surveying the task that Fay was facing in having to find vases to accommodate what seemed to be an endless mass of blooms.

'Her heart's in the right place, and that's all that matters,' said Fay as she searched through her cupboards for containers. She found three large vases and put them on the draining board. 'That's not going to be enough,' she observed sadly. 'I wonder what to do. It seems a pity to leave half of them in a bucket.'

'How about offering some to Joan?' Don suggested.

'Of course,' Fay agreed. 'I'll give her a ring after breakfast. Maybe she and Jim would like to come round for a while this evening.'

Joan was very pleased to be offered some of the flowers, and she and Jim were eager to come round later to catch up on the news.

'I wonder if I'd be able to get either of those CDs in town today?' mused Don. 'I'd like to get their reaction to them.'

'You could phone that big record shop and see,' Fay suggested. She continued to arrange some of the flowers while Don discovered that the shop had one of the CDs in stock.

'I'd like to go and collect it,' he said. 'Do you want to come?'

'Not really,' Fay replied. 'I'd rather get on with these flowers and have a quiet morning. It's been a busy week for me.'

'Okay,' said Don, collecting his car keys from their hook. 'I should be back in about an hour.'

Fay heard him leave. She concentrated on the flowers. They were so beautiful. She could not name them all, but their shapes and colours were familiar. One in particular was heavily scented, and it took her back to a garden of her childhood – the garden next door to where she had lived. She noticed her hand begin to tremble as she selected each flower stem, and she used her other hand to steady it; but this tactic was unsuccessful, and she had to give up trying. She wandered to the sitting room and took up her usual position on the sofa. By now her whole body was shaking.

Oh, no, she thought. But at least this time I'm aware that something's happening. I hate it when the others tell me afterwards that I've been in a strange state. She wondered about picking up the phone to try to contact Don on his mobile, but she gave up that idea because she realised that she was shaking so much that she would not be able to use it. No point in panicking, she thought. I'm sure it'll pass off in time if I sit here and wait.

A few minutes later she heard a key in the front door. That's funny, it's too early for Don to be back, she thought. Then her body seemed to fill with ice. If it isn't Don, who is it? she wondered, paralysed with fear. Fleetingly she realised that she felt she was about three years old. Then everything went black.

'It's a good thing Don phoned us,' said Jim. 'I wonder how long she's been out like this.'

'I'm glad we encouraged him to go on into town,' said Joan. 'There was no need for him to turn back after he found we were free to come over.'

'I don't think we need to do anything at the moment except sit with her,' Jim observed.

'Yes, she's sitting quite well supported,' Joan agreed. 'I must say that finding her like this validates my hunch that I needed to book next week off work. I'm going to insist on staying with her all week.'

'She might want to go back to Helen and Peter's,' Jim reminded her.

'I can go with her,' said Joan decisively. 'I'm sure you and Paul and Diana can manage without me for a few days. After all, they're more or less settled into their house now, and Diana isn't having to go into work.'

'What if Fay's against it?' asked Jim.

'She hasn't any choice,' said Joan. 'She'll quickly see the sense in it when we tell her what's happened this morning.'

Fay moaned quietly.

'It sounds as if she's coming round,' said Joan. 'Fay, it's all right, we're here.'

Fay cowered back in her seat with her hands over her head as if to protect herself.

'Fay,' said Jim. 'It's all right. It's Jim and Joan, your friends.'

But his gentle words appeared only to have the effect of increasing Fay's trauma, and she shrunk further into her seat.

'Perhaps we should try phoning Helen,' said Joan worriedly. 'I don't like the look of this. Maybe if she hears Helen's voice it might help her.'

Jim rang the number, but there was no reply.

'Try Diana,' Joan urged him, 'Fay's in a terrible state.' She wanted to hold her and comfort her, but she could see that any physical contact would be likely to increase her terror.

Jim hurriedly rang Diana's number and was relieved to hear her voice.

'Diana, Fay's in a bit of a state,' he explained. 'And she thinks we're people who are going to harm her. If I put the phone near her head, will you say something to her?'

'Go ahead,' said Diana steadily. She began to speak in gentle measured tones. 'Fay,' she said. 'This is Diana, your daughter. I love you very much and I'm coming over to see you quite soon. Mum and Dad will be there too, and Paul, of course. Do you remember the knitting you've been doing for my baby? It won't be many weeks now before it's born. I want you to be there when I go into hospital. I want you to be with Mum and Dad and Paul.'

'Keep talking, Diana,' Jim encouraged softly. 'She seems a bit calmer.'

Diana continued. 'I think Mum and Dad have arrived already, and I'll be over in a few minutes. Will you talk to them for a while until I get there?'

'Yes,' said Fay, speaking as if from a long way off. 'Joan, are you coming?'

'I'm here already,' replied Joan, taking hold of her hand. 'Jim, tell Diana not to rush. I don't want to feel anxious about her and Paul.'

'Okay, I'll do that,' he said.

Joan sat beside Fay, who leaned on her shoulder. 'I'm glad you've come, Joan,' she said. 'I don't like being on my own.'

It was not long before Diana and Paul arrived.

'Hello Fay,' said Diana cheerfully. 'Mum said you weren't feeling too good.'

'Yes,' said Fay. 'Maybe I should have had some breakfast before I started arranging those flowers. Go and have a look in the kitchen, Diana. I've got far too many. Your mum's going to take some, but I think we should share them out between the three of us.'

'Thanks, Fay,' Diana called from the kitchen. 'That would be lovely.'

'Take some of the carrier bags from the bag behind the cupboard door,' Fay called back, 'and choose the flowers you'd like.'

They were all talking in the sitting room when Don returned carrying the CD. 'Everything fine?' he asked cheerfully.

'Fay's not been feeling too good,' said Joan carefully. 'Maybe we should have a chat about it this evening. What time shall we come over?'

Don took the hint. 'Around six. I'll make something for us all to eat.' He addressed Diana and Paul. 'Can you come as well?'

'Unfortunately not,' said Paul. 'We're seeing some friends this evening, but don't hesitate to phone if you need to speak to us. We'll take our mobiles.'

'See you later,' said Jim as he stood up to leave.

Just then the phone rang. It was Helen, who had checked her callminder when she came in from doing some local shopping and had found her parents' number recorded.

The others waved to Fay and left.

'I think I've had some funny thing again,' Fay explained. 'I'll hear all about it this evening when Joan and Jim come back. Can we phone you after that?'

'Of course,' Helen replied. 'Is Dad there?'

Fay handed the phone to Don. 'Don't worry, Helen,' he said. 'I won't be leaving her on her own. We'll speak to you soon.'

'Do you want me to give you a hand with the flowers, Fay?' he asked after he had put down the phone.

'Maybe I should eat a dry biscuit or something first,' said Fay uncertainly.

'I'll get you something,' Don replied. He soon returned with a plate of oatcakes and a glass of fruit juice. 'Your staple diet,' he joked.

'That's not true any more,' she protested, nibbling at one of the oatcakes.

They spent the day quietly together. Before Joan and Jim returned, Don said, 'I'd better tell you the bit I know. If you remember, I set off to pick up a CD, saying that I'd be away for about an hour.'

'Yes, I remember that,' Fay said.

'I wasn't far down the road before I realised how stupid I'd been to leave you, so I phoned Joan and Jim to see if they could pop round. If I hadn't been able to get them, I would have come straight back myself.'

'I was working with the flowers,' said Fay. 'There was a smell from one of them that reminded me of…' She hesitated.

'Reminded you of what?'

'I…'

'Let's have a look at them together,' Don suggested.

They examined the contents of the three vases and the remaining flowers in the bucket without success.

'Maybe Diana took them away?' said Don.

'That might be it,' said Fay. 'What a relief. Whatever they were, they reminded me of the garden next to ours when I was small.'

'Hm. No wonder you felt odd,' said Don sympathetically. 'Anyway, what happened after that?'

'I went to sit down. No, I was trying to arrange flowers, and my hands started shaking so much I couldn't carry on. After that I sat on the sofa, and I was feeling very pleased with myself because I was aware of what was happening, although there was nothing I could do to stop it. After that, everything went black.'

'So Joan and Jim will have to tell us the rest of it,' said Don. 'Let's get the food together, and then we'll listen to some of the CD while we're waiting for them to come.'

They relaxed in the calming simplicity of the music that filled the room.

When the last notes died away, Don said, 'I don't think it will ever cease to amaze me how deeply this kind of music affects me. There's a complete lack of drama and overstimulation, but at the same time I feel as if I have been taken through some process that I can't even begin to name.'

'I follow exactly what you say,' agreed Fay. 'For me I would add that it's the simplicity that allows me to stay with it a hundred per cent of the time, and I like to listen to each chant several times. I must say I'm looking forward to seeing how Joan and Jim react to it. I'm glad they're coming across quite early. Let's eat as soon as they arrive, and then we've got the rest of the evening to talk and listen to the music.'

Not long afterwards Fay could hear Jim at the letterbox pretending to be Helen by calling through it in a falsetto voice. She collapsed with laughter when she realised what was happening, and went to let him and Joan in. She pushed him playfully as he came past her into the hall.

'That's good,' he encouraged her. 'It's a bit of an improvement on this morning.'

'Stop joking about it,' Joan admonished him. 'It's not funny.'

'I prefer a few jokes,' said Fay slowly. 'It helps me.' She reflected for a moment, but said nothing more about it. 'Come and have something to eat,' she said. 'We've got a lot to talk about.'

After the meal, Fay settled herself in her familiar position on the sofa and said, 'Can you tell me about what happened? Or perhaps I should say what I remember first?'

It did not take her long, and Joan and Jim listened in silence.

'That makes sense. Doesn't it, Joan?' said Jim.

Joan nodded. 'The predominant feeling I had when we arrived was that you were a small child who was terrified of us. I don't know who you thought we were. We just couldn't get through to you.'

Jim continued. 'First we tried to get Helen on the phone, but she wasn't in, so we tried Diana. You soon seemed to realise who she was.'

'I had a chat with her at lunchtime,' said Joan, 'and she told me what she was saying to you.' Joan went on to recount everything she could remember.

'Mm,' said Fay briefly, before lapsing into silence. When she spoke again she said, 'This is different from the other times.'

'I think so,' Jim agreed. 'If you ask me, it looked as if you were remembering something from your own childhood, rather than being in a state that might be a past life of yours, or being taken over by a resonance of someone else's life.'

'Yes,' Joan confirmed, 'that's what it looked like to me too.'

'This leaves me with a lot to think about, but can we leave it for now?' asked Fay. 'Perhaps we could listen to the CD Don was off to get this morning? We wanted your opinion about it.'

'Sounds good to me,' said Jim.

Fay listened to the now familiar music. She felt increasingly clear there must be something in this that was right for the wedding, although she wanted Helen and Peter to be the ones who made the final decision. Maybe it wouldn't be something from this selection. If not, perhaps the man at the music shop could help. Plainchant could surely be a central focus of the ceremony.

When the last track had died away she leaned forward in her seat and said, 'This music allows and engenders thought and reflection. Peter and Helen's wedding day marks the beginning of a journey for them, and also the next stage of the task Helen and I have to accomplish with Peter's aid. For some weddings it is right to have drama and loud celebrations – even fanfares. Sadly, some ceremonies are only a modern designer accessory, something that is all too easy to discard. Peter and Helen's wedding service will be a time for reflection, setting a seal on what marriage really means.' She leaned back in her chair again.

'I feel really affected by what you've just said,' Joan murmured.

Don looked at Fay admiringly. 'It's brought together very succinctly a number of things I've been thinking about of late.'

'Fay,' Jim addressed her. 'I'd like to get down some of what you said. I don't know quite why, but I don't want to lose the essence of it. And I'm sure Helen and Peter would like to hear it.'

'I think we should give them a ring soon,' said Don. 'Time's getting on, and we need to talk to them about Fay's experience of today.'

'Perhaps we'd better have a word about next week first,' Joan began. 'I've booked it off as leave, and I'm going to spend it with you, Fay.'

'But I was thinking of going back to Helen's,' said Fay.

'Yes, I thought you were, but you need someone with you at the moment,' Joan insisted. 'So wherever you're going to be, I'll be around.'

'That's a great offer,' said Don.

'It isn't an offer, it's an order,' said Joan, smiling.

The phone call with Helen and Peter revealed that it was going to be difficult for either of them to take time off work that week, and that they were worried about the consequences for Fay.

'Pass me the phone, Fay,' said Joan. 'Hello, Helen. I'm inviting myself to stay for the week... You like the idea? Good, so do I. Yes, I won't be leaving her on her own.' She handed the phone back to Fay saying, 'Now tell them what happened this morning.'

When Fay had finished, Don took the phone and read out what he and Jim had written down of Fay's statement. 'I thought you'd be impressed,' he said when he heard their reaction. 'I'd like to expand it when we're together, because I've started to wonder if we can write something to give to Reverend Howard to put in the talk he'll be giving during the ceremony. Or better still, perhaps one of us could read something out. I'll be with you again on Wednesday and Thursday evenings, so we could discuss it then.'

When he put the phone down he turned to Joan. 'That's it fixed then,' he said briskly. 'I'll pick you up just after six thirty on Monday morning.'

Chapter Twenty-seven

Joan and Fay shared the spare bedroom in Helen and Peter's house, and insisted on being in charge of the shopping and cooking while they were there. As they did not have access to a car they did not travel far, but there was plenty to occupy their time. Apart from enjoying each other's company, they started more knitting projects for Diana's baby, and they invited Jenny round for a morning so that Fay could help her again. She was surprised and encouraged that Jenny had already been able to incorporate many of her suggestions, and was appreciating the difference this was making. During Wednesday evening they discussed some interesting situations that had arisen in Don's work, and they also spent a little time concentrating on what Fay had been saying. Don couldn't join them on Thursday evening after all, and most of the time was taken up with trying to work out how they were going to organise the following week.

'Quite apart from wanting to support Fay, I've had a really good holiday this week,' said Joan. 'Thank you for having me, Helen and Peter.'

'You're welcome any time,' said Peter warmly.

'I'm pretty sure next week is Dad's last,' mused Helen.

'I wish I had another week,' said Joan regretfully, 'but my job-share is off next week, and I've got to cover for her.'

'Helen and I have been making plans,' said Peter. 'I think we'll be okay, because I've booked Tuesday and Wednesday off.'

'And I've got Thursday and Monday,' Helen added. 'So that's the week more or less covered.'

'And I can go back with Don on the Thursday evening like I did last week,' Fay finished.

'Helen and I are planning to call in at the music shop this weekend,' said Peter. 'I'd like to meet the chap you spoke to now that I've had time to absorb what's on the two CDs. We're going to get our own copy of the one you borrowed from the library.' He addressed Fay. 'When you're here again I'm determined to take you to meet Bruce Steele.'

'That would be wonderful, Peter,' Fay replied.

Unlike the previous one, Fay's weekend seemed quite ordinary. She and Don had a look round some record shops to see if they could find more music that might interest Peter and Helen, but in the end decided against buying anything.

When Don dropped Fay off again on Monday, Helen was keen to let her know straight away that the trip to Bruce Steele's had been fixed for the following day. She regretted that she would not be able to go too, but went on to say that she could go with Peter some other time. She then told Fay about their trip to the music shop, and what they had learned from the discussion there. They all looked forward to Wednesday evening when Don would be with them.

As she and Peter set off the following day, Fay thought how comfortable she felt with him at the wheel. His driving style was impeccable, and she wished that everyone on the road would follow his excellent example. As they travelled, she asked him which driving school he had used.

'There were a number of places with a very good reputation,' he replied, 'but in the end I chose a man who had retired from the police and set up his own business. He was excellent. He'd been a trainer for police drivers.'

Fay said nothing else, but watched the scenery with interest as their journey progressed. It was a hot day, and they had all the car windows open a few inches to allow the air to circulate.

'The maker of Morna's brooch...' she mused. She wondered who had made the original one, and whether or not any others like it had been made at the time. She accepted that the answers to these questions could not be obtained, but it did not stop her from toying with ideas. A fly came in through the window beside her and struggled around on the windscreen, until with the aid of a piece of card she found in the glove compartment she helped it out.

Who knows, she wondered with a smile, Bruce Steele could be a descendant of the craftsman who made the original brooch. It was highly unlikely, but not completely impossible. Of course, Morna's brooch itself could be a copy – possibly of something earlier.

Her mind turned to Don's signet ring, and how they came by it.

'Peter,' she said, 'I wonder what Bruce Steele would make of Don's ring?'

'We should ask him,' he replied. 'He's very knowledgeable.'

'It's a pity we haven't got it with us,' Fay remarked. 'If I'd thought earlier, I could have asked Don to let me have it. Never mind, we can always come again some time if he seems interested.'

'That's right,' Peter agreed. 'By the way, we're about there.'

A few minutes later he drew the car to a halt in a layby outside a row of nondescript buildings, and they got out.

'I can see he's definitely there today,' said Fay, relief showing in her voice. 'The door's slightly ajar.'

The shop was dark inside compared with the bright sunlight they had just left, and Fay waited for her eyes to adjust to the change before she was sure that there was no one in sight.

Peter called out, 'Hello…o!'

At first there was no response, but after a while a long-haired man, who Fay guessed was a little older than Peter, came into the shop by the same door.

'Hi,' he said casually. 'You must be Mrs Bowden…' He smiled and held out his hand. '… alias Morna.'

Fay smiled back at him and took his hand. She felt an immediate affinity with him, and she relaxed. 'First, I want to thank you for making the brooch. It's very important to me,' she began.

'I guessed that from what Peter told me,' he replied. 'I'm glad I was able to help. It was an interesting challenge, and one that drew me immediately.' He lowered his voice and said with an air of confidentiality, 'I put back some of my other commissions so that I could work on it as soon as possible.'

Fay felt embarrassed. 'Oh. We didn't mean you to…'

'I know that,' he reassured her. 'It wasn't anything to do with you. The brooch itself drew me in some indefinable way. It was irresistible.' Here he stopped as if startled by what he was saying, and he changed the subject. 'Have a look round while you're here if you want,' he invited, 'and let me know if you would like to see the workshop. It's a bit of a mess by most people's standards, but I find I work better like that. I have a clear bench, but I let everything else get in a muddle. It helps to concentrate my mind.'

Peter looked puzzled, but did not question the logic of what Bruce had confided. Instead he said, 'There's something we'd like to ask you about.'

Bruce looked interested. 'Another challenge?' he enquired eagerly.

'I can't say,' Peter replied. 'It's about a ring. Unfortunately we haven't got it with us, but we can describe it to you.'

'Carry on,' said Bruce.

They told him all they knew, describing the ring in as much detail as they could.

When they had finished, he said seriously, 'I'd very much like to see that ring, and I hope it won't be long before you're able to bring it to me.'

'It could be quite a while,' Fay replied. 'But I'm sure my husband could photograph it for you, and I can send you an impression of the lettering.'

'I would be indebted to you if you would,' replied Bruce, surprisingly grateful.

'I'll arrange it as soon as I can,' Fay assured him. 'Perhaps we could see your workplace now, and after that we can look round the shop. That way we'll not take up much more of your time.'

'Don't worry about that,' Bruce replied. 'Your visit is at least as important to me as it is to you.'

Peter and Fay did not question the reason behind this statement, but followed him through a door into a room of moderate size. The centre of it was taken up by two heavy wooden tables standing side by side, with lighting arranged around them, and a variety of tools close to hand. As Bruce had warned them, the rest of the room was in confusion. They took great care to weave their way between the piles of unidentifiable items that were interspersed with boxes, chests and packages of every size and shape. Fay noticed that the walls were lined with shelves, and that these too were in gross disarray, with things that seemed about to tumble in any direction – some on to the mess beneath and some sideways, with imminent danger of causing a domino reaction.

Bruce was working on a delicate silver pendant for a necklace. Without saying anything, he let them watch him work, explaining nothing, but demonstrating everything.

Fay's mind flooded with questions, but it seemed entirely wrong to bombard him with the sound of her ignorance, and she decided to concentrate solely on what he was showing to them. She noticed that he became so totally engrossed in what he was doing that he slowly became unaware of their presence, and at length she touched Peter's arm and indicated that they should leave.

Back in the room that was the shop, they examined all the items on display.

'They're all so individual,' whispered Fay. 'He's an amazing man.'

'I agree,' said Peter quietly. 'Fay, when we leave, shall we leave him a note with your address?'

'That's a good idea, Peter,' she replied. 'I think I've got something in my bag that I can write on. I'll add a note to say I'll be in touch soon about the ring.'

'I'm sure he'd appreciate that.'

They stayed for a little while longer, and then reluctantly left.

On the return journey Fay had a sudden thought. 'I wonder what Don would think about coming here on Friday afternoon?' she asked Peter.

'We'll talk to him about it tomorrow evening,' he replied. 'I can't speak for him, but in his shoes I'd be keen under the circumstances.' He considered for a moment before asking, 'Is there anywhere else you'd like to go on our way back to the house?'

'I don't think so, thanks,' said Fay. 'When I went to meet Bruce, I had no idea that so much would come from it, and I've got a feeling there might be more.'

'Me too,' said Peter, 'and if it looks as if Don might not want to go on Friday, I'll be doing my best to persuade him.'

Surprised, Fay glanced across at him and saw his face was set, and his mind was made up. This was uncharacteristic of the Peter she knew, and she asked, 'Can you put into words why you're so determined? I certainly want Don and myself to go on Friday, but I don't think I would be pushing him into it.'

'I don't know,' replied Peter. 'I'm astonished at the intensity of my resolve. As you know, I'm not one for pushing people around, and I can assure you that in this case that's not what I'd be doing. I'd be alerting Don, and I might have to be forceful to get him to see and understand.'

Fay considered this. Then she asked, 'Do you think this might be something to do with supporting Helen in her part of the task?'

'I've no idea,' he replied. 'I hadn't consciously made that connection, and I can't see one now either.'

'Neither can I,' said Fay, 'but it came into my mind quite strongly.'

'Supposing there is a link…' said Peter slowly. 'Shall we assume one and see what comes?'

'Shall we make a start once we get back?'

'Yes. We'll only be about another ten minutes.'

Not long afterwards they were seated in the house, sipping chilled drinks.

'Peter,' Fay addressed him, 'when you were talking about persuading Don, you looked so different.'

'I certainly felt different,' he replied. He looked embarrassed.

'What are you thinking?' asked Fay.

'It felt as if I was taken over.'

'Taken over? What do you mean?'

'That's all I can say. Actually…' Here he faltered before going on. 'Actually, it was as if there was some kind of message coming through me.' He blushed and looked very uncomfortable.

'What makes you think that?' asked Fay, leaning forward in her seat.

'I don't know.'

'Was it a good feeling?' asked Fay, fascinated.

Peter thought for a minute and then said, 'I wouldn't call it good or bad, but it seemed right.'

'So although it felt uncomfortable, you didn't feel that anything wrong was happening?'

'No, not at all. I was taken by surprise. How I was speaking didn't sound like me. But I wasn't worried about the words being said. I was sure they were spoken for a right reason.'

'Mm,' said Fay thoughtfully. 'I think that sort of thing has happened to me once or twice lately. Do you remember how we were all sitting talking when I was in the aftermath of knocking myself out at the chapel?'

'How could I forget? And I think I know what you're going to say. We were talking about how Reverend Howard speaks out, and

Helen was saying she wished she could be like that too.'

'That's right.'

'And you went on to make a pronouncement about how she would be able to speak out in the future.'

'Yes. I felt confident that what I was saying was true, and at the same time I felt it was a message coming through me.'

Peter heaved a sigh of relief. 'That's very much like the feeling I was trying to describe,' he said. 'The only difference is that when I was speaking about Don I worried you might think I was being overbearing.'

Fay chuckled. 'Peter, you're incapable of being overbearing,' she said. 'It's just not in your nature. You can be firm, which is a good quality, but you can't be overbearing. The idea is preposterous.'

'Now I've got that straight in my mind, can we go back to the original reason for this conversation?' asked Peter. 'If there's a link between what I said and my part in the task, what can it be?'

'I have to admit it eludes me,' Fay confessed.

'I suppose the best thing I can do is to encourage Don, believing it's the right thing, see if anything comes from it, and then take it from there,' said Peter.

Fay nodded.

When Helen came home that evening she was intrigued to hear about how their trip had turned out, and she plied them both with questions until she was certain she had squeezed the last detail out of them.

'I'll help to persuade Dad,' she pronounced.

'No,' said Peter. 'You mustn't. That's my job.'

'Okay,' she replied. 'I won't get in the way.'

When the following evening came, Peter had no difficulty in persuading Don to make the journey to see Bruce Steele that Friday.

'You can phone him in the morning to check if he's going to be there,' said Helen. 'I hope he is, but I'll be envious. I wish I could have another day off work and come with you.'

'When you go, it will be with me,' said Peter. He turned to the others. 'Now, there's something I'd like to get on with while we're all together.'

They looked at him expectantly.

'It's only another few weeks to the wedding, and we've got to finalise our ideas about the service. Our contact with Reverend Howard has shown he's very flexible, but he does need to have the details confirmed soon.' He turned to Helen. 'I haven't raised this with you before, but I'd like to ask you what you'd think about our friend at the music shop coming to the church with his group to sing for us?'

'But that would be very expensive,' she objected.

'Could you first answer the question, please?' he persisted gently.

'That would be absolutely wonderful,' she said with longing in her voice. 'I wish it were possible, but the cost would be huge.'

'Now I know what you think, I'll let you into a secret,' said Peter. 'By luck the group happens to be performing the following day somewhere about an hour's journey away from your parents' home. I found this out when I rang to see what they might charge. Like you, I thought the cost would be prohibitive, but I wanted to phone to discuss the whole thing with him. He said he would have to approach the others, and when he got back to me he said they were all in agreement with a proposal he had put to them.'

'What proposal?' asked Helen urgently. 'What did he say?'

'They're willing to sing for us for the price of their accommodation for the night in the modest Bed and Breakfast place they had booked.'

'That's amazing!' exclaimed Helen, as tears welled up in her eyes. 'But what are we going to ask them to sing? We haven't made a final choice yet. It's so difficult.'

'We don't have to worry about that,' Peter reassured her. 'I said I'd discuss their offer with you, and I indicated that it was quite likely we'd decide to leave it up to them to advise us. I've given him a little of the background to what has been happening to us all, and he was more than keen to use his expertise to devise a suitable programme.'

'I must say I'm very touched by this,' said Don. 'How many are in the group?'

'There are six regulars, but only four of them are performing the following day, so it'll be those four,' Peter explained.

Don was impressed at the way Peter had been taking charge of the situation, and he said so. 'What's the chap's name?' he asked.

'Fred Bell,' Peter replied. 'He has an incredible fund of

knowledge.'

'Fred Bell,' mused Fay. 'I won't forget that name.'

'There are some other things I've been investigating too,' Peter continued. 'I've asked Reverend Howard if he would be willing to choose appropriate readings. I explained that I hadn't checked with you, Helen, and I said I would get back to him once I had.'

'Peter, I had no idea you were doing all this,' said Helen.

'We've all had a lot to deal with and think about,' he replied, 'and I felt it best to start making some positive moves about organising things. I thought if I made some provisional arrangements I could then check them with you all, and that this would result in the least stress. But since I spoke to Reverend Howard, I've thought of a reading that *I'd* like to include.'

'Which is that?' asked Helen.

'It's from *Revelation.* It's something about being given a white stone, and on the stone a new name is written which no man knows except he who receives it.'

'I can see why that came to you,' she replied. She paused, savouring it. 'It feels so right. It certainly seems relevant to everything that has been happening in our lives. I don't want to sound fanciful, but its message might even relate to the task.'

'That's exactly how I felt,' Peter replied. 'It came to me in the middle of one night, when I was lying awake trying to think about the task and hoping that we would soon be clearer about what it is.'

'These things that we feel suggest that one or another of us is being directed in some kind of way…' said Don thoughtfully. 'What you've just told us, Peter, is one of them.'

Peter nodded, and then said with authority, 'I want us to talk now about a central part of the wedding ceremony. You remember how we spoke of planning something that would be read out?'

'Of course,' said Fay. 'I've been thinking about it ever since.'

'We need to get something down on paper very soon,' said Don.

'I'd like to draft something while we're all together this evening,' said Peter. 'At the very least I should make some notes, and then Helen and I can work on it together.'

'Yes,' Don agreed. 'Time's quite short now, and we'll need to make some decision about who's to read it. We originally thought it would be me or the Reverend himself, but I think we should consider very carefully before we make the final decision.'

Helen turned to Don and said, 'Dad, I want it to be you. I'm quite clear about that.'

'I agree,' said Peter. 'There's no question in my mind. Please will you do it for us?'

Don looked touched, and his voice was slightly unsteady when he replied, 'Yes, of course I will.' He gathered himself, and added, 'We'd better get on with the content now, hadn't we?' He looked round the others and asked, 'Who's going to be the scribe?'

Peter looked across at him and said, 'Would you mind doing it?'

Helen handed her father a pad and a pen and said, 'If everyone's in agreement, I'd like us to list some of the significant things that have been said, starting with the young man and his statement about the task.'

'That's a good idea,' Don agreed, 'but perhaps we should start by saying something about Fay's illness, and how that led to the search for a ring that would remind her to think carefully before committing herself to anything.'

'Then we could go on to say how that led you to the signet ring with your initials on, and how it fitted the ring finger of your right hand,' said Helen. 'But there's more to that ring, isn't there?' she added slowly.

'Yes,' said Fay. 'I'm convinced that I was directed to buy it.'

Don smiled. 'I remember how determined you were,' he said. 'You were so certain.'

'I was absolutely sure it was the right ring to buy,' Fay confirmed. She turned to Peter. 'When we told you about it you said to Don you thought it was almost as if it had been made for him. That stuck in my mind because I'd had that same feeling.'

'I'll make a couple of headings,' said Don.

Fay's illness
The signet ring

'There's something else we should say about that ring,' said Helen. 'Mum, you thought it was the right ring for two reasons. Have you remembered the other one yet?'

'No, I haven't,' Fay replied. 'It's frustrating. It seemed so clear in my mind at the time, but when I tried to speak, it was gone. I wonder now if it was something about the person who made it. I find it so strange that as far as we know there are no other pieces around that were made by that particular craftsman. Surely he must have made other things?'

'I've thought a lot about that too,' said Don. 'I'm sure you said earlier that they could have been lost, hidden away, or even destroyed, and I think you're probably right.'

'It's going to be difficult to decide how much of this to put in the talk,' sighed Helen.

'We'd better limit it to what we know, and then perhaps add a question or two to prompt people to think about it,' said Peter.

'I'll make a note about that and then we'd better go on,' said Don as he wrote:

There's a lot here. Details and surmise.

'Then we should put in how, in a way, that led to our finding the …' said Helen. She stopped herself just in time, and said instead, '…how we spoke to that young man and what he said to us about the garment and about the task. Of course,' here she looked across at Fay, 'on the day itself, we'll be free to tell everything he told us.'

Peter looked surprised. 'You mean there's more?' he asked.

'Yes,' she replied. 'But if we told you, then you'd know about the garment. It's about the history of the design, and that's all I can say.'

'I think that before you go on to your garment we should say more about Don's ring,' said Peter suddenly. 'As you know I've been keen that Don wears it at our wedding, and so has Fay. I still believe it signifies a deeper union between them, one which I want to be validated at our ceremony.'

Helen nodded emphatically.

'I'll certainly be wearing it on the day,' said Don. 'I know that the pact we made that led to the ring brings us closer, but I think the union you're referring to would go much deeper even than that.' He paused, and for a while he seemed to be lost in thought. 'I wish I knew what it *means*,' he said slowly. 'I'm sure you're right, Peter. I have that same sense.'

‘I agree it goes beyond our pact,’ said Fay reflectively, ‘and I think it might be to do with helping me with the task.’

‘I’d like to talk more about it, but at the moment we should really go on to the task itself,’ said Don. ‘Perhaps we should include exactly what you remember the young man saying.’

Helen and Fay spoke to each other for a while, trying their best to remember the terms he had used, and then Fay took the pad and wrote:

Young man
At some time in the future, you and your mother have a task to complete together. It is one of crucial importance, and you must be sure to recognise it when it manifests to you. Your mother will guide you, and your husband will support you through your part in it.

She showed it to Helen, who nodded.

‘We’re pretty sure that’s it,’ said Fay, as she handed the pad back to Don. ‘I don’t know whether we should refer to the garment itself, and the strange thing he said about payment.’

‘I’ll make a note about that, so we can decide later,’ he replied.

‘Mum,’ said Helen. ‘Do you remember that the man asked for the date of the wedding?’

Fay nodded. ‘And something struck me about his reaction when you told him.’

‘Me too,’ Helen agreed.

‘What was that?’ asked Peter curiously.

‘I thought it connected with something already in his mind,’ said Fay.

‘Yes,’ said Helen, ‘and it was as if it made sense to him.’

‘This sounds important,’ said Don, making notes.

‘It’s so frustrating,’ said Helen impatiently. ‘There are so many unanswered questions.’

‘I think it’s sufficient at the moment to stay alert,’ Fay advised.

Helen agreed with some reluctance, and then said, ‘Perhaps we should think about what else to include in Dad’s talk.’

‘There’s Joan,’ said Fay. ‘Can you remember what was going through her mind about me at the Easter service? We all thought that was important.’

‘Ah, yes,’ Helen replied. ‘Let me see.’ She reached over for the pad and sat for a few minutes deep in thought. 'We'll have to check with her, but I think I can remember it more or less,' she said. She began to write:

Joan
In the Easter service she was thinking...
All the time he (Rev) was speaking she had in her mind the hope that what's happening in Fay's life will mean a renewal for her... She wondered if all that you (Fay) are going through at the moment and in the last months is some kind of preparation for the task the young man told you about.

'That looks right,' said Don as he took back the pad. 'Has anyone got any ideas about what else we should put in?'

'I once came out with something about Mum's illness, which we all thought could be relevant,' said Helen. 'Shall I add what I think it was?'

She took the pad and wrote:

Helen
Maybe you (Fay) have to be ill for long enough to learn certain things.

As she handed the pad back to Don she turned to Fay and said, 'Mum, what about the monk and the two sorts of happenings? Wasn't it the day you were at the hospital clinic that you first started thinking about that?'

'That's right!' exclaimed Fay. 'Well done! Don, make a note of it.'

He wrote:

Fay
Events (including snakes!) around the appointment with Dr Grayling – led to 'a monk was buried here...'

'And it wasn't long afterwards that I had the dream about the monk who devised snake patterns,' said Fay. 'You all thought that was important.'

Don added it to the growing list.

Fay
Dream about a monk who devised snake patterns.

'Where are we up to now?' he asked. 'Perhaps I should read out everything I've got here so far.'

When he had finished, Peter said, 'I've remembered something else that should go in. It was in a conversation between Helen and myself about what the task might be. We were both struck by what we said.' He took the pad and added:

Helen
If I could choose, it would be something that brings a lot of good to many people.

Peter
It could be some small thing, but it could start off a train of events that leads to much good for many people.

He handed the pad back to Don, who read it out before turning to Fay and saying, 'I think I should have something here about the curse.'

'I was just coming round to that,' she replied. 'Quite a bit came to light that day we were at Lawerlocke Hall when I went to find the chapel. I was trying to find a grave, and it was something to do with being saved. I can't remember more than that, but when we were home again and I was resting, I found myself saying something very intensely.'

'I think it's important to try to remember,' said Don.

Silently, he handed Fay the pad and she began to write:

Fay
(Morna's brooch/thumb/monk.)
(Must find the grave. Now I will be saved.)
The curse of the two kinds of happenings. I've got to lay the curse to rest. Helen, that's the task... our task.

She said nothing as she handed it to Helen. 'What do you think?' she asked.

Helen studied it for a moment before passing it on to Don and Peter.

Don said, 'This is central.'

'Absolutely crucial,' said Peter. 'This should be the climax of the talk.' He turned to Helen and said with great tenderness, 'It's our wedding that brings it all together.'

Helen clasped his hand.

After a moment of quietness she said softly, 'There's something I need to add.'

'What is it?' asked Peter.

'I don't want to forget what Mum said when I was expressing my longing to be as good as Reverend Howard at speaking out. It's been in my mind ever since. Will you write it down for me, Mum?'

Fay took the pad, thought for a moment and wrote:

Fay
To Helen
Your confidence will grow and you will speak out for what you believe. You will be able to speak with your own voice, and with the courage of your own convictions. And your convictions will be well grounded, based on proper care and concern for humanity.

'I've got something else to put in,' said Peter. 'After the visit to the Hall we spoke of how a number of our recent experiences have shown that there's something else behind what is at first apparent. Would you add that, Helen, please?'

Helen wrote:

Fay
There's something about being able to see behind what is at first apparent.

Fay started to chuckle, and the others looked at her in surprise.

'I'm remembering the day when I was saying I was sure I'd be given the energy I needed if I was doing the right thing. Poor Jim was very sceptical when he asked how I would know what the right thing might be.'

'Of course,' Don reminded her, 'you were talking about going back to the Hall, and he wasn't feeling too good about that in the light of what had happened to you there. But I'll write it on the list.' He took the pad from Helen and added:

Fay
I know that if I'm doing the right thing I'll be given the energy I need.

'That must be about everything,' said Don. 'Can anyone else think of anything more that should go on this list?'

'I want you to add what Fay said about plainchant,' said Peter. 'It's very important. I made a note of it when you told us on the phone.' He got up and went out of the room. When he returned he was carrying a small notebook. 'This is my wedding notes notebook,' he announced with a smile. He searched the pages. 'Here it is, Don,' he said, handing it across to him. Don copied it:

Fay
The music allows and engenders thought and reflection. Peter and Helen's wedding day marks the beginning of a journey for them, and also the next stage of the task Helen and I have to accomplish with Peter's aid. The service will be a time for reflection, setting a seal on what marriage really means.

Peter continued. 'And I want you to put a note about the conversation Fay and I had yesterday after we'd been to Bruce Steele's.'

'Oh, yes,' said Fay. 'It's about feeling that we sometimes say things that seem to be coming through us from somewhere else. I certainly had that feeling when I was telling Helen how she would grow and mature.'

'And I had it when I was feeling so sure I was going to persuade you to go to Bruce's on Friday, Don,' said Peter.

Don wrote:

Peter and Fay
... as if coming through me.

Peter took the pad, looked through what everyone had written, and commented, 'There's plenty here to guide us when Helen and I are writing something up for you, Don. Perhaps the best thing is if we work on it over the weekend, and then e-mail it to you.'

'Then I can try it out on Fay and the others,' said Don. 'That way I can see how it feels, and we can make suggestions about anything else that we think could go in.'

'How long do you think it should last?' asked Fay.

'Anything up to about fifteen minutes I should say,' Don suggested. 'Talking about time, I should be leaving soon,' he said as he glanced at the clock. 'It's got a bit late, but I'm very glad to have spent time on this. If you think of anything else, add it, and I'll see it tomorrow evening when I come to collect Fay.'

He stood up and went to get his things. After that he kissed Fay and Helen goodbye, put his hand on Peter's shoulder, and was gone.

'I wish he was still here,' said Helen miserably.

Peter hugged her and said, 'So do I. I wish we'd had more time. I know we can work on this again tomorrow evening, but I would have liked to go on tonight.'

'We'll have time to think about what we've put down so far,' said Fay.

'I know,' Peter replied, 'but it felt as if we were in the middle of something that's been broken off, and it feels painful.'

'I'm sure that's why I'm upset,' said Helen. She picked up the pad and began to doodle, tears not far from her eyes.

'You and I can stay up and talk for a while,' Fay suggested. 'It doesn't matter how late we go to bed, because you're not going to work tomorrow.'

Helen's face began to clear. 'Do you mind, Peter?'

'Don't worry about that,' Peter reassured her as he got up to go to the kitchen. 'But don't stay up too late you two. Fay's still trying to get better.'

After he had gone upstairs, Helen said, 'Tomorrow I want to have a long talk about wedding outfits. Have you got any further forward with yours?'

'I haven't,' replied Fay, 'and I know I haven't got much time left. I'll see if Don will help me next week. But one thing's certain, I'll be wearing my brooch!'

'Mum,' said Helen suddenly. 'I want to talk for a while about the two kinds of happenings.'

Fay waited to see what Helen wanted to say.

'These things that have been happening to you over the last months – memories of bad experience in your life as a child, and the things we think might be from previous lives – I've begun to wonder if perhaps everyone is affected like this in one way or another.'

'I hadn't thought about that,' Fay confessed. 'I've been so wrapped up in what's been happening to me.'

'People can go to great lengths to cover things up, can't they?' Helen continued. 'If you look at what was happening to those Benedictine monks, that's quite a good example.'

'You mean that everyone thought of them as people of great integrity, who lived a pure life?'

'That's right, and if what the article said is true, then there were really bad things happening in that community, which they were trying to hide from public view.'

'Trying to keep up a front,' mused Fay. 'You'll remember what Reverend Howard said about Amnesty and about torture going on in secret. I've a feeling that all of this relates to our task.

'My illness has made me stop, and I've had to spend a lot of time thinking and wondering and puzzling about what was wrong. In amongst that I've found parts of myself I hadn't known existed, or I'd pushed to one side so I wasn't aware of them. I think that Joan was absolutely right when she said that this was a preparation for the task. I've had to bring together what I'm aware of and what I hadn't been aware of, and try to make sense of it all. Perhaps that's what you and I have to help others to do, Helen. Perhaps those who inflict pain are people who don't know or understand what is driving them. Maybe the two kinds of happenings are those that are conscious and those that are unconscious.'

Here Helen broke in. 'And there are the happenings that are known, and those that are hidden from general view.'

'Yes,' said Fay, 'and that is a curse that can lead to a lot of misunderstanding at the very least, and at the most it can lead to disaster. Samuel Locke wasn't afraid to speak out against his erstwhile friend once he knew how the curse was affecting Sir William. He tried to take appropriate steps – something that was suitable in the culture at that time. What I would long for now is a way to help people to see more clearly.’

‘If Peter’s right,’ Helen replied, ‘we only have to start off in a small way, and the effect could spread. The wedding would be a chance to make a statement about what our task is, why it’s important and what we hope to do.’

‘We must write something down about this tomorrow,’ said Fay determinedly.

‘Yes,’ said Helen, ‘and we can discuss it with Peter and Don in the evening. But now we should go to bed.’

Chapter Twenty-eight

The following day was overcast and wet. It rained heavily for most of the morning, but this did not interfere with their plan, and Fay and Helen soon settled down to discuss their wedding outfits.

'I've checked the jacket from time to time,' said Fay, 'so I can assure you it's safe. Are the trousers ready yet?'

'I've to phone the dressmaker at the weekend,' Helen replied, 'but there's no harm in giving her a ring now to see how far she's got.' She picked up the phone, and receiving no reply, left a message on the answering service.

'Pearls, jacket, trousers…' mused Fay. 'Did you make a final decision about something for your head?'

'I asked the woman who's making the trousers to make something up from the remaining material. She seemed to know what I meant, so that's in hand. The only thing I'm short of is shoes. I've looked around, but haven't found anything suitable yet. I'll just have to keep trying, I suppose.'

'Have you got a specific style in mind?'

'Not really,' said Helen. 'I certainly want flat ones, but apart from that I'm banking on seeing something that catches my eye. I think cream would be the right colour. But what about you? What are we going to do about getting you a long flowing dress that's gathered at the left shoulder?'

'You remembered!' exclaimed Fay, delight showing in her voice.

'How could I forget, Mum?' said Helen quietly.

'I'd like it to be linen, and the colour should be oatmeal,' said Fay suddenly.

'Wow!' said Helen. 'That's a pretty clear image. When did you decide that?'

'It came into my mind just now.'

'The problem is knowing where we're going to get it,' said Helen worriedly.

'I'm sure Don will help me,' said Fay. 'By the way, I think I'll wear those sandals I bought when I was out with you. I haven't touched them since I took them home. I've got a bag that will go with them, and I've decided I'm going to put a decorative comb in my hair.'

'That's a lovely idea,' said Helen. 'Have you got one in mind?'

'Not yet, but I'm going to enjoy looking.'

'Incidentally, Peter's left the car for us,' said Helen. 'How would you feel about a shopping trip this afternoon?'

'Yes, let's have an early lunch and then go out,' said Fay straight away. She got up and started towards the kitchen.

'We don't have to rush,' said Helen, smiling.

'I know, but I want to use all the time we've got.'

It was not long before they were ready to leave.

'Helen, there's something on my mind about the jacket,' Fay said as they got into the car.

'It's probably the same thing as is on mine,' Helen laughed. 'I bet you're worrying about whether or not we should go back and give the man some money.'

'That's right.'

'I think we should both try not to worry about it. After all, he said we would know if it was right to. That doesn't sound too complicated, does it? If we don't know, then we don't go.'

'Perhaps we could make a donation to a charity,' said Fay. 'I think that might ease my mind.'

'I wondered about that too,' said Helen. 'Maybe that would be the solution. We can talk to Dad and Peter about it after the wedding.'

Although the shopping trip was pleasurable, it yielded nothing that suited either Fay or Helen. They returned home empty-handed, but happy with their outing.

Helen looked at her watch. 'If you want to sit down for a while, I'll start cooking. That way the food will be ready for when the others come in.'

'Thanks,' said Fay gratefully. 'I think I need a rest now.'

She sat down and put her feet up on a stool that Helen brought for her.

When Helen put her head round the door from the kitchen a few minutes later, she saw that Fay was asleep. It was not until Don arrived that she woke.

'Goodness, I must have dropped off!' she exclaimed as she looked at the clock.

Helen chuckled. 'You went out like a light as soon as you sat down,' she said.

'I've got news for you,' said Don. 'I managed to get hold of Bruce Steele, and it's definitely on for tomorrow afternoon.'

'Oh good!' said Fay excitedly. 'I can't wait to see what he says about your ring.'

There was plenty to discuss that evening, and all too soon it was time for Don and Fay to leave.

'You'll have to phone tomorrow evening and tell us how you got on at Bruce's,' Helen called out to them as they made their way to the car.

Friday afternoon at Bruce Steele's workshop turned out to be a very satisfying experience. Fay realised it meant a lot to her for Don to meet Bruce, the creator of her brooch, and see where he worked. Bruce spent a long time studying Don's ring. He said very little, but his attitude conveyed that there was something out of the ordinary about it. He asked if he could make an imprint of the lettering in some wax, and Fay and Don had no difficulty in agreeing to this.

However, Fay felt a stab of disappointment when he finally pronounced, 'I'm puzzled by my reaction to this ring. It affects me in a way I can't define.' She tried to draw him, but he would say nothing more.

He stayed with them as they went round his shop, although he said very little. But when he overheard Fay telling Don how she must look for a comb to wear in her hair at the wedding, he surprised them by offering to make one.

'Are you sure?' Fay asked him. 'It's only four weeks to the wedding.'

He inclined his head and continued his train of thought. 'I can already see a design in my mind that would suit the occasion,' he said solemnly. 'It will be something worthy of the owner of Morna's brooch.'

'Thank you,' said Don. 'We would both like you to do that. Wouldn't we, Fay?'

Fay nodded mutely. She felt overwhelmed.

Outside in the car she turned to Don and said, 'It's almost too much for me.'

'I can see that,' said Don. 'Let's get home now. And I think we need a quiet couple of weeks before Jack comes.'

The intervening days passed slowly and quietly. When Fay told Don of her
wish to find the wedding outfit she had envisaged, he was more than happy to help her. Although they thought it might take quite some time, they were lucky enough to find just what she wanted. It was part of an autumn collection by a designer who provided clothes for one of the local department stores. Fay was delighted with it, and phoned Helen as soon as she could. Helen herself had got her head cover and trousers, and had at last found a pair of simple flat shoes that would be suitable.

Helen and Peter drafted Don's speech and sent it to him. Don and Fay discussed it with Joan and Jim before making a few minor suggestions and sending it back for Helen and Peter to comment on. It was easy to agree about a few changes, and soon the final version arrived for Don, so that he could rehearse it without time pressure.

When the time came for Jack's arrival, Don and Fay drove out to the airport to meet him. Fay's heart lurched when she caught sight of him. At first she thought he had grown several inches, but realised that this was an illusion, due to the fact that he had matured so much since they last saw him. She hugged him tightly with tears in her eyes. After that Don hugged him, before suggesting that they went together to collect his luggage from the carousel.

'How was the journey?' Don enquired.

'Fortunately there weren't any hitches,' Jack replied.

'You had a rough time on the way back last time, didn't you?' said Don.

Jack nodded.

'We phoned the airport before we set off,' said Fay, 'just in case there was a delay of some kind. I must admit I was very relieved when your flight was right on schedule.'

'I can see my bags coming now,' said Jack, as he moved towards the conveyor to retrieve them.

'Let me take one,' Don offered. Jack passed him a sturdy canvas shoulder bag, as he himself took his large backpack.

They made their way to the car, and were soon moving through the exit barrier.

'I'm starving,' Jack remarked. 'The food on these planes isn't enough for me, and I'm often doubtful about the quality.'

Don smiled. 'Don't worry,' he said. 'We've got plenty in, and you'll soon see how I've been adding to my culinary skills over the last while. I'd like to do some showing off while you're here.'

Jack laughed. 'Sounds great!'

'Yes, I've had to take a back seat,' said Fay, 'and I've been enjoying the results.'

Over the evening meal Jack said bluntly, 'It's good to see you both. I've been worried. I know there's a lot to catch up on, and I'd like to make a start now.'

Don and Fay looked at each other, and then Don said, 'I think we should take it slowly, beginning in February. What do you think, Fay?'

'I agree,' said Fay. 'I don't know how long it'll take though. There's so much.'

'We don't need to worry about that,' said Jack. 'As you know, I've got plenty of time now I'm here. I haven't fixed anything up except to be with you and the others. If there's any time in between, I can phone to see if any of my friends are around.' He laughed. 'And I need to think about what to wear for the wedding. I haven't got anything yet.'

'You and I can go together to look for something,' Don offered. 'We haven't been on a shopping trip for a very long time.'

'Thanks, Dad,' Jack replied. 'You can point me in the right direction. Now, will you make a start? I've had to wait a long time since I got your e-mail, and before that I knew there was something in the air.'

Don and Fay took it in turns with their account.

Jack listened quietly for much of the evening, but there were times when he asked a number of pertinent questions that provoked discussion, which they all found helpful.

When Fay began to yawn, Don glanced at the clock. 'It's late,' he said. 'I think we should finish for this evening. I'll stay up to clear away, and then come to bed.'

'There's a lot more to come, Jack,' said Fay.

'I know,' he replied, 'but at least we've made a start.'

The following day, Don and Jack spent much of the time hunting for clothes for Jack. They returned mid-afternoon, triumphantly bearing a smart but casual suit that seemed ideal. He put it on for Fay to see, and she was impressed. Part of the evening was spent in regaling her with amusing accounts of their attempts to find something suitable. After that they progressed further with catching up on the events of the past months.

Over the following week they spent time with Joan and Jim, who added their own memories and perceptions to Don and Fay's growing account, at the same time insisting on discussing Jack's experiences abroad, and his career plans. Jack visited Diana and Paul, and heard their story too. All this, in addition to many long phone conversations with Helen and Peter, meant that he gradually grasped the extent of what had been happening in his family.

'I realise it's been very hard for me, being away when all this was happening,' he said one evening while he and his parents were relaxing together. 'My work can be so pressured that there's no room for anything else, but however far away I am, I'm never cut off from you. I can imagine how difficult it must have been to decide whether or not to let me know about any of this before I came back.'

Don nodded. 'It was on my mind a lot, and I spoke to Fay about it. After that I drafted the e-mail, and we passed it round the others before we made the final decision.'

'You did the right thing,' Jack confirmed. 'Although I came home for Helen and Peter's wedding, this time has been important for learning what's been happening. And there's a lot to take in.'

'If there are any more questions you want to ask, don't hold back,' said Don.

'I won't,' Jack reassured him. 'If anything else happens, or if you realise something new, make sure and let me know.'

'It's a deal,' said Don.

'I won't have any difficulty doing that now we've told you everything,' added Fay. 'And now I want to talk about coming out to see you, Jack. I don't know when I'll be fit enough, but I want to believe that I'll be able to come sometime in November.' She turned to Don. 'What do you think?'

'I think that's a great idea,' he said. 'How about you, Jack?'

Jack smiled. 'Let's plan as much of it as we can without making the actual bookings.'

Fay was encouraged by his enthusiasm, and they spent the rest of the evening exploring options.

Chapter Twenty-nine

As arranged, Helen arrived two days before the wedding. Fay was delighted to see that she was so full of vitality that she seemed to be glowing. The night before the ceremony they tried on their clothes in the privacy of Fay's bedroom. It excited them both to see Helen wearing the jacket again, reminding them of the day they found it, and the importance of the task that was theirs.

'It won't be long now before we can tell Dad and Peter everything about it,' said Helen happily.

'I've found it difficult to make sure I didn't say anything more than we'd agreed,' said Fay.

'I nearly let some of it slip to Peter once or twice,' Helen confided.

They smiled at each other conspiratorially, and then Helen took the rest of her outfit out of the bag she had brought.

'The head cover is perfect!' exclaimed Fay excitedly.

Helen smiled. 'I thought you'd like it,' she said as she put it on carefully. 'I wanted something that was right for my wedding but had a flavour of the head covers you described to me.'

'I can see that,' said Fay. Then she asked seriously, 'Why did you want to do that?'

'It's out of my respect for Morna,' Helen explained simply. 'Whoever Morna was – either you in a past life, or someone whose distress you've sensed – I wanted to represent her. You will be wearing your brooch, and I have my head cover, both of which we associate with the time when she was alive.'

Fay gave her a hug. 'The head cover looks just right on you, and your reason for having it designed like that is perfect. Now put your trousers and shoes on so I can see the full effect. I'll get the pearls.'

A few minutes later they were studying the full impact of Helen's appearance.

'I feel quite overwhelmed,' Helen admitted. 'This is the first time I've tried on the whole outfit. It's one thing having the parts of it, and it's quite another wearing them all together. You put your things on now.'

Fay took out the linen garment that she and Don had bought, and showed it to Helen.

'Oh, Mum!' exclaimed Helen. 'It suits you really well. It's great you found what you wanted. When you described what you had in mind, I was worried about whether or not you'd get something you were happy with. To be honest, I wasn't sure about your idea either. But it's perfect.'

Fay smiled. She knew the dress was right for her. It looked right and it felt right. She was glad that Helen was pleased with it too. She took out her sandals and put them on.

'Where's the brooch?' asked Helen. 'I'd like to pin it on for you.' She smiled at Fay meaningfully and added, 'I don't want you sticking the pin into your thumb!'

Fay took a box out of a drawer and opened it to reveal the brooch. Helen stroked the back of the snake lovingly, before picking it up and pinning it at Fay's left shoulder. Then she stood back to admire the final effect.

'Wait a minute,' Fay instructed. 'There's one more thing.' She reached into the drawer and took out another box, which she handed to Helen.

'The comb!' Helen gasped as she opened it. 'Mum, it's so beautiful. It goes perfectly with M… your brooch.'

'Don hasn't seen it yet,' said Fay. 'I wanted you to see it first. It arrived by special delivery about a week ago, and I put it away, next to Morna's brooch.'

'Don't let him see it until tomorrow,' Helen urged.

'I'd already decided that,' Fay assured her calmly.

Helen turned the comb over. 'Oh, look!' she said. 'There's an inscription on it.' She examined it closely. 'What does it say?'

She looked up to find that Fay was smiling at her.

'Have another look,' Fay encouraged. 'I'm sure you'll be able to work it out.'

'Did Bruce tell you what it says?' asked Helen, puzzled.

'Have another look,' Fay repeated gently.

Helen stared intently at the inscription. Then Fay saw her face change as she began to realise what it said.

'I think it's your initials,' she pronounced. 'They're done in the same kind of lettering as is on Dad's signet ring. I can see the F and the B quite clearly now. But I think there's another letter too.'

'You're getting warmer,' said Fay.

'It's that third letter that got in the way of my seeing your initials to begin with,' Helen complained. 'Why has he put it there? It seems silly to me.' She glanced at her mother, who was still smiling. 'Why are you so happy about it?' she asked.

'Try looking once more, and then I'll tell you.'

Helen gazed at it, and Fay watched her patiently.

'He's added an M, hasn't he?' said Helen.

'I'm glad you worked that out for yourself,' replied Fay. 'I was so pleased and excited when I saw it – the initial of my other name, and in the same style of lettering as Don's ring. It felt as if he'd given me something I needed, something that brings me together.'

Helen stared at her mother with a startled expression. 'Do you know what you've just said?' she asked.

'I do,' replied Fay confidently.

'Shall I try putting the comb in your hair?' Helen suggested.

Fay considered for a moment. 'No. I think I want to save it for tomorrow.'

'Mum, can we talk about my jacket for a bit?' asked Helen. 'There are some things that are bothering me. For instance, I'm still worried about the money.'

'All we can do is to try to follow what we were told – that we should go back only if we learn that we must leave money there,' said Fay. 'I think we've got to trust that we'll somehow know if we have to go back. Apart from that, we can always follow our plan of putting money into something that will help people.'

Helen relaxed. 'It sounds right when you spell it out, but when I'm on my own I can feel quite anxious about it.'

'The thing *I* get worried about is keeping it safe,' said Fay, laughing. 'Remember how I said to the man I thought we wouldn't always have it, and that another person might have need of it later?'

'I wonder who it might be?' mused Helen. 'I suppose it's too soon to tell. But you never know, I might have a daughter one day who'll wear it.' She laughed. 'And if I'm going to be like the person who had the original jacket, I'm going to have a lot of children.'

'I suppose that was common in years gone by,' said Fay. 'In the past it might have been necessary, but now it's not even particularly desirable.'

'Don't worry, Mum. I'm not planning to, but I wouldn't mind the "good health into old age" part of her life.'

'I certainly want that for you,' Fay agreed.

'He said it was part of my destiny to have chosen the jacket,' Helen reflected. 'I wonder what that means?'

'I think it's another question that has to wait for an answer.'

'If you remember, that man knew more than he was telling us,' said Helen. 'I wish he'd been free to tell us everything he knew,' she added, almost desperately.

Fay was sympathetic. 'I can feel impatient too, but we'll have to accept that there's a time and a place for these things, and that it's not time yet.'

'How's Dad been getting on with the talk?' asked Helen suddenly.

'He's almost word perfect, but he'll take a copy of it with him. He's been practising every evening, but there are places where he gets overwhelmed with emotion, and then he worries about forgetting the next bit. He never does, of course.'

That night Helen slept with Fay, and Don slept in the spare room. He had not protested, as he felt he understood why Helen needed to be with her mother. Both Helen and Fay woke in the night, sure that there was someone on the landing, but again they heard nothing.

'This is something else we don't know the answer to yet,' whispered Fay. 'And although it wakes me and startles me, I don't feel it's something bad. It's just something we don't understand.'

'Actually, I've always felt it's something benign,' Helen whispered back, before falling asleep once again.

When they woke the following morning, they were delighted to discover that the day was warm and bright. Helen eagerly bounced out of bed, but found herself unable to eat any breakfast.

'I'll have to wait until later,' she said. 'I'm feeling happy, but I'm probably nervous as well. Dad, I'd like to be at the church quite early.'

'What time shall we aim for?' he asked.

'About eleven. I'd like to sit at the back for a while before anyone else arrives.'

'That's a good idea,' said Fay. 'And the singers are coming for half past?'

'That's right,' replied Helen. 'Why don't we go back upstairs now and get dressed slowly, and I'll work out the best way of putting your comb in your hair?'

They arrived at the church just after eleven to find that the group were there already, in the process of conducting a small rehearsal.

'It's perfect,' whispered Helen, her eyes shining. She was sitting between Don and Fay on some seats next to the rear wall of the church. This position was ideal, as it was sufficiently inconspicuous that anyone entering the building would be unlikely to notice her.

By half past the rehearsal was finished, and the group came over to exchange a few words with them, before positioning themselves for the Service. After the first few people had filtered in, they began to sing once more, and the whole church resonated with the sound. More and more people arrived until the small building was overflowing with people, eager to witness Helen and Peter's ceremony.

The Service was just as Helen and Peter had intended – quiet, calm and intensely meaningful, framed within the context of the plainchant. There was total silence as Don stood up to deliver his address. It was as if everyone sensed that something of great significance was about to be imparted. The whole congregation was spellbound as he spoke, slowly and deliberately, giving his audience time to absorb the meaning of what he had to say.

After the ceremony Helen and Peter made their way arm in arm to the porch at the back of the church, where they greeted everyone as they left. The sound of plainchant continued to fill the body of the church. As well as people from the local community, there were others who had journeyed to be there that day – people from Peter and Helen's schooldays, from their university days, and some friends and colleagues from their life now. The atmosphere between them all was one of pleasure and shared purpose.

Outside in the churchyard, many people crowded round to ask questions about what Don had said. It was more than obvious that they were hungry for more information, and eventually Fay approached the Reverend and suggested they might offer to arrange an informal evening for discussion in a few weeks' time.

The Reverend agreed, and began to pass the word round, saying that a notice would be posted about a suitable time and place.

They stood talking for nearly an hour before Don reminded them that they would have to make their way to the hotel for the reception. This was a buffet, which had been arranged to accommodate everyone who wanted to come. Peter's sister, Marjory, and her husband, together with his mother, had been uncertain about whether or not they could make the journey, but they had arrived just in time for the Service and were now so deep in conversation with Peter that they were unaware of Don's directions. Helen noticed that Peter was very animated as he spoke to them, and she stood beside him, largely silent, allowing them to enjoy their time together. She was only too aware of the fact that Peter rarely had contact with them, and that the infrequent phone calls were usually rather brief and stilted.

After the others had left the churchyard, she put her hand on his arm and said, 'I'm sorry to interrupt, but we should be making our way to the meal now.'

Peter jumped and looked embarrassed. 'Of course. I'm sorry,' he said.

'It's all right,' Helen reassured him, looking straight into his eyes. 'All of this is very important, and I'm only sorry we haven't got more time now.' She addressed the others. 'I've been wondering if Peter and I could come for a visit soon,' she began. 'I'm sure that we could find a small hotel locally…'

Marjory's husband broke in. 'We'd like you to stay with us,' he said firmly. 'We have plenty of room. Let's arrange a weekend sometime between now and Christmas.'

'We'll give you a ring next month and fix it,' said Peter happily.

The hotel had provided an excellent buffet, and there was plenty of good seating available.

It was towards the end of the meal that Diana began to feel quite uncomfortable. She slipped off to the Ladies toilets, hoping not to attract attention. However, she soon began to realise that she was in the early stages of labour, and that she would have to let Paul know. She was washing her hands when Helen joined her.

'I saw you leave,' said Helen, 'and when you didn't come back, I started worrying that something might be wrong. Are you okay?'

'I'm pretty sure I'm in labour,' said Diana, her voice almost a whisper. 'Will you get Paul for me?'

Helen gave her a hug. 'This is so exciting,' she said. 'My wedding day! I hope your baby's born today. Of course I'll go and find him. Sit here, and we'll soon be back.'

Minutes later she put her head round the door and said, 'Here we are. Come on, we'll have to tell the others, and then explain to everyone else why we're having to leave.'

'But you can't leave your wedding reception,' Diana protested.

Helen stared at her meaningfully. 'I'm coming with you, and there's to be no argument,' she said.

'Do you mind if I wait in the hallway?' asked Diana. 'I feel rather wobbly.'

'That's fine,' Helen replied. 'I'll get our parents and tell Peter what's happening. I want him to stay here with the guests. That way I won't feel responsible for them. There are quite a few of his friends here, and of course there's his family.'

'Are you sure you shouldn't be staying?' Diana persisted.

'I know that Peter and I are together in this,' Helen replied. 'As soon as I tell him he'll understand.

She found Don first.

'We should get moving,' he said wisely. 'You never know how long it will take, and we need to get Diana home to collect her other clothes and the bag she's packed.'

After that Helen found Peter, who was talking to some of his friends in a group next to where Joan and Jim were talking to his mother. She took his hand. 'I'm sorry to interrupt,' she said to them before turning to Peter, saying in a low voice, 'Can I have a word with you for a minute?' She drew him towards Joan, Jim and his mother before quickly explaining the situation.

'I'll tell everyone while you're getting ready to go,' said Peter. He took a glass and banged it on a nearby table to attract attention. 'I have a very important announcement to make,' he began. 'You will all have realised that Helen's closest friend, Diana, is about to have a baby.'

A murmur went round the room.

'It is my honour to be in the position to let you know that she is now in labour, and some of us will have to go with her to the hospital. I shall be staying here with you all, but I'll give you any news as it becomes available. I want to say that I hope the baby is born before midnight, so that it's birthday is our wedding day.'

There was a round of sustained applause, and there were calls of 'Good luck' and 'Hope all goes well', as Helen left with her parents and Joan and Jim.

Chapter Thirty

After just over six hours in labour, Diana gave birth to a healthy boy. She and Paul were overjoyed, but when asked what they were going to call him, had to admit that they had not yet chosen a name.

Although Fay was exhausted the following day, she did not feel unwell, and this was important to her. She and Don spent the day quietly with the others. Jack had a few days left, and Helen and Peter were still with them, as they were saving their time away for a holiday in October. However, they would have to leave the next day to return to work.

Joan and Jim and Paul joined them all for the evening.

'I don't expect we'll all be together like this again for a long time,' said Don, 'although of course it would be great if we could be. The only two who are missing are Diana and the baby.'

'They should be home tomorrow lunchtime,' said Joan. 'There was a minor hitch, and the hospital wanted her to stay in for another night to be on the safe side.'

'How are you feeling, Paul?' asked Don.

'Confused, but ecstatic,' he replied honestly.

'You're a dad now, just like me and Don,' said Jim.

'But you're a grandad too, Jim,' Fay pointed out.

'Yes, and that means I've got time to think more about what it means to bring a new person into the world. When I was young, it was something I didn't think about in any detail. We just got on with the day-to-day practicalities as best we could. And in our case it was with Fay's invaluable support. As I've gone through life, and particularly during the events of the past months, I've been quite preoccupied with the subject.'

'One thing is certain,' said Fay. 'We've all got to do our best to ensure our new family member is helped to understand what the world is, and where he is placed in it, and that requires a lot of support and patience. I hope we can help him to understand the kind of things we've been learning about only recently, so that he lives a life that is whole, and is not divided into different parts inside him. If I look at my own life, I can see so much now of how my behaviour and emotions have been affected by how my mother behaved towards me. For someone who has been cared for in a kind and supportive way, the effect is a good one. However, in other cases it is at best unhelpful, and at worst can greatly stunt a life – without a person being aware of those limitations. Now that I understand more about my own situation, I have the opportunity to change the bad effects of my past. It's going to be difficult, but it won't be as bad as not knowing what is affecting me, and being driven by unconscious forces.'

'I wonder where past lives fit into the picture?' said Don. 'We've all been struggling with what we believe might be lives you lived many years ago.'

'I've been thinking about that a lot,' Fay replied. 'In a way, childhood is a past life too. I'm not a child, but I'm affected by what happened to me then. It's obvious that I'm Fay now and not Morna, but I've been affected by what happened to her, whether or not I was she in a past life.'

'I want to help my grandson to understand these things when he gets older,' said Jim determinedly. 'And looking beyond that, I want to be sure that he can recognise corruption where it exists, even when it's hidden away or concealed behind something that looks as if it's right.'

'I've been thinking about something you told me earlier,' said Jack, who had been sitting quietly up until now.

The others turned to him expectantly.

He went on. 'Mum and Helen told me something when I first came home that we should be thinking about.'

'What's that?' asked Helen.

'I might have picked you up wrongly, but I was sure you said the man who gave you the jacket placed a special emphasis on the date of your wedding.'

'You're right,' Helen agreed.

'Yes,' said Fay. 'I had the distinct impression that it was as if the date fitted exactly the circumstances he knew about. It was as if he knew the date, and when it was mentioned he was reminded of it.'

'I had the impression that he knew quite a bit more than he was telling us,' said Helen.

‘So did I,’ Fay agreed, ‘but it was clear he wasn’t going to say any more. Jack, exactly what’s in your mind?’

‘I’m wondering if he knew a baby was going to be born on that day – a child whose life would be special in some deeply significant way,’ said Jack.

Fay stared at her son. What he had said was so simple, so obvious, but something that had not occurred to her. She was struck by how mature and complete he appeared as he sat there.

It was Helen who spoke first. ‘I’m amazed that no one else had thought of this,’ she said. ‘Jack, I’m deeply impressed. You had such a lot to take in when we were telling you about everything that’s been happening, and you’ve just proved that you’ve taken in every detail.’

‘It must be my analytical mind,’ said Jack lightly.

‘I don’t think so,’ said Don. ‘I think it’s because you feel involved, and because you’re concerned about everything that’s been going on in your absence.’

Jack nodded and tried to say something, but failed.

‘Jack, thank you for helping us with this,’ said Fay sincerely.

‘There’s no way we can be sure,’ said Helen, ‘but I think Jack’s right.’

The others nodded.

‘I’m so grateful to have people like all of you while Diana and myself are bringing up our son,’ said Paul. ‘He’ll have a start in life that many other children don’t have. I wish everyone could have this kind of beginning.’

‘I think this could be the start of the task Helen and I have to do,’ said Fay. ‘I have been using nearly all my energy over the past months in trying to get well, and I’ve discovered that a lot of what I’ve needed to do is to bring together different parts of my life – parts of which I was unaware or at best barely aware. I want to help others to do the same, and I want to help Paul and Diana’s son, so that he never gets into the position I was in – one in which I was driven by forces I did not know or understand. I have been trying to lay to rest the curse of the different kinds of happenings for me. If we help other people with this kind of thing, then the world will surely be a better place.’

Mirabelle Maslin
ON A DOG LEAD

Mirabelle Maslin
CARL AND OTHER WRITINGS

BEYOND THE VEIL
MIRABELLE
MASLIN

Letters to my Paper Lover
FLEUR SOIGNON

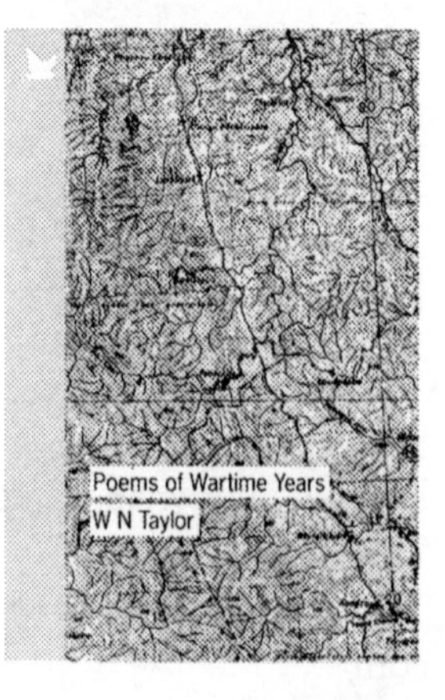
Poems of Wartime Years
W N Taylor

Mirabelle
Maslin
tracy
from the author of Beyond the Veil

Lightning Source UK Ltd.
Milton Keynes UK
29 July 2010

157577UK00001B/1/A